Nessa had longed for this carriage ride home, where she could again practice her fledgling art of seduction on Jack. She slid closer to him. "Thank you for bringing me to the theater tonight."

"The pleasure was mine, I assure you." He draped his arm across her shoulders. "Did you find it to be what you expected?"

"Oh, I found it all fascinating," she assured him. The drive was short, so she moved even closer so as not to waste this opportunity. "I begin to realize just how much I still have to learn of Town life."

"And of life in general?" he asked softly.

She looked up to find him gazing intently at her. "Yes," she whispered. "Fortunately, I have an excellent tutor."

She had thought she was ready for his kiss, but when his lips touched hers she felt, as before, that she might fly into a million pieces. It was an exquisite sensation, starting in her chest and licking outward toward her extremities. Both of his arms were around her now, pulling her even closer. His right hand slid to cup her breast through layers of fabric. Nessa moaned, her senses demanding more and more. . . .

BOOKS BY BRENDA HIATT

Azalea
Bridge over Time
A Christmas Bride
Daring Deception
Lord Dearborn's Destiny
The Ugly Duckling
Gabriella
Scandalous Virtue

SCANDALOUS Virtue

BRENDA HIATT

HarperPaperbacks
A Division of HarperCollins*Publishers*

🔥 HarperPaperbacks
A Division of HarperCollinsPublishers
10 East 53rd Street, New York, NY 10022–5299

This is a work of fiction. The characters, incidents, and dialogues are products of the author's imagination and are not to be construed as real. Any resemblance to actual events or persons, living or dead, is entirely coincidental.

ISBN 0-06-101379-X

Cover illustration © 1999 by Jon Paul Ferrara

First HarperPaperbacks printing: June 1999

Printed in the United States of America

Visit HarperPaperbacks on the World Wide Web at
http://www.harpercollins.com

❖ 10 9 8 7 6 5 4 3 2 1

For the Circle——Anne, Barbara,
Connie, Joy, Mel, Monique, and Russ——
with gratitude for your unwavering support.
You all know just how special you are!

1

Rain beat upon expensively paned windows while in the flickering candlelight within, the boisterous clamor hovered in volume between battlefield and bordello. John Jefferson Ashecroft, equally at home in either setting, relished the wild abandon of this latest celebration of his recent, unexpected elevation to the lofty title of Marquis of Foxhaven.

Lord Peter Northrup, fourth son of the Duke of Marland and his oldest friend, clearly did not share his enthusiasm. "Three near-orgies in three nights is a bit much, don't you think, Jack?" he whispered. "Thought you valued your grandfather's memory. This would have him rolling in his grave!"

"Mausoleum, dear boy. Nothing so crude as earth for a Foxhaven resting place! But the old fellow's gone now, so there's no one to care what I do with my good fortune—or no one whose opinion matters." Jack turned from the card table and his advisor.

"Here, Polly, lass! Bring me another pint and

another kiss!" he called out to a passing maidservant.

Giggling, the girl complied, and Jack slid a hand up her skirts to sweeten his kiss. "Milor' you are a handful!" Polly informed him, wrinkling her freckled nose and winking.

Jack chuckled. "Nay, you're the handful, and a pretty one at that! What say you and I escape upstairs for half an hour? My guests will never miss me." He swept a glance about the sumptuous drawing room and at the dicing, dallying throng there assembled. The marked absence of ladies—of Quality, at any rate—gave evidence that this particular gathering lacked Society's blessing.

Then he caught Lord Peter's eye. "What? Surely you don't begrudge me a bit of revelry after the past few years of privation?"

Lord Peter snorted. "Privation? I don't recall that a light purse ever kept you from revelry in the past. Now you simply have the means to speed yourself to perdition on greased wheels."

"Ah, you have no idea how I suffered during the war," Jack informed his friend with a melodramatic sigh. "Wine, women, and song were hard to come by. The sleep I lost in the search . . . ! Ask Harry over there. He has no fault to find with my present lifestyle."

"No surprise there." Lord Peter turned a judicious eye on Harry Thatcher, Jack's second-oldest friend, who was enthusiastically tossing dice with his one remaining arm. The wars had left his other sleeve empty. "Harry always lived for the moment, even before his injury turned him bitter. Now he just wants company on his journey to hell."

Jack shrugged. "And perhaps I'll oblige him. He saved my life in Spain, after all."

"And you his—twice," Lord Peter reminded him. "I'd say the score's more than even."

"Polly, go ahead and take Ferny another bottle," suggested Jack, nodding toward the gesturing Lord Fernworth across the noisy room. "Perhaps by the time you return, Peter will be done with his moralizing. You're quite the spoilsport tonight, you know," he informed his friend when the wench had gone. "I can't think you accepted my invitation merely to cluck over my shortcomings like some brightly colored mother hen."

Lord Peter smoothed his gold-and-scarlet waistcoat. "I suppose I am acting the prig tonight. Sorry, Jack. It's just—"

A forceful throat-clearing at his elbow interrupted him. The thin, nondescript butler Jack had hired earlier that week announced, "A Mr. Havershaw, milord." The throat-clearing guest, just as thin as the butler but much taller, hovered nearby, scowling.

He'd really have to see about a new butler, thought Jack resignedly. This Carp, or Crump, or whatever his name was, didn't seem to have a grasp of the proper procedures at all.

"Ah, yes, Mr. Havershaw," said Jack with forced cordiality while looking daggers at his oblivious butler. "I do apologize for not keeping our appointment last Wednesday. The press of business, you see—"

"Yes, I certainly do see, my lord." Mr. Havershaw scoured the room with a sour glance. "I would not have presumed to come to you, but some of these papers are quite pressing. If I could have half an hour of your time in the library?"

Jack stared at the man in disbelief. "Now?" He knew that Havershaw had enjoyed an unusually privileged position as both his grandfather's steward and lifelong friend, but this was absurd!

"If you'd be so kind, my lord. I'll not keep you long from your . . . guests."

Aware that Lord Peter, along with a growing number of the revelers, were regarding him with interest, Jack finally shrugged. "I may as well get it over, I suppose. Peter, see that no one's glass goes empty, will you? My staff leaves a bit to be desired. All right, Havershaw, the library's this way."

Havershaw headed for the hallway. "I know, my lord."

How did the man manage to make those two words sound like an insult? He was the marquis now, by God, however unprepared for the role he might be.

Once in the library, he turned to face his nemesis. "I trust you'll make this quick, Mr. Havershaw. It's most irregular for a host to abandon his guests in this manner."

He'd meant to say something far more cutting, but various childhood memories of Havershaw had crowded back. With them came an ingrained respect he was amazed could still constrain him. Other than his grandfather and, more recently, the Duke of Wellington, Jack had never cared about pleasing anyone but himself.

Lord Geoffrey, his spendthrift, gamester father and Lord Foxhaven's second son, had died when Jack was but eight. Two years later, his mother married Sir Findlay Branch, a wealthy, stuffy baronet whose apparent mission in life was to eradicate Lord Geoffrey's influences from his son.

Jack had responded with rebellion, at first subtle, then open, and finally flagrant. Before he reached eleven he was shipped off to boarding school and forbidden to return until he reformed. As a result, he spent all holidays at Fox Manor, where old Lord Foxhaven had become the only stabilizing influence in his early life. There, Mr. Havershaw had been an imposing, authoritative presence, second only to his grandfather in the boy's eyes.

"As I said, my lord, this should take but half an hour, perhaps less," said that former object of awe. Opening the satchel he carried, he pulled out a thick sheaf of papers. "There will be much more for you to go over when you finally see your way clear to visit Fox Manor, of course, but these documents are the most pressing."

Jack eyed the stack doubtfully. "I thought I'd signed all the necessary papers after Uncle Luther's funeral."

"Those to ensure your succession to the title and estates, yes. But Foxhaven encompasses a great many enterprises, some of which have been too long neglected due to your uncle's ill health."

Uncle Luther's ill health. If Jack had known when

his grandfather died last spring that his uncle's health was so poorly, he might have been more prepared for the responsibilities which had descended upon him three weeks since. But no one had seen fit to tell him.

Not that he'd ever inquired.

Jack had sold out of the army a scant six weeks after his grandfather's death—as soon as the public's enthusiasm for the war heroes began to wane, in fact—and left for Paris, where a warm welcome still awaited. He'd nearly exhausted both his funds and the goodwill of those willing to supplement them by the time he returned to England in late August. Though he wouldn't have wished poor old Luther underground, his timing had been Jack's financial salvation.

"Very well, let's get it over with. I imagine I'll feel even less like dealing with all of this in the morning." He hadn't drunk much yet, by his standards, but since his succession not a morning had come that hadn't found him cripplingly hung over. There was no particular reason to believe tomorrow would be any different.

Havershaw managed a chilly smile. "Excellent, my lord. If you would turn your attention to this? It deals with certain investments in Portugal . . . "

Forty minutes later, Jack was heartily regretting his compliance. Not that the various business matters put before him were particularly incomprehensible, or even quite as boring as he'd expected. But being dumped headfirst into Foxhaven business made him far too cognizant of the responsibilities now facing him— responsibilities he had neither the ability nor inclination to take on. Why, the very thought of Jack Ashecroft, family outcast, attempting to play the respectable nobleman was thoroughly laughable. Not that he was laughing at the moment.

He yawned.

Mr. Havershaw regarded him through narrowed eyes. "I believe that will do for this evening, my lord. There is one last thing, however, that you may wish to have now." He pulled a sealed envelope from the satchel. "A personal letter from your grandfather, to be delivered to you in the event of your uncle's death without issue."

Jack took the envelope gingerly, turning it over in his fingers several times before breaking the seal—the seal that was now his. Odd feeling, that.

The letter was but a single sheet, its brief contents scrawled in his grandfather's strong but careless hand.

My dear Jack,

    If you are reading this, you have succeeded to my title and, knowing your attention to family matters, most likely unexpectedly. Rest assured that to me this event was neither unexpected, nor at all undesirable. Luther, while an estimable man, has the strength of neither character nor constitution to effectively carry Foxhaven into the future. You have. In fact, you have it in you to become the finest lord Foxhaven has known in six generations—if you can find it in you to put aside your ongoing pursuit of pleasure to tap into that

inner strength I have long observed and, at
whiles, attempted to nurture. It is up to you,
Jack, to bring Foxhaven into its own by coming
into your own. Consider it my dying request.

> Ever your faithful and loving grandfather,
> Julius Ashecroft, Marquis of Foxhaven

Jack sat back in his chair and read it through again,
hearing his grandfather's dry, sardonically affectionate
voice as he did so. He'd known Jack couldn't refuse this
call to action, a call from beyond the grave from the
only person he'd ever truly cared for—or who had
cared for him.

Clenching the letter in one fist, Jack felt his spine
stiffen with resolve. He gave a single nod. "I'll do it," he
said aloud. John Jefferson Ashecroft, black sheep of the
family, was going to become respectable.

"Very good, my lord," said Havershaw, just as though
he knew what Jack was talking about. "He also penned
an addendum." He held out a folded slip of paper.

Frowning, Jack took and opened it. "The road to
hell is paved with good intentions," it read, "as your
own father proved repeatedly. To assist you in your
effort to reform, I have made certain financial arrangements to act as an incentive. Havershaw will acquaint
you with the terms. —F."

"Terms?" Jack looked up suspiciously.

Havershaw pushed a packet of papers across to him.
"The specifics are spelled out there. In brief, all monies

not attached to the estates are to be held in trust until such time as the trustee determines that you have made the required transformation of character."

"The devil they are!" Jack exploded. "What utter nonsense! And just who is this trustee who will pass judgment upon me?"

"I am," replied Havershaw with a thin smile.

Nessa quietly closed the kitchen door and pulled her cloak and hood tightly about her face. Glancing up at the still-lighted windows of the narrow but imposing townhouse, she hoped her sister would not feel so concerned about her fictitious headache as to come to her room to check on her. If all went as planned, she'd be back inside of two hours. With luck, Prudence would never know she'd been away. Hurrying around the corner to the street, she hailed a passing hackney.

For the hundredth time she told herself she was mad to be doing this, and for the hundredth time she hushed her conscience. "King Street, St. James," she told the driver, climbing into the conveyance.

This evening was a present to herself. From the moment she'd first seen the notice in the papers about this masquerade ball, she'd been determined to attend. In London for the first real visit in her life, Nessa felt she deserved some enjoyment.

As the hackney lurched forward, she took the golden feathered mask she'd bought earlier that day from the pocket of her cloak and fastened it over her eyes. No one would ever know, and she'd have a delicious memory to look back on——the first such memory in her whole sheltered lifetime. It was only fair she have this reward for leading such a virtuous existence, she reasoned.

The one thing that did cause Nessa a pang of guilt was the fact that her year of mourning still lacked nearly three weeks till completion. Not for a moment did she believe her husband would have understood, sharing, as he had, her late father's puritanical outlook on life. But she'd spent all of her four and twenty years conforming to the strictures of first the one and then the other. Now, for the first time in her life, she was free of them both——and ready to enjoy that freedom.

"This be King Street, miss," the hackney driver called back to her just then.

"Thank you," she called back. "Take me to the Upper Assembly Rooms, please. And if you could return in one hour, I'd be most grateful."

The driver assented and pulled the carriage to a halt a moment later. Nessa paid him generously, hoping thereby to ensure his return. Then, lifting her chin, she strode regally up the stairs to those same hallowed rooms that housed Almack's during the Season. Handing her cloak to one waiting lackey and her ticket to another, she swept into the ballroom.

A mere step inside the room she paused, surveying with bewildered delight this, her first masquerade. Gaily costumed revelers moved and shimmered in the candlelight of the chandeliers, dancing to the strains of a country tune or gathering in small groups to converse. Multihued dominoes vied with replicas of every historic personage imaginable.

Nessa glanced down at her own low-cut gown, smiling to think she had feared her costume too risqué. What pains she had taken to alter the gown in secret, hiding it from her sister and sharp-eyed abigail. Removing the ruffles from the neckline had transformed it into an effective cyprian's costume. Prudence would doubtless have a spasm if she found it hidden in the back of Nessa's wardrobe, but it was nothing compared to the plumage she saw here displayed.

"Eh there, me beauty! Might ye care to dance?" inquired a poor imitation of Henry VIII at her elbow.

Abruptly, she remembered her sister's objections when Nessa had first mentioned this masquerade to her, about cits and other vulgar sorts attending. In her excitement and determination to attend she'd shrugged it off, but now the evidence was before her.

"Ah, not just yet, thank you," she replied nervously, taking a step away from the man, who reeked of spirits. Somehow, she hadn't really thought about what she'd do *at* the masquerade. She'd focused all her energies on simply getting here.

The man stepped closer. "'Ere now, you're not refusing to dance with yer monarch, are ye?" he prodded with a leer. "Royal privilege and all that."

Nessa swallowed. "No, it's not that. It's only——"

"She has a prior obligation, to confess her sins," interrupted a tall, brown-robed monk. "Even Your Majesty must admit to the superior claims of the Church in such matters." The monk's accent was cultured, reassuring Nessa that this, at least, was a man of her own class.

The drunkard appeared disposed to argue, but a tilt of the monk's head and an ominous glitter of brilliant blue eyes from behind his mask dissuaded him. Muttering something about more wine, King Henry moved away.

"Thank you, sir," said Nessa, relieved. "He really was becoming most persistent."

"One can hardly blame him." The monk looked her over with a most unclerical gleam in his eye. "What do you here alone? Or is your protector busy procuring you a glass of iced champagne?"

"My—?" Nessa glanced down at her costume again and flushed. Perhaps it was a trifle *too* realistic. "No, I assure you I am here alone—but I do not intend to stay long. No more than an hour."

The monk smiled, and Nessa realized how very handsome he was, even with a mask obscuring much of his face. "Then pray, allow me to act as your escort for the brief time you mean to grace this gathering with your presence."

Nessa frowned, wondering if perhaps she had tumbled from the frying pan into the fire. "I, ah—"

"Surely you cannot feel less than safe with a man of the cloth?" he prompted. "Besides, our costumes complement each other so well."

That forced a chuckle from Nessa, making her instantly more comfortable. Surely a man with a sense of humor could not be too evil. Though why she should think that, she did not know. Neither her father nor her husband had ever shown the slightest hint of whimsy, and both had been regarded by the world as the most upright and estimable of men.

"Very well, Friar, I place myself under the protection of the Church for the present."

The tall, handsome monk took Nessa on a tour of the rooms, pointing out their shortcomings. "Makes one wonder what everyone sees in the place, doesn't it?" he asked. "But during the Season, ladies have been known to pine away or even leave Town in disgrace for being denied admittance to Almack's of a Wednesday night."

"I take it, then, that you are a regular attendee yourself, Friar?" asked Nessa, hoping to discover a bit more about him.

"Me? Hardly!" His laugh was almost a snort. "Not that I've attempted it, of course, especially since——Ah, here comes a tray of champagne! Would you care for some, milady?"

Nessa wondered what he'd been about to say. "No, thank you. Is there lemonade, perhaps?" She suspected her judgment was impaired enough this evening without adding spirits to the mix.

The monk spoke to the servant, who returned in a moment with the required beverage. With a flourish, he presented it to her. "In my present guise, I suppose I dare not request a kiss in return for such gallantry. But allow me to tell you your eyes are most haunting, even through that remarkable mask."

"You flatter me, sir." More than ever, Nessa suspected her escort's costume was decidedly at odds with the man underneath. He might be the greatest rake in all London, for aught she knew. She cast about for some way to discover his name—not that it was likely to mean anything to her, as unfamiliar as she was with London Society.

Apparently she was not alone in her curiosity. "Since you do not intend to remain for the unmasking at midnight, might I know the name of the lady I have taken under my protection?"

Though he was but mimicking her earlier words, his phrasing still caused Nessa a thrill of alarm. Surely he did not truly believe her to be as she dressed tonight, a woman of easy virtue? Considering what her life had been until now, the idea was both outrageous and highly amusing. More than ever, she knew she must guard her identity at all costs.

"You may call me Monique," she informed him. It was a name she'd always liked, and sufficiently French to fit her present role.

His well-shaped lips curved into a smile. For a fleeting moment, she wondered what it would be like to kiss those lips—then cut off such thoughts, shocked at herself. Clearly, she was taking her masquerade role far too seriously!

"Might I request this dance, Monique?" A waltz was just beginning.

"First might I know *your* name, Friar?" she asked boldly.

"In return for the dance, you may call me Brother

Eligius," he said loftily, taking her hand to lead her to the floor.

Nessa hung back. "One might ask what it is you are worthy of, Brother Eligius."

"Ah, a lady who knows her Latin! Worthy of this dance, of course—and anything else you might see fit to bestow upon me," he added with a lascivious wink. She might have been alarmed were it not clear he was teasing—and if his words didn't send her thoughts down most improper channels.

She stood her ground. "I see. Perhaps I shall bestow the next dance upon you, then. This one is nearly over." That was not quite true, but she could not bring herself to admit that she had never learned to waltz. Given her parents', and later her husband's, views on the dance, she had never even dared to ask.

To her relief, the monk did not press the issue, but stood trading quips with her about both of their pseudonyms until the orchestra struck up a country dance. The dance was lively, allowing little opportunity for conversation, and by its conclusion Nessa's hour was nearly up.

The two of them had drawn many curious stares, and as they left the dance floor a lanky man dressed as a harlequin approached them.

"What a sight this is!" he exclaimed. "Have you persuaded your partner to join you in a life of virtue, J— er, Friar?" A quick motion by the monk had prevented him from uttering the monk's name, to Nessa's frustration.

"Indeed, for her I believe it won't be so much of a stretch, despite appearances," he replied, making her wonder how on earth he had guessed that. "Am I not right, milady Monique?"

"Perhaps. Perhaps not," she replied, stung that her attempt to throw off propriety had been such a failure. With sudden recklessness, she swooped up onto her tiptoes to plant a swift kiss square on the monk's mouth. Then, more shocked at her own boldness than he could possibly be, she turned quickly away.

"I really must be going, now," she said breathlessly, not meeting his eye. "I wish you success in your conversions, Brother Eligius." Before he could respond or even react, Nessa fled the scene of the most daring thing she'd ever done in her whole sheltered life.

The hackney was waiting when she stepped outdoors, and as she rode home, Nessa's brief elation ebbed. She should be pleased, she knew, that there was virtually no chance that she would ever again encounter the mysterious monk, as he'd likely identify her if she did. But somehow that reflection brought less than complete satisfaction.

Arriving back at her sister's, she again paid the driver and reentered the house as quietly as she'd left it. Her brief taste of freedom was over, with none the wiser.

2

Jack watched the enigmatic woman in white as she hurried from the ballroom, his lips still tingling pleasurably from that surprising kiss. Surely there'd been no hidden meaning in her parting words. She couldn't know about the real conversion he was attempting—his own.

"So much for that costume reminding you of your new mission, Jack," commented Lord Peter, the bells on his harlequin headpiece jingling as he nodded sagely. "Still running after the demimonde, I see."

Jack shot his friend a sardonic glance. "I shouldn't make remarks about appropriate costumes if I were you, Peter. But that lady . . . I'm not certain—"

"What possessed you to let that pretty piece escape, Jack?" Harry Thatcher, clad in a simple black domino that effectively hid his injury, came up to join them just then. "If you didn't want her, with your newfound virtue, you should have sent her my way. I can still appreciate a toothsome wench—and pleasure one, too. Loss of an arm hasn't slowed me down in *that* department. God preserve me from a title, though!"

Jack regarded his wartime crony with a mixture of sympathy and envy. "As *your* uncle has three sons already, I shouldn't think there's much chance of your being saddled with such a curse." Harry's father, like Jack's, was second son to a peer, in this case the Earl of Balfour. "Had I known Uncle Luther was both sickly and childless, I might have stayed on the Continent. But now I'm stuck with it."

Both of his friends laughed, though they doubtless knew there was more than a grain of truth in Jack's words. He was finding this "conversion" to respectability damnably tedious—and difficult. Much as he hated to admit it, if it weren't for the money his grandfather held over his head, he'd have abandoned the idea already.

"This"—he waved his arm about to indicate the glittering throng—"was to be my final fling, as it were. As of tomorrow, I don the sober mantle of Marquis of Foxhaven, and all that goes with it. God help me." With mock piety, he made the sign of the cross, causing his companions to chuckle anew.

Peter sobered quickly, however. "It ain't going to be easy setting yourself up as a paragon after the reputation you've built over the years, Jack. Too many people know the real you."

"Precisely what I've come to realize. That is why I need your help, both of you."

Harry snorted. "That's well enough for Pete here. Always eager to be the voice of conscience anyway. But you can count me out. I think the whole idea is daft. You've got position, you've got money—more than you ever dreamed. Here you are, with everything you need to have the best time of your life, and you get morality or some such rot." He shook his head. "Never thought I'd live to see it. Makes a man wonder what the point is."

Jack glared at his friend, who only voiced what he himself had felt more than once since reading his grandfather's letter two nights since. "The point is living up to my potential," he said tersely, willing himself to believe it. "Now that I'm Foxhaven, I have a family name to uphold. Besides, as I told you, I *don't* have the money. At least, not enough to continue as I've done and maintain the estates both. Not unless I follow through on this thing."

Before Harry could repeat his thanks for escaping such a fate, Peter spoke up. "Well *I* think it's an admirable attitude, Jack, money or no, and I'll support you however I can. As I said, though, it won't be easy. What you need is some sort of shortcut to respectability." He furrowed his brow, pondering.

"My thoughts exactly," agreed Jack. "Would an irreproachable wife turn the trick, do you think?"

Both of his friends gaped at him, clearly dumbstruck.

"Someone whose reputation is lily-white, beyond question," he continued. "Surely some of that should rub off, in the eyes of Society."

Peter was the first to find his voice. "By George, Jack, I didn't think you were serious, but . . . yes. I think that just might be the ticket."

"And where are you going to find such a paragon of virtue?" asked Harry cynically, belatedly recovering from his own shock. "Never tell me you're acquainted with a woman fitting that description!"

Jack shook his head ruefully. "Any woman willing to admit to an acquaintance with me wouldn't qualify, on that ground alone. But if the three of us do a bit of research, surely we can discover a woman of that caliber somewhere—perhaps even here in London. I hereby commission you both to help me to find her— the perfect wife. One who can polish up my tarnished reputation and thereby secure the balance of my fortune."

"You look a bit hagged this morning, Nessa. Did your headache keep you from sleeping?" asked Lady Creamcroft as her sister entered the brightly sunlit breakfast parlor. The torrential downpours earlier in the week had given way to unseasonably lovely weather for a London autumn.

"Yes, I'm afraid so." Nessa manufactured a yawn. "I'm feeling much better today, however." Lying to her sister was completely out of character and made her feel far guiltier than she'd expected. Still, last night had been worth it. She was almost certain of it.

"I did come up and knock an hour or so after you'd retired, and assumed you were sleeping when you failed to answer."

Nessa paused in the act of filling her plate from the sideboard. "I, ah, may well have been asleep at that time. 'Twas later in the night that I awoke and had trouble nodding off again. I came down to the kitchen for some warm milk, and that helped." That was the excuse she'd given to the scullery maid who'd discovered her sneaking through the lower levels upon her return from the masquerade. Luckily, her cloak and her wrapper were the same color—black—and there'd been too little light for her attire to give her away.

"Nessa! It is not at all the thing for you to be wandering about the house on your own after we were all abed. Why did you not ring for a servant?"

"I didn't wish to wake anyone."

Prudence, like their parents, was an absolute stickler for propriety, Nessa reflected. If the idea of her venturing to the kitchens alone upset her, she didn't like to think what she'd do if she discovered where her sister had really gone last night. Doubtless she'd have Prudence's prostration from apoplexy on her conscience as well.

"That's what servants are for, my dear," her sister assured her. "Things are more lax in the country, I know, but you are in Town now, and must learn to abide by Town customs."

Nessa laughed. "Lax? Not in Lord Haughton's house, I assure you, Prudence. His standards were every bit as high as any you'll find in London—probably higher."

"I was thinking more of how you went on after his passing." Prudence frowned. "I wish I could have had you with me sooner, but with Lord Creamcroft traveling back and forth from Herefordshire to Town all the summer . . . "

"You did invite me to accompany you, if you recall," Nessa reminded her sister. "I preferred to wait till my period of mourning was up, or nearly so, so as not to interfere with your engagements."

She'd also needed time to adjust to the idea of being her own mistress for the first time in her life. Married at eighteen to a man of her father's generation, temperament, and choosing, she'd never known anything but rigid adherence to the rules as laid out by the men in authority over her.

Suddenly finding herself without their firm guidance, she'd been at somewhat of a loss. Had her parents still been alive, she might have returned home to Worcestershire during the early months of her widowhood, simply to have her decisions made for her, as they'd always been. Living under the thumb of her Cousin Filmore held no appeal, however, so she had remained at Haughton until her late husband's nephew and heir was due to arrive.

Gradually, tentatively, she had taken up the reins of the house and estate, showing an unexpected flair for both business and domestic organization. By the time she'd left, on the arrival of the new Lord Haughton a fortnight ago, even the dour, efficient housekeeper, Mrs. Cobb, frequently sought her direction.

Nessa settled herself across from her sister with a plate of eggs and creamed sole and thoughtfully sipped her coffee. She had mourned her husband's passing, of course, just as she had her father's two years earlier. But, like her father, her husband had been so distant that she had been unable to develop more than the mildest affection for him—an affection tainted by more than a hint of bitterness. It would not be true to say she'd felt relief at finding herself on her own, but it would be equally untrue to say she was prostrated by grief.

Now that she'd finally made the adjustment, she felt ready and more than ready to taste her newfound freedom. Last night had been a promising start.

"Oh!" Prudence broke into her musings. "Mention of your mourning period reminds me that I have received an invitation which includes you."

Nessa blinked in surprise. "An invitation? Will it be proper for me to go anywhere just yet?" she asked innocently. "I'll not be out of my weeds for more than two weeks, you know."

"Yes, I know, and I consulted Lord Creamcroft on that very point. He seems to think me overscrupulous in this—as in a few other matters." She primmed her lips. "But in this particular case, I believe he may be right. Lady Mountheath is hostessing a musicale three days hence, and 'tis she who issued the invitation. She knows of your circumstances and surely would not have invited you had she thought your attendance ineligible."

"A musicale. So there will be no dancing?"

Prudence looked stricken. "Heavens no! There could be no question of your attending then, of course.

But a quiet evening in company, listening to a few noted performers, seems a very proper way to ease you back into Society."

Not that she'd ever been in Society to begin with, thought Nessa sourly. A three-day visit to London for her presentation at Court a few weeks after her wedding scarcely counted. Idly, she wondered whether any of those who'd attended last night's masquerade were likely to be present—especially one in particular. Given what she'd heard of Lady Mountheath, it seemed unlikely.

Still, she found herself looking forward to the musicale. It would be the next step, albeit a small one, toward her new life of freedom.

A somber trio gathered before the library fire at Foxhaven House the following night. At least, Jack felt weighed down by doom and depression at the idea of marriage, whatever his companions might feel. If their spirits were higher than his own, they were discreet enough not to show it.

"We may as well compare notes," he suggested heavily as he passed the brandy decanter around for the second time. The thought of walking willfully into parson's mousetrap set his teeth on edge, but he really had no choice. Just that afternoon he'd received a note from Havershaw informing him that the roof of the west wing at Fox Manor required repairs that would eat up the remainder of his quarter's allowance.

Lord Peter pulled a sheet of paper from his pocket

with a flourish. "Have my list right here, old boy," he said, waving away the spirits.

Harry took the bottle and poured himself a generous measure to compensate for Peter's forbearance. "You actually wrote 'em down? Egad, but you're taking this project seriously. Must have been an amusing sight, you quizzing all the biddies and taking notes the while."

"I didn't jot down the names until later, when I was back at my lodgings," Peter assured him. "Wouldn't have been at all the thing to let on what I was about. That would queer the whole deal."

Harry laughed heartily. "Jack might thank you for that, judging by his face. You look like you've downed a quart of spoilt milk, old boy," he advised his friend.

Jack only scowled more fiercely. "If you're not going to help, you may as well remain silent, Harry—or take your leave."

"While the bottle's still half full? Heaven forfend! But I have had my ear to the ground, as it happens, though I may not be as organized in my approach as Pete here." He chuckled again. "Two or three names cropped up in Boodle's betting book as those least likely to disgrace themselves this winter. Starched up, butter-wouldn't-melt-in-their-mouths misses, just as you're wanting."

Wanting? Hardly that, Jack thought. "Let's have them."

"There were two chits listed there—can't say as I've ever met either of them, not that that's surprising. Lucinda Melks, Lord Jeller's daughter, and Lady Beatrice Bagford, daughter to the Earl of Sherbourne."

Jack nodded gloomily. "I've been introduced, briefly, to both of them. Just out of the schoolroom, I believe."

Harry shrugged. "Easier to train that way, I should think." He studied Jack's morose expression. "Antidotes, are they?"

"No, no, not really. Miss Melks' nose is a bit long, but otherwise she's quite handsome. And Lady Beatrice is tall, blond, and nobly formed, as I recall." And brainless, as well. Jack had not the least desire to wed either, even if one of them would have him. "What of your list, Peter?"

His friend peered down at the sheet in his hand. "Lady Beatrice is on mine as well, but I left off Miss Melks because of a rumor that her maternal grandfather had dabbled in trade. Other contenders include Miss Varens, though she's been out nearly two years, and Lady Constance Throckwaite, Claridge's daughter. Both fairly attractive and eminently respectable."

Peter paused, then said, "I hear Mrs. Dempsey has called here twice in the last week, and you were seen in Covent Garden with Selena Riverton. If you're at all serious about this, Jack, you'll have to give up your paramours, at least until you've been safely wed for awhile."

"Your sources are appallingly thorough, Peter! Miranda Dempsey has just returned from Paris, but I've carefully been 'not at home' to her, if you must know, and Selena accosted me by chance as I was passing the theater where she performs. Can I help it that women find me irresistible?" He grinned, his mood momentarily lightening. "Have you anyone else on your list?"

"There were a few others, but—of the debutantes— those I have already named were mentioned most often."

"Of the debutantes?" echoed Jack. "What else is there?"

"Widows," said Harry succinctly. Peter nodded.

Jack looked from one to the other with a frown. "A widow? I'll admit that idea has more appeal than a virgin child." His tastes had always tended to run to more experienced women—which had resulted in more than one near-miss with an irate husband. "But would that serve my purpose as well? After all—"

"One would," Peter declared. "Except that I can't vouch for her appearance, as no one seems to have seen her. Lady Haughton should just be coming out of her weeds this month."

"Old Haughton was married?" asked Jack incredulously. "Hard to imagine, somehow."

"Yes, scary old fellow, wasn't he? Can't say I'd have envied his wife. Kept her immured in the country."

Jack frowned again. "But she'd be far older than I, wouldn't she? I don't know that I need rebel quite that thoroughly against the young chits."

"Not at all," Peter assured him. "Haughton married late. She's no more than four- or five-and-twenty."

Harry spoke up. "Now that you mention it, Pete, I heard something about her as well. Lady Creamcroft's sister, isn't she?"

"That's right. The late Lord Cherryhurst's daughter. Between them, he and old Haughton pretty well cornered the market on straitlaced respectability."

Jack had met Lord Cherryhurst at his stepfather's house when he was a lad, and retained an impression of a nose and chin jutting skyward. Any daughters would no doubt reflect their father's starched-up formality. Truth to tell, a young woman who was the product of Cherryhurst's upbringing and several years' marriage to Haughton sounded terrifying—but perfect for his purposes.

"What's her first name?"

Peter checked his notes. "Agnes."

Harry snorted. "And her sister is Prudence, I seem to recall. No doubt both were well trained to live up to their names."

Jack winced. Agnes. Purity. "I suppose I could at least meet her," he said at last, remembering Fox Manor's leaking roof. "I'll also seek a reintroduction to Lady Beatrice. Perhaps she's matured a bit since the summer."

"Excellent!" Peter rose to slap him on the back. "We just need to arrange invitations to some of the same dos. Lady Beatrice is certain to be at the Mountheath's musicale, and there's an outside chance Lady Haughton may attend as well, for all she's still in blacks."

Jack snorted. "Lady Mountheath? She won't have me under her roof. She's the biggest gossipmonger in London—probably knows more about my reputation than I do."

"Just show up," Harry suggested with a grin. Over Peter's indignant exclamation, he continued, "No one's more terrified of a scandal than Lady Mountheath—too many people would jump at the chance to spread it, after all the dirt she's dished over the years. And wouldn't it create just that if she attempted to have the Marquis of Foxhaven ejected from her house? She'd never do it! Mark my word, she may look daggers at you, but she'll never let on you weren't invited if you appear at her door."

Both Jack and Peter had to chuckle at the truth of Harry's words. No one had a greater fear of exposure than someone who'd thrived for years on exposing others.

"I'll try it," said Jack with sudden decision. "And I'll be everything that's proper while I'm there, which in itself should go a long way toward repairing my reputation. Lady Mountheath's rumor mill is legendary."

"I'll accompany you," offered Peter. "I happen to have an invitation, which may mitigate your lack of one."

Harry poured himself yet another measure of brandy. "I won't wish you a good time, as I see little chance of that. I'll bide my time more pleasantly at the club, and you can meet me there afterward to tell me how the first foray went."

Nessa regarded her reflection in the dressing mirror with vague dissatisfaction. Her rich chestnut brown hair looked well enough piled high on her head, if a little severe. Simmons, her abigail, was weaving a spray of tiny silver silk flowers through the crown as an accent, though a few curls about her face would have made for a softer effect. Her complexion was well enough, but black had never been particularly flattering on her. And after nearly a full year wearing nothing but that hue, she was heartily tired of it.

No doubt the world—and her sister—would see it as vastly disrespectful when she discarded every black gown she owned (which numbered in the dozens) in two weeks' time, but that was precisely what she intended to do. Perhaps giving them all to some charitable organization would mute criticism a bit. But whether it did or not, she never intended to wear black again come mid-October.

"Thank you, Simmons, that looks lovely," she said, though privately she thought the silver flowers gave the impression that her hair was beginning to gray. But anything more colorful would have been frowned upon—particularly by her sister.

At least the lines of her black satin gown—as with all of her gowns—were elegant, if a bit high in the neckline for fashion. That would change too, she vowed, no matter what Prudence had to say to the matter. Taking up her black lace fan, she left her chamber.

"Nessa, you look lovely this evening," her sister greeted her as they met at the head of the stairs. "Those silver flowers are a nice touch."

Lord Creamcroft, at her side, murmured agreement with his wife's words, but Nessa noticed that his eyes were all for Prudence. Did her sister have any idea of how her husband worshipped her? Nessa wondered. Probably not—she wouldn't consider it proper for a husband to care so much for his wife. It was sad, in a way, for both of them. What might her own marriage have been like, had Lord Haughton loved her?

She forced a smile. "Thank you, Prudence. They were Simmons' idea. Shall we go?"

Once inside the carriage, she resumed her musings. Most likely, had Lord Haughton cared more deeply for her he would simply have demanded sexual intimacy more frequently than those few incidents early in their marriage. Nessa shuddered.

"Are you cold, sister?" asked Lord Creamcroft kindly. He was an attractive man, with light brown hair and eyes, only a few years older than her sister. Nessa felt a brief, unexpected surge of envy.

"Thank you, no," she replied. "Just a passing chill." No, she would not envy any married woman! She knew, all too well, what the marriage state entailed: obedience, subordination and occasional subjection to distasteful physical contact. Even with a man closer to her own age than her father's, or one reasonably attractive, it was nothing to be desired.

To be fair, since her arrival in London ten days ago she had seen no sign of Lord Creamcroft bullying her sister. Of course, he held her in affection, which might make a difference, she supposed. Unaccountably, her thoughts strayed back to the masked monk at the masquerade.

"Here we are," Prudence announced just then, interrupting her errant thoughts—which was probably just as well. "Is not the Mountheath house lovely?"

Nessa peered out of the carriage window as they slowly approached the entrance, waiting their turn behind a few other carriages. Lovely was not quite the word she'd have chosen. Imposing, certainly, with its enormous columns and frowning gray façade. She murmured something noncommittal.

A few minutes later, they stepped down from the carriage and entered the impressive edifice. The interior of the Mountheath Townhouse was as formally elegant as the exterior, Nessa noted. Both her father and husband would have approved of this place. She found it rather oppressive.

"Prudence, my dear," a large, turbaned woman greeted them at the head of the stairs. "And Lord Creamcroft. Such a handsome couple, as I always tell everyone. And this must be the mysterious Lady Haughton!" Her eyes gleamed with avid curiosity.

Nessa dropped a half-curtsey. Her rank was equal to Lady Mountheath's, but the latter's age and role as hostess demanded the tribute. "Guilty as charged," she assented daringly, and was not surprised to hear a soft gasp from her sister. Prudence had warned her that Lady Mountheath thrived on scandal, and she could not resist teasing a bit.

Their hostess, however, merely nodded, raking Nessa with her eyes. "Everyone has been wondering what you were like, my dear. I believe you will throw out the suppositions of the majority. But come, you must meet my daughters. New to London as you are, you'll wish to make friends as soon as may be, I doubt not."

Nessa very shortly decided that she'd as soon not number Miss Lucy and Miss Fanny among her close friends, even though both girls—she kindly refrained from calling them spinsters even in her thoughts—were near her in age. They both possessed their mother's penchant for malicious gossip, as well as her tiny, sharp eyes and double chins.

"I can't think why Mamma invited Miss Islington," Lucy was confiding in a loud whisper as the three of them stood not far from the top of the stairs, where they had a good view of those entering. "Her cousin married well beneath him, you know. It must sink the whole family's social standing to be associated with trade, even two generations removed."

Nessa wished she had stayed with her sister and brother-in-law. She was searching for a reply that would neither condemn Miss Islington for her cousin's connections nor offend her hostess' daughters when Fanny gasped.

"Look! Look there, Lucy!" she hissed. "Is that not Jack Ashecroft? Or Lord Foxhaven, I suppose we must say, now. I am positively certain Mamma did not invite him!"

Her sister turned. "You're right, Fanny! It *is* he! Do you suppose Mamma will have him removed?"

Nessa was forgotten as both sisters avidly watched

the tableau unfolding at the entrance to the large room.
She herself found the situation interesting, the more so
when she got a good look at the man in question. Lord
Foxhaven was without a doubt the handsomest man
she'd ever seen, with thick, jet-black hair, noble profile,
and breathtakingly athletic physique.

As she watched, Lady Mountheath greeted the gentleman accompanying him, then turned to face the sup-
posedly uninvited guest. Her color rose precipitously
as she apparently realized who he was. Nessa had
thought her hostess' smiles insincere before, but they
were nothing to the strained expression she now wore.
The corners of her lips looked as though a puppeteer's
strings pulled them upwards against her will. Nessa
edged closer in hopes of hearing the exchange.

"Why, my lord, such a, er, delightful surprise," Lady
Mountheath was saying stiffly. "Had I but known you
were in town . . ."

"Yes, I thought as much, my lady. Knowing your
unfailing hospitality, I presumed on your kindness to
accompany Lord Peter, praying that you'd not turn me
away."

Nessa swallowed, hard. She was almost certain
she'd heard that voice before. But no, she must be mistaken. This appeared to be a man of some consequence,
as did his companion.

Lady Mountheath managed to force a trill of laughter. "Turn you away! La, my lord, how droll you are.
Come, both of you, and join the assemblage. You've
met my daughters, I believe?" Behind her back, out of

sight of the gentlemen, she beckoned Fanny and Lucy with one actively twitching hand.

"Charmed to see you again," said Lord Peter, bending over the hand of first one, then the other suddenly simpering miss. He introduced Lord Foxhaven, who had apparently not made their acquaintance for all they'd recognized him on sight.

Nessa tried to move unobtrusively away as her suspicions sharpened. Unfortunately, Lady Mountheath recollected her manners before she could escape.

"Here is someone you'll not have met," she said, appearing oddly eager to call the interloper's attention away from her daughters. "Lady Haughton is but newly come to Town, staying with her sister, Lady Creamcroft. Lady Haughton, may I present Lord Peter Northrup, son of the Duke of Marland, and His Lordship the Marquis of Foxhaven."

Both gentlemen regarded Nessa with sudden interest, which was unsettling enough. But far more unsettling were the brilliant blue eyes of the marquis—eyes she had seen once before, through the slits of a brown mask!

Nessa had just presence of mind enough to modulate her voice into a softer, lower tone than she normally used, praying that Lord Foxhaven would not recognize her, as she made her answer. "I'm happy to make your acquaintance, gentlemen." She dropped a perfectly proper half-curtsey.

"Lady Haughton, what a sur—that is, how nice to meet you here tonight." Lord Peter winced visibly from the surreptitious kick the marquis had given him.

Nessa realized with a jolt that this had been the harlequin at the masquerade. She fought down her panic as Lord Foxhaven spoke.

"This is indeed a pleasure," he agreed smoothly, succeeding in making her wonder whether she'd imagined that kick. "You are highly spoken of in all the best circles, my lady. It is my honor to make your acquaintance." The bow accompanying this speech was the very picture of polished elegance.

"You are too kind, my lord," she murmured, beginning to breathe somewhat easier, though she kept her eyes lowered. He hadn't recognized her. At least, she cautioned herself, not yet.

3

Jack glanced quickly at Lord Peter, then back to Lady Haughton. For a moment, he'd been almost certain he'd met her before, but now he began to doubt. Clearly Peter was showing no signs of recognition— not that he was the most perceptive of fellows. Besides, it seemed so unlikely, after all he'd been able to learn of Lady Haughton.

He'd done a bit of research since Peter had brought her name to his notice. As his friends had said, no one had seen her since her arrival in London two weeks ago, so he had not really expected her to attend tonight. Not only had she been in virtual seclusion since her husband's death, but both she and Lady Creamcroft were complete sticklers for propriety—so much so as not to allow her appearance in public before her year of mourning was up.

Which made the possibility of her being the same woman he'd met at last week's masquerade impossibly remote. "Monique," whoever she'd been, had certainly not been a grief-stricken widow! Even if she had possessed melting brown eyes remarkably similar to Lady Haughton's.

Still, he decided to attempt a small test. "Might I procure a glass of lemonade for you, my lady, before the entertainment begins?"

Though she kept her eyes demurely lowered, the long, mink-brown lashes fluttered at his words. "No, thank you, my lord," she said after just the slightest hesitation. "I do not particularly care for lemonade."

Jack watched her closely. Could it possibly be . . . ? But he decided not to press the matter—not just now, at any rate. If this really were the woman from the masquerade, he would find out soon enough. That could be very useful information. Very useful indeed.

"Ratafia, then, perhaps?"

She nodded then, not deigning—or daring?—to meet his eyes again. "Thank you, my lord. That would be pleasant."

Peter accompanied Jack to the buffet table. "Not quite the antidote you predicted, eh, Jack?" he commented as they obtained beverages for themselves along with Lady Haughton's ratafia. "Rather prim, of course, but I'd say she shows potential."

Jack smiled, remembering the luscious Monique. "Potential indeed, I suspect. Still, I don't want to limit my options just yet. Did you notice whether Lady Beatrice is here tonight?"

"Over there, with her father." Peter nodded toward the archway of the music room.

Following his glance, Jack saw Lady Beatrice, surrounded by half a dozen gallants, looking just as cool and lovely as he remembered. After meeting Lady Haughton, however, he found his enthusiasm for the blond debutante at a lower ebb than ever.

"Let's see whether my new position will garner me more than the stiff nod plain Jack Ashecroft received when I first met her, shall we?"

Lady Haughton's ratafia in hand, he detoured past the music room. "Good evening, Lady Beatrice, Sherbourne." He nodded to the lady in question and her father, in turn. "How nice to see you again."

Lord Sherbourne frowned at him suspiciously. "Evening, Foxhaven," he said with a stiff nod. "Didn't expect to see you here."

Jack allowed himself a half-smile. "Ah, sometimes I surprise even myself." He turned to face Lady Beatrice.

She smiled limpidly, darted a quick, curious glance at her father's sour expression, then regarded Jack again, more warily. "Good evening, my lord. I had not realized you had returned to London."

Jack wasn't surprised. His exploits since his return to the metropolis had hardly been of the sort to reach such a sheltered miss's ears.

It seemed her father was thinking along similar lines. "Come, Beatrice," he said before Jack could respond. "Your mother will be expecting us to join her within for the performance." With a warning glance over his shoulder, he led his daughter away from Jack's dangerous influence.

Chuckling, Jack continued back to where Lady Haughton had now been joined by Lord and Lady Creamcroft. "The reputation is still ascendant, it would seem," he said in an undertone to Peter as they approached the trio. "Is Lady Creamcroft such a dragon in the defense of her sister, do you suppose?"

"I'd imagine Lady Haughton can defend herself, after a lifetime of the sort of tutelage she's had." Peter motioned off to the left with his head. "There's Miss Varens. Perhaps you'll need to lower your standards just a hair."

Jack glanced at his friend in surprise. "You wound me, Peter! At any rate, I must bring Lady Haughton the refreshment I promised her before pursuing other game." This last was said a shade too loudly, Jack realized belatedly. Lady Haughton appeared not to have heard, but her sister was frowning—whether at his words or at him in general, he couldn't tell.

"Your ratafia, Lady Haughton." He presented the drink with a flourish. "I believe the entertainment will be beginning in a moment."

"Thank you, my lord." The expression in her brown eyes, when she lifted them briefly, was wary but not censorious. "Have you met my sister and her husband, Lord and Lady Creamcroft?" She seemed anxious to turn his attention away from herself.

"Creamcroft, we've met at Boodle's, have we not?" The young baron nodded his assent. He seemed a pleasant enough fellow, at least. "Lady Creamcroft, I don't believe I've had the pleasure. Charmed."

Lady Creamcroft responded most properly, but her expression told him she'd heard all the worst tales about him—most of them true, unfortunately. She edged herself almost imperceptibly in front of her sister. A dragon indeed, albeit a young and pretty one— nearly as pretty as Lady Haughton, in fact, her brown hair touched with golden highlights instead of red ones. Amazing that poker-faced old Cherryhurst could have produced these two beauties.

"My lord," she said formally. "If you'll excuse us, we'd best take our seats."

As the trio retreated, Jack just caught the curious glance Lady Haughton sent her sister. Doubtless by the end of the evening she'd have heard everything her sister knew of him.

He frowned. He'd just faced almost the identical situation with Lady Beatrice and her father, and it had afforded him only amusement. So why should the thought of Lady Haughton learning of his reputation cost him a pang? He didn't know, but couldn't deny that it did.

"Cross off another one," said Peter in his ear. "Looks like this won't be so easy as you thought."

"I never said it would be easy." Jack couldn't quite hide his irritation. "There's your Miss Varens. Care to introduce me?"

Peter performed the office, but though they said all that was proper, Jack was greeted by cold stares, not only from Sir Arnold and Lady Varens, but from the young lady herself. He'd intended asking her to go driving with him tomorrow, for she was a pretty little thing, but suddenly opted against it.

Cursing himself for a craven, but feeling decidedly out of his element, Jack went to find a chair for the performance which was just beginning.

"What was that about, Prudence?" asked Nessa in an undertone as their party moved toward their seats. "That was the nearest thing to rudeness I've ever seen in you!"

Her sister glanced over her shoulder before answering in an even lower tone. "Lord Foxhaven is not the sort of man with whom you should be encouraging an acquaintance," she whispered repressively. "I can't conceive why Lady Mountheath should have invited him here tonight. I had thought her more discriminating."

Nessa decided against revealing what she'd learned from that lady's sharp-tongued daughters, or the scene she'd witnessed earlier. "Why? What is wrong with Lord Foxhaven?"

"Pray lower your voice!" Prudence admonished her. "He is but very lately come into his title and seems—how shall I put it?—ill prepared for the role. His life has been one of unremitting license, if all I hear is to be believed. 'Twill take more than a marquisate to establish him in Society, I assure you."

Settling into the chair beside her sister, Nessa commented, "I never knew you to put such stock in gossip, Prudence. Are any specific evils laid at his door, or merely the general ones that jealousy might account for?" At her sister's questioning look, she clarified. "A young, handsome man coming so suddenly into a high position is bound to excite envy."

But Prudence shook her head. "Jack Ashecroft's scandalous reputation had been bruited about London long before he inherited. For all that he was feted as a hero last May, after our army's victory over Napoleon, he has never had the entrée to the better circles."

"He was a soldier, then?"

"A major, I believe—or perhaps he was promoted to colonel. His *military* career was distinguished, I'll grant you that. One of Wellington's finest, 'tis said. But he is at least as well known for his paramours"—even in the dim light, Nessa could see her sister's flush at this bold reference to the man's improprieties—"and his association with all manner of low types. 'Twas even rumored that he occasionally acted as a spy while on the Continent, and you must know what is said of spies."

"Yes, of course, but—"

"Hush," said Prudence, clearly desirous of dropping such a distressing topic. "The music is beginning."

Though she tried, Nessa found it difficult to concentrate on the flutist's performance. Instead of the music—though adequate in execution—she found her thoughts straying again to Lord Foxhaven, whom she'd noticed slipping into a seat only two rows back.

Had he recognized her? She thought not, but when he made the offer of lemonade, she had wondered. One thing was certain, however: If *he* were not going to betray their earlier meeting, *she* most assuredly would not!

The very thought of Prudence's reaction if she learned the truth made her quail. Nessa didn't want to be responsible for her sister's almost certain collapse, especially after Prudence had been so kind to her.

Momentarily diverted, she wondered why she and her sister had never been particularly close, considering that they had no other siblings. Of course, any sort of affectionate display had been frowned upon by their parents—perhaps because it would have made that particular lack in their marriage all the more apparent.

Nessa sighed. As a young girl, a love match had been a cherished dream of hers, one she'd never dared divulge to anyone, as she'd known no one who would have understood. Even though she'd long come to recognize that dream as pure fantasy, she had never entirely given it up as an ideal—if not for her, then perhaps for her sister.

She glanced at Prudence, who appeared riveted by the music, surprising a surreptitiously longing look from her brother-in-law, directed at the same object. How could her sister be so blind to the potential happiness that awaited her, if she would only allow herself to return her husband's obvious affection? The more she saw of their marriage, the more Nessa came to realize that it was quite unlike her own had been—and could be even more unlike, if only Prudence would unbend a little. Again she felt that tiny pang of envy.

A slight movement to her right recalled her attention to Lord Foxhaven. Even behind a mask, he'd been remarkably handsome. Without it . . . She thought again over what Prudence had said about his unsavory reputation.

Nessa had no reason to doubt her sister's words. At their first meeting she'd been sure he was anything but monklike, despite his costume. But the knowledge that she'd been right excited more than repelled her. She'd never known a rake before. Not that Prudence would countenance such an acquaintance, of course. And her father—and late husband—would likely spin in their graves should she at all encourage a man of his stamp.

With such conflicting thoughts Nessa was occupied for the remainder of the performance, her visceral attraction to the scandalous Lord Foxhaven warring with the propriety ingrained in her since birth, as well as a certain sense of responsibility toward her sister.

When Lady Mountheath announced the end of the formal performance, advising her guests to partake of the buffet while sundry other musicians added to the ambiance, the assemblage rose en masse to comply with her instructions. As they left the music room, Nessa's party was again accosted by Lord Foxhaven, giving her the opportunity to choose between her battling inclinations.

"Lady Haughton, I realize it would be improper of me to ask you to go out driving"—this with a glance at Prudence—"but would you perhaps allow me to call upon you at your sister's home tomorrow?"

Nessa cursed her blacks yet again, for the thought of

a drive sent her spirits soaring. She saw Prudence frown and open her mouth, no doubt to deny him even the visit.

"That would be quite acceptable, Lord Foxhaven," Nessa said quickly, refusing to meet her sister's eye. "I shall look forward to it."

He bowed over her hand, also avoiding Prudence's glance, she noticed. "Until tomorrow, then." He turned and walked away before Lady Creamcroft could rescind her sister's invitation.

Prudence, however, was for the moment too flabbergasted to speak. "Well!" she exclaimed when she finally found her tongue several seconds later. "That is the outside of enough, I must say. Nessa, did I not tell you Lord Foxhaven has a less than savory reputation? What can you be thinking, to invite him under my roof?"

Nessa rather wondered the same thing, but answered her sister readily enough. "Why, it would have been most impolite, would it not, to have refused him? Besides, what evil can he possibly commit in your drawing room, with people all about? Perhaps he has turned over a new leaf, in which case he should be encouraged, don't you agree?" This last seemed most unlikely when she recalled his behavior at the masquerade, but it gave Prudence pause.

"I suppose that is possible," she conceded, "though Lady Mountheath told me a tale about his exploits since inheriting his title that shocked me exceedingly. Not for the world would I repeat it! Still, if he acts the gentleman, I'll not turn him out. If we reward proper behavior in him, perhaps he'll be encouraged to turn away from debauchery."

Nessa tried not to smile at the idea of her sister's acceptance being more rewarding to a dashing young man like Lord Foxhaven than debauchery could be. For a taste of debauchery, she herself might be willing to forego Prudence's approval! Not that she had the least idea how to go about finding any such taste, of course.

"That's right, Prudence, we'll win him to respectability in spite of himself," she agreed, her expression solemn. She hoped that might prove impossible, however. A respectable Lord Foxhaven would not be nearly so intriguing as the rake her sister had described.

"Until tomorrow," he'd said. She could scarcely wait.

❧ 4 ❧

Harry was well into his second bottle of port when Jack and Lord Peter joined him at their accustomed table at the Guards Club on St. James Street. "How went the first volley?" he inquired almost cheerily, as two more glasses were placed.

Peter shook his head sorrowfully. "Even worse than you predicted, Harry."

"What, Lady M. turned you away from her door? I could have told you she would."

The other two stared at him in disbelief. "You *do* need to cut back on the spirits, old boy!" Peter exclaimed. "But no, you were right the first time—she wasn't willing to risk a scene by turning Jack away. It was once we were inside the trouble began."

"Oh come now, Peter, it wasn't so bad as all that," Jack protested, irrationally nettled by his friend's gloomy prospect. "No one gave me the cut direct, which I more than half expected."

"Old Sherbourne came close, and Claridge managed to keep you from getting close enough to Lady

Constance for an introduction," Peter pointed out. "We'll have to come up with another plan to whitewash your reputation. That's all there is to it."

Harry raised his glass. "I'll certainly drink to that! Damned idiotic thing to contemplate in the first place, marriage. Don't know what you were thinking, Jack."

Jack regarded his two longtime friends with mingled amusement and irritation. "Ready to turn tail after the first skirmish? I'm disappointed in you both. I'll not give up so easily, I assure you, especially after the brilliant flanking maneuver I executed toward the evening's close."

Two pairs of eyes turned to him expectantly. "Eh? What?" Peter blinked owlishly, giving the appearance of having imbibed more than Harry had.

"I'll have you know that I am engaged to call upon Lady Haughton at her sister's house tomorrow morning." He twirled his wineglass with a flourish, awaiting their reactions.

Harry gave a sour guffaw, but Peter gaped carpishly. Several seconds passed before he found his voice. "Never say Lady Creamcroft agreed to that? I saw how quickly she pulled her sister away from you when she found out who you were."

"Lady Creamcroft is nothing if not proper. It would have been most unseemly for her to refuse my request after her sister had already acquiesced." He saw no point in adding that he had not given Lady Creamcroft a chance to do so.

"So Lady Haughton is hanging out for another husband already?" Harry asked with a twisted grin. "How bitter a pill will she be to swallow? Must be pretty desperate to encourage you her first evening back in Society."

Jack glared, but it was Peter who answered. "You have it all wrong, Harry, I assure you. Lady Haughton is quite a taking little thing, even in her blacks. Chestnut hair, big brown eyes, creamy complexion. When she's back in colors, I daresay she'll turn out a diamond of the first water. I can't believe——" He broke off as Jack's malevolent eye shifted to him. "That is to say, I'm delighted you'll have a chance to speak with her again, Jack. Still . . . "

"Yes?" Though Jack's tone was dangerous, it didn't deter his friend.

"Try not to get your hopes too high, eh? I mean, I wish you the best of luck and all that, but it's likely Lady Haughton is allowing the visit merely because she's lived too secluded to hear the gossip. Could be that once she does, she'll be as cool as all the others. And even your best drawing room manners are likely to shock her, with Cherryhurst and Haughton as her standard."

He looked so worried that Jack had to laugh.

"Egad, Peter, it's not as though I've developed a *tendre* for the woman! You of all people know I've never believed all that poets' rot about love and such. My heart's in no danger, I assure you. I merely see this as a promising opening for my campaign. If nothing else, being received at Creamcroft's house is sure to nudge my respectability up a notch—and put me that much closer to those funds I need."

In fact, he hoped far more might come of tomorrow's visit, but he had no intention of revealing the true reason for his optimism to his friends. Not until he was sure. Maybe not even then.

"Besides," he continued, "this will be good practice for me. The worst that can happen is that I'll have to go to an alternate strategy—in which case Harry and I can share a toast to my escape. But for the sake of both my grandfather and that money, I'm determined to give my initial battle plan a fair shot."

Nessa sat in her sister's tasteful drawing room attempting to concentrate on her needlework while wishing for the twentieth time that she could wear something other than black today, of all days. A sidelong glance showed Prudence the model sober matron in her high-necked gray silk, industriously netting a purse. Prudence would benefit from colors as much as herself, in Nessa's opinion.

Though she didn't actually fidget—her father and husband had trained that out of her years ago—Nessa felt inwardly jumpy. Would Lord Foxhaven really come to call? *Had* he recognized her from the masquerade? More importantly, would he say anything in front of Prudence if he had? Refocusing her attention on the fabric she held, Nessa realized she'd been working the wrong row. With an impatient click of her tongue, which for her was tantamount to cursing, she began undoing the work of the past ten minutes.

The front knocker sounded as she pulled out the last errant stitch, and she found herself holding her breath until Clarendon entered to announce Lord Foxhaven. She dared a quick glance as he followed the butler into the room, his beaver under his arm.

Against the prim formality of Prudence's drawing room, he appeared more outrageously handsome than ever—and perhaps the slightest bit ill at ease. Prudence's expression, as she rose gracefully to greet their guest, showed more acute discomfort.

"How nice to see you again, my lord," she said stiffly.

Lord Foxhaven bowed over her hand with perfect propriety. "Lady Creamcroft." Then, with another bow in Nessa's direction, "Lady Haughton. I'm honored to have this chance to pay my respects to you both."

Nessa bobbed her head in return. "Good morning, my lord." She kept her voice low, as she had last night, and watched him closely for any sign of flirtation, or of a secret shared.

It did not come.

"Pray take a seat, my lord, while I ring for a tray," suggested Prudence, motioning to a gold and white striped armchair.

He complied, then made an innocuous comment about the unseasonably fair weather. "So much more pleasant than our usual autumn rains, don't you agree?"

Prudence assented with a further comment on the weather and Nessa nodded again, feeling oddly disappointed. *This* was the scandalous rake her sister had warned her against?

"You are abroad early, my lord," Nessa observed. "You must not have kept particularly late hours last night."

Prudence cast her a startled glance, and Nessa herself was nearly as shocked at her own boldness. But her eagerness for even a tiny glimpse into a rake's night life had overset her well-learned reticence. What must it be like, to——?

"No, I retired shortly after returning from Lady Mountheath's entertainment. I am finding that late nights do not agree with me so well as they once did."

Nessa regarded him suspiciously, but he appeared perfectly serious. Only for the briefest instant did she imagine that she caught a hint of amusement deep in his blue eyes——but whether directed at himself or at her she had no idea.

"That's very commendable, Lord Foxhaven," Prudence said approvingly. "Rationality and restraint generally develop with maturity, I have observed."

"Indeed, Lady Creamcroft," he agreed. "I've also found that dissipation, while passingly enjoyable, leaves no lasting reward."

Though Prudence's eyebrows arched ceilingward at even this oblique reference to his purported wildness, Nessa stifled a sigh. Was all his debauchery behind him, then? No doubt she should be pleased, for his sake, but . . . how very dreary.

Indeed, he and Prudence seemed to be trying to outmatch each other in moral platitudes. "So I have always been taught, my lord. One need look no further than the Book of Proverbs for numerous examples."

With difficulty, Nessa refrained from rolling her eyes at her sister's words—and wondered at herself. Whence had come this new impatience with propriety? Or . . . was it so new? Hadn't she always secretly—so secretly—chafed at the strictures laid upon her? Her chafing was becoming more overt after a year of relative freedom, that was all.

Lord Foxhaven nodded as sententiously as any octogenarian at Prudence's moralizing, making Nessa wonder if he could possibly be the same man she had met at the masquerade. Where was the humor that had attracted her?

As though aware of her thoughts, he turned toward her. "I'm more familiar with the Song of Solomon than with Proverbs, I must confess, but I am willing to be instructed." The slightest of winks accompanied his words, making Nessa's pulse flutter unexpectedly. For a moment she found herself drowning in his deep blue gaze.

A faint gasp from Prudence recalled her abruptly, reminding her that she should be equally shocked at his reference to the one book of the Bible their father had forbidden them to read.

"Very commendable, my lord." Nessa managed to keep her voice from quivering with the laughter that threatened. "Don't you agree, Prudence?"

"Certainly," Prudence replied stiffly, with a pointed glance at the clock on the mantelpiece.

Lord Foxhaven took the hint at once. "I see I have

exceeded my quarter hour," he said, rising. "The fascinating company must be my excuse."

Seeing him about to depart, Prudence unbent to the extent of a genuine smile. "You are too kind, my lord."

"I will bid you both good day, ladies," he said. "I leave tomorrow for Kent, to deal with various estate matters, but I hope to see you again upon my return in a fortnight." Then, to Nessa, "Perhaps then you will permit me to take you for that drive."

With a start, Nessa realized—as Lord Foxhaven must—that in a fortnight her year of mourning would be over. Her spirit seemed to expand within her at the thought. Conscious of Prudence stiffening again at her side, however, she only said, "That might be pleasant, my lord."

"Until then." Lord Foxhaven bent over Prudence's hand and then her own, his gloved fingertips lingering on hers for just a fraction longer than was strictly proper.

And then he was gone.

The next two weeks seemed an eternity to Nessa. No further invitations included her, beyond an art viewing followed by tea one afternoon. Prudence's circle of friends seemed more staid and, yes, boring, than ever.

"You were unusually quiet today," observed her sister as they rode back to Upper Brook Street. "Mrs. Heatherton twice asked you about Warwickshire, but you gave her only the briefest of answers."

"I am sorry, Prudence. I must have been woolgathering. I hope Mrs. Heatherton was not offended."

"No, I think not. She mentioned something privately to me about your grief still preoccupying you."

Nessa nodded absently. "May we go shopping tomorrow?"

Prudence blinked. "Why . . . I suppose so. Is there something in particular that you need? A new bonnet, perhaps? The milliner at the corner of—"

"Oh, let's make a day of it," said Nessa, as though on impulse. "I haven't been shopping for an age." *And I plan to make up for it over the next few days*, she vowed.

Though clearly puzzled, Prudence did not hesitate to agree. Half-guiltily, Nessa hoped her sister wouldn't overly regret her compliance.

The next morning they left early, at Nessa's urging. "Let's start with Madame Fanchot's," she suggested as they stepped into the carriage.

Prudence gaped, for Madame Fanchot was the most *au courant* modiste in Town, dressing those at the very pinnacle of fashion. She offered no objection, however, to Nessa's relief. If her sister had balked at this early stage, there was no knowing how she might react once she had a hint of what Nessa was really about.

She soon found out.

"Look at this pearl gray, Nessa," said Prudence only minutes after they were ushered into the display room by Madame Fanchot herself. "This would be the very thing to ease you out of your blacks when you are ready."

Nessa looked, then winced. Her sister had unerringly chosen the only drab swath of fabric in sight, and looked as though she thought even that might be too daring. It was now or never.

"Oh, I am quite ready, Prudence," she said, steeling herself against the shock on her sister's face. "My proscribed year ends two days hence, and I wish to be ready. Madame, might I see that jonquil silk over there?"

"But that is so . . . *bright*," Prudence hissed as the modiste went to fetch the bolt of yellow fabric. "It scarcely seems proper. I had thought you might go to half-mourning soon—grays, browns, perhaps a subdued lilac—"

"No."

Prudence's eyes widened further.

"Many widows, I've observed, go to half-mourning after the first six months of their bereavement. I feel I've done my duty and over by wearing nothing but unrelieved black for the full twelve."

"But . . . but Father—" Prudence sputtered, her pretty head shaking helplessly from side to side.

"Hasn't it occurred to you yet that Father's standards were hardly those of the world in which we now live?"

"He was very proud of that," Prudence reminded her severely.

Nessa sighed. "Yes, I know. Lord Haughton was the same. Admirable men, both of them. Most admirable. But now I am ready to experience life on my own terms, and wearing color—more color than I was allowed even as a daughter or wife—is a way to begin. Can you not understand that?"

Prudence still looked doubtful. She, of course, had never rebelled against their father's tutelage, even though her husband was of a different stamp entirely—more was the pity. Still, she looked a fraction less shocked than she had a moment ago. "Perhaps," she finally said. "Though I am still not certain—"

"Here we are, Lady Haughton!" Madame Fanchot spread the jonquil silk upon a low table for her inspection. "Will you want this made up before or after presenting it?"

"Presenting it?" Now Nessa was puzzled.

"It is to be a gift, is it not?"

This was becoming more difficult than she'd anticipated, but she refused to waver. "No indeed, Madame. It is for me. However, that rose muslin would complement my sister's coloring nicely. May we see it? Pray bring us a few pattern books as well. I expect we shall be here for a while."

Two and a half hours later, a well-satisfied Nessa and a dazed Prudence left the shop laden with various accessories to round out the six gowns Nessa had ordered for herself and the two she had ordered for Prudence, after wearing down her protests. The jonquil silk was to be delivered Friday, the day after her year would be up, and the others would follow over the next week.

"Come, Prudence, let us stop for coffee and ices at Gunter's so that you can rally a bit before we go on."

Prudence paused in the act of handing her parcels to the coachman. "Go on?"

"Certainly. I said we would make a day of this, did I

not?" Nessa resisted the urge to glance over her shoulder. She had the oddest feeling that her father and husband were watching her with disapproval. Defiantly, she raised her chin. "I've only just begun," she declared, as much to those dour shades as to Prudence.

"Is that the last one, Havershaw?" Jack stretched his arms high over his head to relieve the tension in his shoulders, produced by several hours bent over a desk.

"Yes, my lord. I must say, you have kept at it. You've made it through this backlog of paperwork in record time." The respect in the steward's voice made Jack glance up in surprise.

"Really? I can't imagine that I've been as efficient as my grandfather in dealing with the estate business. I'm still learning as I go, after all."

Havershaw smiled his thin smile, but Jack was further startled to see a trace of genuine warmth in it. "Indeed, my lord, you're doing far better as a novice than your Uncle Luther ever managed, and though you have not yet his experience, you are in a fair way to match your grandfather in cutting to the heart of most business matters. I believe you may have a natural bent for this sort of thing."

Jack grimaced. Three weeks ago, he'd have sworn on everything sacred that he'd be a terrible landowner and that the details of running a large estate would drive him to distraction or drink—or worse. Reluctant as he was to admit it, however, he'd almost enjoyed these past two weeks immersed in tenancies, harvests, land improvements, and foreign investments. Jack Ashecroft, responsible landowner? It seemed so unlikely.

"Have I passed the test, then?" he asked with a grin. "Do you deem me respectable? With that trust money, I could have the roof leaded and drain the lower acreage before the winter rains set in."

"No doubt you could," said Havershaw dryly, "but this quarter's rents will just cover those items, I believe. True reformation takes time."

Jack bit back a curse. If the rents all went for repairs, he'd have precious little spending money when he got back to Town. "Can you perhaps give me a clue as to what your standards are to be, Havershaw? I've no mind to spend years at this endeavor while Foxhaven falls into ruin for lack of funds."

"I rather doubt that is a serious risk, my lord."

And of course it wasn't. It was Jack's lifestyle that was at risk. "A wife, then. If I marry a woman of unimpeachable reputation, will you count me reformed?"

He held his breath while Havershaw hesitated. If he said no, Jack realized, he wouldn't have to get leg-shackled after all.

But the steward finally nodded. "If you can get such a woman to marry you—willingly—I suppose that would be as objective a measure as any."

Jack let out his breath, his brief hope gone. Pushing the mound of finished paperwork aside, he stood. "In that case, I shall make it my first priority. On the morrow I'll head back to Town for what remains of the Little Season."

"Will you be returning for Yuletide, my lord?" Haver-shaw, imperturbable as ever, began gathering up the papers.

"That will depend on how my wooing goes, won't it?" replied Jack sourly. "I'll send word."

When he reached his chamber, Jack rang for Parker, his valet. A few years older than he, though slighter in build, Parker had been with him throughout his military career and held a position of trust with his employer enjoyed by vanishingly few servants.

"Yes, my lord?"

"We leave in the morning, Parker. Be good enough to get everything ready for our departure."

"I've done so already, my lord." The valet proceeded to remove his master's boots.

Jack shook his head. "Don't know why I trouble myself to tell you anything. You've been reading my mind with ease for years now. Know me better than I know myself."

Parker only smiled.

"Being that's the case," Jack continued, "perhaps you can enlighten me as to my conflicting inclinations on matrimony. Think you it's too high a price to pay for mere money?"

Parker turned to regard him, pale hair falling across his high forehead. "I think the right woman could be the making of you, my lord, if not of your reputation."

"Blast it, Parker, the making of my reputation is the whole point of the thing! What do you mean by that?"

But Parker merely shrugged and seized his other

boot. Explaining his cryptic pronouncements had never been his way, though they almost invariably proved true in time.

They left for London before the morning was far advanced. Jack reflected that the habit of retiring and rising early, which he had adopted almost without thought while in the country, appeared to agree with his constitution. Very odd, that—and not a little disturbing.

As he neared Town a few hours later, Jack could almost feel the calm of the country seeping from him, to be replaced by the excitement of the city. Yes, surely *this* was where he truly belonged, amid the bustle of humanity. Here, he could live by his wits and the cards, as he'd done before, and to hell with that damned trust. If it weren't for his grandfather's memory, that's just what he'd do. Perhaps respectability wasn't meant for the likes of him after all.

But even as he said this to himself, he found his thoughts turning to what he had hoped might be the means to that respectability: Lady Haughton. Her period of mourning should have ended three days since, by his calculations. With her puritanical upbringing, of course, she might well intend to observe half-mourning for another twelvemonth. It would not surprise him, in fact, if Lady Creamcroft demanded it of her. If that were the case, pursuing a courtship could be problematic.

Pondering his options, Jack disembarked from his traveling coach and climbed the stairs to Foxhaven House—one of the finer establishments on Berkley

Square. The effect was somewhat marred by the disheveled appearance of his butler, who'd clearly hurried into his coat to answer the door.

Jack handed his hat and cloak to the man with some degree of misgiving. "I'll be going out after I've had a wash and a change," he advised Carp, or whatever his name was. "Tell Cook I will most likely dine at my club."

Once in his bedchamber, Jack returned to the matter of Lady Haughton. Ought he to call upon her this afternoon? He glanced at the clock on the mantelpiece. Were she in the whirl of Society, he might find her in Hyde Park in a couple of hours, but that seemed unlikely. No, he would wait and call upon her in the morning, as was proper, and invite her out for a drive the next afternoon.

"My blue coat, I believe, Parker."

His valet, with customary prescience, already had the requested garment in his capable hands. Jack stripped off his travel clothes and splashed his face with cold water from the ewer, all the while working out his strategy.

Surely, he thought as Parker helped him to shrug into the blue superfine, he would be able to cajole the fair Lady Haughton out of her blacks in fairly short order. If she *had* masqueraded as the lovely "Monique," she could not be nearly so trammeled by propriety as her sister. The occasional sparkle he had glimpsed in her eyes suggested a sense of humor, as well. Still, a lifetime under the thumbs of Lords Cherryhurst and Haughton would have left its mark.

He would go slowly, he decided, tying his cravat with a flourish. He did not wish to shock his quarry—particularly this early in the campaign. If on the morrow he found her in half-mourning rather than unrelieved black, he would take it as a hopeful sign and proceed from there. He had no particular desire to rush matters—as long as the roof at Fox Manor didn't spring another leak, anyway.

Well satisfied with this remarkably prudent decision, Jack set out for his club, hoping that Harry or Peter might be there to catch him up on the news of the past two weeks.

5

Neither of his closest friends was at the Guards when Jack arrived, so he ordered a bottle of port and settled in to wait. He was refilling his glass for the first time an hour later when Harry turned up.

"Jack! Good to see you back in Town!" he exclaimed, signaling for another glass. "I see you've only just arrived." He nodded at the nearly full bottle.

Jack didn't bother to correct him. "Hello, Harry. Is it my imagination, or is London already a bit thin of company?"

Harry's glass arrived then, and he filled it before answering. "Perhaps a bit. Hadn't really noticed. Fair number of house parties, I believe—that might account for it." He tossed off half of his port at a single swallow, making Jack wince slightly.

What was the matter with him? Normally he'd be matching Harry glass for glass, not deploring his habits! Still, it was borne in upon him for the first time that Harry had begun to drift toward the outer fringes of Society over the past few months—and not unintentionally. He wasn't likely to get the sort of news he'd hoped for here.

At that moment, however, a better source manifested itself, in the form of Lord Peter. "Jack!" he called out as he strode toward them. "Fernworth said you were back in Town."

"Ferny? Don't recall seeing him since arriving."

"Said he saw your coach at Foxhaven House," explained Peter, taking a chair. "Wondered when your next . . . entertainment might be. I tried to put the damper on such expectations." He regarded Jack questioningly, as did Harry.

"I'm back in Town but two hours and already you're playing the mother hen." But Jack's jibe lacked rancor. The truth was, he had no burning desire to return to the excessive lifestyle he'd enjoyed last month, even if he could have afforded it. An unsettling thought.

Harry clearly did not share his change of heart. "Really, Pete, what a damned interfering nodcock you are. High time Jack threw another party, in my opinion. What say you, Jack?"

Jack shook his head. "Much as it pains me to admit it, Peter is right. I've made great strides toward respectability in recent weeks, and would hate to see such heroic effort go for naught."

With a sound of disgust, Harry refilled his glass. "I'd hoped two weeks sequestered in the country would bring you to your senses. You're on your way to becoming as dashedly dull as Pete here, I hope you realize."

"Why thank you, Harry!" Jack shared an amused

glance with Peter. Harry merely snorted again and turned his attention to his wine. "So, Peter, what news? Has Society managed to carry on without me for a fortnight?"

Some of the amusement left Peter's face. "There is one tidbit you may find of interest, actually," he said. "It concerns Lady Haughton, who, I believe, was your prime candidate when you left, was she not?"

"What is it?" Jack asked, more sharply than he intended. "Has she left Town? Or—surely she hasn't already accepted another offer?" He wasn't sure why either of those possibilities should weigh him down so.

"No, no, nothing so bad as that," Peter assured him. "It's just that I saw her Saturday night at Mrs. Westercott's soiree. She's well and truly reentered Society now, it appears."

Jack felt a surge of relief. "But that's all to the good," he exclaimed. "I'd been wondering whether I'd have to persuade her out of her weeds, even though her year is up. Feared it might be difficult."

"Not difficult at all, I'd say," said Peter wryly, "considering that she was dancing at Mrs. Westercott's—and wearing bright yellow."

Jack blinked. "Yellow? When only days ago she was in heavy blacks? Hmmm . . . " He lapsed into thought.

"Yellow," Peter repeated. "Not quite the thing, if you ask me, and certainly not what I'd have expected of Cherryhurst's daughter and Haughton's widow. Lady Creamcroft was with her, and looked more than a little embarrassed."

"So your supremely respectable widow has decided to cut a dash, has she?" Harry clearly found the situation highly entertaining. "Mayhap she's a better match for you than we suspected, Jack!"

Even Peter chuckled, though he still looked somewhat worried. "She may not be the best choice for your plan after all," he suggested. "More than a few eyebrows were raised Saturday night. Perhaps you should give one of the debutantes another look." His lips twitched slightly in response to Harry's continued laughter.

But Jack was not amused. Upon Havershaw's promise that marriage would turn the trick, his intention to wed Lady Haughton had firmed to the point of resolve, though he had not fully realized it until now. He had no desire to look elsewhere.

"I'll simply have to move more quickly than I'd intended. Any idea, Peter, where she's likely to be tonight? Anything of importance going on?"

Lord Peter thought for a moment. "There's the Plumfield ball, and Lady Trumball's card party. Various smaller dos—supper parties and the like. Perhaps the theater. What have you invitations for? Or do you plan to use the same tactic as at the Mountheath do?"

"Actually, I've no idea what invitations I might have. I left the house before checking my letters. I'll go do that now. Care to join me, gentlemen?"

Peter tossed off the remainder of his glass and stood. "Wouldn't miss it, I assure you. Harry?"

"I'll be along in a bit," he replied, refilling his glass

from the now nearly empty bottle. "Sounds like we might have an amusing evening ahead."

"A productive one, as well," Jack promised them both. "Mark my words, I'll have Lady Haughton betrothed to me before the month is out."

Lord Peter regarded him with surprise, but Harry grimaced. "Hope for your sake you're wrong, Jack."

Leaving with Peter, Jack wondered whether he didn't hope the same thing—and if not, why not.

"Nessa, we simply *must* go!" Prudence insisted in a whisper, fluttering anxiously at her sister's elbow. "Lord Plumfield is a good friend of Lord Creamcroft's, and I have more than a passing acquaintance with Lady Plumfield. It simply won't do for us to be any later to their ball."

Nessa looked up from the cards in her hand. "But I'm having a marvelous run of luck, Prudence," she whispered back. "Why don't you and Lord Creamcroft go on and I'll join you there later?"

Prudence fanned herself vigorously. "Leave you here *alone?*" Her hiss nearly became a squeak. She glanced apprehensively around the table lest the others were attending to their words, but the two gentlemen and other lady appeared intent on their own cards. "You know we cannot do that."

Instead of responding, Nessa played her next card. She'd had only a very few chances to play whist since learning, as Lord Haughton had disapproved of cards except with the vicar and his wife. She was pleased to discover she had a flair for the game.

"I'm not a schoolgirl, you know." She continued the whispered conversation. "At four-and-twenty, I scarcely need a chaperone."

Prudence's fan waved more frantically. "Nessa, you know as well as I what would be said, were you to stay here without us. Do you wish to be thought *fast?*"

Secretly Nessa confessed that she did, but realized that it was unfair to distress her sister so, after all of her kindness. "Very well. Let me finish this hand, and then we will go."

For a moment, she thought Prudence might faint from relief. "Thank you, Nessa. I'll go inform Lord Creamcroft."

Nessa knew she should feel guilty, but decided to defer that until later. Just now, she preferred to savor the brief remainder of her game.

"That gives us the rubber, Mr. Galloway," she said five minutes later, laying down her last card. "I have enjoyed this immensely. Thank you all for allowing me to make your foursome."

Miss Cheevers smiled a bit sourly, either at having lost or because Nessa had claimed more attention than herself from the two gentlemen present. "We must do this again sometime, Lady Haughton."

The gentlemen echoed the sentiment with more sincerity, and Nessa favored them all with a bright smile, just as Prudence returned to her elbow, Lord Creamcroft in tow. Saying her farewells, she accompanied them to the door.

"I'm glad to see you making friends, sister," com-

mented Lord Creamcroft amiably as they waited for
their carriage.

"I thank you and Prudence for the opportunity,
Philip," she replied, conscious of her sister's faint gasp.
Prudence had only once or twice used her husband's
Christian name in Nessa's hearing. Nessa rather hoped,
by example, to change that.

Her brother-in-law did not appear scandalized in
the least. In fact, Nessa caught a twinkle in his eyes that
indicated he suspected what she was about—and
approved. More and more, Nessa was certain that
Philip would prefer a much less formal relationship
with his wife. If only Prudence could be persuaded to
unbend a little . . .

"I pray you two will not allow concern for me to
interfere with your own enjoyments," Nessa continued, with a meaning glance at her sister. "I find myself
quite able to take care of myself. In fact, I hope that I'll
not have to impose upon your hospitality for much
longer. I believe it is high time I set up my own Town
establishment."

Prudence's strangled protest was cut short by the
arrival of the carriage. Once they were all ensconced
inside, however, she turned horrified eyes upon her
sister.

"You cannot be serious about living alone in Town,
can you, Nessa? Only think of the talk that would
ensue. Propriety demands—"

"Oh, you needn't worry, Prudence. I will engage a
suitable companion when the time comes. And it is not

as though I intend to move out in the morning!"

In fact, the idea of setting up her own household in London had only just occurred to her—but it suddenly seemed an excellent one.

"Move out!" Prudence was plying her fan again, leaning weakly back against the squabs. "But you have nowhere to go! Promise me you will not even think of such a thing, Nessa."

"I can scarcely impose upon your hospitality for the rest of my life, Prudence. Surely you must see that."

But Prudence shook her head. "I see no such thing. You may stay with us until you decide to return to the dower house at Haughton—or remarry. There will no doubt be several eligible and respectable gentlemen at the Plumfields'—far more respectable than that card-player, Mr. Galloway. I will endeavor to introduce you."

Nessa smiled at her sister, but said firmly, "I have no plans to return to the country in the near future. That dower house is positively grim, I assure you. And I do *not* intend to remarry, in even the distant future. I simply wish to settle in Town for the present." *And live on my own terms*, she added silently.

"While I understand your feelings, sister, remember that your cousin would have to authorize the release of your funds for such a move," Lord Creamcroft reminded her. "In any event, I hope you will let no thought of inconveniencing *us* cause you to hasten such a decision. We are more than happy to have you with us for as long as you will stay."

"Thank you, Philip," Nessa replied warmly, though

she cringed at the thought of what Cousin Filmore's response to such a request would likely be. She'd quite forgotten that her small fortune was under his control, as he'd been generous with her allowance. "I'm sure I can convince my cousin—" She broke off, noticing that her sister appeared to be on the verge of a faint. "I, er, believe Prudence requires your attention."

Turning, Lord Creamcroft perceived his wife's distress and took both her hands most tenderly in his own. "There, there, my dear. It'll all work out for the best, you'll see." As she was unresisting, he dared a quick kiss on her cheek.

That brought Prudence to her senses immediately. "Philip! I mean, my lord! I mean—"

Nessa began to chuckle, earning a reproachful glance from her sister. "Oh, never mind me. I'll just watch Mayfair go by." She directed her gaze resolutely to the carriage window and was gratified to hear her sister's indignant exclamation suddenly muffled by what could only be a kiss. Yes, there was hope for true happiness there yet!

But what of her own?

"Where to next, Jack?"

Lord Peter still sounded remarkably chipper, but Jack favored him with a sour look. They'd gone first to the Plumfield ball, but the Creamcroft party had not arrived, though they were generally expected—a fact that took some forty-five minutes to ascertain. Then they'd gone to the Trumball card party, only to discover that Lady Haughton, her sister, and brother-in-law had left twenty minutes earlier.

Next they'd stopped in at a ridotto at the Peckerings, which Peter had suddenly recalled, but with no luck. The Creamcrofts had neither been nor were they particularly expected, though they had been invited.

Miranda Dempsey, the vivacious, redheaded widow with whom Jack had dallied in Paris, had been there, however. She was clearly more than eager to rekindle their brief, torrid romance, and he had only extricated himself with some difficulty.

"Let's go back to Plumfields'," suggested Jack, once he and Peter had made their escape. At the moment, he was far more inclined to head back to the club, or even home, but it was not in him to give up—not yet.

"Just what I was going to suggest myself," agreed Peter cheerily. "Off we go, then!"

Jack settled back into the carriage for the fourth time that evening, reflecting, as they clattered along the streets of Mayfair, that his friend was enjoying this mad search far too much. Blast it, did Peter *want* him legshackled for life? His own enthusiasm for the plan was waning rapidly.

Lord and Lady Plumfield had abandoned their posts at the head of the stairs by the time Jack and Peter returned, so at least they were spared immediate comment upon their odd schedule for the evening. Harry, however, had arrived in their absence, and spotted them at once.

He accosted them reproachfully when they were

but a few steps inside the ballroom. "Devil take it, Jack, I thought you meant to come here first. I've been cooling my heels here for half an hour, at least."

"It appears you've been well rewarded for your time." Jack nodded toward the glass of fine champagne in Harry's hand. "Do you never purchase your own spirits?" The cut was beneath him, he knew, but the evening's fruitless hunt had set his temper on edge.

Harry appeared cheered by his remark, however. "Not if I can avoid it, old boy!" He drained the glass that had been recalled to his notice and signaled a passing waiter for another. "Oh, your quarry is in the dance at the moment, I believe."

Jack experienced an inexplicable lightening of his mood. "Lady Haughton is finally here, then?"

"Oh, so you *were* here before? Wench is leading you a merry chase, is she? Quite an active social life for a widow just out of her weeds."

Jack's mood became just a shade less light.

Harry now turned to his companion. "You were right, by the bye, Pete. She *is* a taking little thing. Begin to understand Jack's determination, though given her current course, I'm not sure he need go so far as parson's mousetrap. Offer her a slip on the shoulder first, Jack," he advised his friend kindly.

Though he glared at Harry, Jack couldn't keep his lips from twitching slightly. "You forget the point, Harry. The idea is for Lady Haughton to repair *my* reputation, not for me to ruin hers." He couldn't deny, however, that the notion held more than a modicum of appeal.

"You'd best hurry, then." Harry indicated the near lefthand side of the ballroom with a motion of his head.

Jack followed his glance and then stiffened, an odd mixture of vexation and elation welling up inside him. There stood the object of his quest, resplendent in deep rose silk. Flowers of the same shade adorned her chestnut curls, which she wore loose to her bare shoulders. Though her gown was cut no lower than most of the others there, its contrast to the high-necked black dress he'd last seen her wearing made it seem outrageously seductive.

Momentarily rendered speechless by the vision before him, Jack merely observed—only to realize abruptly that Lady Haughton was surrounded by no fewer than six gentlemen, with all of whom she seemed to be conducting a flirtation! Excusing himself from his companions, he strode toward her.

Nessa was certain she had never enjoyed an evening so much in her life. The Westercotts' soiree on Saturday had been but a trial run. In fact, she had dared only two dances there, so severe was Prudence's disapproval—and so rusty were her skills. Though her parents had permitted their daughters to learn all of the approved dances, they'd been afforded very few opportunities to practice in public—and after her marriage, Nessa had danced only once or twice, at small country gatherings.

Tonight, she had a mind to throw caution to the winds. Winning at whist while tentatively flirting with Mr. Galloway had been a highly entertaining novelty, and now she had just concluded her third dance, with the promise of several more to come.

And such attentive young men! She turned a blind eye to Prudence's reproachful looks from across the room, just as she had earlier turned a deaf ear to her sister's strictures on which gentlemen were respectable enough to be worthy of her notice. Respectability was the very *last* thing she was seeking tonight!

"Why, what a charming thing to say, Sir Lawrence," she responded to a particularly outrageous compliment, flitting her fan experimentally. The fan was something else she needed proper instruction on, she realized. Else she might send signals she did not intend. But so what if she did? she asked herself with sudden recklessness.

"No more than the truth, I assure you, Lady Haughton," said her young cavalier. "You outshine every other woman present."

"Indisputably," agreed Mr. Pottinger, a handsome man of more mature years but with a decided lisp. "You have given new life to the Little Season, my lady."

It was nice, Nessa reflected, to know that not everyone disapproved of her as Prudence did. Resolutely, she squelched the twinge of conscience that threatened to assail her.

"You are all very kind," she assured the small cluster of gentlemen surrounding her. "As new to the social scene as I am, it is most pleasant to have made so many friends already."

A clamor arose as they all attempted to convey how

very honored they were to be counted among her friends, and Nessa positively basked in the attention. Surely, enjoying such harmless flattery could not be so evil as she'd always been led to believe.

The orchestra struck up the opening strains of the next dance—a waltz. At least three of her gallants stepped forward to lead her out, but before she could formulate a suitable excuse, another voice spoke from behind her.

"I beg your pardon, gentlemen, but I believe the lady has promised this particular dance to me."

Whirling, she found herself transfixed by the piercing blue eyes of Lord Foxhaven. Why her heart should leap so at his appearance she had no idea, unless it were sudden fear that now she was wearing colors, he might recognize her as the masked Monique. Bemused, she allowed him to take her hand in his. As he led her toward the assembling dancers, however, sanity abruptly returned.

"I . . . I fear I cannot oblige you, my lord," she stammered.

He gazed down at her, his expression unreadable. "Engaged to someone else, are you?"

"Yes. That is, no. That is . . . " Nessa gave it up, realizing that glib excuses would not work on this man—not that she was precisely managing glibness. "I'm afraid I do not waltz, my lord," she finally said in a small voice.

To her surprise, Lord Foxhaven broke into a wide smile. "Do you not indeed? Then, my lady, it is high time you began." Ignoring her inarticulate protests, he whirled her out onto the floor, then placed one hand lightly on her waist.

Nessa quickly moved from under his hand. "My lord, you do not understand," she whispered frantically. "I do not know *how* to waltz! I never learned."

For the barest moment the marquis looked surprised, but then he gave her a reassuring smile. "'Tis really a very simple dance: three steps repeated, in time to the music. Just follow my lead. I promise not to attempt any of the fancier movements—not until you've learned the basics."

A half-wink gave his words a deeper meaning, and Nessa felt herself flushing. The sensation was not unpleasant, however. "Very well, my lord. I shall hold you to your word." She let added meaning color her own words as well, and saw his eyes light in response.

He again placed his hand at her waist, its warmth seeming to spread in all directions. Though the dance was not quite so easy as he had implied, Nessa found that with some concentration she was able to overcome the distracting effect of his touch enough to follow his steps. Occasional, surreptitious glances at the other dancers assisted her as well.

Still, she could not deny that this particular dance was a disturbingly intimate experience. No wonder her father had so strongly disapproved of the waltz! Though Lord Foxhaven took no liberties, she was acutely aware of the placement of each long finger against her body, pressing and releasing as they moved to the music. By the time the music ended, she believed she could cautiously claim to be able to waltz—a gratifying accomplishment—but she would never look upon the dance in the same way again.

"I thank you for the lesson, Lord Foxhaven," she said breathlessly as they twirled to a stop.

He shook his head. "The lady does not thank the gentleman for the dance, Lady Haughton. I see you are more unschooled in the ways of polite Society than you pretend. The honor, by the dictates of custom, must be mine."

Placing her hand on his arm to accompany him from the floor, she regarded him uncertainly. "By the dictates of custom?" She tried to keep the disappointment from her voice.

But then his eyes smiled into hers, warming her again. "Not only by custom," he said, his voice silken. "I quite enjoyed the experience of instructing you. It is an experience I look forward to repeating, perhaps in other areas."

Nessa's face flamed as she read a meaning into his words that was doubtless far more lascivious than he had intended. Why did her mind always seem to run along such paths when she was near this man?

"Thank you, my lord," she managed to murmur as they reached the crowd surrounding the dance floor. Prudence was waiting for her, looking thoroughly shocked.

"Lady Creamcroft." Lord Foxhaven executed a respectful bow. "Might I procure refreshment for you both? Ratafia, perhaps?"

"Thank you, no, my lord," replied Prudence stiffly. Nessa stopped herself on the verge of requesting a lemonade, and instead shook her head, but accompanied her refusal with a smile.

Lord Foxhaven bowed again and left them.

"Nessa, what can you have been thinking?" Prudence demanded the moment he was out of earshot. "And where on earth did you learn to waltz? Not in Lord Haughton's household, I'll take my oath."

Nessa suddenly found her sister's overbearing propriety almost amusing, where a month ago she'd considered it the norm. "Actually, Prudence, you just witnessed my first lesson. Was it not kind of Lord Foxhaven to offer to instruct me?"

"Kind?" Prudence was obliged to fan herself vigorously before she could continue. "I'll have you know that I myself have *never* waltzed—not even with my husband! You know what Father always—"

"Father said a great many things," interrupted Nessa. "But we are adults now, Prudence, and must make our own decisions. Truly, you should try the waltz. It is really quite easy. I'm sure Philip would be more than happy to teach you."

For a moment Prudence appeared to waver, but then she frowned. "I should never be able to bring myself to ask such a thing of Phil—that is, Lord Creamcroft. What might he think of me?"

"He might think his wife was becoming a living, breathing woman, instead of the stone statue her father raised," Nessa suggested.

"Nessa, really!" Prudence's eyes reproached her. "I begin to think you must always have harbored these . . . irregular propensities. Did Lord Haughton never suspect?"

Nessa shook her head. "If I *have* always harbored them—and I don't believe they're in the least irregular or unnatural—then I managed to hide them almost as well from myself as from the rest of the world. I begin to see that it was the strictures laid upon us by our father—and upon me by Lord Haughton—that were unnatural. I wish that you could see it too, Prudence."

But Prudence merely clicked her tongue and hurried away to her husband's side, to put an end to what was clearly becoming a most disturbing conversation.

Nessa watched her sister's retreat with mingled pity and amusement. So much happiness awaited poor Prudence, if she would only reach out her hand to grasp it! If she herself were married to a man of her own generation, one who actually loved her . . .

No. Marriage was a trap, a cage. Five years' experience had made that abundantly clear. Her own happiness must lie along a different path from her sister's. But when she saw it offered, she was determined that *she* would not hesitate to seize it!

⤙ 6 ⤚

Nessa came downstairs rather later than usual the next day, to find her sister awaiting her in the drawing room.

"So there you are, Nessa! I'd begun to fear you meant to sleep the day away," Prudence greeted her. "I wished to have a word with you before your first caller arrives."

Nessa's heart sank at the prospect of another lecture. But—"My first caller? Am I expecting callers?"

"After your tremendous success last night, I would be most surprised if you did not have several. Three bouquets of flowers have already arrived, as you can see."

Nessa regarded the elaborate arrangements her sister indicated with wide eyes.

Prudence continued. "You are still very innocent of the ways of Society, I see. Therefore, I wished to, ah, advise you with respect to some of the gentlemen you met last night, and who might possibly come to call."

"Advise me?" Nessa asked suspiciously. "Why did you not do so during the drive home?"

"With Lord Creamcroft in the carriage?" Prudence was aghast. "'Twould have been most unseemly. However, now that we have a moment alone, I consider it my duty, as your sister and as one more acquainted with those who make up London Society, to put you on your guard. It is quite possible that some of the gentlemen with whom you danced last night do not intend marriage."

Despite her sister's serious expression, Nessa laughed. "Marriage? Prudence, did I not tell you last night that I have no desire to marry again? Perhaps you can warn me about the ones who *do* intend marriage, so that I can avoid them in the future."

"But . . . but, surely you weren't serious? You've made it amply clear"——she indicated the cerulean-blue round dress Nessa wore——"that you are not pining for Lord Haughton's memory. A widow as young as yourself . . . what respectable alternative is there?"

Nessa hesitated a moment before speaking. "I wish to explore my options, Prudence," she finally said in as reasonable a tone as she could manage, "and not be rushed into anything I could regret for the rest of my life. I had no choice in the matter of my marriage to Lord Haughton, but now I have. If I choose not to marry, that is my concern."

Prudence tried once more. "Please, Nessa, listen to me. There are some gentlemen you simply must not encourage—most particularly if you do not intend to marry right away. Some are mere fortune hunters, but a few of them would be only too eager to ruin you. That

Mr. Galloway, with whom you played whist, may be one. But by far the most dangerous must be—"

The butler entered just then, as though to complete Prudence's sentence by announcing the very name she'd been about to utter. "Lord Foxhaven," he intoned.

Jack was in exceptionally fine spirits today. Though Lady Creamcroft had rebuffed him at every turn last night, her sister had not. In fact, she had rather obviously enjoyed his attentiveness, granting him one more dance (though not a waltz) near the end of the evening. He felt certain that he would have her securely betrothed to him well within the month he had set as his goal. Perhaps even within the week.

In this optimistic frame of mind, he presented himself at the Creamcroft Townhouse promptly at eleven o'clock, the earliest acceptable hour for callers. After Lady Haughton's success last night, he did not deceive himself into believing he would be her only suitor, but he intended to be the first.

"I bid you good day, ladies," he said jovially as soon as he was announced. Advancing into Lady Creamcroft's pristine drawing room, he bowed first over his hostess' hand, ignoring her chilly response, and then over Lady Haughton's.

Deliberately, he brushed one gloved finger across her wrist, where it lay bare between glove and sleeve, as he lifted her hand to his lips. While he did not— quite—kiss her hand, he brought it a full inch closer to his lips than the prescribed custom. A slight widening of her eyes showed him that she noticed—and did not necessarily disapprove.

Lady Creamcroft's throat-clearing indicated that she also had noticed, and quite definitely disapproved. "How nice to see you again so soon, my lord," she said, her tone conveying exactly the opposite.

"I could not bear to stay away." Some devil of mischief prompted Jack to accompany his broad smile with a wink. He was rewarded by seeing Lady Creamcroft stiffen until he could almost see her quills. He wouldn't have believed such a young, pretty thing could be so starched up.

"We are most flattered, are we not, Prudence?" responded Lady Haughton, as her sister was clearly incapable of speech at the moment. Lady Creamcroft gave a single, frigid nod.

"Pray do not reduce to flattery words that are the simple truth, my lady." Seating himself near his object, Jack turned the full force of his charm—which numerous ladies had led him to believe was considerable—upon her. "Lovely as you were last night, I find you even more so in the light of day, and free of distracting adornments."

"My adornments were excessive, then, my lord?" she asked with a smile. Yes, she was definitely learning to flirt.

"I said no such thing, of course. Did I not already pay tribute to the effect you achieved? Such loveliness as yours, however, shines the brighter with less to conceal it."

She pinkened slightly, clearly taking his meaning. "I . . . I see, my lord." Her confusion told him that while she might enjoy pretending to sophistication, she had not yet achieved it—which was all to the good.

Lady Creamcroft now found her tongue again, just as her sister appeared to have momentarily lost hers. "Lord Foxhaven," she said severely, "I must ask you not to trifle with my sister. She is unused to the ways of Society—particularly the more . . . unrestrained ones."

"Trifle?" Jack placed one hand melodramatically upon his chest. "You wound me, madam! I would not dream of trifling with Lady Haughton, I assure you. I give you my word that my intentions toward your sister are entirely honorable."

"Oh." Lady Creamcroft blinked, clearly surprised, but only slightly mollified. "I . . . I am very glad to hear that, of course, my lord."

He inclined his head in a half-bow he hoped did not betray any mockery. After all, he could not claim that Lady Creamcroft's suspicions were unjustified, given what his life had been up to this point.

Turning back to Lady Haughton, he found her watching him with an expression he could not decipher. A trace of alarm, certainly, but also something else—disappointment? But no, that made no sense.

"I trust the thought of me as a serious suitor is not distasteful, my lady?"

Her small smile did seem somewhat forced. "I am honored, of course, my lord, if a bit surprised. I had not thought you the serious sort, I must confess."

Yes, his campaign was progressing nicely, no doubt about it. "Then I must endeavor to alter your perception of me."

Nessa, however, did not wish her perception altered. *Honorable intentions?* Lord Foxhaven had honorable intentions toward her? That could only mean he intended to make her an offer of marriage—not at all what she wanted from him! She had hoped he might help her to enjoy her new freedom, but now it appeared he wished to curtail it instead, just as Prudence did.

The butler reentered the drawing room just then, to announce the arrival of Sir Hadley Leverton and his sister.

Lord Foxhaven rose. "Before I take my leave, might I persuade you to come driving with me in the Park this afternoon, Lady Haughton?"

Perhaps, Nessa thought hopefully, he had only said that "honorable" bit to appease Prudence. Her spirits recovering, she nodded. "Why, thank you, my lord. I should enjoy that."

Bowing first to her, then to the clearly suspicious Prudence, he took his leave, greeting the newcomers on his way out.

Though she smiled and said all that was proper, Nessa scarcely attended to Sir Hadley's greeting, or to the introduction of his sister, Miss Amanda Leverton. She had danced twice with Sir Hadley last night, after Prudence had arranged an introduction. Nessa found him handsome enough, and he was not so many years older than herself, but his conversation was decidedly dull.

"How very kind of you, Sir Hadley, to acquaint your sister with mine. She has so few friends in London, as yet, that every suitable acquaintance must be welcome." Prudence gave Nessa a meaningful glance as she spoke, to reinforce that Sir Hadley and his sister met her exacting standards for approval.

Sir Hadley bowed formally. "I assure you, Lady Creamcroft, that Amanda was most eager to make Lady Haughton's acquaintance after hearing all that I said in her praise. I myself come prepared again to admire, and to make myself agreeable."

Prudence smiled benignly.

Nessa, however, felt as if she were being driven toward the altar like a hapless beast to the slaughter. But she would not go tamely. Not this time!

"Sir Hadley tells me you are but recently come to Town, Lady Haughton." Miss Leverton, an angular young woman with an unfortunately long nose, seated herself on Nessa's left. Her brother took the spot so recently vacated by Lord Foxhaven, on her other side. "I know how overwhelming it must be to one who has spent so little time in Society. I should like to offer my assistance in helping you to fit in. I'm really quite good at that, am I not, Sir Hadley?"

"She is indeed," agreed her brother. "I daresay Amanda was almost singlehandedly responsible for Miss Henderson's rise to popularity, and subsequent betrothal to Lord Durkle."

Miss Leverton nodded. "Mrs. Henderson was ever so grateful to me, for it was a far better match than she had expected for her daughter. Not that Miss Henderson is so very plain, you understand. She simply needed polish."

So *this* was why Prudence was encouraging this acquaintance! She must be hoping that the talented Miss Leverton might smooth away Nessa's own rough edges.

"And you were able to provide that polish, I presume." Nessa shot an accusatory glare at Prudence, who had the grace to look vaguely embarrassed.

"She was indeed." Sir Hadley was quick to praise his sister's accomplishment. "Nor is Miss Henderson— soon to be Lady Durkle—the only young lady Amanda has so benefited."

A shame the young lady could not similarly benefit herself, thought Nessa sourly. "Quite the philanthropist, I perceive." She did not take great pains to disguise the sarcasm in her voice, but the Levertons appeared not to notice. That Prudence did was evidenced by a quick, cautionary shake of her head.

Luckily for them all, other callers were announced at that juncture, allowing for a natural turn in the conversation.

Jack returned to Foxhaven House well satisfied with the progress of his campaign to acquire Lady Haughton for the benefit of his reputation. She was by no means immune to his charm, of that he was certain. Perhaps a leisurely courtship would be possible after all. If a stick-in-the-mud like Sir Hadley Leverton was willing to introduce his sister to Lady Haughton, her respectability must still be intact, colorful wardrobe or no.

"A gentleman awaits you in the library," his butler informed him as Jack cheerfully divested himself of hat and cloak.

"Lord Peter Northrup?" He'd heard some new *on dit*, no doubt, that he felt Jack should know about.

"No, milord, a Mr. Woolsey. He arrived a quarter of an hour ago and insisted on staying. He says his business is urgent."

Jack raised an eyebrow, intrigued. The name tickled at his memory, but he could not place it. "Thank you, Crump, er, Culp."

When he entered the library, a tall, thin man rose to greet him. Jack thought he looked vaguely familiar, but did not fully recognize him until he spoke.

"I give you good day, Lord Foxhaven," he said, bowing. "I have been sent with a message from the War Office."

"Good to see you again, Woolsey," Jack greeted the senior clerk, one known for his self-importance. "How goes the peace process?"

Mr. Woolsey produced a grimace that might possibly have been a smile, along with a sealed letter. "It progresses on various fronts. This message will no doubt tell you whatever it is you have need to know."

Jack glanced at the envelope and his eyebrows rose at the sight of the Duke of Wellington's seal. "No doubt it will. I presume I may send any response to White-hall?"

Mr. Woolsey sniffed. "You'll not wish to keep His Grace waiting. I am willing to remain while you compose it, my lord."

"This instant?" Jack was incredulous. "Surely it can't be as urgent as all that, now we're at peace. I'm a busy man now, you know, with estates to consider." He no longer had to jump at Wellington's command—or anyone else's. The knowledge gave him a perverse delight.

Unwilling respect colored Mr. Woolsey's response, pleasing him further. "Of . . . of course, my lord. You may send your response to Whitehall."

"Thank you, Mr. Woolsey. I'll be in touch."

Jack waited until the man was gone to break the seal on the duke's letter. Its contents were brief and to the point.

Recently appointed to the post of ambassador to Louis XVIII's court, Wellington had reason to believe certain factions intended his removal, not only from Paris but from life. Given that climate, he wished to surround himself with a few people he could trust. In particular, he felt that Major Ashecroft's experience as an unorthodox but clever strategist, combined with his other distinctive abilities, would be of great benefit in exposing any plots before they came to fruition. He was therefore "invited" to join his former commander at the royal court in Paris.

Jack perused the letter again, thoughtfully. He had no doubt that there were many in France who would count it quite a coup to dispose of the great Duke of Wellington who had so embarrassed Napoleon's forces. He was surely in far greater danger than he implied in writing, for Wellington was no coward.

Jack had made quite a name for himself over the course of his military career, he knew, for his ability to extract information, supplies, and other, more personal favors, from sources of all ranks and nationalities. Wellington plainly thought those particular abilities could be put to good use in Paris just now. Just as plainly, the Iron Duke had not yet heard of Jack's succession to his title.

A post in Paris, working again under Wellington—the only man other than his grandfather whose respect had ever mattered to him. The idea appealed to Jack, on various levels. But it would be the death of any chance of fulfilling his grandfather's dying wish. Once back amid the licentious atmosphere there, he had no doubt that he would give way to temptation in short order, making his previous excesses seem tame by comparison. His character—and reputation—would be fixed, as the most debauched Lord Foxhaven England had ever known.

Unless . . .

Unless he married first, and brought his bride along. Surely Lady Haughton would be proof against the temptations of Paris. With a respectable wife, he might strike a blow for England and still keep his resolution to honor his grandfather's wishes. It was the only way.

So a leisurely courtship was out after all. This very

afternoon he would attempt to obtain Lady Haughton's promise. And the moment he had her secure—by this evening, no doubt—he would send his response to the Iron Duke.

Lady Haughton did not keep him waiting above two minutes, which Jack took as an excellent sign. Then she apologized for that brief delay, which augured even better.

"I left my muff upstairs," she explained as she joined him and Lady Creamcroft downstairs, "and Prudence reminded me that I'd be chilly without it—at least in an open carriage. Is yours?"

"It is indeed." Endeavoring to hide his amusement, he indicated his high-perch phaeton through the drawing room window. For a moment he thought Lady Haughton would clap her hands, but she merely clasped them tightly together instead.

"How famous! I've never ridden in such a conveyance in my life. Shall we go?"

A chuckle escaped him despite his efforts, so childlike was her delight. "Very well, my lady. Lady Creamcroft, your servant." He bowed to the wooden-faced Prudence and escorted her lively young sister from the house.

Jack assisted Lady Haughton up the short ladder into the phaeton. "I fear your sister does not entirely approve of me," he commented, once they were out of earshot.

"Oh, pray do not mind Prudence." She settled herself into the seat, then looked over the edge as if to judge the distance to the ground. "She truly believes she is looking out for my best interests." The face she turned back to him showed no trace of alarm at the height of the carriage.

Jack smiled his approval. More worldly ladies than she had exhibited substantial nervousness at being suspended nearly six feet above the street. "You are fortunate to have someone to watch over you so carefully." He whipped up the horses.

"Yes, I suppose so," she replied with a noticeable lack of enthusiasm. Her face brightened again as the pair of bays broke into a brisk trot. "Are these carriages as dangerous as Prudence says?"

"Only in the hands of an inept driver," Jack assured her, though she seemed to need no such reassurance. The smile she sent his way in response nearly took his breath away. He realized again how very lovely she was. "A diamond of the first water," Peter had said. By Jove, the man was right.

It was no more than three blocks from Upper Brook Street to the Grosvenor gate of Hyde Park. Only moments later they turned in to join the throng already assembled along the paths to enjoy the fine October day. Jack had already decided that this would be the proper moment to launch the next stage of his campaign: achieving a first-name acquaintanceship.

"That deep shade of green particularly becomes you, Lady Haughton . . . or may I call you Agnes?"

To his surprise, she laughed at him. "Not if you wish

me to answer, my lord." Her eyes danced merrily, so she could not be offended. "I've always detested that name. Family and friends call me Nessa," she explained. "You may do so as well."

Only as the feeling subsided did Jack realize how dismayed he'd been for a moment, thinking she had rebuffed him. Now he grinned in relief. "And you may call me Jack. I, too, prefer a nickname to my given one."

She inclined her head playfully. "Very well then, Jack. The name suits you, I think."

"And Nessa, you. I confess I'd had difficulty thinking of you as an 'Agnes.'"

"I'm relieved to hear it!" she replied, and they laughed together, drawing stares from two nearby carriages and a few pedestrians.

As he had with so many of the gambles he'd taken throughout his career, Jack decided to hazard everything upon a single throw.

"Lady Haughton—Nessa. I enjoy your company as much as that of any woman I've ever known. In fact, I believe we deal remarkably well together. It is my wish that we might always do so."

Her eyes widened to astonished pools of liquid brown, but she did not pretend to misunderstand him. "I had hoped, when you implied such an intention this morning, that 'twas merely to mollify Prudence, but I see now it was not so. I must apologize, Jack, if I have in any way led you to believe I expected such a declaration."

Jack felt the first stirrings of misgiving, though he took her continued use of his name as a hopeful sign. "This is entirely my own inclination, I assure you, Nessa." He transferred the reins to one hand so that he could take hers with the other. "I wish you to become my wife. Will you?"

Gently but firmly, she extricated her hand from his clasp. "I'm most honored, of course, but I fear my answer must be no. I have no intention of marrying again, ever, no matter how much I might like a man."

As stunned as though she had dumped cold water upon his head, Jack nearly let the reins go slack, before the sidling of his spirited horses recalled him. Bringing them quickly under control, he turned back to this most startling woman. "You are certain?"

She nodded. "I am absolutely resolved, and have been so for some time. I'm sorry, Jack."

7

Nessa watched the rapid play of emotions across Jack's face with some concern. Was it possible that he actually cared enough for her to be wounded by her refusal? It seemed highly unlikely. More reasonable was the theory that he needed her wealth, though Prudence had implied he was quite well set-up financially.

"Jack?" she prompted softly, when he made no response to her final words.

He blinked, her voice apparently jarring him out of his thoughts. "I beg your pardon, Lady Haughton, and hope I have not offended you by my precipitousness." His tone was distracted, as though his mind were not on his words.

"I gave you leave to call me Nessa, remember? I'm not at all offended, and do hope we can remain friends."

The smile he gave her was rather twisted. "Friends. Of course." He studied her for a moment, consideringly, then leaned toward her. "Very *good* friends, perhaps?" His voice was now low and suggestive.

Nessa felt a shiver of mingled alarm and excitement. But surely, this was what she'd been hoping for? "That . . . that might be pleasant." Though she tried for a seductive tone, the words came out rather high and breathless.

Jack drove on for a few moments, and Nessa realized that he was guiding the phaeton down one of the less-traveled side paths of the Park. Again, that curious mixture of fear and anticipation coursed through her. What might he be intending?

A minute or two later, he pulled the horses to a halt. They'd rounded a bend and trees now screened them from any onlookers. Transferring the reins to one hand, he turned toward her.

"I'd like to be your very good friend, Nessa." With his free hand, he reached out to gently—so gently— stroke her cheek. A wild jumble of feelings assailed her at his touch, so unlike any touch she'd experienced before.

Unconsciously, she leaned into his hand. "I . . . I should like that, Jack." Again her voice trembled, defying her control.

Stroking again from temple to jawline, he then curled his fingers at the nape of her neck and drew her, again so gently, toward him. For just the barest second Nessa resisted, then became pliable under his touch, swaying forward until their lips were only inches apart.

"I should like that, too," he said softly. Tilting his head slightly, he brought their lips together.

His kiss was not precisely demanding, but it was very thorough. He began by gliding his lips along the outer edges of hers, then delicately explored her lips with the very tip of his tongue. Finally he pressed his mouth firmly upon hers, and she felt her own soft and yielding beneath his. And then it was over.

Nessa realized she was breathing very quickly. Lord Haughton had never kissed her like that! His infrequent kisses had been either dry, fatherly pecks, or wet and unpleasant—the latter during their occasional couplings. Lord Foxhaven's kiss was something else entirely.

And most pleasant.

She smiled up at him and thought he looked startled for a moment. "Is that how a rake kisses?" she asked. "I suppose there is something to be said for experience."

He was undeniably startled now. "Lady Haughton—Nessa—you are a woman of continual surprises." His hand, still on the nape of her neck, tightened there for an instant, as though to pull her to him again—but then he released her.

"I should take you back to your sister's. The fashionable driving hour is nearly over."

Nessa tried to hide her disappointment. "Certainly, if you think it best, my lord."

He gave her another lingering look that set her pulse, only beginning to slow, into another gallop. But then he turned his attention resolutely to the horses, taking the reins again in both hands. "There should be a place to turn around just ahead," he said, flicking the pair to a trot.

They drove back to Upper Brook Street in silence, but Nessa scarcely noticed, her mind was so busy. Had this been but a prelude to a future seduction, or had her kiss disappointed him into abandoning the idea? She wished she had the courage to ask, but could think of no remotely delicate way to do so.

Certainly *she* had not been put off by that kiss, so much more enjoyable than the quick one she'd stolen at the masquerade. If that was a sample of what a notorious rake could do, perhaps she should peruse the entire catalogue of his skills. She shivered naughtily at the thought—one no gently bred lady should have allowed to cross her mind. But it appeared she might never have the chance to do more than think about it.

"Here we are, my lady," said Jack, pulling the phaeton smartly to a halt in front of the Creamcroft house. Jumping down, he came around to help her from the carriage, then escorted her to the door. Frantically, she tried to think of some way to appease her curiosity.

"Will I see you again, my lord?" she finally asked in a rush, just as he plied the knocker. The door was opened immediately by the vigilant butler.

"Most assuredly, my lady," he replied, to her vast relief. "I've never been one to surrender after a single setback."

Leaving both Nessa and the butler to wonder what on earth he meant by that remark, he bowed, then walked briskly back to his phaeton.

"I tell you, Peter, the easiest course by far would be to compromise her so that she has no choice in the matter.

I would never have believed a widow with five years of marriage behind her could be such an innocent."

Lord Peter, stretched at his ease before the fire in the Foxhaven House library, sat up to eye him with alarm. "Jack, you haven't already—that is—surely not in the Park?"

Jack laughed at him. "Of course not. 'Sdeath, Peter, I didn't think *you* believed all of those stories about me! It was damned tempting, however, I must admit. She seems surprisingly willing to enter into an *affaire*."

Peter regarded him with interest. "So what stopped you?"

Jack frowned and flicked an invisible speck from his well-fitted tobacco-brown pantaloons. "Do you know, Peter, I'm not quite sure. I nearly crossed the line, thinking to force her to wed me in that way, but I've a profound dislike for changing my battle strategy without proper planning. Didn't expect her to refuse an honorable offer, you see."

Peter blinked. "You mean to say you made her an offer in form? So soon? And she actually refused you?"

"Things were going exceptionally well," Jack explained with a sigh. "She had let down her guard— she's really quite animated when away from Lady Creamcroft's influence, you know. We'd agreed to use each other's Christian names. The moment seemed propitious." He stared moodily into the fire.

"Did she give a reason for her refusal? Has she formed an attachment for someone else?"

Jack's head snapped up. "No, of course not! In fact, she said that she was resolved against marriage, period. To me, or to anyone."

For some reason, Peter seemed almost pleased. "She *is* but a week out of her weeds," he reminded Jack. "Perhaps, given more time . . . "

But Jack shook his head. "Time is something I don't have. Wellington has requested my presence in Paris—and I've more than half a mind to go. But if I cannot secure Lady Haughton first—"

"You'll never have a prayer of becoming respectable," Peter finished, "or of securing the balance of your inheritance." He frowned. "You needn't go, surely? You've sold your commission, and as Foxhaven you certainly have no need to jump to Old Nosey's bidding."

"True enough," Jack agreed. "But to know Wellington thinks highly enough of my abilities to ask . . . I find myself reluctant to disappoint him."

Peter thought for a moment. "Perhaps you could go to Creamcroft directly, in the matter of his sister-in-law? Is he in a position to give consent to a match?"

Jack snorted. "Of course not. She is of age, and quite well placed, as I understand it. And even if he were, it seems an underhanded way to do things. Wouldn't augur well for future happiness, I shouldn't think."

"I suppose that's true," Peter agreed with a grin. "But compromising her ain't the answer either, Jack. The whole point, as you recall, was to elevate your respectability—not to lower hers."

"Yes, yes, I know. Why do you think I stopped short of seduction this afternoon?" Jack had been asking himself that question ever since.

"You'll just have to persuade her, then. Woo her more conventionally—flowers, drives, poetry, that sort of thing."

"Poetry?" Jack laughed. "Not my style, I assure you. Besides, as I said, there's no time. No, it'll have to be blackmail. I see no other way."

Peter's jaw dropped. "Blackmail? What on earth can Lady Haughton have done to warrant that? Going so abruptly from blacks to colors ain't quite enough, in my opinion. Besides, everyone knows of it already. Surely old Haughton didn't do anything that you could hold over her head?"

Jack merely smiled and shook his head. "To be effective, I'm afraid it must remain my secret, Peter—and I still have some research to do on the matter. You'll know soon enough whether it works. Either there will be a betrothal announcement within the week, or I shall be on my way to Paris."

"And perdition," Peter muttered. "Whatever your scheme is, I hope for your sake it will be successful."

"Oh, I think it will." For now Jack had a weapon—one that should give him just the leverage he needed.

Immediately after entering the main ballroom of Hightower House that evening, Nessa resumed her campaign to convince her sister to waltz. Not only was she convinced it would do Prudence a world of good, it was also a way to distract her own mind from the disturbing events in the Park that afternoon.

"Philip, have you never tried to induce Prudence to learn the waltz?" she asked her brother-in-law. "Surely you can convince her that it is not nearly so difficult or risqué as she seems to believe."

Lord Creamcroft gazed fondly down at his wife. "Nothing would please me more than to waltz with her, but I have no wish to tease her into doing anything she finds objectionable."

Prudence smiled her thanks at her husband, but Nessa chose to focus on the first part of his response.

"There, you see, Prudence? Nothing would please him more. Haven't you a duty to please your husband?" She knew that particular responsibility had been drilled as forcibly into her sister as herself.

"Oh!" Clearly Prudence had not considered the matter in that light before—nor, likely, had Philip ever spoken so plainly, without Nessa's prompting. "Is it true, Philip? *Do* you wish me to waltz?"

Lord Creamcroft placed an arm around his lady's shoulders and gave her a very discreet squeeze which nevertheless made her squeak. "Not if you don't want to, my dear. But should you ever wish to try it, I'd be more than agreeable."

Prudence looked charmingly confused, but Nessa was distracted from this promising scene by the arrival of Sir Hadley and Amanda Leverton.

"Lady Haughton! How delightful to see you again so soon." Miss Leverton accosted her. "I do hope you haven't had time to fill your dance card, as Sir Hadley most particularly wished to have a spot on it."

Her brother stepped forward to agree, and to claim as many dances as she would grant him. Though Nessa had not yet been claimed for a single dance, having only just arrived, she allowed him but one—for now.

Other gentlemen were hurrying toward her by then, to renew acquaintances from the evening before or to seek introductions, rather to Nessa's relief. She wasn't sure whether it was Sir Hadley himself or Prudence's too-obvious approval of him which put her off, but she knew for certain she did not wish him to dominate her evening.

"Good evening, Mr. Galloway," she said, half turning from the Levertons. "I see no card tables here, alas, so I fear we shall not have the opportunity of another victory." She regarded the dashing young redhead with added interest, now that Prudence had indicated him as someone to avoid. Perhaps *he* would show her the wilder side of London life, if Lord Foxhaven—

She cut off that line of thought abruptly.

"Indeed, Lady Haughton, I had hopes of discovering whether you dance as well as you play at whist," responded Mr. Galloway with a deep bow. A throat-clearing at his elbow made him glance over his shoulder. "Ah, yes. And I promised an introduction to my cousin, Mr. Gregory Orrin. Gregory, Lady Haughton. My claim for a dance comes before yours, however."

In ten minutes, Nessa found herself committed for more than half the sets—though she kept the two waltzes free. She told herself it was because she hadn't yet enough experience with that dance to risk exposing herself or embarrassing her partner with a misstep.

Despite her inattention, the Levertons refused to leave her side, though Prudence and Lord Creamcroft were now chatting with other friends a few feet away. Perhaps Prudence felt the Levertons offered sufficient protection for the moment. Nessa might almost have suspected she'd arranged it with them.

"My dear, you must strive to appear less eager," Amanda Leverton advised Nessa in an undertone during a lull in the conversation. "Try to cultivate an air of aloofness toward the gentlemen. 'Twill enhance your popularity, I assure you."

"I thank you for your counsel to one so inexperienced as I." Nessa glanced away before Miss Leverton could see the twinkle in her eye. Amanda, she had noticed, was engaged for but two dances thus far—one with her own brother.

The orchestra struck up the first dance then, and Sir Hadley stepped forward to lead Nessa onto the floor. Happily, it was a country dance, offering little opportunity for conversation. As they went down the dance, however, Nessa could not help noticing one or two details about her partner.

Though undeniably attractive and dressed both impeccably and respectably, Sir Hadley's coat showed faint signs of wear at the elbows and hem. The fit, while passable, did not speak of Weston or any of the other premier tailors in Town. Certainly, it was not up to Lord Foxhaven's standards. . . .

Almost unconsciously, Nessa scanned the room. No, he was not here. *Would* she see him again, as he had promised, or had either her refusal or her subsequent behavior given him a disgust of her? Not that it mattered of course!

She favored poor Sir Hadley with a brilliant smile, causing him to miss his next step and earning him a glare from the young lady whose hand he had been supposed to grasp just then. Sir Hadley did not appear to notice.

Her next dance was with Mr. Galloway, and it was quite clear from Prudence's raised eyebrows that she did not approve. Nessa merely gave her sister a slight shrug, telling herself as she had last night that she'd set aside time for guilt later on.

Mr. Galloway proved a bit of a disappointment as a dancer, however, his conversation far more practiced than his steps. Still, he flattered her at every opportunity, lightening her mood considerably.

"Having discovered you have two such talents makes me eager to uncover any others," he said as he led her from the floor.

Nessa knew she should blush at such a statement, but somehow Mr. Galloway did not cause the same delightful confusion she felt when Lord Foxhaven used similar words. Still, she brought her fan into play, fluttering it between them in mock rebuff.

"La, sir," she said, trying for a flirtatious tone, "Were

I to fathom your meaning, I'm certain I should be quite shocked."

"Shall I speak plainer?" Mr. Galloway asked, his eyes beginning to smolder.

A deep voice from behind Nessa spoke, "I'd advise against it. Shocking a lady is a far worse offense than confusing her."

Nessa whipped around toward the speaker to find Lord Foxhaven regarding her with apparent amusement. Now her color did rise, as those shared moments in the Park that afternoon came flooding back.

He continued, speaking to Mr. Galloway rather than to her. "I know whereof I speak, believe me. Unexpected pronouncements may lead to equally unexpected results."

Rather to Nessa's irritation, Mr. Galloway appeared intimidated by this new arrival. Dropping his arm from under her hand as though it had suddenly become hot as a poker, he bowed.

"Foxhaven. I must acknowledge you the authority in such matters. My lady." Bowing again, he hastily decamped, leaving Nessa to stare after him in surprise.

"Is this how you intend to handle all rivals?" she demanded of Lord Foxhaven. "I presume you must be a crack shot, to have frightened poor Mr. Galloway so." She could not help being nettled by that young man's abrupt defection, after all the flattery he had heaped upon her during their dance.

Jack chuckled, exasperating her further, even while something within her thrilled at the sound. "I probably have that reputation, yes. And once a reputation is established, I have found, little action is necessary to maintain it."

Nessa regarded him uncertainly. Was he trying to tell her he was not a rake after all? Or, at least, not anymore? "I should imagine that depends on how thoroughly one's reputation was established to begin with, and through what means, my lord."

"My lord? I thought we were Jack and Nessa now—or have you reconsidered?" The look in his eyes, even more than his words, recalled to her again the events in his phaeton that afternoon—and the feelings that had accompanied them.

"Er, yes, of course. I mean, no, I haven't reconsidered," she amended hastily, wondering if he alluded to his offer, as well as their use of Christian names. As her disjointed response elicited further amusement rather than disappointment, she decided not.

His smile was knowing now, as though he divined the nature of her conflict, but he only said, "Good. I should hate to have to retake the ground I had already gained."

She had no idea how to respond to that, so turned slightly from him as though to observe the room, in an attempt to display that aloofness Miss Leverton had advised. What an abysmal failure as a flirt she was turning out to be!

"Are you looking for someone?" he asked, and she wondered if she imagined the slight edge to his voice.

"My sister," she replied, only belatedly realizing

she'd have done better to name another gentleman. She didn't want Lord Foxhaven feeling too secure of her, particularly if he intended a renewal of his "honorable" courtship. "I've been trying to convince her to waltz," she added by way of explanation, as the orchestra struck up the opening strains of that very dance.

"Then allow me to do the same with you. 'Tis time for your next lesson, I believe." Jack held out his hand with a smile and Nessa responded by placing hers into it after only the slightest hesitation.

As they took their places, she finally spotted Prudence and Lord Creamcroft, moving toward one of the curtained arches leading into the hallway, rather than the dance floor. As she watched, the pair disappeared through the arch.

"Are you so proficient at the waltz now that you can dance it with your head turned backwards?" Jack's question brought her belatedly back to her own situation.

"Oh! I beg your pardon."

With that encouragement, he led her into the steps of the dance. It really *was* as simple as she'd told Prudence, if more unsettling. Taking his hand from her waist, Jack twirled her for the first time, quite successfully. Her confidence rose.

"I meant what I said about refusing to surrender," he commented then, as though it stemmed from their current conversation.

Though they were attempting no fancy steps at the moment, Nessa nearly stumbled. "I beg your pardon?"

Instead of repeating his statement, Jack asked a question of his own. "You like me, do you not, Nessa? You implied as much this afternoon."

Nessa blinked. "Why . . . yes, of course, Jack. I find you quite, er, amiable." *Interesting* or *exciting* would have been nearer the truth, but she settled on a safer word.

"Then perhaps you'd care to share your reasons for refusing my offer? If you find me *amiable*"—his emphasis on the word gave her the uncomfortable feeling that he was reading her thoughts—"then surely you must agree that we would deal well together."

She focused on her steps for a moment before answering. "As well as could be expected in marriage, I suppose."

"It sounds as though you have a poor opinion of the wedded state. While I have frequently encountered that attitude among those of my own sex, it is surely an unusual one for yours."

Nessa met his quizzical gaze directly. "I can't imagine why. In my experience, the institution of marriage is tailored to serve the needs and desires of your sex rather than mine. For most women, wedlock is little more than indentured servitude, often to a capricious and exacting master."

It was his turn to blink, rather to her satisfaction. She was also proud to note that she had not missed a step during the exchange. He twirled her again, and again she completed the turn successfully.

"Are you not basing your opinion on a somewhat limited sample, my lady?" he asked then. "What marriages have you been in a position to observe, other than your own and that of your parents and sister?"

She had no answer to that. Her life had been so sheltered until three weeks ago that she had no more than a passing knowledge of any others—as he seemed well aware.

"Are not those enough?" she finally responded. "Surely you are familiar with the Scottish saying, 'Fool me once, shame on you; fool me twice, shame on me'? I should like to think I have learned from my experience, limited as it may have been."

Looking up at him, she saw he was smiling. It provoked her into adding, "And as limited as my experience of marriage might be, my lord, I'll warrant it is greater than your own—or are you hiding a wife somewhere?"

He laughed aloud, drawing a few curious stares from other couples in the dance. "If I were, I would scarcely have made you an offer! But I acknowledge your hit, Nessa. I have no *firsthand* experience of the married state. Will you not consider tutoring me, in exchange for the dancing lessons?"

She grinned at his absurdity in spite of herself. "Hardly a fair bargain, Jack. A dance can be taught in a few hours."

Forcing herself to greater sobriety, she continued, "I can't think why you should be so eager to wed, in any event. Surely the need to produce an heir cannot be terribly urgent to a man of your age and health." Though faintly shocked at her own plain speaking, she awaited his response with interest—though why it should matter so vitally, she was uncertain.

"Is it so impossible to believe that I am smitten by your charms?" He twirled her yet again. They were really getting quite good at it. "I must marry eventually," he continued before she could answer, "and I prefer to have the matter settled sooner rather than later. You seem an ideal choice, for a variety of reasons."

Nessa still felt sure he was not telling her all. His response was too glib to bespeak a true attachment to her. "Might I know a few of those reasons?" she prompted, realizing belatedly that she might seem to be fishing for compliments.

"You are lovely, of course, and intelligent," he replied seriously. "I quite enjoy your company, in fact. And, as I intimated to your sister, I am endeavoring to reform my ways. I believe you might help me to do so."

To Nessa's relief, the dance ended just then. She was not certain she could have continued it, so chaotic were her thoughts. He wanted her for her *respectability?* She didn't know whether to laugh, cry, or slap him across the face. If she had repented of her earlier refusal for even an instant, it was now clear she'd made the right decision. Such a marriage would be far worse than the worst she had imagined!

"I'm sorry, my lord," she began in a cold voice, but he had not finished.

"I had hoped to secure your consent in the conventional manner," he continued, "but make no mistake that I shall obtain it nonetheless."

She gaped at him. "You seem remarkably sure of yourself for a man who has been unequivocally refused."

The smile he slanted down at her held a steely determination she had never marked in him before. "Yes, I suppose I am . . . Monique."

∾ 8 ∾

Nessa felt every vestige of color drain from her face. She must have paled visibly, for Jack tightened his grip on her arm.

"'Sdeath! You're not going to faint on me, are you?"

Though more than a bit disoriented by the sudden shock, Nessa found herself oddly touched by his obvious concern. Shaking her head slightly, she pulled herself together. "No, of course not. Unhand me, if you please."

He did so, and she continued. "How long have you known? I presume you have been planning this . . . this bit of extortion all along." Fully recovered now, her tone was as quelling as she could make it.

Lord Foxhaven appeared far from quelled, however. "Actually, though I had my suspicions earlier, it was not until this afternoon that I was certain. Though I may occasionally forget a face or a name, I never forget a kiss."

Nessa felt her face flame. Fighting down her panic and embarrassment, she said, "You have no proof, my lord. Do you honestly think anyone will believe your story, should you choose to tell it?"

Infuriatingly, he continued to smile. "A week ago, perhaps not. But given your more recent behavior, I suspect the truth would spread like wildfire. Such a delicious bit of gossip, don't you think?"

Nessa's heart sank, but she forced herself to speak bravely. "Do what you will, then. I will not be forced."

She had the satisfaction of seeing his eyes harden, though his smile never wavered. "Indeed? Have you so little regard for your own reputation—and your sister's—as that?"

Doubt crept in. "Prudence? What has she to do with it? I attended that masquerade entirely without her knowledge." Belatedly, Nessa glanced around to ascertain that no one had heard her indiscreet words.

"Oh, come now, Nessa. You can't be so ignorant of Society and its ways as all that. Surely you are aware that whatever you do, particularly while residing in your sister's household, must reflect upon Lord and Lady Creamcroft."

"I shall move out, then," she retorted, her head held high. "I'd planned to do so anyway."

Jack nodded sagely. "Of course you will. Your cousin, the present Lord Cherryhurst, will no doubt be quite willing to arrange it once he knows how you have comported yourself in London." Nessa stared. "I've done my research, you see," he explained.

She knew she was trapped. Tears threatened, but anger overcame them. "I will *not* be dictated to—not by Cousin Filmore, not by Prudence, and most particularly not by you!"

He arched one brow. "Wherever did you get the idea that I intended to dictate to you?"

"You are doing so right now!" she flared. Then, deliberately calming herself, "You wish me to marry you, do you not?" She enunciated her words clearly, as though speaking to a slow child. "Husbands dictate to their wives. It is the way of the world." Even as she spoke, however, it occurred to her that she had never heard Philip "dictate" anything to Prudence.

"The way of *your* world to date, perhaps," replied Jack softly, as they were now near the crowd at the edge of the floor. Glancing quickly up, she was surprised to see that his expression had softened considerably as well. "Tyranny has no part in my plans for you, Nessa. In fact, you will almost certainly have more freedom as my wife than ever you'd have unmarried."

Nessa frowned. "But you said you wished to marry me for my respectability. Surely you intend to ensure that I *remain* respectable after marriage?"

He opened his mouth and then closed it, clearly taken aback by her phrasing. "I did not precisely say that I wanted to marry you for your respectability—" he began.

"Not in those words, perhaps, but I well understood your meaning. I have played the paragon of virtue my entire life—first as daughter and then as wife. I had hoped to try my hand at other roles now."

Before he could respond, Sir Lawrence hurried forward to remind her that the next dance was his. With great relief, she relinquished Lord Foxhaven's arm and returned to the floor for the *contredanse* just forming.

She tried to concentrate on the intricate steps of the dance, to keep her mind from her dilemma. Unfortunately, Sir Lawrence's conversation required little in the way of attention, consisting almost entirely of banalities.

Even had she not been burningly conscious of Lord Foxhaven's eyes following her about the room, Nessa would scarcely have been able to keep her thoughts from the remarkable conversation which had just taken place. Marrying him was out of the question, of course. Surely his threats against her reputation, and Prudence's, must be hollow, for he did not seem a vindictive man. . . .

Her eyes strayed to his position at the edge of the ballroom. To her dismay, she saw that he was talking to her sister and brother-in-law. Surely he would not—

"You dance like a feather on the wind, Lady Haughton." Sir Lawrence took her hand briefly as the figures brought them back together. "You must have kept in practice while living secluded in the country."

She merely smiled. In fact, she'd done very little dancing during her marriage, though it was an exercise she had always enjoyed. No doubt if Lord Foxhaven had his way, she'd be forced to give it up again. Though he *had* been the one to insist she learn to waltz . . .

Again she looked in his direction, but now saw only Prudence standing there. Jack was nowhere to be seen.

Perhaps the Creamcrofts had sent him packing. She knew the thought should relieve her, but somehow it did not. Or—a horrifying thought occurred to her—suppose Philip had called him out for insulting her? She didn't *think* her brother-in-law was the sort to react so, but suppose she was wrong?

The rest of the dance seemed to last an eternity, so impatient was she to discover what had passed between the others. It ended at last, and she wasted no time in hurrying to her sister's side.

"Why are you not dancing, Prudence?" she began, uncertain how to broach the subject that obsessed her.

Lady Creamcroft looked at her in surprise. "I have danced twice already, Nessa. You know that I am not in the habit of romping at a ball."

"No, no, of course not, Prudence. I, er, had not realized you had—that is, I've been so occupied myself—"

"Yes, I had noticed." Rather to Nessa's surprise, Prudence did not sound *quite* so disapproving as she had expected. "Really, Nessa, I cannot fathom why you wish to encourage that Mr. Galloway. He is not at all the thing. And as for Lord Foxhaven—"

Nessa held her breath when she paused.

"Well, I must admit that he has behaved unexceptionably in my presence, or almost so," Prudence continued. "Had the stories about him not come from unimpeachable sources, I would doubt their veracity. But still, I pray you will be cautious."

So he had apparently said nothing of consequence to her sister after all. Nessa let out her breath. "Thank you, Prudence. I will endeavor to follow your advice."

Mr. Pottinger approached then to claim the next dance and Nessa accompanied him willingly enough, her mind somewhat calmer. They had taken only a step or two, however, when Lady Mountheath swept up to Prudence, just behind them.

"My dear Lady Creamcroft," she said in carrying tones, "I am most grieved by what I hear——and by what I have observed with my own eyes, as well."

Nessa slowed her pace somewhat, though her escort gave no sign that he had heard. Prudence's reply was inaudible, spoken as it was at a more seemly volume, but from Lady Mountheath's response it appeared she had claimed ignorance.

"Oh, come, my dear. The whole room, nay, the whole of Society is discussing your sister's scandalous behavior, and this very evening she has danced with more than one gentleman whom I'd have expected you to warn away from her. You know that you have always been dear to me, but of course I have my daughters' reputations to consider. Therefore, I am confident that you will not take it amiss when I say that I will not be the least offended should you find you have another engagement on the night of my next dinner party."

Nessa froze, and would have turned back, but Mr. Pottinger urged her forward. "Ignore her," he whispered. "'Tis the only thing you can do. Otherwise you lend credence to her words."

Mechanically, she began moving again. Rage, pain, and shame battled for mastery of her feelings. That horrible, horrible woman! Somehow, she managed to go through the opening movements of the dance, but surreptitiously peeped at Prudence as soon as she could. Lady Mountheath had gone, and Philip was back at her side, much to her relief. Still, even from this distance, she could see that her sister was greatly distressed. What else had that hateful woman said? Had Jack already begun spreading the story of the masquerade?

By the time the dance ended, Nessa had forced herself to face the full consequences of flouting Society's rigid code. She had been deluding herself to think that she could live her life as she chose without serious repercussions. Her choices at this point were limited.

If she retired to the country, she would have to live under the watchful eye of either her Cousin Filmore or the current Lord Haughton. She shuddered. At any rate, leaving Town now might only serve to fuel the gossip further. Try as she might, she could think of only one thing that would save Prudence further embarrassment and, just perhaps, give her the freedom she craved.

Marriage.

Jack took a final puff from one of the fine cigars provided by Lord Hightower for his gentlemen guests in the library. He very much feared that Nessa would call his bluff—for bluff, he now realized, it was. He respected Nessa's feelings too much to force her into marriage if the notion was truly repugnant to her. A most inconvenient scruple, in light of his situation, but there it was.

He tossed the butt of the cigar into an ashtray, nod-ded to the two gentlemen conversing on the other side of the room, and headed back to the ballroom. His first order of business must be to gauge her feelings, now that she'd had some time to think things over.

Lord Creamcroft, who had accompanied him to the library, had already returned to his wife's side, but Nessa was not with them. Jack's attention was caught, however, by the unusual pallor of Lady Creamcroft's complexion, combined with her husband's thunderous expression.

Jack's heart sank. Had Nessa already told her sister of his ultimatum? That would certainly complicate things. For all he knew, Creamcroft might even call him out—which would be awkward in the extreme. Odd that such a scenario had not occurred to him before, during the course of all his careful planning.

Taking a deep breath, Jack headed toward the Creamcrofts, prepared to undo whatever damage he had caused. Restoring his respectability, or even gain-ing the balance of his inheritance, he realized belatedly, was not important enough to justify ruining anyone else's life—most particularly Nessa's. No, not even important enough for him to be easy about upsetting the prudish Lady Creamcroft or her more pleasant hus-band.

He would simply go to Paris alone, if need be, and endeavor to exert some self-control for the first time in his life. It could not be so hard as he imagined. Others managed it all the time.

When he was but a few strides away from Lord and Lady Creamcroft, he saw Nessa returning from the dance on the arm of some aging roué—Pottingly or something like that. She looked up just then and caught sight of Jack. Whispering something to her companion, she disengaged herself from his arm and hurried forward, intercepting Jack before he reached his destination.

"I'm happy to see you are still here, my lord," she began breathlessly. "I feared . . . But that is neither here nor there. I have been thinking on what you said earlier." She spoke quickly, as though to say something before she could change her mind, but Jack interrupted her anyway.

"So have I, Nessa." He kept his voice low, but urgent. "I handled things poorly. If you would allow me to—"

"No, Jack, let me finish." Her face set, she focused on a spot somewhere over his right shoulder. "I have decided I will marry you after all," she said in a strained monotone. "You have only to name the date."

Jack felt as if the earth had shifted on its axis beneath his very feet. A bolt of elation lanced through him, staggering in its intensity. "You . . . you have?"

She nodded, her pretty face still rigid and unsmiling.

Hard on the heels of his startling jubilation, doubt assailed him. Clearly she did not make this decision willingly. "Might I ask the reason for your *volte-face?*" he asked gently.

She did not quite meet his eyes. "Prudence. Lady

Mountheath was quite abominable to her, because of me. I——I have realized that I cannot allow her to be dragged down in disgrace on my account, after all of her kindness to me."

Inwardly, Jack cursed himself for being such a bungler. He had successfully wooed dozens of women. Why had he botched it the one time it mattered? He should let the matter drop——allow her to live her life as she wished. It was the only fair thing to do.

As he opened his mouth to do just that, he suddenly recalled the letter he'd received only that afternoon from Havershaw. Fire had destroyed one of his tenants' cottages. Until it could be rebuilt, a family of five would be homeless. Without that trust money . . .

"Do you not wish to marry me after all, my lord?" Nessa prompted as he hesitated.

"Yes. Yes, of course! I was simply . . . surprised by your sudden change of heart." But he was all too aware that it was not truly a change of *heart*. Her expression was determined, resigned, but certainly not happy.

Sir Hadley came up behind her just then, no doubt to claim another dance, but Jack waved him away. "Lady Haughton is feeling overcome by the heat," he said. "Be a good fellow and fetch her some lemonade. I shall escort her out onto the terrace, where it is cooler." Sir Hadley bowed in some confusion and hurried off.

Jack led her through the French doors a short distance away, then paused. It certainly *was* cooler out here. In fact, it was downright frigid——not surprisingly, as it was late October. What had he been thinking?

What the devil had happened to his vaunted ability to plan for every contingency? Nessa shivered.

"My apologies. Let's go into the parlor instead." Leading her back inside, he indicated an archway. A few moments later they were seated on a divan, alone in the room but with the door discreetly half open. Taking both her hands in his, he said, "I will marry you, Nessa, but only upon two conditions."

Despite her obvious distress, a spurt of laughter escaped her. "My, how the tables have turned! An hour ago you were bargaining for my hand. Now it appears I am to bargain for yours. What are your conditions?"

Jack reached out to stroke her cheek, pleased to see she was still in possession of her sense of humor. "Brave girl. Only these: first, that we schedule our wedding to take place before Christmas." He paused and she nodded, accepting that. "Secondly," he continued, "that you come with me to Paris."

"Paris?" she breathed, her eyes wide.

He nodded. "I've been invited to a post at Louis' court. We would leave just after the first of the year. Consider it a honeymoon," he added with a grin.

Though she frowned at that, Nessa nodded slowly. "Very well, Jack. I will go with you to Paris. And now," she finally met his eyes, "I have a few conditions of my own."

"Indeed? Let's have them, then."

She ignored his teasing tone. "First, as I said before, I will not be dictated to. Or bullied. Or abandoned in the country while you pursue your pleasures in Town."

He nodded solemnly. "You have my word."

Though she looked startled, a smile flitted across her face. "And—I want the rest of those waltzing lessons you promised me."

Jack laughed aloud at this conclusion, but quickly sobered. "We shall consider it settled, then." He regarded her quizzically. "Surely a kiss would be appropriate, to seal our troth?"

She looked wary, but did not shy away when he leaned toward her. He covered her mouth with his, savoring the light, slightly floral scent of her skin and hair. She truly was exquisite—an excellent choice. As he deepened the kiss, she seemed to melt beneath him—much as she had that afternoon in the park. Her breath quickened and mingled with his, and again it took all of his self-control to pull away.

"Is this how you mean to bend me to your will, my lord, now you have agreed not to dictate?" she asked as soon as she could speak.

Her quick recovery surprised him, but he answered readily enough. "Do you not find me persuasive? That is but one of many weapons in my arsenal, I assure you."

She eyed him speculatively. "Indeed. I asked you this afternoon whether that was how a rake kisses. I don't recall that you ever answered me."

He tried to choke back a laugh, but failed utterly. "No, I suppose I didn't. How should I answer? That is how *I* kiss. If I am to be categorized as a rake, then I suppose the answer must be yes."

The sparkle did not leave her eyes. "Ah, but you

aren't truly a rake anymore, are you? Perhaps I shall never know for certain how a *real* rake behaves toward a lady."

Nessa would never bore him, of that Jack was absolutely certain. "You little minx! How on earth did you ever attain such a spotless reputation in the first place?"

"By being relentlessly respectable, of course," she replied. "Did I not tell you I was heartily tired of it?"

"You did. And sometime you must tell me what it was like and just why you developed such an aversion . . . but not now. I perceive Sir Hadley and your lemonade have found us."

Practiced in such matters, Jack expertly and surreptitiously straightened a ruffle of Nessa's rose gown and one of his lapels before turning to face the interloper. "My apologies, Leverton. It was too cold on the terrace for Lady Haughton's comfort, so we changed our venue for her recovery. She seems much more the thing now."

Sir Hadley glanced suspiciously from one to the other, but Jack regarded him serenely—as did Nessa, he noted with approval.

"Is that my lemonade, Sir Hadley? You are a dear, thank you. I'm quite parched." She took the glass from her erstwhile suitor with a breathtaking smile, earning a grudging one in return.

"My honor to be of service, my lady," he said, bowing. "My very great honor. Perhaps I might persuade you to accompany me back to the ballroom?" He sent a darkling glance at Jack.

"An excellent idea. I'll come with you." Jack rose and extended a hand to help Nessa to her feet, forestalling Sir Hadley, who had perforce to precede them from the room. Jack took the opportunity to whisper, "Shall I approach the Creamcrofts, or do you wish to speak with them first?"

The look she flashed him held a hint of alarm. "Let me do it, please! I'm not certain how——" But Sir Hadley had turned back, so she broke off. "Thank you, my lord," she concluded more audibly.

Her face giving no hint of the turmoil she doubtless felt, Nessa proceeded regally to the ballroom to dance the next set with Sir Hadley. Jack wasn't certain he could have performed any better himself, under the circumstances. Yes, she'd do quite nicely.

The remainder of the evening passed far too quickly for Nessa, dreading as she was the announcement she must make to Prudence during the drive home. She danced one more waltz with Jack, and honored her other, previous commitments on the floor, but sat out the remainder of the dances to give herself time to think.

Her newfound popularity was an impediment to this goal, however. Between Miss Leverton and various interested gentlemen, she was given little time to herself.

"Are you certain you do not wish for another glass of ratafia?" Mr. Galloway asked, seating himself rather too close to her on the bench where she'd sought refuge behind a potted palm.

"Quite certain, thank you," she replied, scooting an inch or two away from him. "I am merely a bit tired. Pray go and enjoy the dance."

No sooner had he left her than Miss Leverton appeared with a fresh volley of advice for Lady Haughton's improvement. Nessa smiled and nodded at what she hoped were appropriate intervals while her mind traveled other paths.

Was she doing the right thing? If not, what alternative did she have? She imagined life in the country, at Haughton Abbey's dower house—an intolerable prospect. Or at Cherry Oaks, where her Cousin Filmore now held sway—a man after her father's heart. Even worse.

No, marriage to Lord Foxhaven must be superior to either of those alternatives. Mustn't it? He had promised much, but of course she had no way to enforce those promises. She hoped she could trust him. And Paris . . . !

"You understand what I mean, do you not, Lady Haughton?"

"Oh, certainly, Miss Leverton. Thank you for advising me."

Whatever instructions she had just imparted, her self-appointed mentor was not finished. She launched into yet another monologue.

What would it be like to live with Jack in Paris? Nessa was unable to suppress an anticipatory shiver. And that "persuasion" he'd alluded to—he'd implied he meant to do more than kiss her, but did she really want him to? Certainly, his kisses were completely different from Lord Haughton's, but kissing had always been the least unpleasant part of marital intimacy. Would . . . *that* be different, too? Her thoughts shied away from the subject.

"I'm sorry, Lady Haughton, I did not mean to embarrass you with my plain speaking."

Nessa had no idea what Miss Leverton had been saying, but it was clear her own musings had brought a blush to her cheeks. Happily, it served to deter her advisor from further counsel. As Amanda Leverton stood, Prudence approached.

"Will you be ready to leave soon, my dear? Supper is not to be served until after midnight, and I confess myself quite tired."

Though not surprised, as the Creamcrofts frequently left such functions early, Nessa wondered whether Lady Mountheath's hatefulness had contributed to her sister's fatigue. She felt a moment of panic on realizing that the moment she'd been dreading was almost upon her. Best to get it over, though. "Certainly, Prudence. I am rather fagged myself."

When they were all ensconced in the carriage a short time later, Prudence commented, "I could not help overhearing just a bit of what Miss Leverton was saying to you as I walked over, Nessa. Perhaps you should not rely too heavily on her advice after all. It seems most improper to me for a lady to hint that she might like to be kissed in order to prompt a gentleman to a declaration."

Nessa coughed. Was that what Amanda had thought put her to the blush? It was too funny, after the occurrences of this day, though a mere month ago, such advice probably *would* have shocked her, she realized. What a change Lord Foxhaven had wrought in her! Perhaps he really was a bad influence, she thought with a secret grin.

"Prudence, I have something to tell you," she said while her courage was still high. Her sister and brother-in-law regarded her expectantly. Philip still wore grim lines about his mouth, she noticed. He, at least, should be pleased that Prudence would be spared further embarrassment on her behalf.

Taking a deep breath, she plunged ahead. "Lord Foxhaven has made me an offer of marriage, and I have accepted him," she said in a rush, then braced herself for her sister's reaction.

For a full minute, it did not come. Then Prudence said, faintly, "Oh, Nessa, are you certain? He is so . . . That is, you have been accustomed to such . . . I am very happy for you, of course, but . . . "

Her husband broke in, firmly. "Our heartiest congratulations, sister. Though Lady Creamcroft may doubt it, I believe you and Foxhaven will deal very well together. Had a few words with him earlier this evening and he seems a fine chap."

Prudence regarded her husband uncertainly. "But the stories—"

"Overblown, or at least ancient history. I'm certain of it." Prudence appeared to need further reassurance, so he put his arm about her shoulders. "I'm sure your sister can tame whatever wild tendencies might remain in him, my dear. A good wife always can. We'll send an announcement to the papers in the morning."

Nessa knew Philip's eagerness stemmed from his wish to protect his wife, but she felt the tiniest bit hurt nonetheless. Did he want her out of their house so badly as all that? But then she considered the rest of what he'd said.

Tame Jack's remaining wild tendencies? If he truly had any left, her preference would be to coax them back into full vigor. This promised to be a most interesting engagement, whatever befell.

9

Jack hummed to himself as he mounted the stairs to his bedchamber. The evening had gone surprisingly well, all things considered. For a while he thought he'd ruined everything, but it had turned out right after all.

"Congratulate me, Parker," he greeted his waiting valet. "I am betrothed."

Though betraying no real surprise, Parker regarded him closely for a moment before responding. Then, breaking into a wide smile, he heartily congratulated his employer. "I am truly happy for you, my lord."

It was Jack's turn to attempt deciphering Parker's visage, but with as little success as usual. "So you think I've done the right thing, do you?"

"I do, my lord. I feared for a moment that you had been too precipitate, but I see now it is not the case."

"How the devil can you know that?" Jack demanded. "I met the woman less than a month ago, after all."

Parker merely smiled and proceeded to help him out of his coat, but Jack felt oddly reassured. He could not recall a time in their long acquaintance when Parker's judgment had been faulty.

Lord Peter and Harry presented themselves at Foxhaven House at the unheard-of hour of ten o'clock the next morning, eager for news.

"'Sdeath, Harry, did Peter have to drag you from your bed to have you here so early? Get yourself some coffee from the sideboard."

Harry, decidedly groggy, complied. "Don't know why Pete couldn't have told me whatever news after he had it. Rising early ain't good for my constitution, I'm sure of it. So what is it? Do you leave for Paris in the morning?"

Helping himself to a cup of coffee as well, Lord Peter turned toward Jack with interest. "I scarcely slept for the anticipation, Jack. Out with it!"

Jack leaned back in his chair, extending his legs toward the library hearth. "Both of you clearly need more to occupy your time—and minds. To think that my small doings should hold such fascination for two such purportedly worldly gentlemen . . . "

The worldly gentlemen advanced menacingly toward him, and he threw up a hand. "Very well, very well. No need to douse me with hot liquids. Lady Haughton and I are betrothed, with the wedding to take place before Yuletide. Satisfied?"

The two faces before him were a study in contrasts, Harry's evincing distaste and pity, Lord Peter's disbelieving joy. The latter spoke first.

"Congratulations, old fellow! I knew you had it in

you. Well done!" He clasped Jack's hand and pumped it heartily.

But Harry shook his head gloomily and dropped into a chair. "I was afraid it would come to this. Really going to go through with it, are you? Set up a nursery, the whole bit?"

That thought hadn't occurred to Jack before, and sobered him abruptly. A nursery? Children? Him, a father? It seemed awfully unlikely, somehow——not to mention more responsibility than he'd bargained for, far outstripping the others that went with his title.

"I, er, yes. I suppose so," he said lamely. "The announcement may not appear in the papers for a day or two, so I'd prefer you keep the news to yourselves until then, by the way."

"So, Jack, tell us how you pulled it off," prompted Lord Peter, pulling a chair close. "I take it your blackmail, whatever it was, was effective?"

Harry raised an eyebrow at that, his interest reviving. "Blackmail, say you? There's a new courtship technique."

But Jack shook his head, cursing himself for ever using the word aloud. "Merely a figure of speech, Peter. Oddly enough, Lady Mountheath made herself useful in my cause."

"What? She never——" began Lord Peter.

"Not intentionally, I assure you. She was apparently rude to Lady Creamcroft on account of her sister's choice of dancing partners. I managed to parlay Lady Haughton's anxiety for her sister's social standing into an agreement to marry me, that is all." Jack hoped they would be satisfied with that, but he was not to be so fortunate.

"Just like that?" Peter was openly suspicious. "She insisted upon no conditions? No unusual promises?"

Jack grinned, remembering. "Actually, she did." The moment the words were out, he regretted them, but now he was forced to elaborate. "She, ah, wants me to teach her to waltz."

"What else?" his friends said together.

"There are times it is damned inconvenient to have close friends," Jack observed. "There *are* things a man prefers to keep private, you know."

"Oh, come, Jack!" Peter protested. "We've been with you on this campaign from the outset. Surely we deserve the details of the final coup."

Now Jack felt distinctly embarrassed, but had to agree he owed that much to his compatriots. "All right, then. I promised not to dictate to her, or leave her alone in the country. It would seem old Haughton was quite the bully, judging by her disinclination to remarry. I've no doubt if I were to begin ordering her about she would cry off at once."

Harry brightened at once. "By Jove, a loophole! Well done, old boy! You can get your inheritance before the wedding, then play the tyrant, eh? I should have known that if anyone could devise a way to have his cake and eat it too, it'd be Jack Ashecroft!" He rose to bow in tribute, spilling the last drops of his coffee on the thick Turkish carpet in the process.

Lord Peter frowned. "That's not your intent, is it? To have her cry off before the wedding? Paris——"

"What would he want with a wife in Paris?" demanded Harry with a laugh. "If Old Nosey had asked me, I'd have gone like a shot. I hear there's a grand time to be had. Don't have the blunt handy to go on my own, or I'd be there now."

"I don't doubt it," said Lord Peter in obvious disgust. "You'd happily drink and wench yourself to death, and be found in some gutter within a sixmonth."

Harry grinned. "Wouldn't I, though? And what a way to go! I'd thought to do it here in London, only Jack stopped giving his parties too soon. You'll need to celebrate your betrothal, though, eh?" He turned hopefully to his host.

But Jack was lost in thought. *Did* he want to go through with the wedding? Harry was right that he might possibly implement his original plan without doing so. Surely he should snatch at the chance. His freedom had always been very precious to him. All he'd have to do was give Nessa a disgust of him. Merely tossing a few orders her way would no doubt do the trick. After all, it appeared she valued her own freedom as much as he did his. So why should he find such a plan so distasteful?

"Jack?" Harry prompted.

Prodded out of his reverie, Jack shook his head. "The whole plan hinges upon my behaving myself till Christmas, remember? A betrothal orgy hardly qualifies. If I give a party, it'll be of a more respectable sort—though you'll still have ample access to my cellars, Harry, so not to worry."

Harry looked only partially mollified. Lord Peter did not appear pleased at all, however.

"*Is* that the way of it then, Jack? You don't mean to go through with the actual wedding?"

Jack met his friend's eyes and saw the concern in them. "I *had* planned to carry it out. In fact, I rather doubt old Havershaw will release the trust if I don't. If he could be convinced, though . . . "

"Then don't let Harry's blather dissuade you," said Peter firmly—as firmly as Jack had heard him speak since selling out his commission. "If your inclination is to marry Lady Haughton, then you should do it. Have to marry sometime anyway, for the succession. Do you honestly think you can do better?"

He was certain he couldn't. But could Nessa?

"You'll wish to write to the present Lord Haughton and to our Cousin Filmore before sending an announcement to the papers, will you not?"

Nessa looked up from her breakfast to regard her sister with raised brows. "Whatever for? I scarcely need the permission of either to wed. I've only met Lord Haughton's nephew once, at the funeral, and Cousin Filmore has shown little interest in how I go on, for all he holds my purse strings."

Though her husband had left a tidy sum to Nessa, rather to her surprise, he had left it under Lord Cherryhurst's control—a circumstance that had no doubt irritated Lord Haughton's heir as much as it had Nessa. Once she married, however, Lord Cherryhurst's—and Lord Haughton's—last vestige of control over her would vanish. Regaining control of her fortune had played a large part in her decision—not that Jack needed to know that, of course.

"It simply seems the proper way to go about things," argued Prudence. "Surely there is no great hurry to make an announcement, so you and Lord Foxhaven will hardly be inconvenienced by observing such a protocol."

"That's very thoughtful of you, Prudence, considering that our announcement will likely deflect the gossips' attention." Nessa hoped that consideration might moderate Prudence's resistance to the match. "However, as Lord Foxhaven and I are agreed on a December wedding, I'd really prefer not to wait. I can send notice to both gentlemen in the same post which carries the announcement to the papers."

But Prudence fixed on only one portion of her reply. "December! This very December that is but a few weeks distant? Oh, Nessa, surely not!"

"Lord Foxhaven wishes me to spend the Christmas season at Fox Manor," Nessa explained reasonably, but without regard to her betrothed's true plans, whatever they might be. "We saw no reason to delay the match, once we had agreed it should take place."

Prudence was clearly aghast, however. "But . . . but Nessa, only think! You'll have no time to shop properly for a trousseau, or to arrange for an engagement party without conflicting with other entertainments. And

I'm certain you do not wish Society to think that you are rushing into marriage."

This last, Nessa knew, was the real concern. "'Twill be six weeks at least between the announcement and the wedding, Prudence. No one will suspect it to be . . . *necessary*, with a delay of that length."

Her sister flushed scarlet and groped for her fan at such plain speaking, even if it *was* what she'd been hinting at.

Nessa gave her a moment to compose herself, then continued. "The primary reason for haste—surely one which Society will approve—is that Jack, I mean Lord Foxhaven, has been asked to join the court of King Louis XVIII in Paris as soon as possible. He wishes us to marry first, that I may accompany him. Given that, I cannot think anyone will find our haste unseemly. 'Tis a great honor, after all!" she finished grandly, striving to convince herself as much as her sister.

Prudence appeared suitably impressed by this final argument. "I suppose . . . Has he really been bidden to the Royal Court?"

"By the Duke of Wellington himself," Nessa affirmed.

"Oh, my." Prudence was visibly impressed. "I knew that Lord Foxhaven was a war hero, but I hadn't realized—that is—but of course he mustn't refuse. Are you certain *you* wish to go to Paris, however, Nessa? 'Tis said the Society there is most indecorous."

"Is it?" she asked with interest.

Prudence nodded, but with obvious reluctance. "I'll not repeat most of what I have heard, of course, but shocking tales have been drifting back from Paris since the summer. Lord Foxhaven will be right at home, I should think." She primmed her lips. "But you, Nessa, must be very much on your guard. Truly, I cannot imagine what Papa would have said."

To forestall another homily, Nessa changed the subject. "I meant to ask you last night, Prudence. Where did you and Philip go when you disappeared during the Hightower's ball?"

Her sister flushed scarlet and began to stammer something about fresh air. Nessa grinned, but by the time Prudence concluded her disjointed explanation, her mind was busy with other possibilities. If the stories of Paris were true, a stay there could be the very thing to introduce her to a wider—and wilder—world. Perhaps this marriage would not be so unpleasant after all.

Only half an hour after Prudence had read the announcement aloud to Nessa over their breakfast table the next morning, Jack presented himself at the door.

"I've come to take my bride-to-be driving," he explained, smiling past Prudence to Nessa in the way that quickened her pulse. "I thought perhaps she might wish to have a hand in the selection of her engagement ring."

That sobered Nessa at once, bringing as it did a sense of finality and . . . bondage. Prudence, however, was most agreeable.

"How kind of you, my lord. I take it there is no family piece you wish her to wear?"

He shook his head with a rueful smile. "'Tis still in my mother's possession, and I fear she'd not take kindly to my reclaiming it. I suppose I should write her, on the off chance that she'll offer, but it's an antique-looking thing anyway. At the very least, it would have to be reset, and I wish Nessa to have a bauble to display at once."

No doubt he meant it as a compliment, but to Nessa both his words and the meaning look he sent her smacked of possessiveness. Again, she felt the walls of a prison closing in on her, and it was all she could do to smile back.

"You have not written your mother of your betrothal?" Prudence exclaimed, missing the interchange. "Oh, my lord, you must do so without delay! Whatever will she think, that we were so forward as to publish an announcement without her knowledge!"

Jack merely shrugged. "I doubt she'll know, as she never reads the papers when she's in the country. And even if she did . . . well, I cannot imagine that it would concern her unduly."

Nessa regarded him curiously. Clearly he and his mother were not on good terms, but just as clearly— to her, at least—the estrangement was painful to him, though he hid it well. She really knew very little about this man she was pledged to marry.

"Pray get a note off to her today, my lord," Prudence urged, still distressed. "Women care more about such matters than men realize, I assure you."

"Very well, I promise to do so. And now, my

betrothed, if you will fetch your wrap, we can be on our way."

Despite her earlier misgivings, Nessa could not but be flattered by his apparently affectionate attention. Of course, it could all be a ruse, for Prudence's sake. . . . She hurried to get her cloak.

Jack had brought a closed carriage today, as the weather had turned damp and chilly with the approach of November. "I thought we'd begin at New Bond Street, progress to Old, then finish up in Piccadilly," he explained as they settled themselves inside.

"Goodness! All of that shopping for a single ring?"

The intimacy of the smile he sent her made Nessa catch her breath. "I had a few other things in mind, as well. You'll want to be well outfitted for Paris, I doubt not. Besides, this will give me a chance to show you off to the fashionable world."

Nessa bristled at once. "I am not a possession to be displayed for the envy of others, and then tucked safely away in a box," she warned him.

"Who said anything about possessions or boxes?" He seemed genuinely startled by her response.

Realizing that she had overreacted, she tried, somewhat haltingly, to explain. "Forgive me. But it has been my experience that many husbands treat their wives so—as pretty baubles to wear on their arms in public, and to lock away when not in use. Not an enjoyable existence for the bauble, I assure you."

Jack frowned. "I had never thought of it in that way, but you are right. Many men *do* behave so. I begin to perceive your reluctance to remarry." His eyes searched her face, and she felt it grow warm under his examination. "Will it help if I promise never to regard you as a possession? For I do not, Nessa, truly."

She met his eyes. "As what *do* you regard me?" She held her breath, waiting for his answer.

"A person in your own right," he replied, "with a mind and will of your own. Rather a strong will, I might add." His eyes were twinkling now, and she felt her own expression soften in response.

She had hoped he would say he regarded her as an equal, but of course that was absurd. No man ever considered his wife so, not even those who, like Philip, clearly loved their mates. And from what Nessa had seen of fashionable ladies, she could scarcely say they were in the wrong. She inclined her head. "Very well, my lord, that will do—for now."

A few moments later the carriage pulled to a stop before one of the premier jewelers in London. The experience of selecting her own jewelry was a novel one for Nessa, and she enjoyed it thoroughly. As she tried on the third ring, a large rectangular diamond surrounded by tiny sapphires, she realized that she was the only woman in the shop. Jack was according her an honor—and freedom—very few enjoyed. Gratitude colored the smile she gave him.

"Is that the one, then?" He returned her look warmly.

"Oh!" She looked down again at the ring she wore. "No, 'tis still a bit flashy for my taste, I believe. Perhaps that one, there, with the smaller stone?"

"But my lady," the jeweler protested, "a man of Lord Foxhaven's consequence will surely wish—"

"That smaller one," said Jack decisively, cutting him off. "She is the one who will wear it, not I. What have my wishes to do with it?"

Trying on the smaller diamond, Nessa felt an unexpected lightness of heart. Jack had passed his first test with flying colors.

Soon after, Nessa left the jeweler's with a lovely but tasteful diamond solitaire on her finger. They progressed down Bond Street on foot, the coachman having been given instructions to pace them. A few shops down, Jack purchased a silk scarf for Nessa, again of her own choosing. She was finding him a far more pleasant shopping companion than her sister.

Upon leaving the drapers, they nearly walked into Lady Mountheath and her daughters. Jack bowed and tipped his hat, and Nessa greeted them as cordially as she could manage. The woman's words to Prudence two nights since still rankled.

Lady Mountheath favored them both with a sour smile. "I understand that felicitations are in order. No doubt you will be very happy," she said in a tone that implied just the opposite.

Miss Lucy tittered, while Miss Fanny's small eyes raked over Nessa from head to toe, lingering meaningfully on her midsection. With a stern look, their mother called them to order, and they dutifully echoed her insincere well wishes.

"I have observed," continued Lady Mountheath,

"that marriage often has a . . . stabilizing influence upon young people. I hope that it will be so for your sake, Lady Haughton. An unreformed rake can cause his wife both embarrassment and heartache."

With a parting glare at Jack, she turned to go, but Nessa's precarious hold on her temper snapped.

"No doubt Your Ladyship speaks from experience," she said smoothly. From what Mr. Pottinger had told her, Lord Mountheath was not known for his discretion. "I shall endeavor to learn from your example and thereby avoid making the same mistakes."

Taking Jack's arm, she turned her back on the open-mouthed trio and walked briskly down the street. Her face was flaming, she knew, but from anger rather than embarrassment. Suddenly realizing that Jack had said not a word, she glanced up in some trepidation only to see his face contorting comically.

Catching her eye, he relinquished the struggle and began to chortle. "Oh, my dear," he gasped after a moment, "you were magnificent! You can't imagine how many women—and men too, for that matter—have dreamed of dealing that gorgon such a set-down!"

Nessa's own lips began to twitch, her anger subsiding in the face of his merriment. "No doubt she will find a way to repay me, but I cannot help but feel 'twas worth it. Did you see the look on her face?"

He nodded, and they were both obliged to lean on one another for support as they dissolved into laughter. After a moment, becoming aware of curious stares from passersby, Nessa straightened. "Come, my lord, I believe we have a bit more shopping to do."

Over the next hour, as they passed in and out of the shops, Nessa found herself enjoying his company more than ever. The incident with Lady Mountheath had somehow bound them more closely together, inspiring a camaraderie she found most pleasant.

Along the way they encountered several acquaintances, all of whom stopped to offer congratulations on their betrothal with varying degrees of sincerity. Mrs. Heatherton, one of Prudence's close friends, seemed genuinely delighted, but her companion, a Mrs. Renfrew, regarded her with undisguised pity. This Nessa found more unsettling than spite or curiosity, but decided to credit it to ignorance.

Jack, meanwhile, congratulated himself on the progress he was making in winning Nessa's trust, if not her affection. He could not recall ever having enjoyed a woman's company and conversation the way he did hers. The prospect of spending a lifetime tied to just one woman was appearing less and less onerous with each passing moment. Really, he had been most fortunate.

They had just agreed to return to the Creamcrofts' for some luncheon when they were accosted by a stunningly beautiful flame-haired woman, dressed in the absolute pinnacle of fashion. Jack stifled an oath, realizing that his luck had just run out.

"Why, Jack," the woman cooed, with a smile that failed to soften the glitter in her emerald eyes, "I understand congratulations are in order. Do introduce me to your sweet little bride-to-be."

Beside him, Nessa pulled herself to her full height—which still lacked several inches to that of the redhead. Jack felt her grip on his arm tighten slightly.

Resisting the urge to pat her hand, he bowed formally to the newcomer. "Nessa, my dear, this is Mrs. Dempsey. Mrs. Dempsey, my fiancée, Lady Haughton."

His erstwhile paramour's eyes narrowed, raking over every detail of Nessa's appearance, though the smile never left her lips. "Ah, so it's to be Mrs. Dempsey now, is it? But of course, we don't want to offend the delicacy of the little wife."

If anything, Nessa stood even taller. Despite his deucedly awkward situation, Jack could not help being proud of her. Then she spoke.

"Charmed to make your acquaintance, Mrs. Dempsey, and my thanks for your felicitations. I perceive that you are an old friend of Jack's?" Though Miranda Dempsey could be no more than a year or two Nessa's senior, she slightly emphasized the adjective.

Miranda's smile slipped for a moment, but she quickly recovered. "I suppose 'friend' is the most diplomatic way to describe it," she retorted, then turned the full power of her smile upon Jack. "Should you find your proper little wife tedious, darling, you'll still know where to find me."

She extended her expensively gloved hand to him in farewell, but Jack accorded her only the merest bow and the slightest touch of his fingertips to hers. Her eyes blazed at the perfunctory nature of his farewell, but he turned quickly away before she could direct any more barbs his—or Nessa's—way.

One glance showed him that Nessa had in no way mistaken Miranda's meaning. Jack mentally cursed the woman. Though in honesty he knew such encounters were inevitable, he'd hoped to have Nessa secure before one occurred. Anger and panic warring within him, he propelled his unresisting fiancée away from the site of his worst setback yet.

10

Nessa paid little attention to the direction Jack was leading her, mechanically putting one foot in front of the other. There was room in her mind for only one thought. Though she'd done her best to evade it, the truth had struck with blinding clarity.

That woman was Jack's mistress.

She couldn't understand why she was so hurt by the knowledge. Evidence that Jack was still a rake should be just what she wanted. But the hurt was as undeniable as it was baffling.

"I know what you must be thinking," he said, the moment they were out of earshot.

Nessa glanced up at his handsome profile, then quickly away. "I'm not an idiot, my lord. Mrs. Dempsey's meaning was quite clear."

"So it's to be 'my lord' every time my past rears its unattractive head?" His tone was teasing, but she thought she detected a hint of anxiety as well.

They had reached the waiting carriage but she paused to regard him searchingly. "Your past, Jack?

Mrs. Dempsey implied otherwise. And one would be blind to consider her unattractive."

Jack grasped her shoulder, gently but firmly. "Nessa, I've never once denied that my past is somewhat unsavory. There are those, like Mrs. Dempsey, who will be unwilling to believe that I've put it behind me, and so encounters similar to the one you just witnessed may occur—for a while. But I *have* renounced my old, debauched lifestyle, and eventually everyone will realize that. I will do my utmost to spare you any future embarrassment connected with my past in the meantime."

His deep blue eyes fairly glowed with sincerity, and Nessa found herself almost desperate to believe him—a far cry from the disappointment she'd felt previously, at the idea of his wild ways being behind him.

Though her hurt eased only slightly, she nodded. "Very well, Jack. I suppose it would be hypocritical of me to condemn you for having enjoyed the very lifestyle I have envied." She managed a semblance of a smile.

Undisguised relief spread over Jack's features, mingled with something else—something that warmed her to her toes, despite the light drizzle which had begun to fall and the lingering chill in her heart. "Thank you, Nessa. I'm determined you won't regret your faith in me."

Nessa met his eyes squarely. "So am I," she said.

"Are you certain you do not wish to accompany us to the theater tonight, Prudence?" Nessa asked a few days later, as a maid removed the tea tray. "I know you have not been in the habit of going, but it is a perfectly acceptable amusement."

Her sister shook her head. "No, we are promised to Lady Trumball this evening, but Lord Creamcroft has suggested the theater once or twice of late, so I doubt not we will attend sometime. Though Papa never approved of it, I did not find the theater so very depraved the one time I went last Season."

Nessa allowed herself a small hope that Prudence might finally be beginning to think for herself. "I am glad to hear that, though I should rather have liked you along for my first visit."

Prudence regarded her for a long moment, her pretty brow furrowed. "Do you find it . . . difficult . . . being alone with Lord Foxhaven, then? There is still time to cry off, you know."

"Difficult? No, not at all." Nessa had never mentioned the encounter with Mrs. Dempsey to her sister. "He and I deal very well together, as I have told you. 'Tis simply that Simmons will feel obliged to play the chaperone, I know, and I've no desire to listen to her sermonizing."

Simmons had been Nessa's abigail from the first year of her marriage to Lord Haughton and, if anything, was more of a stickler for the proprieties than her late master had been. She seemed to have a genuine fondness for her mistress, but her moralizing could be tedious—and Nessa had heard a fair share of it lately, especially on the subjects of her wardrobe and fiancé.

Yet more was forthcoming as she dressed for the theater a few hours later.

"Milady, are you certain you would not prefer to wear the peach? Its neckline is more becoming than that of the lilac." Simmons held up the more modestly cut peach gown hopefully.

Nessa sighed. There was simply no pleasing the woman. "I thought you might consider lilac a more seemly color, Simmons. 'Tis approved for half-mourning, after all."

The rail-thin abigail twitched her long nose. "Not when it is so vivid a shade—nor when cut so revealingly. Milady would not wish to be mistaken for one of the vulgar young women who perform on the stage, I am sure."

Secretly, Nessa thought she might like that very much, but Simmons was speaking again.

"Though Lord Foxhaven's exploits with such women are well known, you must strive to rise above any vulgar competition and set him a virtuous example—if you are really set upon this marriage."

"Of course I am," said Nessa automatically, as she had a dozen times since the betrothal was announced. But now her attention was caught by Simmons' earlier words. Though she knew it was not at all the thing to encourage servants' gossip, she could not resist a bit of probing. "Exploits?"

The abigail nodded her mousy brown head sententiously. "Indeed, milady. Lord Foxhaven is known to visit the theaters frequently, and not for the performances. At least, not those upon the stage."

Her pale blue eyes gleamed, though whether with outrage or curiosity, Nessa was not completely certain. Though she knew she should remonstrate, she remained silent in hopes of hearing more. Simmons did not disappoint her.

"One of the downstairs maids told me that he's been known to carry on with two actresses at the same time, on alternate days of the week. And each trying to outdo the other with her wicked, seductive ways in an attempt to have him to herself!"

Reluctantly, Nessa stopped this fascinating but disturbing flow of information. "That will be enough, Simmons. Pray remember that you are speaking of my fiancé. And put the peach away. I have already decided upon the lilac for tonight."

Simmons pursed her lips disapprovingly. "As you wish, milady." She finished Nessa's toilette in silence, but Nessa scarcely noticed, so tumultuous were her thoughts.

Here was yet more evidence that Jack really had been—and perhaps still was?—a rake, not that she'd doubted it after that encounter with Mrs. Dempsey a few days since. Again she felt that oddly painful squeezing of her heart at the thought of Jack with other women. At the same time, however, she felt avid curiosity. Just what sorts of things *had* Jack been in the habit of doing with all of these women? Surely, if anyone should know, it was his betrothed.

By the time she descended for dinner, Nessa had

decided to devote the evening to finding out. Even if Jack really had put his debauchery behind him, as he said, there must be enough of the rake left in him to satisfy her curiosity.

"What a, er, striking gown that is," Prudence commented as Nessa entered the drawing room. While her pretty young face could not pucker in the way Simmons' did, her disapproval was quite as pronounced as the abigail's. "Perhaps a shawl . . . ?"

With a sigh, Nessa allowed the maid to fetch one from her room. Jack was to join them for dinner, but her brother-in-law would be present as well. And Nessa wanted Philip to notice his wife, after all, not herself. Lord Creamcroft arrived before the shawl did, but Nessa needn't have worried. He had eyes only for Prudence.

"You look lovely tonight, my dear. That shade of blue particularly becomes you. It matches your eyes."

"Why thank you, my lord. Nessa convinced me to buy it, saying that very thing."

Philip shot a grateful smile Nessa's way before returning his full focus to his lady. "Perhaps you should take her shopping with you more often," he suggested.

Prudence pinkened, but with pleasure, Nessa thought. At this interesting moment, Lord Foxhaven was announced. The maid bearing the shawl slipped into the room just ahead of the butler, but Nessa delayed putting it on. Jack's greeting rewarded her procrastination.

"Good evening, my dear." He bowed over her hand, his eyes frankly admiring. "I hope you'll not be barred from the theater, for fear you'll eclipse the performance with your beauty."

Remembering Simmons' words earlier, Nessa was unable to suppress a chuckle. "Is not much of the point of attending the theater to see and be seen, my lord?" she responded playfully. "I'd not wish anyone to cast aspersions on your vaunted taste in women on my account."

He raised an eyebrow at that, while Prudence emitted an audible gasp from the other side of the room. "No chance of that, I assure you, my lady," he said in the same tone, though his expression was wary. He then turned to bow to his hosts. "Lady Creamcroft, it is a delight, as always. Creamcroft, your servant."

They returned his greeting cordially, though Prudence shot a cautionary glance Nessa's way. She responded by pointedly draping the exquisite lace shawl across her bare shoulders, while smiling innocently at her sister. It would have been impossible to carry on the sort of flirtation with Jack she intended tonight with her sister along, she realized. Just as well she was not coming to the theater after all. Could she safely leave Simmons behind as well?

Dinner was an intimate affair with only the four of them at table. Even so, Prudence directed the conversation so efficiently along acceptable channels that Nessa was unable to do more than send the occasional suggestive glance Jack's way. At the close of the meal, she and Prudence left the men to their cigars and brandy, retiring to the drawing room.

"Simmons did not sound particularly well this

evening," Nessa commented as they seated themselves to await the men. "'Twould be unkind to drag her out on such a chilly evening. I believe I can do without her this once." She spoke with studied casualness, picking up a periodical and leafing through it without glancing at her sister.

Prudence, however, responded just as she'd feared she might. "I'll have one of the other maids accompany you, in that case."

"I don't see that it's necessary. There will be people all about us at the theater, after all." She still avoided Prudence's eye.

"Nessa! You can't mean you intend to go entirely *alone* with Lord Foxhaven?"

Finally she met her sister's shocked gaze. "I'm not a schoolroom miss, Prudence, but a woman who was married five years. Lord Foxhaven and I are betrothed, to be wed in a month's time. Surely sharing a carriage alone, with a coachman just outside on the box, cannot be so very scandalous."

Prudence frowned—an expression Nessa was beginning to find more than a little bit irritating. "Perhaps not for just anyone, I admit, but in our family things have always been done with an eye to the proprieties. You know that."

Nessa stifled an urge to say, "Proprieties be damned," and instead pressed her slight advantage. "Then it's not unknown for a woman—even a respectable woman—in my situation to attend an evening entertainment with her betrothed unchaperoned?"

Prudence hesitated a long moment, then reluctantly shook her head. A wave of exultation and burgeoning freedom swept through Nessa. What other fictitious restrictions had Prudence led her to assume were de rigueur, she wondered? Of course, as a widow, she must have far more freedom than a young girl making her comeout. Why had she not realized it before? And now, betrothed, she should have yet more liberty—and she intended to take advantage of it.

Impulsively, she rose to give her sister a hug. "Pray do not fret, Prudence. With my upbringing, I doubt I am capable of shaming you in any way. But I must learn more about Lord Foxhaven before I marry him, and having a servant present makes that difficult—particularly when the servant is Simmons."

The gentlemen joined them at that juncture, sparing Prudence a reply, but Nessa feared from her expression that she still had reservations. Given her own intentions for the evening, she could not in conscience claim they were unfounded. To reassure her sister further, however, she refrained from any open flirtation with Jack until they all departed—the Creamcrofts for Lady Trumball's musicale and she and Jack for the theater.

Jack had been observing Nessa with mingled admiration and amusement all evening. No other woman he knew could have looked so alluring and flirted so subtly while staying strictly within the bounds of propriety. Now that they were alone in the carriage—a circumstance he had scarcely dared hope for—she surprised him yet again.

Shifting to sit next to him rather than across, she smiled up at him. "Pray tell me what I may expect at the theater. Your experience is far greater than mine."

Jack raised an eyebrow at the apparent double entendre. "The performances vary greatly, of course," he responded, casually draping one arm across her shoulders. She made no protest. "Leda Varens' Titania is generally held to be excellent, I hear, and John Kemble always does a creditable job. I'm sure his Oberon will be no exception."

Nessa nodded, though a bit impatiently. That wasn't the sort of thing she'd meant, as he well knew. "I've no doubt I'll enjoy the play immensely. I've read it, and 'tis one of my favorites. But what of the theater itself? I've never been, you know."

He blinked. "Never? Ah yes, I keep forgetting how very sheltered a life you've led. You have a gift, my dear, for appearing more worldly than you truly are." It was something he needed to keep in mind. For all her seductive flirtation, Nessa would be extremely easy to shock—and perhaps frighten.

"Why thank you, my lord." She smiled at him, taking his words as a compliment. "I'm pleased to know I don't always give the impression of a country bumpkin, even if it is how I've primarily lived."

Jack gave her shoulder a squeeze, feeling suddenly protective of her—a feeling alien to his experience. "Never that, my dear, I assure you." He proceeded to tell her more about the Covent Garden Theater: the deep stage, allowing for elaborate scenery, the tier upon tier of box seats along the sides.

"And the actresses?" she prompted when he paused. "I'm certain you can tell me whether they are as beautiful and talented as I've heard?"

He hesitated, wondering just what she *had* heard. This was the second time tonight she'd referred obliquely to women with whom he'd dallied. No doubt the high-sticklers surrounding her were only too eager to spread tales about him—mostly true, unfortunately. It was only natural she would be curious.

"Of course a woman must be extremely attractive, as well as talented, to tread the boards at one of the premier theaters in London," he said carefully. "As I said before, Miss Varens is thought to be quite good."

Nessa leaned toward him. Her clean, fresh scent filled his senses, headier than any exotic perfume. "And what is *your* opinion of her, Jack? Do you have any particular favorites among the actresses?"

He'd have liked to think she was jealous, but she sounded simply curious to learn about something outside her experience. "I have had, from time to time," he admitted, grinning down at her. "Recently, however, I fear I haven't given any of them much thought. I've been rather taken up with other pursuits." He pulled her against him, and she snuggled under his arm in a most satisfying manner.

"I can't help but wonder just how one goes about becoming such a favorite," she said then, tilting her face up to him in an obvious invitation——one he was quite incapable of refusing.

"This is one way," he responded, lowering his lips to hers.

As before, he found her surprisingly inexperienced for a woman with five years of marriage behind her, but her very innocence inflamed him. She seemed as eager to learn as he was to teach. He teased her lips apart with his tongue, probing the sweet depths of her mouth. Her momentary stiffening told him this was a new experience for her. Then, tentatively——almost experimentally——she touched his tongue with her own. A faint moan escaped him.

With extreme reluctance, and drawing on considerable self-control, he ended the kiss. "We'd best stop while we still can, my dear." He tried to speak lightly, but his voice actually held a slight tremor. Where was his practiced sophistication with the ladies now? This particular one seemed to cut right through it.

"Of course, Jack, if you think it best." Her words were prim, but her voice breathless with what just might be desire. He'd find out later, he promised himself. Just now, however, the carriage was pulling to a stop in front of the theater.

A few moments later, they mounted the imposing staircase of the Covent Garden Theater, greeting various acquaintances on the way to their box. Nessa's rapt expression and occasional exclamations forced Jack to see the glittering chandeliers and sumptuous decor through her eyes, as though for the first time. It *was*

rather grand, he supposed. Until now, he hadn't realized just how jaded he'd become with Town life.

"Look!" She clutched his arm just then. "Is that one
of the actresses?"

Following her gaze, he had to stifle a laugh. "No, that
is the Countess Lieven, wife of the Russian ambassador
and one of the patronesses of Almack's. She is rather
exotic looking, I'll grant you."

Nessa blinked, glanced down at her own attire, then
back at the countess. "And to think Simmons and Prudence thought *my* gown too immodest!"

Jack was forced to resort to a fit of coughing, which
drew a few stares, but was preferable to the attention a
roar of laughter would have attracted.

"Are you all right?" Nessa asked in some concern.

"Perfectly," he said as soon as he could safely do so.
"I simply find your candor refreshing."

She looked rather confused. "I hope not to choke
you with it. Is this our box?"

It was. Harry and Lord Peter were already within.
Jack had forgotten until that moment that he'd invited
them. Still aroused by that kiss in the carriage, he felt a
surge of irritation, then realized it was for the best.
Alone in the box with Nessa, he'd have run a grave risk
of bringing her reputation down to the level of his own.
Tempting as that seemed right now, it was the last thing
either of them needed.

"Here you are at last," Peter greeted them. "The cur-
tain's due to rise in five minutes. Lady Haughton, I bid
you good evening. You look lovely tonight." He bowed.

Nessa smiled prettily. "I thank you, Lord Peter. 'Tis nice to see you and Mr. Thatcher again." She extended her smile to Harry, who stepped forward with alacrity.

"The pleasure is entirely ours, I assure you, my lady." He lifted her gloved hand to his lips to plant a lingering kiss on the back of it.

Jack's irritation returned abruptly. "If the play is about to start, we'd best take our seats." He all but snatched Nessa's hand away from Harry, and was rewarded by a stare from the lady and a knowing smirk from his friend. What the devil was the matter with him?

The possible answers to that question plagued him throughout the first act. He distracted himself by pointing out various aspects of the set, performance, and actors to Nessa in an undertone.

"And who is the young lady playing Cobweb?" she whispered near the close of the act. "She's lovely, and displays great energy!"

"That is Selena Riverton," replied Jack in an even lower tone. "A relative newcomer to the London stage."

Nessa turned to give him a long look. "You know her, do you not?"

Now how the devil had she deduced that? He'd have sworn his voice gave no hint. "I, er, we've met, yes," he responded lamely.

Her half smile was enigmatic. "Then your taste has not been overrated, it would seem." She turned her attention back to the stage, leaving him in greater turmoil than before.

❧ 11 ❧

Nessa tried to follow the familiar play, but her own story seemed far more dramatic at the moment. The only object upon the stage that truly claimed her attention was Selena Riverton. She wasn't sure what had prompted her to make that guess, but Jack's reaction had proved her intuition correct. That sprightly beauty was one of the actresses with whom he'd dallied.

No, she certainly couldn't fault his taste. The willowy blonde was enchanting, with just enough of a lisp to suggest an innocence she surely did not possess. Nessa had not yet determined her feelings on the matter, however.

Jealousy, she told herself, was far beneath her, particularly with a cyprian as its object. Still, she could not deny a surge of *something*—envy, perhaps?—as she watched Jack's erstwhile paramour cavort upon the stage. What freedom such a woman enjoyed! How could a prim and proper widow like Nessa compete with such unbridled joie de vivre? And did she want to?

Yes, she admitted, she did. She wanted to turn

men's heads—particularly Jack's—to tempt him to indiscretions, throwing propriety and judgment to the winds. A mere fantasy, of course, but . . . that kiss in the carriage tonight had shown that Jack desired her. Was it just possible her fantasy had a chance of fulfillment?

Sneaking a glance at Jack, she found him regarding her thoughtfully—almost confusedly. She smiled mysteriously before turning back to the stage, her thoughts an exciting, alarming jumble.

Their group ventured out of the box between acts, exchanging greetings with others doing the same. Between an array of bobbing turbans and feathers, Nessa saw Mrs. Dempsey a short distance away, clad in a gown that made the Countess Lieven's look positively modest. The other woman was clearly trying to catch Jack's eye, but caught Nessa's instead. Tilting up her chin, Nessa smiled brightly to show she knew what she was about before turning back to Jack. With the tail of her eye, she caught the affronted surprise on Mrs. Dempsey's face.

"How long before we should return to our box?" she whispered to Jack—not so much because she wanted to know, but because she wanted Mrs. Dempsey to wonder what she was telling him.

He smiled down at her. "Anxious to see more of the play, my dear? I'm pleased that you're enjoying your first foray to the theater. We have another five minutes, I should think."

Nessa wasn't sure she could call the jumble of emotions in her breast enjoyment, but she was certainly finding the evening educational. Still, she was far more eager for the close of the play than its continuance. She longed for the carriage ride home, where she could again practice her fledgling art of seduction.

Nessa was just as glad the dim interior of the carriage concealed the tint of her cheeks, for she was certain they were flaming. How was she to play the seductress when she was blushing like a schoolgirl at the mere memory of her last kiss in these confines?

Lord Haughton had never kissed her with such intimacy, even when in her bed. Indeed, his kisses had always inspired distaste and dread rather than pleasure. Were the feelings aroused by that mingling of tongues normal? Whether they were or not, she wanted to experience them again, to decipher them. She slid closer to Jack.

"Thank you for bringing me to the theater tonight," she said, wishing she could come up with something more interesting. No doubt the women to whom he was accustomed were scintillating conversationalists.

"The pleasure was mine, I assure you." He again draped his arm across her shoulders. "Did you find it to be what you expected?"

She tilted her head to one side. "Yes and no. The performance was very good, very much as I'd imagined *A Midsummer Night's Dream* would appear on the stage. But the audience was rather a surprise. Few of them seemed to be there to watch the play."

"Very true," he agreed with a chuckle. "You must

realize, of course, that most of them have seen it several times previously. They attend for the social aspects, not considering that their activities are distracting to newer theater attendees."

"Oh, I found it all fascinating," she assured him. The drive was short, so she moved even closer so as not to waste this opportunity. "I begin to realize just how much I still have to learn of Town life."

"And of life in general?" he asked softly.

She looked up to find him gazing intently at her. "Yes," she whispered. "Fortunately, I have an excellent tutor."

She had thought she was ready for his kiss, but when his lips touched hers she felt, as before, that she might fly into a million pieces. It was an exquisite sensation, starting in her chest and licking outward toward her extremities. This time she parted her lips at the first touch of his tongue, allowing him inside, sliding her own tongue along his.

Both of his arms were around her now, pulling her even closer. With one hand, he stroked her back. In return, she threaded her fingers through his hair, exploring the sides of his face, his ears, his throat with her touch. His right hand slid from her back to her side, then up to cup her breast through layers of fabric. Now she was the one to moan, her senses demanding more and more of these strange new stimuli.

But as before, he pulled away, though lingeringly. His breathing was fast and loud in the darkness. "My love, you spur me to heights for which this is hardly the time or place." His voice was unsteady, but she scarcely noticed, focusing instead on his first two words. But then he continued.

"Given my lack of self-control when with you, I believe it might be best if I were to retire to Fox Manor until our wedding. It will be safer so."

"Safer?" Nessa was not certain she completely understood.

He nodded. "Pray forgive my bluntness. Though I know neither of us are, ah, untouched, I am determined to wait until we are wed to consummate our union."

Nessa caught her breath at such plain speaking. Of course he must see that as the inevitable end of such activity as they were just now sharing. Any man would. Absurdly, stupidly, she had not thought it through in that way, never having before felt anything akin to desire for any man.

"I am sorry, Jack. I did not mean . . . "

"No, I didn't really think you did." His voice was gentle, not at all accusing. "You cannot help being irresistible." Now his tone was teasing, and again she was thankful he could not see her blush. "There are various preparations I wish to oversee at Fox Manor, in any event. I should have been there already."

Nessa nodded, not trusting her voice as a cold finger of apprehension touched the back of her neck. She'd deliberately avoided thinking about the marriage bed, but now it loomed large—that most unpleasant aspect of marriage. The one she'd tried hardest to forget.

Kisses were one thing, and with Jack, quite pleasurable. The marriage act was something else entirely. Though she knew it was the price she would have to pay for the freedom Jack offered her, she was in no hurry to pay it.

"Yes, that makes sense," she finally managed to say. "You'll let me know when the Creamcrofts and I are to join you there?"

"Of course." The carriage pulled to a halt before the house. "I'll call tomorrow so that we may work out the details."

"'Tis settled, then." Jack rose to take his leave of Nessa and her sister. "I'll look to see you the afternoon of December seventh."

"With the wedding to take place on the tenth," agreed Prudence. "It still seems very rushed, but Nessa has convinced me that your obligation to the Duke of Wellington makes it necessary."

Again Nessa felt a thrill of excitement at the thought of Paris. "We shall put the intervening time to good use," she assured Jack. "I've my wedding clothes and trousseau to purchase, among other things." She deliberately kept her tone playful to disguise her conflicting feelings about his departure. London would seem quite dull without Jack in it, she feared.

He took her hand. "I eagerly look forward to the results." Pressing a lingering kiss to her wrist, just above her glove, he lifted his eyes to hers. The promise she saw there snatched her breath. Fortunately, Prudence saved her from the necessity of speaking.

"Pray have a safe journey, my lord. I confess, I am nearly as eager to see Fox Manor as Nessa is. We shall join you there in a month's time."

Nessa murmured her agreement, hoping that her eyes spoke more eloquently than her words. And then he was gone, for four long weeks. She stifled a small sigh.

Prudence, showing herself more perceptive than expected, suggested that they begin shopping that very afternoon. Nessa agreed, eager for any employment to take her mind off of Jack's absence—and what would follow their reunion. She still had not shaken off the trepidation which had seized her last night at the thought of her approaching wedding night. Her last one had been such a nightmare. . . .

Lord Haughton had given her an hour to prepare, though she'd had no idea how to do so. Her mother's advice had consisted only of: "Try to think pleasant thoughts, and don't move too much." Not precisely helpful. So she'd changed quickly into her nightrail and climbed beneath the covers of the big, strange bed to await him.

She'd had a vague idea of the mechanics of coupling from her visits to tenant farms during breeding season, though of course she was not expected to notice such things. But applying such limited knowledge to her own body was no easy thing, despite her rather vivid imagination.

Her husband had not made it any easier. Joining her after precisely one hour, he had expressed approval that she was ready—though she felt anything but. Dropping his dressing gown a brief second before crawling under the covers, he'd afforded Nessa her first glimpse of male nudity—and an unappetizing glimpse it was. In his prime, Lord Haughton could not have been called a fine figure of a man, with his spindly legs and thin chest. At nearly fifty, with the addition of a decided paunch, he was less so.

What he did next made Nessa forget his appearance, however. Rolling on top of her, he pinned her to the bed. For an instant she tried to struggle, before remembering her mother's words. Clenching her teeth, she forced herself to remain motionless while her new husband pulled up her nightgown and inserted something foreign and surprisingly hard between her legs.

The rest was a blur in her memory, a blur of panic and pain, and of chanting her mother's brief advice over and over in her head while her husband moved above her, his face contorting strangely. After perhaps ten minutes of this—though it seemed like hours—Lord Haughton ceased his movements. Kissing her lightly on the cheek, he thanked her formally, resumed his dressing gown, and left.

Over the months that followed, the same scenario was repeated, every week or two at first, then less and less frequently. Nessa's panic had abated once she knew what to expect, but the pain had grown only a little less. Certainly, she'd never learned to anticipate her husband's nocturnal visits with anything other than dread.

Surely, though, surely, Jack would be different? His

kisses were enjoyable where Lord Haughton's had not been, so perhaps his lovemaking would be—if not pleasant, then not entirely distasteful. She could only hope so.

"Nessa, did you hear me?" Prudence sounded mildly exasperated.

Blinking, Nessa realized she'd forgotten her sister's presence during her musings. "I'm sorry. What did you say?"

"I was merely asking whether you wished to take a light luncheon before we begin our shopping." She smiled. "You truly must hold Lord Foxhaven in affection to be daydreaming about him only moments after he has gone."

Nessa only wished her thoughts had been so agreeably employed.

Shopping distracted Nessa from her fears to a great extent, and for the next few weeks she was able to immerse herself in fabrics, lace, ribbons, stockings, and buttons. Prudence appeared to enjoy the process nearly as much as she did, and Nessa made certain her sister added more touches of color to her own wardrobe with her occasional purchases.

Oddly, Nessa felt less inclined toward flamboyance than she had during her first post-mourning shopping spree, though she still tended toward cheerful shades. The gowns she bought now were respectable, but definitely not dull. In fact, more than one modiste complimented her on her keen fashion sense.

Leaving a milliner's shop about a week after Jack's departure, she and Prudence encountered Amanda Leverton, who eagerly accepted an invitation to accompany them home for tea.

"I wish to thank you for your kind note of congratulations," Nessa told her as they arrived back at the Creamcrofts'. Other than that formal little message, she'd heard nothing from Miss Leverton since her betrothal, and had wondered how she and her brother had taken the news.

Amanda's smile did not quite reach her eyes. "I did not wish you to think Sir Hadley or I might think the less of you, though you *did* raise his hopes briefly. We realize now, of course, that you and he would not have suited."

"Of course," Nessa murmured, hoping her amusement did not show. "I'm pleased that I was not an instrument of pain to Sir Hadley." She had suspected from the start that his affection was more for her inheritance than her person.

Prudence, meanwhile, had rung for the tea tray and now bade them be seated in the drawing room. Nessa thought her sister looked a bit wary of Miss Leverton, but she was determined that she would cause Prudence no distress. That this was her object soon became apparent.

"Lady Haughton, as your erstwhile advisor, I feel obligated to give you my thoughts on your impending nuptials," she announced as she took her chair.

Nessa shot a reassuring smile Prudence's way

before replying. "I am all eagerness to hear them, of course."

"You will both forgive me, I know, for speaking frankly," she informed them. "Word of Lord Foxhaven's deplorable reputation must surely have come to your ears by now, so that will be no news. I hope to advise you on how to achieve the maximum happiness that can reasonably be expected in marriage to such a one as he."

Nessa considered telling the presumptuous wretch to leave, but knew that would embarrass Prudence more than anything this woman might have to say. So she smiled instead, with dangerous sweetness. "How very generous of you to concern yourself so with my happiness."

"Just so." Oblivious as ever, Amanda's smile held more than a hint of self-satisfaction. "My dear Lady Haughton, however great the temptation, you must *never* attempt to compete with your husband's various paramours. No, nor even acknowledge that you are aware of their existence. Determined ignorance can be a wife's best friend in such circumstances."

Out of the corner of her eye, Nessa saw Prudence's fan fluttering at a great pace, but she faced her adversary without flinching. "I can certainly see how such advice would benefit yourself, were you in my situation, and therefore I thank you kindly for it. I have noted, however, that many wives who follow your recommended course of action seem far from content in their marriages. You will forgive me then, I know, if I choose my own path in this matter. I have, after all, been married before."

Miss Leverton appeared momentarily speechless at this startling evidence that Nessa had a mind of her own. Prudence, much to Nessa's surprise, filled the silence.

"Of course my sister must do as she thinks best. I cannot help but find your counsel on such a matter ill advised, Miss Leverton, as well as impertinent. Whether you are motivated by jealousy or disappointment on your brother's behalf, I'm afraid I cannot allow you to speak so beneath my roof."

Amanda rose hastily, her face flaming. "I beg your pardon, indeed, Lady Creamcroft. I have just remembered an engagement elsewhere."

"You'd best hurry, then," replied Prudence, her tone as bland as her expression. Amanda Leverton hastened from the room.

When the front door was heard to close behind her, Nessa began to chuckle. "Oh, well done, Prudence! And to think I restrained myself from throwing her out to spare *your* sensibilities."

A small smile hovered at the corners of Prudence's lips, quickly suppressed. "'Twas not your place to do so, as this is my home. Her behavior was inexcusable, however, so I had no such compunction. Impudent upstart! I hope you will not allow her words to carry any weight with you, Nessa, and I apologize for ever suggesting that her advice might be of help to you."

Inordinately pleased to discover that her sister had

such backbone, at least when her sense of propriety was offended, Nessa gave her a quick hug. "I know you meant it for the best, Prudence. Let us say no more about it. And now, what say you to a few hands of piquet before we dress for dinner?"

12

It was a blustery day in early December. Cloud-shadows scudded across gently rolling fields as the carriage bore Nessa southeastward—to the next stage of her life. Kent's reputation as "the garden of England" was scarcely apparent at this season, though it did seem a kinder landscape than Worcestershire, where she'd grown up.

"We must be nearly there," commented Prudence, sitting across from her. "How fortunate for Lord Foxhaven to have his estates such a comfortable distance from London."

Nessa had to agree. Even if Jack did leave her here alone, contrary to his promise, she'd feel far less isolated than she had in Warwickshire, knowing that London was but a few hours away.

The carriage slowed, then turned down a smooth drive between two imposing stone gateposts. Peering ahead, Nessa caught her breath. A single shaft of sunlight escaped from the hurrying clouds to illuminate the loveliest edifice she had ever seen. Situated on a slight rise, lovingly sculpted of mellow, rose-hued stone, Fox Manor dominated the surrounding landscape like a benign matriarch smiling upon her extended family.

A little village nestled cozily in a dell half a mile away, stone walls and thatched roofs gleaming cleanly in the brief sunshine. Even the cows in a nearby byre yard looked happy and wholesome. What a contrast to Haughton Abbey or Cherry Oaks, with walls and villages both grimed by the continual smoke from nearby chimney stacks.

Clouds covered the sun again, but that first impression kept Nessa's spirits from reflecting the comparative bleakness of the now-dull December day. Surely that sunbeam on her first glimpse of her new home was a hopeful omen?

"Why, what a lovely house and park!" Prudence exclaimed.

"I perceive Inigo Jones' influence in the design," agreed Philip, pointing out the subdued classical touches ornamenting the three-storied house with its square towers at each corner.

Nessa scarcely heard this brief lesson in architectural history, however, besieged as she was with a sudden attack of shyness at seeing Jack again after a month apart. In another few moments the carriage swept to a stop before the columned portico. Fortifying herself with a deep breath, Nessa allowed her brother-in-law to help her to the graveled drive.

The house was even more imposing at close quarters, though still lovely. Somehow, she'd received the impression from Jack that Fox Manor was a modest country house—which it certainly was not! The double front doors opened, and the owner's approach cut short her musings on his house.

"Welcome to Fox Manor," Jack greeted them with a bow and a flourish. "You've made good time, I see. Come inside and get warm." He sent Nessa a meaning glance, though clearly his words were intended for the whole party. She felt that tingling flutter beginning to stir again.

The Creamcrofts thanked him and moved toward the house, but Nessa said, "Even in December I can scarcely call Kent cold, my lord." She smiled, meaning it as a compliment, but he frowned slightly.

"I hope that will remain true," he said, softly enough that the others could not hear. "My mother arrived last night and awaits us in the parlor."

Nessa's eyes widened at this news, remembering how Jack had spoken of his mother's indifference previously. Had Lady Branch come to pass judgment on her son's choice of a bride? Jack had turned back toward the house so that she could not read his expression, but he had not seemed pleased.

She quickened her pace to walk by his side, just behind Prudence and Philip, wondering what to expect but unable to think of a discreet way to inquire. Her month-long separation from Jack made her awkward in his presence.

They passed into the marble-floored, two-story foyer, and then through a wide, arched doorway on the right. At once a stylish middle-aged woman with improbably black hair rose to greet them.

"This must be Lady Haughton, and Lord and Lady Creamcroft. Welcome to Fox Manor. I am Lord Foxhaven's mother, Lady Branch," she said without waiting for Jack to make introductions. "Pray do sit down. I have already rung for tea."

My, we've made ourselves right at home, haven't we? But Nessa quickly scolded herself for such an uncharitable thought. Surely she should be pleased if Jack's mother wished to heal the rift between them upon the occasion of his marriage.

"I am delighted to make your acquaintance, Lady Branch," she responded with what she hoped was a natural smile.

Prudence, of course, said everything that was proper before taking her seat, as did Philip. Jack, however, appeared decidedly ill at ease, though he said nothing beyond a suggestion that they move their chairs closer to the fire to take away the chill of winter travel.

"Oh, yes, I despise traveling in winter myself," declared Lady Branch, pouring out the tea which had just arrived. "But for an occasion such as this, I felt obliged to exert myself. Lord Foxhaven is my only son, you know."

"Was your husband, Sir Findlay, unable to come?" Nessa asked politely, wondering whether the woman ever referred to her son by his Christian name. "I should like to meet him as well."

Lady Branch fidgeted with the edge of her sleeve. "He was busy with estate business," she explained after the tiniest hesitation. "Otherwise I'm sure—that is, he very much wished to be here." She kept her gaze averted from Jack's as she spoke, but turned a shrewd eye upon Nessa.

"Tell me, Lady Haughton, were you but recently come to London when you met my son?"

"Indeed, yes," Nessa replied. "I'd been there no more than a fortnight when we were introduced."

"Time to hear of his ascendance to his new position, I presume."

Nessa took a fortifying sip of her tea before responding, fairly certain now that she understood the direction of Lady Branch's thoughts. "I confess that, immured in the country as I had been for most of my life, Lord Foxhaven's very existence had escaped my notice until the evening we met at Lady Mountheath's musicale."

"Which fact was very much to my advantage," Jack put in, moving to sit next to her. "Had she known anything of me prior to our meeting, I doubt not that my suit would have held little hope." He turned slightly away from his mother. "Would you care for a tour of the house, my dear?"

But Lady Branch would not be put off so easily. "I understand that you were living as a dependent in your sister's household while in Town, having been very recently widowed."

Carefully keeping her expression bland, Nessa set down her cup. "I was a guest in my sister's home, yes, but scarcely dependent. Your sources must have neglected to inform you that my late husband provided quite amply for me upon his passing—which was nigh on fourteen months ago."

She knew she should not allow Lady Branch's questions to nettle her, as the woman was doubtless merely concerned for her son, but she could not help feeling a bit defensive.

That Jack was at least equally nettled now became apparent. "Your sudden interest in my affairs is touching, madam, but I'm afraid I cannot allow you to badger my bride-to-be before she has progressed beyond the parlor. I'd much prefer her first impressions of Fox Manor were favorable."

Standing, he suggested that his guests might like to freshen up in their chambers before going over the house. "The ladies, perhaps, would prefer to wait for a sunnier day to walk outdoors, but if you'd care to see the grounds and fishpond, Creamcroft, you'll be more than welcome."

Prudence looked even more relieved than Nessa felt to have the barbed exchange cut short. Rising with alacrity, she expressed eagerness to see the house, taking flawlessly proper leave of Lady Branch, as did Nessa. She preferred to be on good terms with her future mother-in-law, but refused to be intimidated.

Lady Branch's smile, however, did not reach her eyes. With a silent sigh, Nessa turned away. This battle, apparently, was far from over.

Jack led the way up the broad oaken staircase, seething with barely concealed anger. What the devil was his mother up to, anyway? After ignoring his existence for nearly twenty of his twenty-eight years, she had no business attempting to insert herself back into his life now. Certainly, he would not allow her to make Nessa uncomfortable in any way.

"What a charming prospect," Lady Creamcroft commented, turning at the top of the stairs to look back toward the great hall below. "Had you a hand in the decorating, Lord Foxhaven?"

He shook his head. "I've spent little time here since inheriting, so most of the house is just as my grand-father left it. Fortunately, my grandmother had impeccable taste, and he was wise enough to give her her head in such matters."

"So what *have* you been doing for the past month, if not redecorating Fox Manor?" Nessa looked up at him with a glimmer of amusement in her eyes, and Jack found himself inordinately relieved that she showed no sign of unease after his mother's questioning.

"Trying to get ahead on the estate business, mostly, so I wouldn't have it hanging over my head for the next few weeks," he replied candidly. "Also hiring additional servants and ordering extra food to accommodate those we've invited for the festivities, that sort of thing—though Havershaw, my steward, has handled most of the details, I confess.

"I have done one bit of decorating, however." He opened the door to the chamber that was to be Nessa's, then stood back. "I hope you'll approve."

He found himself holding his breath as she took a

hesitant step into the room and looked around at the fresh peach-and-green decor he had selected. He'd noticed those colors in her wardrobe repeatedly, so he had operated on the assumption that they were among her favorites. Not for the first time, he asked himself why it should matter so much.

Jack had provided more than one lady friend with lodgings decorated to her tastes, so he had no particular reason to doubt his skill in this area. It was an essential part of the game of courtship men and women played—a game he'd been adept at for years. This was just another round in the same game, though with slightly higher stakes.

Wasn't it?

"It's perfect, Jack." Nessa turned to him, her liquid brown eyes beautifully expressing her pleasure, her lips softly parted in a smile. "You couldn't have done better if I'd told you precisely how I wanted it. Thank you."

Slowly, he released his breath. While away from her, he'd managed to convince himself that he'd merely imagined her overwhelming effect upon him. Now he knew he'd only been fooling himself.

"I'm pleased you like it," he said, holding her gaze— a gaze which seemed to offer him tangible proof of her gratitude. An offer he was far too ready to accept, after only half an hour in her presence.

She took a deep breath, her breasts rising and falling provocatively, even under the layers of her winter traveling gown, her expression altering subtly as she interpreted his own. Her color deepened and she dropped her eyes.

Jack hastily cleared his throat. "Lord and Lady Creamcroft, your chambers are just across the way, here." He indicated their adjoining rooms, wondering if he'd have been wiser to have Nessa stay away until the eve of their wedding. The next three days promised to be exquisite torture.

A short time later, changed and refreshed, his guests emerged from their chambers for the promised tour. Lady Branch insisted upon being one of the party, to Jack's vexation.

"I haven't been in this house in twenty years," she explained. "I'm interested to see if everything is as I remember it."

As they moved from room to room, floor to floor, however, it became clear—to Jack, at least—that her real motive was to continue digging into Nessa's background and motivation for marrying him.

"I made Lord Haughton's acquaintance some years ago," she commented as they all traversed the length of the ballroom. "It would have been before your marriage, of course, but I recall him as eminently solid and respectable. He must have been a most satisfactory husband—much like my Sir Findlay."

Nessa murmured something noncommittal, then gestured toward the Rococo plasterwork of the ballroom ceiling. "What a lovely effect that has!" she exclaimed. "Like a light and airy fairyland. I can just imagine how this room must look with all of the candles lit for a ball."

"Takes a small army of servants to keep it dusted." Jack spoke teasingly, but then looked around, seeing the ballroom afresh. She was right—it *was* a beautiful room. But his imagination ran to visualizing Nessa as his hostess here, graciously welcoming the neighboring gentry to their home. It was an oddly appealing image.

His mother snorted delicately. "That's what servants are for, of course. But Lady Haughton, I cannot help but wonder . . . That is . . . Do you not worry that after growing accustomed to a husband such as the late Lord Haughton, you may find yourself, well, disappointed by one who may not measure up to his standard?"

Nessa turned to her in evident surprise. "My dear Lady Branch! Surely you are not suggesting that your own son could possibly fall into that category?"

Jack silently ground his teeth. This was far, far worse than he'd imagined—nor could he think of a way to intervene, as he himself was now the topic of conversation. He glanced frantically toward the Creamcrofts, who were studying the giltwork with an interest all out of proportion to the workmanship.

His mother lowered her voice now, but Jack had no trouble hearing her next words, much as he'd have preferred not to. "It must seem terribly unmaternal of me, I know, but ten years of marriage to Lord Foxhaven's father showed me just how unsettling it can be to find oneself dependent upon a rake and a gamester. Of course, it is entirely possible that Lord Geoffrey's son may by now have got the better of those propensities he inherited. For your sake, I do hope so."

Jack groaned inwardly, though he could at least hope that the Creamcrofts were now out of earshot of his mother's words. He'd barely managed to convince Nessa that his rakish ways were behind him. But now, with his own mother bringing evidence against him . . .

"Lady Branch, I assure you that I am fully aware of your son's *previous* reputation," Nessa responded firmly. "I go into this union with my eyes open, and feel that he and I shall suit very well indeed. I hope that in time you will discover those sterling qualities in your son that I have already come to appreciate."

His mother stared, openmouthed, and Jack had all he could do to refrain from doing the same. Keeping the jubilation from his voice with an effort, he said, "I thank you, my dear, for that endorsement, and will do everything in my power to live up to it."

Nessa met his eyes then, with an expression that said as clearly as words: *You will. You'd better.*

"I find myself suddenly fatigued," declared Lady Branch before Nessa could respond aloud. "I believe I shall retire to my chamber until dinner." With a swirl of skirts, she swept from the room, her rigid back expressing her indignation at what had passed.

The four people remaining released a collective sigh of relief. "Shall we move on to the gallery?" Jack suggested.

The others agreed with alacrity, apparently well content to pretend that the recent exchange had never taken place.

*　　　*　　　*

Nessa continued her tour of Fox Manor, absorbing Jack's explanations of the rooms and furnishings. All were lovely, but she was far more intrigued by the man at her side. What had it been like, growing up with a mother who must have always expected the worst of him? She'd thought her own childhood repressive, but at least her parents had believed her capable of reasonable, respectable behavior—believed her incapable of anything else, in fact. She felt a sudden spurt of panic. How little she knew about this man she was about to marry!

"That's really all that is worth seeing indoors," Jack said all too soon. "The gardens and grounds are fairly extensive, but of course this is not the most pleasant season to view them." He glanced out the window of the morning room, where they had concluded. "We may get a drizzle in an hour or so, but if any of you would care to see what we can in the meantime? Creamcroft?"

Philip demurred, however, when Prudence confessed herself wearied. "I believe I'll defer it if you don't mind, Foxhaven, and take Lady Creamcroft upstairs to rest for a bit. She's not been used to much travel of late."

"My apologies! I should not have dragged you over the entire house so soon after your arrival. Of course you'll want to rest before dinner." He turned expectantly toward Nessa, clearly expecting her to accompany the Creamcrofts.

She smiled up at him, however. "I am not in the least

tired, my lord. If you are still willing, I should very much like to see as much of the gardens as the weather will allow." It was a bit daring, she knew, but she wanted to ask him a question or two without prying ears about.

"Certainly, my lady." He seemed genuinely pleased at her response. With a bow to the Creamcrofts, he led her out of the room through French doors, which opened onto a stone terrace. "The ornamental gardens are ahead and to the left, the kitchen garden to the right, and the orchard beyond both. Which would you like to see first?"

"Is there a maze?" She thought she'd glimpsed one from one of the upper windows earlier.

"In a manner of speaking." Placing her hand in the crook of his arm, he headed straight down the path. "It's more ornament than puzzle, and not really tall enough to get lost in, but rather interesting all the same."

Nessa fell into step beside him. "As a child, I always wished for a maze, but my father considered them frivolous."

"What did Lord Cherryhurst *not* consider frivolous?" The question was rhetorical but Nessa answered him anyway.

"Sewing, so long as it had a purpose besides the purely ornamental; embroidery, however, was frowned upon. Bible reading, of course—"

"Except for the Song of Solomon," Jack put in mischievously.

She grinned up at him. "Yes, except for that. It was expressly forbidden—in fact, my father removed it from the family Bible so that we girls would not be tempted to read it in his absence." Jack looked as though he couldn't decide whether to laugh or swear, so Nessa hurried on. "Singing was an approved activity, so long as it was limited to hymns. Dancing was not, though he did finally consent to allow us to learn the minuet and a few country dances."

"At your urging, I'll wager."

Nessa nodded, remembering how much difficulty she'd had getting Prudence to add her pleas to her own. Finally, with their mother's grudging support, they had persuaded him. One of the few such victories she could recall.

"But enough about my childhood. What of yours? To hear your mother speak, it would seem that little frivolity was allowed you, either."

They had reached the maze now. Its thick hedge of yew was green even now, and while it was a little less than Jack's height, Nessa could not see over it. He pointed to the entrance and she nodded eagerly. Not until they were within the deep green walls did he reply to her question.

"While my father lived, frivolity was not only allowed, it was the order of the day. My mother spoke truth when she called him a gamester and a rake, I suppose, but I primarily recall him as an entertaining companion. Not until after his death did I understand how little she approved of our lifestyle."

Nessa frowned. "Was she forced to marry him, then? How old were you when he died?"

"Eight. And I don't doubt she married him willingly enough. He was thoroughly charming, as well as the second son of a marquis. But I presume he lost heavily at the tables, judging by the frequency with which we moved, always to cheaper lodgings. My grandfather, I believe, had washed his hands of him years before."

Nessa tried to imagine what Jack's life had been like, living, if not quite on the brink of poverty, then without many of the things she'd always taken for granted. But with a father who did not condemn his every errant thought, who had been "an entertaining companion." On the whole, she believed she envied him.

"And after he died?"

"Mother dismissed most of the servants and rented out one of the extra rooms. She must have written to my grandfather, for he stepped in soon afterward, making such exigencies unnecessary. As she was as thrifty as my father had been extravagant, we never lacked again—at least, not in material things."

His expression had become somber, and it was clear to Nessa that to the boy Jack had been at the time, the change was not for the better. "And then she remarried?" she prompted.

He nodded. "Two years later. Sir Findlay is a man after your own father's heart. He rose from the middle classes to his baronetcy, and retains the morality and work ethic he was born to. I was a reminder of my father, and of everything Sir Findlay opposed. Needless to say, we did not get on."

Clearly, that was a massive understatement. "But

you spent time with your grandfather, did you not?"

"Yes, here at Fox Manor. From the age of eleven onward, all of my school holidays were spent here, and it was he who arranged for me to attend Oxford, and who purchased my commission. Even he, however, was unable to restrain those, ah, tendencies, which my mother claims I inherited from my father."

Both his expression and his tone had softened, Nessa noticed, when he spoke of the late Lord Foxhaven. "You loved your grandfather very much, didn't you, Jack?" she asked gently.

He started visibly. "Love? Er, well, yes, I suppose so. Certainly, he was the only person on earth who wielded the least bit of influence with me during those years. Sir Findlay's attempts, and my mother's, achieved just the opposite effect."

His tone was light again, but Nessa suspected it was to conceal deeper feelings—feelings he was not yet ready to explore. But Nessa probed further, needing to know more about this man she was to marry, and about his reasons for marrying her.

"So you regret not following your grandfather's wishes while he was alive, and now wish to make up for it?"

Jack stopped abruptly and she realized they had reached the center of the maze. "Would you care to sit down?" He indicated a stone bench with large urns at either end, which doubtless held flowers in spring and summer. "Or would you prefer to keep moving? There is less wind in here, but it is still chilly."

By way of response, Nessa sat, but kept her eyes on his face, awaiting the answer to her question. Jack looked away, toward the house she supposed, though she could not see it from where she sat. Finally he took his place beside her on the bench.

The silence had lengthened uncomfortably before he spoke. "I'm not sure that regret is the proper word," he said at last. "However wild I was, I never hurt anyone . . . well, no one who didn't deserve it."

She met his crooked grin with calm expectancy, determined not to be dissuaded.

With a sigh, he continued. "My grandfather did much for me—more than any other human being, alive or dead. The only way I know to repay him is to honor his dying request."

This was news to Nessa. "Dying request? But I thought you were on the Continent with the army when he passed away."

"So I was. Therefore, with his customary thoroughness, Grandfather put his wishes in writing." Reaching inside his greatcoat, he pulled a much-folded piece of paper from his breast pocket.

"No eyes but mine have read this until now. Under the circumstances, I suppose it is only fair that you do so." His usual humor replaced by wariness, he extended the paper to her.

Greatly curious, she took it, unfolded it, and read its brief contents. Swallowing, she read it through again, then raised wide eyes to Jack's.

"I . . . I believe I finally understand. You feel that a

respectable marriage——or rather, marriage to a woman with a respectable reputation——will help you to fulfill his request." Though she'd rather suspected something of the sort, having it verified in ink on parchment gave her little satisfaction.

Jack's nod depressed her spirits further. "It . . . seemed the least I could do for him." Then, apparently perceiving something of her feelings, he hastened to add, "I have become genuinely fond of you, however. Whatever my original motives, I truly believe we shall rub along very well together. Don't you?"

She saw real anxiety in his eyes. This, she knew, was her last chance to cry off. Clearly, he knew it as well. But was he concerned because he cared for her, or because she had the power to overset his grandfather's wishes? Either way, she realized, her response must be the same. The letter from the late Lord Foxhaven had moved her deeply, coming on the heels of Jack's revelations about his childhood.

Swallowing hard, she gave the reply that would be the deathknell of her dreams of freedom, of frivolity, of *fun*. "Yes, Jack, I do. I will help you restore your reputation and the Foxhaven name by playing the respectable wife to perfection. It is, after all, the role I've trained for all my life."

And would now be doomed to play for the rest of it.

13

Jack was reminded of St. Joan of Arc as Nessa vowed to behave respectably and restore his reputation. Beautiful, noble, willing to sacrifice herself for something she believed in—for *him*. He was both touched and shaken. Could he, Jack Ashecroft, possibly have inspired such devotion?

No, it was the letter, of course. It had affected him similarly, after all, even before he'd read the postscript—which he didn't dare show Nessa. He released a small sigh of relief.

"Thank you, Nessa. You have no idea how much this means to me. I'll try very hard never to make you sorry."

The martyred expression faded from her face. "I shall hold you to that, Jack. Perhaps if I am allowed to be a little bit wicked in private, I shall not mind so much playing the paragon in public." The twinkle was back in her eyes, and something within him stirred in response.

"Only a little bit wicked?" he asked softly, leaning toward her.

Her cheeks, already pink from the cold, pinkened further, but she did not pull away. "Wickedness is very new to me, you know. By my father's standards, waltzing and wearing bright colors qualify."

"And how about this?" He covered her unresisting mouth with his own. Her response was immediate, her lips soft and pliable beneath his, her hands coming up to encircle his neck as he pulled her closer. His own response was even more profound, desire racing through him like a flame in dry tinder. Luckily——or was it unluckily?——the cold stone bench was not conducive to further intimacies.

Slowly, reluctantly, he released her. He'd intended to keep his distance until they were wed, but it went against his nature to refuse a kiss to a woman who wanted one. Who needed one. "The next three days can't pass quickly enough." His voice was still husky with passion.

To his surprise, the matching desire in Nessa's deep brown eyes was suddenly shot through with alarm. "Three days. Yes," she agreed shakily, now avoiding his gaze.

As Jack regarded her thoughtfully, a large drop appeared on her cheek. For a moment he thought, incredibly, that she was crying, but then similar drops began to fall all about them. "We'd best return to the house," he suggested, standing.

She nodded and took his proffered hand, still strangely subdued after that all-too-brief burst of passion. He led her back through the maze amid the pattering of raindrops, wondering what had wrought her sudden withdrawal.

Could she be dreading their wedding night? That seemed unlikely, as she'd been married before and would know what to expect. Besides, she'd shown herself far from indifferent to him. Perhaps it was marriage itself she was nervous about. It would be perfectly natural, he supposed, given her feelings about the state.

So why was he not similarly reluctant to permanently bind himself to one woman for the rest of his life? He had been before, but he realized that was no longer the case. What had changed?

"No, here, to the left," he murmured as Nessa began to take a wrong turn. In a moment they were out of the maze and back on the flagged path, rain still falling about them. As they hurried toward the house, Jack lapsed back into thought.

That he'd developed an affection for Nessa he could not deny. But he'd held dozens of women in affection—and lust—without wishing to spend a lifetime with any of them. Was this love? Immediately he rejected the disturbing notion. Love was a myth. He'd determined that years ago. Something invented by poets and pretended by women in an attempt to bind men to their will.

Even between family members he'd seen little evidence that such an emotion existed. Nessa had asked whether he'd loved his Grandfather. He hadn't denied it, as his reverence for the old man was doubtless what many would call love, but his feelings there were based on admiration and mutual respect rather than any mystical state of the heart. Certainly it was not the same thing numerous women had claimed to feel—something composed of lust and a desire for control.

What he felt for Nessa was doubtless similar—mutual respect and admiration . . . with some lust thrown in as well, yes, but that was simply because she was female and beautiful.

"Will dinner in an hour and a half suit you?" he asked as they reached the house. "I generally dine early in the country."

For the first time since leaving the center of the maze, she met his gaze, her eyes still oddly shadowed. "That will be fine. I'll go upstairs to change." She started to turn away, then stopped. "Thank you, Jack, for showing me the maze. Fox Manor is a lovely estate."

He smiled, trying to lighten her mood. "I'm glad you approve, as you will be mistress of it inside of a week."

Her attempt at a smile in return was not particularly convincing. "So I shall. Until dinner, then." With only a faint rustle of her skirts, she turned and was gone, leaving Jack to his own, rather disturbing thoughts.

During dinner, Nessa still appeared strangely subdued to Jack. She responded to Lady Branch's continued queries with perfect politeness but no elaboration. When Jack and Creamcroft joined the ladies in the drawing room after the meal, she was quietly engaged in reading and acknowledged his appearance with only a nod before returning to that pursuit. When the gentlemen suggested the ladies join them at whist, Nessa demurely echoed her sister's refusal, leaving them to piquet to while away the evening.

Jack found himself completely unable to concentrate on his cards—a novelty, that, making him glad they had agreed to imaginary stakes. The ladies retired early, leaving him none the wiser as to the reason for Nessa's change of spirits.

Early the next day, guests began arriving for the wedding, keeping Jack busy with greetings, as well as last-minute questions from the butler and housekeeper. Relatives he had not seen in a decade or more—as much by their choice as his—greeted him in return with smiles and congratulations which rang hollow to his ears. By early afternoon he felt decidedly out of sorts, restraining himself from outright rudeness only by extreme effort.

Nessa, however, was magnificent. Dressed in a gown of subdued rose and modest cut, she acknowledged all introductions with exactly the right blend of deference and assurance. Her voice soft and well modulated, she responded to even impertinent questions with unruffled dignity.

When Jack's mother stepped forward to play hostess, Nessa calmly moved to the background. When Lady Branch retired to fortify herself before dinner, Nessa effortlessly moved into the breach. Not even Lady Creamcroft was a more perfect model of proper English womanhood. She was behaving just as Jack had hoped she would, and there was growing respect in

even his Aunt Gwendolyn's eyes—she who had frequently urged his grandfather to cast Jack off entirely.
That respect began to extend to him as well, in perfect
accordance with his plan.

So why was he so damned irritated by it all?

Shortly before dinner, Harry and Lord Peter
arrived. Jack's spirits lifted at once as he hurried out to
the graveled drive to greet them. "Come in, come in!"
he cried jovially. "Finally, some relief from this plague
of relatives besetting me!"

Harry shook his hand enthusiastically. "Respectability not all you'd hoped, eh? Don't say I didn't warn you.
One good thing about being a black sheep—relatives
generally pretend they don't know you."

"Buck up, Jack," Lord Peter advised him with a slap
on the back. "It's only for a few days, after all—or are
this lot staying till the New Year?" They all headed up
the front steps.

"Heaven forbid! No, all but one or two will leave a
day or two after the wedding, at latest. They feel
obliged to turn out en masse to officially sanction my
return to the family fold, but not to disrupt their own
holiday plans—thank God!"

"Unless you can drive them away even earlier."
Harry grinned with anticipation. "I'll help in any way I
can, of course."

Jack chuckled. "Hope I won't have to ask that of
you. Seriously, though, Nessa—Lady Haughton—is
doing a stellar job of keeping them all under control,
and off my back. She may have raised a few eyebrows in

London, but she still has the propriety thing down pat, believe me. Even Aunt Gwendolyn is in raptures over her."

"Sounds as if your plan has been a stunning success," Peter congratulated him.

"Yes. Yes, indeed," agreed Jack, stifling a sigh. He led them through the front hall, barely hearing their comments on its noble proportions. "Dinner will be served in under an hour. Care for a glass of sherry first, or would you prefer to go up and change?"

"Sherry for me," said Harry predictably.

"A quick glass, but then we really must get out of our dust before meeting anyone." Lord Peter gestured at Harry's boots and trousers, as well as his own.

A few voices still emanated from the parlor, so Jack bypassed it in favor of the library. Already he felt in better spirits and less out of his element with the arrival of his friends. Perhaps the next two days would not be so insupportable after all.

Nessa was heartily tired of playing the proper hostess, but at least it served as an effective distraction. Of course, the role was more properly Lady Branch's, but as she often abdicated in favor of her bedchamber, the task fell to Nessa—when one of Jack's aunts did not step forward, which they frequently did.

It had taken some effort, but she finally had all of the names and relationships sorted out. There was Lady Gwendolyn, the late Lord Foxhaven's eldest sister, an intimidating dragon of a woman who could have made even Lord Haughton cower, Nessa was sure. Then there was Esther, the Dowager Lady Foxhaven, widow of Jack's Uncle Luther, a frail, soft-spoken woman of middle years. It appeared neither she nor Luther had ever taken up residence at Fox Manor, due to their mutual ill health, which necessitated a seaside abode.

Lady Margaret, sister to Luther and Jack's father, was second only to Lady Gwendolyn in overbearing importance. Her husband, Lord Garvey, though standing more than six feet tall, seemed almost afraid of his diminutive spouse. Add to that various cousins—children and grandchildren of Lady Gwendolyn, their spouses and children, as well as Lady Margaret's younger brood—and Fox Manor was filled to capacity, large as it was.

Now, however, on the very eve of the wedding, Nessa's conflicting emotions were in such a state that she scarcely trusted herself to manage any conversation beyond polite nothings. Fortunately, little more seemed required of her, and most of the guests retired early to their beds as the wedding was to take place at nine o'clock the next morning.

Nessa, resigning herself to sleeplessness for yet another night, pulled out some embroidery. On arriving in London, she'd been pleased to discover that, contrary to her father's strictures, this activity was not considered the least bit improper by polite society. After two or three months of practicing it, however, she'd decided it was one of the duller pursuits open to ladies—which made it perfect for lulling herself to sleep on this, her last night of relative freedom.

Needlework did nothing to occupy her thoughts, however, which persisted in replaying the days immediately before and after her first wedding. Determined to block out her father's lectures and her mother's advice, and especially her memories of the marriage bed, she set the embroidery aside and took up pen and paper.

With sudden fancy, she decided to write a letter to herself—a letter from the woman she hoped to be twenty or thirty years hence, offering advice to the woman she was now. Writing quickly, she captured her hopes and dreams on paper as though they had already occurred. She wrote about the births of her three children, a campaign to see English girls better educated, the acquisition of a dog and a cat, which she'd always been forbidden.

Weaving this rosy future for herself as though it were a memory to look back on, she felt her eyes grow heavy. She extinguished the candle and climbed into bed, to fall into a deep, refreshing sleep, untroubled by her fears of the morrow.

When her abigail awakened her at dawn, her anxieties came crowding back. Thrusting them to the back of her mind, she allowed herself to be dressed, curled and adorned for the looming ceremony. She couldn't help but be pleased by the effect of her ivory silk gown, overlaid by costly ivory lace and accented at neckline, wrists, and hem with tiny seed pearls. Her veil, of matching lace, cascaded from her chestnut curls to the floor, where it trailed behind with her silken train.

Prudence was to act in the stead of their late mother, but thankfully subjected her to little in the way of motherly advice. "I need not tell you what to expect, as you've been married before," she said, tucking back a stray wisp of Nessa's hair a few moments before they were to go down. "Besides, I doubt not our mother gave you the same advice she gave me upon my own marriage. 'Twill still hold good."

Nessa stared at her sister. "Prudence! Never tell me you still abide by, 'Think pleasant thoughts and don't move too much!'"

Prudence's cheeks flamed scarlet. Without meeting Nessa's interested gaze, she replied, "If it was good enough for Mother, why should it not be good enough for her daughters?"

Sudden panic gripped Nessa. "But . . . but Philip *loves* you! Surely that must mean . . . that is . . . " Prudence's averted face reddened further, so she desisted. "I just thought that might make a difference, that's all."

"I . . . have no complaints," said Prudence breathlessly. "But we must hurry downstairs. The carriage to take us to the chapel will be at the door by now."

No complaints, Nessa mused as she obediently accompanied her sister from the room. Did that mean Prudence found the physical aspects of marriage less unpleasant than she had, or was that merely a polite nothing to get her to drop the subject? She wished now she had attempted a discussion on this topic with her sister earlier. It was too late now.

The carriage was indeed waiting, along with others

already crammed with house guests. The day was overcast and windy, with an occasional spate of freezing drizzle. Had the day been fine, many of the guests would no doubt have walked, as the chapel was less than half a mile from the house. Nessa did not see Jack, and supposed he must have gone ahead to the chapel already.

The drive lasted only moments. The carriage door was opened by two liveried footmen, then Lady Gwendolyn hurried Nessa through a faceless crowd into an anteroom in the ivied stone building.

"All is in readiness," she told Nessa, raking her from head to toe with a critical eye. Apparently satisfied, she informed her in a gentler tone that she was to remain there until the organ music began in a few moments.

Too preoccupied to reply coherently, Nessa merely nodded, and Lady Gwendolyn conducted Prudence from the room to her appointed place near the front of the chapel. Prudence sent Nessa what was no doubt intended to be an encouraging smile over her shoulder as she left the anteroom, but Nessa felt no noticeable abatement of her nervousness.

Had she been insane to agree to yet another marriage—a lifetime of servitude—so soon after gaining her freedom from her first one? And what of the physical side? Though Jack had presented his offer as a means to benefit them both, she had no doubt he would claim every right as a husband. What she couldn't decide was how she felt about that.

The next five minutes seemed an eternity, as the

rest of the guests filed into the church and took their seats. Finally the music began. Nessa closed her eyes, took a deep breath, and stepped out of the anteroom as though going to the gallows.

Philip awaited her at the rear of the chapel, as he was to give her away, and the sight of his kind face bolstered her spirits somewhat. Taking his extended arm, she paced slowly up an aisle that seemed impossibly long for such a small church.

Suddenly aware of all eyes upon her, Nessa lifted her chin and then her eyes. There, next to the altar, stood Jack, looking supremely handsome in a dark blue superfine coat and knee breeches. His face was as serious as she'd ever seen it, though when she caught his eye the familiar twinkle was still there.

He turned to face the altar as she reached it, but that one glimpse had fortified her. The ceremony itself was a blur, Nessa far more aware of the man by her side than anything the vicar was saying. Still, she managed to repeat the proper words at the proper times, and could not suppress a tremor at the sound of Jack's voice doing the same.

In less time than it seemed she had spent traversing the aisle, the ceremony was over. Lifting her veil, Jack bestowed the requisite kiss. Though it was more ritual than real, a mere touch of his lips upon hers, she was forcefully reminded of other kisses they had shared— and would share again. They turned to face the guests, who murmured their approval.

Nessa's thoughts flew ahead to the coming night,

and she knew her cheeks betrayed her, but the onlookers appeared to find her blushes charming as Jack led her back down the aisle. Emerging into the wintry daylight, they were greeted by shouts of congratulation. Gathered about the little church were dozens and dozens of people no longer faceless—tenants and other local folk, ready to welcome the new Marchioness into their midst.

Though she smiled and waved, Nessa could not help remembering a similar scene outside the village chapel at Haughton six years ago. That crowd had seemed less cheerful than this, though perhaps that had been due to her own depressed and fearful spirits. Then, as now, she had been overwhelmed at the prospect of her new responsibilities as Lady of the Manor.

As it had turned out, Lord Haughton had scarcely allowed her any such responsibility. At Fox Manor, however, things would be different. Thank goodness she'd had those last months at Haughton Abbey to teach her what her duties were and how to perform them!

She was brought back to the present with a welcome start as Jack handed her into the carriage, now decorated with hothouse flowers and greenery. Had it been so before? She hadn't noticed.

Once they were shut inside, she breathed a small sigh of relief. At the same moment, Jack breathed a larger one. Their eyes met, and they began to laugh.

"'Tis wearing, is it not, living up to the expectations of others?" he asked. "We have the rest of the day's festivities to get through yet, but for this brief moment, at least, we can relax." He then knocked on the little door at the top of the carriage and told the driver to take his time.

"I'd forgotten how very public a wedding is," Nessa confessed. "By the end of the day, both our faces will ache from smiling."

Jack sobered. "So you smiled for most of your first wedding day, did you? I suppose I should be glad to know that."

"Smiling because one is expected to is far more tiring than smiling because one is happy." Nessa remembered vividly her exhaustion at the end of that earlier wedding day, after hours of striving to appear the perfect, happy bride for fear of her father's or husband's censure should her smile slip. Then, despite her efforts, she recalled how that day had concluded. She managed not to shudder.

"Then I shall take it as a personal affront if you are too wearied by bedtime," Jack said with a wink. "Not that I intend for that to be too many hours distant."

Nessa was spared from replying by their arrival at Fox Manor. It was just as well, for his mention of bedtime, on the heels of her unfortunate recollection, rendered her speechless, a cold hand of apprehension gripping her by the throat. Resolutely, she swallowed her fear and allowed Jack to help her from the carriage, to be met by yet another noisy throng.

The tenants, she knew, had been bidden to a sort of auxiliary wedding breakfast, laid out in the ballroom. Many had either run ahead of the carriage or gone directly to the house, for dozens of people were here already. Women curtsied and men doffed their hats as she passed, some murmuring well-wishes and blessings. Her heart swelled, crowding out anxiety for the moment.

She had nearly reached the wide steps, the crowd growing thicker all the time, when she heard a young woman's voice from somewhere behind her.

"I dunno, May. She seems a slip of a thing to be woman enough for our Jack! Mayhap he'll need us still."

It took every bit of Nessa's control and breeding to pretend she had not heard, when her instinct was to turn and locate the speaker. Nervous titters and shushing sounds followed, but she had no doubt the comment had been intentionally audible. Keeping her benevolent smile pinned to her face, she proceeded through the open doors of Fox Manor—her new home.

Taking up their posts by the door, she and Jack welcomed every guest, noble, gentry, or common, as they filed past. Though she tried to squelch the impulse, Nessa could not quite help scrutinizing every maid of above average appearance, and wondering.

More than one such examined her in turn, with an expression less than welcoming. Surely, though, it was natural that the local lasses would idolize Jack, and resent the woman who put him out of their reach forever? Even unrealistic fantasies—as theirs must have been!—would be only reluctantly abandoned. Nessa chose to interpret the occasional hostile stare as a compliment to Jack rather than an insult to herself. In time, she would prove herself to the villagers—all of them.

Finally the interminable receiving line was at an end, and she and Jack were free to join family and gentry in the dining room. Nessa was ravenous, as there had been no opportunity for more than a cup of tea before the ceremony. Now it was near noon. So many polite comments were addressed to her, however, requiring equally polite responses, that she was unable to do more than snatch an occasional bite from her plate.

This carnival atmosphere was not at all what she remembered from her first wedding breakfast—but then, Lord Haughton would never have dreamed of inviting any commoners into his house except as servants. Only family and the more prominent local gentry had been present at the ceremony or reception. With him and her own father presiding, of course hilarity had been out of the question.

This was more pleasant, she decided, even if she was in danger of starving. By early afternoon, the villagers and local gentry had departed, along with one or two of Jack's relations as well. Two days hence, the rest would have departed for their various estates, leaving only the Creamcrofts and perhaps Lord Peter and Mr. Thatcher.

Nessa stifled a small sigh as the final dinner course was served that evening, looking forward to that calmer time. This wedding day might be far less unpleasant than her first had been, but it was more hectic, and just as interminable. Would it never end?

Jack rose from the table, a wineglass in his hand. "A toast to my bride, Lady Foxhaven." Though it was by no means the first toast drunk in her honor that day, the guests dutifully echoed the sentiment.

"And now," Jack continued, still standing, "my bride and I shall take our leave. I bid you all a good night." Draining the last drops in his glass, he extended a hand to Nessa. Startled, she rose to take it.

Murmuring a farewell to family and friends, she accompanied Jack from the room. Panic belatedly set in as she set her foot on the first step of the great stairway, but she strove to conceal it.

Only a moment ago she had been wishing for the day to end. Had she been mad? The tall windows flanking the front door showed that the light was long gone, but it could not be more than six o'clock. The others would not be going up to bed for hours yet. Nessa's panic intensified.

"Are . . . are you certain you wish to leave the festivities so soon?" she asked breathlessly.

Jack gave her what was perhaps meant to be a reassuring smile, but which had quite the opposite effect. "I find all of these people wearying, don't you? I didn't wish either of us to become totally exhausted—yet."

Nessa bobbed her head in mechanical agreement, her breath coming quick and shallow. Speaking was totally beyond her now. At the door of her room, she paused in some confusion. Jack had not indicated where she was to stay after the wedding.

"Why don't you go ahead and allow your maid to help you out of that gown. It's lovely, but looks devilish uncomfortable. I'll see whether Parker has finished restoring my things to my room." He nodded at the chamber adjoining hers, which his Aunt Esther had occupied until that afternoon.

"Then . . . this is to remain my room?"

He nodded. "You did say you liked it." His tone was teasing, but she thought she detected an undercurrent of uncertainty.

"Oh, I do! Thank you, Jack." Pleased and grateful, Nessa realized now that he had vacated his own chamber for the past week rather than add to her strain by forcing her to change rooms on this already stressful day.

He dropped a light kiss upon her forehead. "I'll join you in half an hour, my dear."

Abruptly, the chill returned to Nessa's midsection, driving out pleasure, but she managed to nod and turn the handle. Simmons came forward at once to close the door behind her and began unfastening the intricate wedding gown.

"Would my lady care for a glass of something to calm her nerves?" She carefully laid the veil back in its folds of tissue.

Was her anxiety that obvious? This would never do. "Of course not, Simmons. I *have* been married before, you know."

The abigail put away the veil and returned to finish unpinning the gown, helping Nessa to step out of the creamy confection. "Marriage to an upright, respectable, *and* respectful man like Lord Haughton will hardly have prepared you for this night, milady."

Nessa knew she should rebuke Simmons for such outspokenness, but instead swallowed convulsively. "What . . . what do you mean?"

"Lord Haughton was an older man, and a gentleman," said Simmons, shaking out the gown. "It stands to reason he would be less . . . demanding . . . in the marriage bed."

"Lord Foxhaven is a gentleman as well," Nessa pointed out feebly, but she knew her words lacked conviction. Lord Haughton had not come to her bed frequently, it was true—as Simmons was no doubt aware. But he had simply taken what he wished when he did visit her, with no consideration for Nessa's feelings or comfort. Would Jack truly be even more . . . demanding? She shuddered.

Yet weighing upon her more heavily than a fear of pain or discomfort was the certainty that after this night she and Jack could no longer be friends. She would miss that terribly.

For a moment she considered asking Simmons after all to fetch her some brandy or sherry—anything to make the looming experience less disagreeable. But that would be to admit her abigail was right about Jack, and she was not ready to do that. So she sat in determined silence while Simmons brushed out her hair and turned down the counterpane.

"Thank you, Simmons. That will be all."

With a pitying look Nessa would rather not have seen, the maid left her. Alone, but not for long.

Just as she had on her first wedding night, Nessa climbed under the covers and waited, trying not to think about the painful ordeal to come.

14

Jack flicked a speck of dust from the lapel of the midnight-blue dressing gown he'd purchased in London for this particular occasion. Though not normally a vain man, he could not refrain from a glance in the looking-glass before reaching for the handle to the door separating his chamber from Nessa's. He wanted to look his best for her, tonight of all nights.

Turning the handle, he blessed his luck that Nessa was a widow. As two experienced adults, they could delve straight into the pleasures of their union, with none of the coaxing, cajoling, and tears an untried girl would have occasioned. He could not imagine a virginal miss holding a fraction of the appeal that Nessa did, in any event.

An oil lamp on the nightstand gave Nessa's green-and-peach room a soft, romantic glow. And Nessa herself awaited him in the bed, her rich chestnut hair loosed from its bonds to drape seductively over her shoulders. Jack felt his anticipation grow, along with a certain portion of his anatomy.

"I hope I didn't keep you waiting too long, my dear," he said, his voice husky with desire.

Nessa gave an odd little twitch before replying, "No! Not at all. Of course not." Her voice was high and breathless, even strained. If it weren't absurd, he might think she sounded frightened.

He moved closer to the bed. "Nessa, is everything all right?"

She nodded almost convulsively, her eyes unnaturally wide.

"No, I don't think everything is." He sat on the edge of the bed to regard her with a frown. "Are you unwell? Is it your time of month? Did that dragon of an abigail say something to worry you?"

Each question was answered by a sideways shake of her head, but the panic—yes, he could only call it panic—did not leave her eyes. Baffled, he reached out a hand to stroke her hair, hoping that his touch might calm her. Instead, she flinched away. Startled, he dropped his hand.

"I've never seen you like this, Nessa. Clearly, something has frightened you badly. Will you not tell me what it is?"

She closed her eyes and swallowed visibly. "Please, Jack, can't we just . . . get it over?"

He nearly fell off the bed in his astonishment, suddenly deflated in more than an emotional sense. "What?"

Nessa opened her eyes and fearfully met his frowning gaze. "I . . . I know what is expected, of course. And I am ready, truly."

"Are you indeed? I rather doubt that, my dear." Though he kept his voice gentle, mentally he cursed the late Lord Haughton. What a bumbler the man must have been, to make Nessa so terrified of the physical side of marriage! He'd been wrong, very wrong, he realized. This was going to require far more skill than a virgin bride would have, for he had damage as well as ignorance to undo.

Now that he'd divined the cause of her reluctance, Jack's anticipation swelled again. He'd always loved a challenge. Moving closer to her, he said, "I won't consider you ready until you want me as much as I want you, Nessa. And I'll bring you to that point, if it takes me all night."

Nessa had tried to blank her mind, steeling herself for the inevitable, but Jack's words startled her into unwelcome awareness. "What—what do you mean?"

"I mean," he explained, "that before this night is done, you will discover what the marriage bed was truly designed for—mutual pleasure, not the unilateral satisfaction of one party. Kiss me, Nessa." He lowered his lips to hers just as he'd done in the maze, and in his carriage in London.

At first she was unresponsive, still struggling to understand. But then, as her fear began to dissipate, her lips softened beneath his, just as they had when no dread of lovemaking had constrained her. He deepened the kiss slowly, very slowly.

Soon, those pleasurable feelings he had aroused

before stirred within her. Her lack of resistance became active participation, as she twined her tongue with his. Slowly, Jack shifted his position until he lay beside her, never breaking the kiss. With one hand, he cupped her cheek, stroking gently. Finally, he lifted his head to murmur, "See? Not so terrible after all."

She managed a small smile, but she still doubted him. That was all well and good, she thought, but still just a kiss. She knew there was worse to come yet.

"No, that's not all." She blinked at this evidence he'd guessed her thoughts. "But things will get better, not worse. You'll see." Moving away from her briefly, he peeled back the coverlet to join her beneath it.

She stiffened when he lay against her, now separated only by their thin garments, but when he did nothing but kiss her again, she relaxed once more. Again pleasurable sensations welled up—more quickly this time—and she began to respond eagerly.

Gently, so gently, Jack slid his hand lower, from her cheek to her throat, and then to her collarbone. Whenever she tensed even a fraction, he paused. Finally, his hand cupped her breast. This did not frighten her particularly, as it was something Lord Haughton had never done. Indeed, it served to intensify what she was beginning to suspect might be desire.

Trailing kisses from her lips to her throat, Jack followed the path his hand had taken until he reached the low neckline of her nightgown. With nimble fingers, he undid the first tiny button, then continued on, unbuttoning it as he went, until his lips reached her other breast.

When he touched the nipple with his tongue, she gasped, but not with fear. Still, he took his time. Circling both nipples, one with his tongue, the other with his thumb, he then returned to her lips for another long, deep kiss.

Emboldened by the delicious sensations Jack aroused, Nessa began her own exploration, skimming her hands over his shoulders, first above and then beneath his dressing gown. So heightened were her senses by this time that the touch of her fingers upon his bare skin was almost a shock. Apparently he felt it, too.

"Oh, my dear," he whispered. "Have I told you how very exciting I find you?"

Timidly, curiously, she shook her head. "Let me pleasure you, Nessa," he said. "Let me excite you as much as you excite me. I want you to know just how good it can be."

She swallowed, but managed an almost imperceptible nod. Smiling, he resumed his attentions, stroking, touching, kissing. First tentatively, then more eagerly, Nessa stroked his back and shoulders in return.

His dressing gown had fallen open by now, and she saw that he wore nothing beneath it—but the knowledge no longer frightened her. She slid her hands lower, exploring areas she would never before have dreamed of touching.

Jack moved his own hands lower as well, massaging her breasts, her waist, her hips, her belly. Finally, with one finger, he brushed the mound of curls below, and the cleft they concealed. At that touch she stiffened again, pulling back from him, reminded again of her first wedding night. At once he retreated, but only back to her belly.

Kissing her again, he whispered, "I won't hurt you, Nessa. I'll never hurt you."

She opened her eyes, searching his. "I trust you," she said.

For an instant she wondered if his vow extended beyond physical pain—and whether it was a vow he could keep. Surely he'd loved and left dozens of women over the years, never intending to hurt any of them. . . .

Desire superseded such anomalous reflection then, as Jack again gave Nessa his undivided attention. This time when he touched her most sensitive spot she did not flinch away. Softly, gently, he stroked and massaged, all the while kissing her mouth, her earlobes, her throat. When he slid one finger inside her she gasped— but with desire, not dismay.

Slowly, then more quickly, he eased his finger in and out, giving her a foretaste of what was to come on a grander scale. She tightened around his finger with a small moan.

He shrugged his dressing gown the rest of the way off. As he'd already unbuttoned the entire length of her nightgown, nothing now separated them. He rolled to cover her body with his own, but at once her eyes flew open, the fear returning.

"No, no, it's all right," he whispered. "We'll do this another way, so that you can stop any time you wish to."

Rolling back onto his side, he turned her to face him, kissing and caressing until her fear again faded into desire.

When she again convulsed around his finger, he moved his hips forward until his swollen member rested against her mound. He moved slowly, gently, though by now she felt more than ready to receive him. Removing his finger, he replaced it with the very tip of his manhood, teasing her moist lips apart until he was just inside her.

Rocking ever so slightly back and forth, he duplicated the action he'd begun with his finger, at the same time massaging her tiny, sensitive nubbin. Nessa matched his rhythm, moving her own hips to meet him. Now it was his turn to groan as he covered her mouth with his, stifling her gasps of pleasure.

Nessa had gone beyond wonderment by now, lost in a sea of sensation she had never dreamed existed. Jack had promised he would make her want him, and oh! She did, she did! She quickened the thrusting of her hips, parting her legs slightly to impale herself upon him. Over and over she thrust her hips against his, reveling in how he filled her, reveling in the absence of pain. An even more intense surge overwhelmed her and she went over the edge into a world of pure pleasure that had her shuddering with ecstasy.

As she began her descent from the heights, Jack accelerated his own movements, driving himself into her once, twice, again. He tensed then and shuddered, just as she had, gradually slowing his movements.

Nessa's body still throbbed around him, but now a warm languor began to steal over her, replacing the urgency she'd felt a moment ago.

Her breathing slowed, and she could hear his doing the same. Speaking seemed out of the question, and yet she felt a need to express her thanks for the new world he had opened to her. Never again would she fear him, fear the physical aspect of marriage. Tentatively, shyly, she touched his cheek with her fingertips.

Jack opened his eyes, pools of midnight blue, and smiled. "Did I keep my promise?" he asked.

She nodded. "And it didn't take all night, either."

He gave a bark of laughter, then hugged her to him. "Nessa, you are truly a remarkable woman. I'm glad I married you."

A warm glow filled her, as pleasurable as the one his physical loving had aroused. "I'm glad too, Jack. Thank you. For everything."

He raised a quizzical brow, making her blush. "Oh, that wasn't everything, not by a long shot."

"No?" She felt breathless, but daring. "I seem to recall a discussion of lessons . . . "

"And that was but the first. Come, my wife, let me demonstrate the full range of my instructional abilities." He pulled her to him again and she felt not the smallest desire to resist.

By morning, Nessa felt as if she'd acquired years of experience, if not much sleep. Marriage to a rake had much to recommend it after all, she had decided well before midnight. Now she found herself a bit sore, but happy. She'd longed to throw off all those years of propriety and, in one glorious night, she'd done it. And would again——and again.

She smiled up at the plaster flowers on the ceiling. Three days ago, she'd promised to play the paragon in public if she could be wicked in private. Now that she knew just how much fun "private wickedness" could be, she realized such a life was her ideal. She could enjoy frequent——nightly!——tastes of wildness without visiting scandal upon Prudence, Jack, or anyone else.

At that thought, she suddenly sat up with a gasp, awakening Jack, who still slumbered at her side. "The guests! What time is it?" A glance at the clock above the fireplace showed the morning well advanced, though still wintry-dull.

Jack turned toward her with a smile. "Does it matter? No one will expect newlyweds to appear early for breakfast." He reached out to pull her to him once again, apparently revived enough by a few hours' sleep for more lovemaking.

But Nessa evaded him and scrambled out of the bed. "No, Jack, I promised——*you* made me promise. I am now officially hostess of Fox Manor, and your mother and Lady Gwendolyn leave this morning. 'Twould be a dreadful insult were I not to see them off."

"Would it?" Jack frowned. "I can't see how. You've been everything proper since they arrived——more gracious than they deserve, by a long sight. Surely it's for *them* to take leave of *us*."

Nessa began splashing her face at the basin. "Yes, yes, but if we are not available for their leave-taking, then the onus is upon us. One of the frightful things about propriety is that one misstep wipes out any number of perfect ones."

Jack snorted, but sat up and groped for his dressing gown. "I suppose you're right, though that's why all the resolve in the world will probably never restore my reputation. How can one stay on one's guard every minute of the day?"

Drying her face, Nessa went to give him a quick hug. "I can, so long as I may drop it at night."

His deep chuckle quickened her pulse, but she ducked away when he would have pushed her back onto the bed. "At night, I said."

"I'm glad the days are short just now." With a wink, he returned to his chamber to ring for his valet.

Though she knew it was foolish, Nessa quickly tidied both the bed and herself before signaling Simmons to attend her. The maid must know, of course, what sort of activity had transpired here overnight, but she preferred not to flaunt it. Besides, keeping the wildness of their passion a secret made it seem more wicked—and fun.

Half an hour later, Jack had to admit that Nessa looked every inch the proper Lady of the Manor as she descended with him to join the guests assembled in the morning room.

"Such a lovely couple, as I've been telling everyone,"

Lady Gwendolyn declared, brushing aside Nessa's apology for their tardiness. "This young lady will be the making of you, Jack, you mark my words. I see marked improvement already."

Grinning, he stepped to Nessa's side. "I don't doubt it, Aunt Gwendolyn. I do feel much improved." He shot Nessa a quick wink, which she valiantly ignored, though her color rose.

"Incorrigible boy!" exclaimed Lady Gwendolyn, but her tone was indulgent rather than censorious. "And now, I really must be on my way if I am to reach Lewes before nightfall. The days are short, you know."

"Yes, I know." Jack kept both voice and face innocently solemn, but sent Nessa a sidelong glance that set her blushing again.

"Claudia, it appears your son has turned out rather well after all," Lady Gwendolyn commented then.

Lady Branch now stepped forward, with the warmest smile Jack had ever seen her wear. "Indeed he has. And I thank you for it, my dear." She gave Nessa a quick peck on the cheek before turning to Jack. "I can honestly say I'm proud of you—Jack."

For a moment, he found himself speechless. Since her arrival, his mother had called him nothing but Lord Foxhaven, and even in his youth she had despised his nickname, insisting upon "John." Something else to put to Nessa's credit.

"Thank you, Mother," he said after a pause. "I'm pleased to hear you say so." He bent to kiss her cheek, and was surprised when she squeezed his arm in return. It was not much, perhaps, but it was a start.

As his first full day as a married man progressed, Jack reflected with satisfaction that so far he had no cause for regrets. Nessa was the ideal hostess, dividing her attention among the house guests and taking gracious leave of those departing. Already she was consulting with Cook about the menus and making a few changes in servants' schedules to improve efficiency.

And, of course, she had proven even more delightful in bed than he'd envisioned. What a wedding night! Jack had been with several world-renowned courtesans over the years, women known both in England and abroad for their skill, but never had he been so well satisfied so many times in one night. What Nessa lacked in experience, she more than made up in enthusiasm.

Watching her skillfully settle a debate between Lord Peter and Harry that had threatened to become heated, he frowned. A night like that after a year and more of abstinence was bound to have certain physical effects upon her. He'd have to be extremely gentle tonight, or even desist altogether—if she'd let him!

As though feeling his eyes upon her, she turned just then and gave him a saucy half-wink when no one was looking. Jack grinned, but hastily seated himself next to Lord Peter to conceal her effect upon him. He'd let her decide what she was ready for tonight, he decided. Who was he to deny her, after all?

That evening, as Jack was on the point of knocking on the door to Nessa's chamber, a tap sounded on the other side. Opening it, he stared, too overcome for the moment to speak.

Clad in the low-cut gown and feathered mask she'd worn the night he met her, Nessa stood in the doorway.

"May I come in?" At his feeble nod, the vision swept past him, then paused to survey the room. "Not quite the monkish cell I was led to believe, Brother Eligius. Why! What a big bed you have."

Jack emerged from his momentary trance and grinned. "The better to please you with, my Lady Monique." Taking her hand, he lifted it to his lips. "Observe this poor friar overcome by the honor of your visit. How might I be of service?"

Her brown eyes sparkled at him through the mask. "I have come to you for religious instruction, of course." When he blinked in surprise, she continued, "I should like to learn more about the Song of Solomon. 'Tis a facet of my theological education which has been sadly neglected, and I have reason to believe you are well suited to fill the gaps in my knowledge."

He began to chuckle. "My lady, you have come to the right monk." Tightening his grip on her hand, he led her toward the bed.

Jack proceeded to instruct Nessa on ways of pleasuring each other that would not exacerbate her soreness—to which she only reluctantly admitted.

"I promised not to hurt you, remember?" he said when she insisted it did not matter. "I want you to think of our marriage bed only in terms of pleasure, never of pain."

"For enough pleasure, I'm willing to endure a modicum of pain," she assured him, "but if 'tis possible to forego the pain entirely, so much the better."

He demonstrated that it was, pleasuring her with touch and tongue and giving her subtle cues on how to do likewise for him. She proved an apt pupil—so apt that though they'd both skimped on sleep the night before, neither felt inclined to rest until well after midnight. Then they fell into an exhausted but happy slumber that again lasted until the morning was well advanced.

By two hours past noon, the remainder of the house guests had gone, save Peter, Harry, and the Creamcrofts. Jack found himself looking forward to a quiet Yuletide with just his bride and closest friends. Time enough later to contemplate their trip to Paris and the complications awaiting him there. For now, he could relax.

He was rather surprised, therefore, to hear a loud knock at the door only half an hour after the last guests had taken their leave. Curious, he rose languidly from his place beside Nessa on the drawing room sofa, where he'd been awaiting tea along with the others. Peering into the hall, he was in time to hear a familiar voice say to Hackett, "I've an urgent message for Lord Foxhaven from the Duke of Wellington. I understand he is in residence."

Jack strode forward, his mind quickly shifting from indolence to curiosity. "I am indeed, Mr. Woolsey."

At once the man reached into his pocket and extended an envelope to him. "I thank you. Hackett will see that you are provided with the means to refresh yourself. Pray join me in the library in half an hour."

A moment later, seated at his desk by the crackling library fire, Jack read through Wellington's latest missive with a deepening frown.

Two weeks earlier, Lord Liverpool had written to the duke to warn·him of another assassination plot and the official opinion that his situation in Paris was now judged unacceptably dangerous. As soon as a plausible reason could be formulated, one that would not smack of retreat, Wellington would be recalled, probably to take a post at the Congress of Vienna now underway.

Though Jack would no longer be able to serve as originally requested, Wellington felt he could still be of use here in England. The assassination plot, incredibly, appeared to be of British origin, and two of the primary suspects were known to have spent time in the company of Miranda Dempsey after Jack left Paris in August. Now that Jack had attained a degree of social influence as Lord Foxhaven, the duke felt he might be in a position to extract valuable information from Mrs. Dempsey—information that could bring these traitors to justice and protect England from any further outrage.

Jack scowled down at the letter and drummed his fingers on the desk. Though he typically did not say so, Wellington's life was very likely on the line here. If Jack refused to act, these would-be assassins might very well follow the duke to Vienna, to carry out their dastardly plot there. But to accede to Wellington's wishes would be to betray the wedding vows he had taken only two days since—and his grandfather's wishes, as well.

What the devil was he to do?

His struggle was sharp but brief. Whatever befell him personally, Jack could not refuse his erstwhile commander's request. He would simply have to devise a way to extract the necessary information from Miranda while doing minimal damage to his marriage and reputation. A strategist of his caliber should be able to manage it—shouldn't he?

By the time Mr. Woolsey joined him several minutes later, his response to the Duke of Wellington was already written.

A few moments later, Jack reentered the drawing room to resume his seat beside Nessa, just as though his life had not suddenly been turned upside down. "It occurs to me," he said casually, "that you haven't yet seen the rest of the grounds. The weather has turned clear for the moment. What say you to a walk?"

"That would be lovely," Nessa exclaimed. "If you'll wait a moment, I'll go up to change my shoes and fetch a wrap. Perhaps the others would like to come too?"

"No, no," said Lady Creamcroft, correctly interpreting Jack's quick frown. "You two newlyweds run along."

Though her phrasing only added to his burden, Jack smiled his gratitude. For what he needed to say to Nessa, he preferred they be alone.

❧ 15 ❧

Nessa took a deep breath of the bright, wintry air. Lovely as Fox Manor was, she'd begun to feel a bit enclosed. Some outdoor exercise was just what she needed. "What's beyond that small rise over there?" she asked, pointing.

"The east end of the orchard, with a brook and small wilderness beyond. It's quite pretty in summer, but I doubt it's much to look at now. There's a path, but parts of it may be muddy."

"I'm game if you are." Alone with Jack, she could shed her mantle of propriety for awhile—not that it was so onerous now, with most of the guests gone.

"Off we go, then," he said, stepping out at a fairly brisk pace. In five minutes they crested the rise, and in two more they were out of sight of the house. Both slowed their pace then, in unspoken agreement.

Nessa chuckled. "I believe we've successfully escaped. Is that the wilderness you spoke of, off to our right?"

Jack nodded, his expression unexpectedly serious.

Folding her gloved hands over his arm, Nessa regarded him curiously. After a walking a minute or two in silence, he spoke.

"Nessa, were you . . . very much looking forward to Paris?"

She immediately noticed his use of the past tense, and swallowed. He meant to go without her. Perhaps he had intended it all along. Despite a crushing sense of disappointment, pride forced her to say, "A bit, but not so very much. Why?"

He regarded her for a long moment, but she refused to meet his eyes, afraid of what her own might reveal. Instead, she gazed ahead as though trying to spot the brook and held her breath.

"There has been a change in plans. The Duke of Wellington is to leave Paris for Vienna shortly, so my presence is no longer needed."

Nessa released her breath and lifted wide eyes to his face. "You're not going to Paris?" He shook his head, and relief washed through her. He wasn't leaving her behind after all! "That visitor, just now," she exclaimed with sudden insight.

"It was the message from Wellington, yes. So you don't mind too terribly?"

She smiled up at him. "I did rather wish to see what all the fuss was about, but I'll be happy to stay in England, as long as I am with you, Jack. Thank you for telling me right away."

His nod was rather brusque, she thought, as though something in her answer displeased him, though he only said, "Good, good." He lapsed into silence then, as they continued on their way, leaving her to wonder at his reaction.

Had she been too outspoken about her happiness at being with him? Though they'd spent hours getting to know each other physically, little had been said between them of feelings. While she felt certain that Jack's fondness for her went beyond simple lust, perhaps he was not yet ready for emotional declarations—which she had come perilously close to making just now.

To demonstrate that it had already passed from her mind, she made a general comment about the extent of the orchard, and he replied in kind. She would *not* allow herself to brood upon the subject. No talk of love had ever entered into her agreement with Jack, nor his with her. 'Twould be absurd to allow sentiment to mar the happiness she had found thus far in marriage.

Compared to her first marriage, to countless marriages she'd seen, theirs had the potential to be exceedingly pleasant, not to mention exciting. That should be good enough for anyone.

Shouldn't it?

That evening, after supper, Jack decided to bring Harry and Peter into his confidence, as part of his decision concerned them. Ushering them into the library, he poured a small measure of brandy for each of them before beginning.

"I received another missive from Wellington today.

He's had wind of my title, and now feels I can serve him better here in England, as I have property interests to attend to."

Harry sat up straighter than Jack had believed him capable this late in the evening. "The devil he did! Rescinded your invitation to Paris? Oh, hard luck, old boy! And after you already got yourself leg-shackled and everything. Well, at least you got the money signed over—didn't you?"

Jack nodded, smiling at his friend's genuine distress on his behalf. "Yesterday afternoon. I'm not nearly so devastated as you seem to be, I assure you. And you won't be, either, once I've told you the sequel."

He settled himself into a chair near the fire. "Wellington is going to Vienna, and asked my recommendations for a post or two with him there. I've already dispatched my suggestions. I doubt not you'll be hearing from him before many weeks have passed."

Harry choked on the sip of brandy he'd injudiciously taken as Jack dropped his bombshell. Coughing and sputtering, eyes streaming, he nevertheless managed a grin. "Damn, that was good of you, Jack," he said when he could. "Even if Old Nosey laughs and tosses your recommendation in the fire, which is not unlikely, it was a handsome thing for you to do."

"That it was," agreed Lord Peter, getting up to slap Harry on the shoulder. "I congratulate you, though I doubt not you'll make poor use of the opportunity. Vienna's even worse than Paris, from what I hear." His tone was only half jesting.

"All depends on your perspective," Harry retorted. "I intend to make *very* good use of some of the opportunities to be found in Vienna——if I get the chance." He couldn't seem to stop grinning.

Pleased with the result of his news, Jack grinned back at him, then turned to Peter. "You could always go along to keep an eye on our boy, you know. I did mention your suitability as well."

Lord Peter looked alarmed, then thoughtful. "Should the offer come, I'll give it some consideration. But tell us, Jack, what has Wellington in mind for you to do here in England? Tending your fields is all very nice for the economy, I suppose, but surely it's not all he mentioned?"

Caught off guard, Jack hesitated, then decided against dissembling to these two who knew him best. "No, he seems to think I hold a degree of influence over someone who may have information on certain traitors. He wishes me to exert it."

"Miranda Dempsey, I'll be bound!" exclaimed Harry, startling Jack with his perspicacity. Drink clearly hadn't fuddled his wits completely. "Heard she was thick with Jameson and Cranshall, who I never trusted a hairsbreadth."

Jack merely inclined his head slightly. "I'm impressed. It appears my recommendation was more astute than even I guessed."

But Lord Peter was frowning. "You didn't agree, surely, Jack! You've been married but two days, after all."

"Puts a new twist on the term 'affairs of state,' don't it?" quipped Harry, earning a glare from both of the others.

"I didn't agree to a dalliance with Miranda, no. But I did offer to find out what I could," Jack admitted, shifting uncomfortably in his well-upholstered chair.

Peter regarded him shrewdly. "Still can't bear to let the Iron Duke down, can you? He can't have known about your marriage, though, or he'd never have suggested it."

"Yes, I know. Still . . . I thought perhaps I could find out something of use, without, er, resuming a relationship with Miranda. She hasn't given up, you know."

Peter snorted. "That I can well believe. If she can't have your name, she'll settle for your money. But think, Jack!" He was all earnestness now. "How will it look to your wife if you remain on friendly—if not intimate—terms with a former mistress?"

That was the very problem that had plagued Jack since first reading the duke's letter. "I'll simply make certain she doesn't hear of it," he replied, with more confidence than he felt. "In any event, I needn't do anything about it one way or the other just yet. We don't return to London until after the holidays."

They seemed content with that, and the conversation turned back to the Congress of Vienna and the latest news to come out of it. Jack was just as glad. Weighty matters of national security were far less unsettling than those pertaining to his marriage—and his feelings about it.

*   *   *

The next two weeks passed almost too quickly for Nessa, so enjoyable was this Christmas season, unmarred by the heavy puritanical overtones of all her previous ones.

She found preparing gift baskets of food and other necessities for the poorer villagers particularly satisfying. Together, she and Jack drove or walked about the lands beholden to Foxhaven, delivering the baskets along with well wishes, in what he told her had long been a Foxhaven Christmas custom.

At Fox Manor itself, she reveled in the baking, roasting, and hanging of greenery, which reached a frenzied peak on Christmas Eve. Prudence, however, voiced some reservations.

"Ought you really to condone such things, Nessa?" she asked as they watched the hanging of yet another enormous kissing bough, this one in the morning room. "Father always said such things were pagan barbarisms."

"He said that of the yule log as well, Prudence, but we intend to have one tonight—in fact, here come the men now from their expedition to find a suitable one. Why do you not ask Philip what he thinks of these traditions?"

Prudence obediently approached her husband, where he had paused under the just-hung mass of greenery, ribbons, and mistletoe. To Nessa's delight, her brother-in-law was not at all slow to take advantage of time-honored custom, reaching up to pluck a mistletoe berry before claiming a resounding kiss from his startled wife.

"Philip!" Cheeks as scarlet as the ribbons above them, Prudence glanced wildly about at the appreciative onlookers.

"I believe you may take that as an answer to the question you were about to ask," Nessa suggested wickedly. Prudence sent her a speaking glance, but then she smiled shyly up at her husband.

"*Have* you felt deprived of Christmas traditions these past few years, my lord?" she asked.

Philip encircled his wife's shoulders with an arm and gave her a quick hug. "Only a bit, my dear. Not enough to make you uncomfortable over. I know you were not brought up to them."

Prudence's brow furrowed prettily as she considered his words, but she said nothing. Shortly thereafter, the men went back outdoors to strip the remaining branches from the yule log before bringing it in, and Nessa took the opportunity for a few more words with her sister on the subject.

"Are you still opposed to *celebrating* Christmas, Prudence? Everyone else seems to enjoy it enormously."

Again her sister looked thoughtful. "Yes, they do. Even Philip." Nessa had been pleased to note that she often called her husband by his Christian name now, unless many people were present.

"Perhaps 'tis not such a pagan thing to do after all," Nessa suggested. "It occurs to me that many of the traditions Father despised involve charity to one's fellow man—Boxing Day, gift baskets to the poor, that sort of thing. How can such customs possibly violate the spirit of the season?"

Prudence nodded. "I believe you may be right, Nessa. Father, for all his virtue, was not a particularly charitable man."

Though she said nothing more, Nessa took great hope from that statement, the first one critical of their father that she'd ever heard Prudence utter. Yes, her sister was well on her way to becoming her own person—and a far happier one, she suspected.

Celebrating with the villagers and servants in the biggest of the barns on Boxing Day, Nessa found that Jack and Philip enjoyed children as much as she and Prudence did. She watched with delight as they carried a succession of little boys about on their shoulders and danced with every little girl old enough to stand.

When the motley group of local musicians struck up a waltz, Jack charmed the assembly by dancing it with his wife. Nessa was pleased to see that most of the local lasses appeared to have accepted her already. Glancing to her right, she was even more pleased—and amazed—to see Prudence and Philip waltzing!

"You were splendid!" she declared to them when the dance was over. "However did you convince her to learn, Philip?"

Her brother-in-law chuckled. "Actually, it was her suggestion. It began with a private lesson in a corridor at the Hightower ball, followed by—" But at this point he was silenced by a poke in the ribs from a blushing—but smiling—Prudence.

"No matter. I'm happy for you both," said Nessa sincerely. For a moment she felt the faintest twinge of old envy, but pushed it aside.

Time enough once the festivities were over to worry about the emotional state of her own marriage. For now, she was content with the novel joys of the season—and of the marriage bed, where her education continued apace.

At times, Nessa almost wondered how she could ever have found lovemaking distasteful. Then she would remember Lord Haughton and shudder, turning to Jack with renewed gratitude for everything he'd shown her marriage could hold. If a tiny voice murmured, *everything but love*, she ignored it. She and Jack had affection and trust, which was surely more than many couples shared.

Throughout the Twelve Days of Christmas, they discovered more and more interests in common. Nessa beat Jack at whist, and he taught her to play vingt-et-un and euchre. When the weather permitted, they took more and longer walks until she felt familiar with most of the Foxhaven estate and longed to see it in other seasons. Never much of a horsewoman, Jack taught her some of the finer points of riding until she began to enjoy the exercise and even earned his grudging praise.

When sleet drove everyone indoors, they discussed books. To her surprise, Jack had read most of the same ones she had, with both professing a fondness for the tales of Walter Scott—novels of the sort Nessa had always been obliged to read in secret.

All too soon, Twelfth Night arrived. On the morrow, January seventh, they were all to head back to London. The decorations were taken down and, after dinner, the Twelfth Cake was brought in to close the holiday season.

Jack raised his glass. "To good times and good friends. May we often gather again in the future."

All drank to that, Harry draining his glass as was his wont and signaling the servant to refill it. He then lifted his own wineglass for a toast. "To our host, Jack, the best of good friends. May Wellington's faith in you be justified, as well as yours in me. I wish you the best of both worlds," he concluded, with a broad wink.

Though Nessa didn't understand the reference, she drank with the rest.

Jack could see that Nessa was not as impressed by her first sight of his London house as she had been by Fox Manor. Though she politely refrained from making any criticism of Foxhaven House, she looked about at the dark front hallway with its nude statuary, gilt ornaments, and hunting trophies with something akin to horror.

Seeing it through her eyes, he was inclined to agree. In the first flush of excitement at his newfound wealth and title, he'd filled the Townhouse with various things he'd collected over his years of wandering, in an attempt to make it feel like home. The result was . . . tasteless, to say the least.

"You'll, er, want to redecorate, most likely," he said cautiously. "I rather threw things in any which way after I inherited last autumn."

Nessa seemed to breathe a bit easier. "I believe I would prefer to make a few changes, if you won't mind terribly."

Jack grinned at her diplomacy. "Oh, it's dreadful and I know it. I should have left well enough alone, of course, but now I give you free rein to do what you like with it. I've no doubt you'll do me proud."

She colored slightly, but lifted her chin. "I'll do my best. But perhaps I should see what other atrocities you've committed before making any bold claims."

Jack took her through the four-story house, holding his breath each time he opened a door, trying to recall what might be waiting on the other side.

"Never tell me this belonged to your grandmother," exclaimed Nessa, holding up an extremely sheer scarlet negligee she found in her own wardrobe. "Nor these!" Reaching in again, she produced a pair of lacy black garters adorned with saucy red ribbons.

Vividly remembering the evening—and the party— that had occasioned those particular garments being left in this particular room, Jack could only groan. Had it really been only four months ago? What a wastrel he'd been!

But Nessa was chuckling. "Oh, come, Jack. I'll not hold you accountable for everything you did before we married—or even met. 'Twas the fact that you were a rake which first fascinated me, if you recall. Don't worry that I'll become missish now, when I find occasional evidence of it."

He managed a crooked grin, remembering his promise to Wellington. "Not many wives would be so understanding, I suspect. Shall we have a ball to introduce the new Lady Foxhaven to Society and to show off the house when it is done?"

The twinkle in her eyes told him she was aware he had deliberately changed the subject, but she answered readily enough. "Of course. It will be an essential step in restoring you to respectability. I'm not certain how long these renovations will take, however, so let's not send out the invitations just yet."

Over the next week or two, however, Jack had occasion to wonder once more whether respectability was worth the cost. A continuous stream of tradesmen came to call, with samples of wallpaper, fabrics, carpet, and every other item that might conceivably play a role in redecorating a house. Nessa reviewed everything, made choices, and directed the resultant workmen.

Soon, no room was safe. Bolts of fabric, rolls of paper, tubs of glue, and boxes of pins were everywhere. The furniture went missing or in pieces as it was reupholstered, windows went uncurtained, and all was in disarray.

At first Jack felt like a coward taking refuge at his club, but soon even that offered scant relief. Wellington had written asking Harry and Peter to precede him to Vienna, and they had gone at once. Few of his other erstwhile cronies had yet returned to Town. Staring morosely out the Guards' front window at White's across the street, he decided he needed a change.

Back outside, he considered White's again, wondering whether his reputation was yet restored enough to attempt entry there. Deciding not to risk it just yet, he turned to stroll aimlessly down St. James Street, considering various other clubs. Brooks', Boodle's, Arthur's, Graham's—none really appealed. Instead, he found his steps turning to Jermyn Street, home of some of his old, disreputable haunts.

"Jack, m'boy!" exclaimed a once-familiar voice as he passed one of the more notorious gaming hells. "Didn't know you were back in Town. Let me buy you a drink, for old times' sake."

"Hello, Ferny," he greeted the obviously tipsy young man. "How have you been?"

Lord Fernworth shook his head and heaved a dramatic sigh. "It ain't been the same with you gone, and that's the truth." Jack did not resist when he took him by the arm and led him inside. "And then to take Pete and Harry away as well! I ask you!" He signaled for wine and a pretty serving wench obliged.

"Now you're back," he continued as their glasses were filled, "things are bound to improve. Look at this lot." He gestured around the large room in disgust. "Not a decent card player in the bunch, or none willing to play for decent stakes. How much fun can one have in a hole like this, anyway? But with you back at Fox-haven House . . ."

"I'm married now, remember?"

Lord Fernworth focused on his face with some difficulty. "Yes, yes, of course, but what's that to do with it? What the little lady in the country don't know won't hurt her."

"Lady Foxhaven is here in London, refurbishing Foxhaven House even as we speak." Jack recalled the chaos at home with slightly less than his earlier aversion.

"Here in Town? Man, are you mad? What the devil did you want to bring a wife here for? You *have* changed, Jack." Lord Fernworth glared at him balefully before tossing off the rest of his drink.

Jack regarded him impassively, then allowed his gaze to take in the rest of the establishment where he'd spent a significant portion of his time last September. The clientele consisted of those on the outer fringes of Society, as well as the occasional younger son hoping to achieve Town bronze in short order. Though it was but late afternoon, most were already deep in their cups. What on earth was he doing here?

"Yes, I suppose I have." Pushing his untouched glass across to Ferny, he stood. "Or maybe I've just grown up." Leaving his onetime crony to ponder the meaning of that statement, he strode from the place, vowing never to return.

Walking along Piccadilly on his way back to Foxhaven House, yet another familiar voice hailed him, this one feminine. "Jack! What a delightful surprise!"

"You're looking well, Miranda," he cautiously

greeted the stunning woman before him. "I take it you remained in Town during the holidays?"

She pouted prettily. "I had no choice, unless I wished to join my odious brother and his starched-up wife in Suffolk. I'd planned to attend Lady Hartshorn's house party, but she took ill and canceled it."

"How very discourteous of her, to be sure." Though his tone was light and bantering, Jack's thoughts were in turmoil. Here was his first opportunity to carry out Wellington's request. He'd best make good use of it.

"My sentiments exactly," Miranda replied, trilling one of her lovely laughs.

Jack started before realizing she'd responded to his careless words, not his thoughts. Carefully, he said, "A pity you've had such a dull time of it."

"Ah, but now you're back in Town, that will change, will it not?" She lowered her voice seductively and laid a hand on his sleeve. "By now you've no doubt had time to become bored with your proper little wife and will welcome some excitement as much as I."

"Surely you haven't spent the past month entirely alone?" he asked, though his conscience smote him for failing to defend Nessa. Not that the details of his marriage were any business of Miranda's, he reminded himself.

"It does seem at times as though all the world's in Paris—or Vienna—but I've had escorts to the theater and what few entertainments are available with Town so thin of company. Don't think I'm *that* dependent upon you, Jack!" She fluttered her eyelashes at him.

"Of course not. An attractive woman like you must have so many admirers I'm amazed you missed me at all." Jack was almost startled to discover he could still spout insincerities so effortlessly.

"Ah, but you are in a class of your own, Jack." Miranda sidled even closer to him.

"I'm flattered. Say, do you still see anything of Jameson these days?" he asked casually. "There was something I wished to ask him about." He was becoming impatient with her flirting. Evening was coming on, and he wished to get home.

Miranda smiled. "Owes you money, does he? You're not the only one, but I may have some information you'll find useful. If we combine forces—" She stopped, her attention caught by something over his shoulder. "Why, good afternoon, Lord and Lady Creamcroft! I was just having the most delightful coze with your new brother-in-law."

Damn. Jack turned to face the newcomers, unobtrusively disengaging Miranda's hand from his sleeve. "I give you good day, Philip, my lady. I was just returning to Foxhaven House. Would you care to see how the redecorating is coming along?"

Prudence glanced from Jack to Miranda, a concerned question in her eyes, while Philip replied, "We're on our way home ourselves, to dress for dinner at the Glaedons'. I believe Lady Foxhaven has requested we wait until all is finished before calling in any event, has she not, my dear?"

Recovering herself, Prudence nodded. "Yes, she's

determined to do it all herself, though I offered my guidance. I managed a quick peek a few days since, when I brought a few things she'd left at our house, but she shooed me out before I could see much."

Apparently bored with the turn in conversation, Miranda spoke. "I'll leave you all to your domestic concerns, then. Jack, I propose we continue our discussion later. If you'll call on me tomorrow, we can no doubt arrange a more private venue." With a saucy smile, she continued along the street.

Cursing her impudence but unwilling to make explanations to the Creamcrofts, Jack took his leave as well. "I need to hurry along myself, as Nessa will be expecting me. If the workmen adhere to her schedule, we should be able to invite you to view the finished result in a matter of days."

A moment later he was on his way, thankful that it lay in the opposite direction to Miranda's. He wondered who else had seen them together on the street. He quickened his pace, suddenly eager to see Nessa again.

Bounding up the front steps, he opened the front door himself, unwilling to wait for his incompetent butler. This proved a mistake. The door bumped a ladder propped near one of the front windows. It teetered, then fell with a crash, barely missing him. A decorative urn near the stairway was not so lucky, however.

Sweeping the shards to one side with his boot, Jack waited for Nessa and the servants to come running to investigate the commotion——but no one did. "Nessa?" Frowning, he headed up the stairs. "Anyone?"

Jack continued up to the second landing, then glanced around. In which of the four bedrooms was Nessa likely to be occupied? He glanced into her chamber first, but found only Simmons there, clucking and shaking her head as she bundled up stray bits of fabric and wallpaper and brushed ineffectually at the dust.

The doors of the two spare bedchambers stood open, and as he heard no sound from their direction, he opened the door to his own room——and stood blinking on the threshold. A remarkable change had been wrought since he'd left early in the day. The new paper was hung, in blue and gray stripes, as were fresh curtains and bed-hangings. The carpet was still rolled up at one end of the room, but everything else appeared finished.

And Nessa herself sat upon the floor, hemming the new curtains!

"My dear, whatever are you doing?" he asked, recovering his wits and striding forward. "Are we not paying an army of people to do such chores as this?"

Nessa turned to him with a smile. "Hello, Jack! I'd hoped to have this finished before you returned. Do you like it?"

He glanced about the room again, but his attention was on Nessa herself. Seated on the floor like a servant, her hair coming loose from its pins, a smudge on the tip of her nose, she looked . . . beautiful. And tired, he realized, looking closer.

"It's far better than I expected," he admitted, "but you have not answered my question. Why are you doing such a menial task yourself?"

Her smile faltered. "Mrs. Latham, the seamstress, wished to get home, for her son is ill. As there was only this last length to hem, I decided to complete it myself. And"—she turned back to the folds of fabric in her hands and tied off a knot—"'tis done. I'll go consult with Cook about dinner." She scrambled to her feet before he could move to assist her, and hurried from the room.

Jack frowned after her, then turned to examine more closely the results of her labors. Remarkable! Clearly, she'd made a real effort to have it done quickly, in order to cause him a minimum of inconvenience. Smiling, he rang for Parker to help him change for dinner.

Joining Nessa in the drawing room a short while later, he was surprised to find a small table set for their meal.

"The dining room table has paper and glue pots on it, so this made more sense," she explained apologetically. "It should be only for one night, or perhaps two."

"I begin to think we should have returned to Fox Manor until the renovations were complete," he commented, seating first Nessa and then himself at the little table. "But I know that you prefer to oversee the process yourself."

"I'm sorry, Jack. I know you don't like all of this disorder, but it will be over soon, I promise you." She took a spoonful of soup—and grimaced. "I fear we'll have to look for a new cook before holding a major entertainment. I hope this one has not been with you long."

He shook his head. "All of Grandfather's servants left when the house was shut up during the time my Uncle Luther held the title. I fear I never paid proper attention to hiring a competent staff to replace them, but relied solely on an employment agency."

"Then I won't have the slightest reservation about seeking a new staff at once. I'll begin tomorrow."

When Jack's after-dinner brandy was served, she rose. "As we are already in the drawing room, I'll withdraw to my chamber upstairs, if you do not mind. I imagine Simmons will need direction on where to bestow some of the clutter."

He considered asking her to remain, but then nodded. An early night would do them both good. "As you wish, my dear. I'll join you shortly." She responded to his wink with a grin, then left the room.

Scarcely twenty minutes later, Jack followed her upstairs. Somehow she had managed to have the carpet laid in his bedchamber while they were below, he noticed. Shaking his head in awe at her efficiency, he quickly changed into his dressing gown and opened the connecting door to her room.

A lone candle burned on the nightstand, and Nessa lay beneath the coverlet—sound asleep. Smiling tenderly, Jack leaned over and kissed her cheek, careful not to awaken her. Extinguishing the candle, he quietly returned to his own bedchamber. Climbing into his own bed, alone for the first night since their marriage, he stared up at the ceiling.

Two hours later, with sleep as far away as ever, he rose and went down to the library, to clear a chair of debris. Poking the banked fire into a small blaze, he poured himself a measure of brandy and sat down to consider his options—and the exact nature of these disturbing feelings he had for his own wife.

☙ 16 ❧

Nessa awoke from the deepest sleep imaginable to find the room dark and the bed empty, save for herself. Momentarily confused, she fumbled for a candle, then rose to light it at the fireplace. She must have fallen asleep before Jack joined her. Not surprising, considering how tired she'd been. No doubt he'd returned to his own chamber rather than wake her, which was considerate of him, if a trifle disappointing.

Softly, she opened the adjoining door and tiptoed across the fresh-laid carpet to his bed—only to find it empty. Confused again, she went to look at the clock on his mantelpiece. Why, it was after two o'clock in the morning! His bed appeared to have been slept in, but where could he be now?

She returned to her room to don a wrapper, but then stopped. Doubtless he was simply downstairs in the library, reading. He had done so once or twice before when unable to sleep, she knew. And what would it look like if she went padding down after him? Might he think she didn't trust him? Climbing back into bed, she decided to distract herself by thinking about finishing the house this week.

It was clear Jack did not care for the disorder the workmen had created, though he was good enough not to say so. She would take care he did not catch her acting like a servant again, as he had clearly disapproved. That thought rankled a bit, reminding her too vividly of her childhood and first marriage, but she pushed it aside. She would direct her energies to more efficient delegation, hiring more and better servants, and carefully supervising the workmen. Inside of a week, Foxhaven House would do its master credit, she was determined.

By their third meeting, Jack was convinced he'd extracted all the useful information he could from Miranda. Jameson and Cranshall had indeed been important links in the abortive assassination plot—as had Miranda herself. For a handsome fee, she had passed along certain information about Wellington's plans while in Paris last fall, which they in turn had forwarded to the would-be assassin—whose name Jack had finally discovered.

"Surely you needn't leave so early today, Jack." Miranda pouted across the little table at Bellamy's coffeehouse, where they'd shared luncheon. "If you'll just come home with me for a moment, I've a new gown to show you that I think you'll approve." She leaned forward to give him an unobstructed view of her ample cleavage.

Though once or twice Jack had felt the stirrings of old lust, he had by now learned enough about Miranda to effectively douse any admiration. There was nothing, seemingly, that the woman wouldn't do for money. She'd betrayed her country for it, and now that her coconspirators had lost their funds, she just as readily betrayed them. Jack had to force himself to smile.

"I fear not, my dear. I've decided to take up my duties in Parliament at last, and have much to catch up on there. Besides, we don't wish to arouse gossip, do we?"

She shrugged negligently. "It's a bit late for that, don't you think? Even with your string of excuses to avoid being entirely alone with me, we've been seen in public often enough. If all London believes me to be in your pocket anyway, you may as well enjoy the advantages." She lowered her lashes seductively.

With an effort, Jack restrained himself from glancing around the room. He'd tried to be discreet, meeting with her at times and places when fewer people would be about, but he feared she might be right. It was time to break things off, now that he had that all-important name to pass along to the Home Office.

He stood. "If we've become an object of gossip, as you say, then we'd best not meet again. I don't want my wife hurt."

Miranda remained seated. "Goodness, we can't offend the sensibilities of the oh-so-proper Lady Foxhaven, can we, Jack?" She trilled a laugh, a shade too loudly. "Do you really think she's as innocent as all that?"

When he didn't reply, she rose languidly and tried another ploy. "I've heard Cranshall is about to open a gaming hall. If you'll come give me your opinion of that gown, I'll tell you all about it."

Jack shook his head. "I think not, Miranda. Here's the money Jameson owed you. I was able to put your information to good use, as you'd promised." He held out a folded wad of notes, money authorized by the Home Office.

Her eyes blazed, but she snatched the money from him. "So pleased we could be of use to each other," she snapped.

"As am I." Bowing so that she could not see the irony in his expression, Jack turned and walked away from her for good.

Nessa could not suppress a tendency to smugness as she surveyed the results of her hard work and management. She had consulted with experts and read dozens of periodicals and was now satisfied that Foxhaven House was smack up to the nines—and just happened to suit her own taste as well. Bright, cheerful, new upholstery, carpets, and drapes throughout, but nothing that would soon go out of style.

In addition, she had hired an entire new staff. Daniels, the new butler, had arrived two days since, as had the new cook, and already meals were much improved. Mrs. Blessing seemed destined to live up to her name in the capacity of housekeeper. Nessa had gladly turned the keys over to her this very morning.

How Jack had managed without a housekeeper was beyond her.

Now it was midafternoon, and Nessa was occupied in writing out the invitations to the soiree—to be held on the last day of January—which was to formally open the house and introduce her to Society in her new role. After weeks of answering servants, tradesmen, and workers, she was becoming accustomed to the name of Lady Foxhaven. But would she ever get used to her husband?

Jack had become rather an enigma of late. Out all day, he would return for dinner but say little about how he'd spent his time. The night after the one she'd spent alone in bed, Nessa had made a point of encouraging him to new heights of passion—and he'd seemed more than willing to be encouraged. The next day, however, her monthly courses had commenced, so there had been no further opportunities.

Nessa sighed and addressed the next envelope. Jack had been most understanding, of course, but she herself was more than a little frustrated—and disappointed. And now she must find a way to let Jack know that she was once more approachable.

Her courses had come late, and not until their arrival did she realize how much she'd hoped to discover she was with child. If Jack were similarly disappointed, he'd given no hint of it—unlike Lord Haughton, who had always contrived somehow to make Nessa feel guilty for failing to produce an heir.

Throat-clearing from the open parlor doorway

interrupted her musings. "Lady Creamcroft, milady," Daniels informed her.

Nessa set down her pen and turned with a smile. "Prudence! Welcome to Foxhaven House at last." She rose to greet her sister with outstretched hands.

"I've been all impatience to see what you've done here, Nessa!" exclaimed Prudence, returning her kiss. "What I've seen so far is charming. I insist on a full tour before you ring for tea."

Nessa complied, as eager to show off the house as Prudence was to see it. "Now, you must be totally honest with me," she said when at length they returned to the parlor. "What have I forgotten? What would you have done differently?"

"Not a thing," Prudence assured her. "In fact, I'm now itching to make changes to my own Townhouse in an effort to duplicate the light, airy feel you've given yours. Did you really direct all of the redecorating yourself?"

Nessa rang for the tea tray then, and they were soon deep in a discussion of fabrics, colors, and furniture arrangement. They were still so when Jack returned, half an hour later. At once, Prudence rose to take her leave.

"I'll give you good day, Nessa, and you as well, my lord. You must realize by now that your wife is a woman of many talents. I've no doubt that she will do you great credit . . . if you will allow it." With those enigmatic words, Prudence departed.

Nessa regarded Jack questioningly. "What was that

about? Have you been antagonizing Prudence in some way?"

He had been frowning after her sister, but summoned a smile—with an effort, she thought—when he turned to face her. "Antagonizing? I? Certainly not. Perhaps she is still waiting for me to prove I have reformed my ways."

"You're most likely right," Nessa agreed. "Prudence still feels herself responsible for me at times, I believe."

"Commendable, of course, but I should hope unnecessary. My lady wife, let me congratulate you upon what you've accomplished. I wish now I'd taken bets on how quickly the transformation of this house could be achieved—I might have been able to double our fortune!"

Nessa dimpled at the compliment. "I trust I have not depleted it to the extent that such measures will be necessary."

Jack walked across the room to survey her writing desk. "I see you are in the throes of invitation-writing. We are still on for next Tuesday night, I presume?" Without turning to see her nod, he picked up the address list and perused it, then gave a low whistle.

"Very ambitious, my dear! Do you really believe most of these paragons will be willing to set foot under the notorious Jack Ashecroft's roof?"

Nessa crossed to stand beside him. "Not all will come, of course. Prudence tells me that the Prince Regent is indisposed just now. But if even one of the royal dukes attends, it will set the seal on your acceptance, so I felt it imperative to extend the invitations."

She did not add that Edward, Duke of Kent, had been an intimate of both her father and Lord Haughton, and was at least somewhat likely to attend on that consideration. No sense elevating Jack's hopes just yet.

His hopes, however, did not appear in need of elevating. He grinned at her. "So you have some of the gambler in you after all, Nessa! I suspected it when you revealed yourself such an excellent whist player, but now I see you're willing to play for much higher stakes."

She sniffed at him in mock reproof. "My lord, I assure you that the eminently respectable Marchioness of Foxhaven would never deign to engage in deep play. 'Twould be most unseemly!" But her lips twitched even as she spoke.

"Would it indeed? And what of this?" He suddenly caught her to him for a kiss that was anything but seemly, in full view of the open parlor door.

She giggled when he finally released her, though she darted a glance out the door to be certain no passing servants had witnessed their embrace. "Should word get about that Lord Foxhaven treats his wife with such affectionate abandon, it could wreck all, of course. Such behavior, my good sir, should be reserved for the bedchamber."

"Madam!" he exclaimed in feigned shock. "Are you propositioning me, and before dinner?"

Nessa gave him a look of wide-eyed innocence. "Dinner will not be for an hour and more, my lord, I assure you."

His eyes narrowed to devilish slits of glittering blue. "In that case, we must find some way to pass the time, must we not? I've a mind to see the new decor of your chamber, my lady—in intimate detail."

"I'd been hoping you'd ask." And she accompanied him upstairs most willingly, more than ready to resume her interrupted education.

The day of the Foxhaven soirée dawned dull, with fog and freezing drizzle. Nessa prayed the weather would not keep everyone at home—though surely Londoners must be well accustomed to this vile winter climate! At least Prudence had been able to assure her that no other important functions were being held this evening to draw off attendance.

Food and flowers were delivered, but the weather worsened as the day drew on. Nessa's anxiety increased, and she was just as happy Jack was not at home to witness it. Parliament was back in session now, and rather to her surprise he had made a regular habit of occupying his seat in the House of Lords. Thus, she had still seen little of him during the daytime, though their nights together were more satisfactory than ever.

Still, Nessa was beginning to wonder whether lovemaking, however skilled, was truly enough to sustain a marriage. She and Jack traded witticisms across the dinner table, of course, and she found that nearly as pleasant as their time in bed, but they rarely discussed anything of substance. At times, in fact, she almost had the impression that Jack was avoiding anything approach-

ing serious conversation. There was much she still did
not know about him, she had to admit.

She walked once more to the drawing room window, which afforded a fine view of Berkley Square
below. Just as she reached it, a shy beam of sunlight
escaped the lowering clouds to turn the drizzle to silver
for a moment. Nessa's heart lifted in response. Everything would turn out right, she was certain, if she just
had faith and patience.

A few hours later, it seemed that her optimism was
justified. Only an hour into the soirée, the ballroom was
filled nearly to capacity, which was quite a feat as thin of
company as London yet was. And only moments ago, the
Duke of Kent had arrived, just as she had hoped. She still
found him overbearing and pompous and far too similar
in demeanor to her father for comfort, but his presence
must put an incontestable stamp of approval upon the
evening—and upon Lord and Lady Foxhaven.

"My dear, I congratulate you yet again," murmured
Jack in her ear during a brief lull. "Not that I ever really
doubted you, of course."

"Did you not?" She gazed around at the thronged
ballroom from her place at the open double doors,
where she and Jack still stood to greet their guests. "I
confess I spent much of the day doubting intensely, and
am most relieved to find my fears were groundless."

More guests arrived then to add to the crush—
among them, Lord and Lady Mountheath. Both parties
managed to behave as though their uncomfortable last
encounter had never taken place.

"I heard you had done wonders with the house over the past month," said Lady Mountheath after cool but cordial greetings were exchanged, "and I see 'tis true. Of course——" Her eyes widened and her words ceased. Surreptitiously following her gaze, Nessa realized she had just caught sight of the royal duke.

"Thank you, my lady," Nessa responded, keeping her expression solemn with an effort.

Recovering herself with a start, Lady Mountheath colored slightly before continuing, explaining that she had not been inside Foxhaven House for several years. After she left them to join the throng, Jack began to chuckle.

"Shh!" Nessa cautioned him. "You'll start me laughing too, and then all my hard work to restore you to respectability will be for naught."

"Hardly that, I think. Why, with one of the royals *and* Lady Mountheath here, our social position should be well nigh unassailable, should it not?"

"I admit, I never expected Lady Mountheath to attend. I only sent the invitation for fear it might cause gossip if I did not."

Jack draped an arm over her shoulders and gave her a quick squeeze. "As always, your judgment was unerring." Before Nessa could protest such a public display of affection, the Creamcrofts approached, accompanied by the Heathertons.

"Oh, Nessa, I'm so proud of you!" whispered Prudence excitedly when she reached her sister's side. "Such a success! The papers will be full of it tomorrow.

I had no idea so many of the *ton* were even in London!"

Mrs. Heatherton agreed. "I daresay nearly every important personage in residence is here tonight. A triumph, Lady Foxhaven. No doubt about it."

"A most enjoyable evening, if a bit crowded," chimed in Mr. Heatherton, a good-natured, heavyset man nearing middle age. "The food is first-rate, the servants most attentive—no glass allowed to go empty. And, of course, it always increases everyone's enjoyment to be around happy newlyweds. So much to be said for a love match! Can't imagine why some old biddies frown on them." He winked at his own wife, and Mrs. Heatherton's plain but pleasant face flushed, making her almost pretty.

Though Jack had released her when the foursome approached, Nessa's shoulder tingled where his arm had so recently lain. She willed her own color not to rise. *Love match?* Was that what people assumed? But of course, they must. What other explanation would occur to people, after all? Certainly not the true one. She did not dare to meet Jack's eyes.

"You are all most kind," she responded warmly, relieved to detect no quaver in her voice. "I merely put a lifetime of training to good use, and am as delighted as anyone that it has turned out so well."

"My wife is too modest." Jack's voice was warm with approval, so Nessa dared a glance at him. "She oversaw every detail, both of the redecorating of Foxhaven House and of the preparations for tonight. I doubt a stray leaf from one of the flower arrangements could have escaped her notice."

His smile was as warm as his voice, and Nessa relaxed. He seemed unaffected by Mr. Heatherton's assumption, so she would not allow it to fluster her. Really, she was being unforgivably silly.

"Will you not come join your guests now, both of you?" Prudence suggested. "You've more than done your duty, standing here an hour and more. Come and sample some of the excellent refreshments you have provided."

Nessa thought her sister seemed a shade less constrained in Jack's presence than previously, and she was glad of it. She wished for no friction between her two favorite people. "Yes, I believe we shall. My lord?"

Jack was more than willing to abandon his post, so they moved slowly toward the laden tables at the far end of the ballroom, exchanging pleasantries and fielding compliments from innumerable guests as they went. "Charming," "Such a pleasant couple," and similar comments followed in their wake.

While Nessa could not claim to thoroughly enjoy the balance of the evening, so vigilant was she in supervising the servants and caterers, she felt no small measure of satisfaction. Bringing this off had been work, hard work, but it had been well repaid. She had kept her promise, both to Jack and to herself.

The royal duke had departed, and several other guests were queuing up to take leave of their hosts as well, when a flash of color by the door drew Nessa's attention. Dressed in a clinging gown of red even more vivid than her hair, Miranda Dempsey wafted into the room. Nessa sensed Jack's sudden tenseness, though he made no other sign that he had seen the late arrival.

Whatever the woman had been to her husband in the past, Nessa would no more risk a scandal tonight than Lady Mountheath had on one previous occasion. Graciously, she greeted the uninvited guest. "My dear Mrs. Dempsey, how kind of you to come."

Though the woman seemed rather startled by her reception, she managed a curtsy—a shade less deep than Nessa's rank required, but not so perfunctory as to be an insult. "Thank you, Lady Foxhaven, *Lord* Foxhaven." She gazed lingeringly at him. "I apologize for my lateness."

Jack bowed stiffly but said nothing, so Nessa smiled brightly to make up for her husband's reticence and assured her that she need think nothing of it. Returning Nessa's smile rather uncertainly, Mrs. Dempsey moved off into the crowd to make way for the next couple taking their leave.

Less than half an hour later, Mrs. Dempsey departed as well, looking, Nessa thought with secret satisfaction, rather nettled. Jack had not left her own side since the woman's arrival, nor spoken a word to her. The crowd had thinned considerably by now—only a dozen or so couples remained.

"I must make certain the caterer understands what he is to do with the uneaten food," she murmured to Jack when they found themselves briefly alone near the door. "I'll be back in a moment."

Just as she reached the tables, Prudence joined her.

"You were splendid, Nessa," she whispered in a surprisingly conspiratorial tone. "You kept your composure admirably. But the nerve of that woman! How could she be so bold?"

"Mrs. Dempsey, you mean?" Nessa spoke lightly, though it unnerved her to think Prudence should have such precise knowledge of Jack's past indiscretions. "No doubt 'twas a rather desperate bid for Jack's attention. I could almost feel sorry for her."

Prudence stared. "Sorry! For a woman who has enjoyed more of your husband's time than you have these past weeks? That is carrying charity to unprecedented lengths, I must say."

Nessa felt a cold fist squeeze her heart. Though her breath came fast, she ruthlessly schooled her expression into one of only polite interest. "I'm sure you exaggerate, Prudence. Jack has been spending the bulk of his time in Parliament." *Hasn't he?* She prayed her sister would not contradict her.

Nor did she. "Yes, that was an exaggeration. I'm sorry, Nessa." Her words were as much sympathy as apology, though, and did little to soothe Nessa's sudden pain.

Mechanically, she gave the caterer his final instructions, then returned to where the last guests were taking their leave. She said all that was proper, but her mind was in chaos.

Sensitized now by Prudence's words, she thought she detected pity in many of the departing guests' faces. Did all London know more about her husband's doings than she did herself? Always she had despised the willful blindness of libertines' wives, and here she was, as blind as any of them!

"That's the last of them!" exclaimed Jack gleefully as the front door closed behind the final guests. "The house is ours again, and I intend to take full advantage of it. To quote Mrs. Heatherton, 'A triumph, Lady Fox-haven. No doubt about it.'" He swept her an exaggerated bow.

"So everyone has said." She felt not the least bit triumphant, however.

Jack, however, was clearly in high spirits. "Because it is true. Will you join me in a waltz?" Playfully, he held out his arms, though the only music was the tinkle of plates and glasses as they were collected by the servants.

Nessa felt a tightening in her throat. Could he truly act so if what Prudence had implied were true? "I'm sorry, Jack, but I have the most abominable headache. Perhaps another time."

Immediately he was all concern. "Oh, my darling, why did you not say so? I feared you were taking too much upon yourself. I'll take you right up to bed, then come back to supervise the cleanup myself."

The tightening in her throat became a lump. Afraid to speak for fear of loosing the tears that threatened, she merely nodded and allowed him to lead her up the stairs. She maintained a stoic silence while Simmons undressed her, unwilling to betray her emotions and perhaps provoke unwanted confidences from the abigail. Clucking over how tired her mistress must be, Simmons helped her to complete her toilette in short order, then tucked her into bed.

Alone in the darkened room, Nessa finally allowed her tears to flow. Exhaustion soon provided relief, however, and despite her turmoil she fell into a deep, dreamless sleep.

Thin sunlight awakened her, filtering through the partially drawn peach curtains. Stirring, Nessa realized that Jack lay beside her, still soundly asleep. The events of last night came flooding back—both the triumph and the heartache. In the light of morning, however, with a good night's sleep behind her, Nessa felt far less ready to believe the worst—or to let it devastate her even if it proved to be true.

For a moment she smiled down at her husband's slumbering form, marveling at how boyish and innocent he appeared, when she knew he was neither. Moving gingerly so as not to wake him, she slipped out of bed and dressed in a simple gown that did not require Simmons' assistance. Pulling her hair back with a matching ribbon, she softly opened the door and went downstairs for breakfast and uninterrupted thought.

By the time Jack joined her, nearly an hour later, she had come to a decision.

"Prudence tells me you have been spending considerable time with Mrs. Dempsey of late," she informed him before she could change her mind.

Jack paused in the act of taking his seat and glanced about, as though to assure himself that they were alone in the room. "She has been to call already this morning?"

Nessa narrowed her eyes slightly. Was he stalling? "No, she mentioned it last night. Apparently 'tis common knowledge." Prudence had not actually said that, but she did not think she had imagined the pitying glances from their guests as they left.

"Hardly that, I should think!" exclaimed Jack. Then, apparently realizing what he'd said, he muttered an oath. "Nessa, it's not what you think, I promise you."

"How do you know what I think?" she demanded, stung by his near admission. "Until last night, I *thought* you were spending all of those hours on government business."

"I—I was, in a way." He leaned forward to take her hand where it lay on the table, but she snatched it away. "Honestly, Nessa, my time with Miranda—I did not enjoy it, I assure you—was for the purpose of discovering certain information for the Home Office."

"How convenient." Her tone was as biting as she could make it. "And were you successful, or will you require yet more trysts on behalf of the Crown?" She hadn't known she was capable of such sarcasm.

"No, no, it is over, I promise you." He regarded her uncertainly. "You don't believe me."

"Whether I do or not is of little moment, Jack. I have spent all my waking hours for the past three weeks—nay, longer than that, considering our time at Fox Manor—attempting to elevate you to respectability despite your *well-deserved* reputation. I have done my part in our bargain, Jack, but all the while you have been sabotaging my efforts."

He looked uneasy now, as well he should. "What do you intend to do?"

"What I please," she snapped. "I no longer consider myself bound by my promise to play the respectable wife for the sake of a reputation for which you clearly care so little."

Standing, she made a regal exit, leaving him to ponder just what she meant by that.

As it happened, she had no earthly idea herself.

∞ 17 ∞

Jack stared after Nessa, stunned to his bones. Not for several seconds did he realize his mouth had dropped open. Belatedly, he closed it, still staring at the doorway she had just vacated.

This was a hell of a wrinkle.

Just when he'd finally fulfilled his awkward obligation to the Duke of Wellington, when he could finally devote all of his energies to his marriage, this had to happen. He thought he'd made it clear to Miranda that any further relationship was out of the question—but she was unwilling to take the hint, as evidenced by her uninvited appearance last night.

Jack dropped his head into his hands and groaned. He'd made a botch of it, just as he had so many other things in his life. This particular mistake mattered more than any of the others, though, because it affected Nessa—and she mattered greatly.

Raising his head to stare out at the gray February day, he finally admitted to himself what he'd been denying for weeks: He'd fallen in love with his wife. It was a shattering thing to a man who'd built his life on the firm belief that love was a myth, but there it was. Now, what the devil was he to do about it?

The first thing, clearly, was to determine the true extent of the damage. He would go at once to speak with Lady Creamcroft. He'd not thought her the sort to carry tales, but it seemed he'd misjudged her. Once he knew precisely what he was up against, he would face Nessa again—this very day—and have everything out in the open.

Leaving his breakfast untouched, he rose and called for his greatcoat, then strode from the house.

His plans received a setback when he discovered that Lady Creamcroft was not at home. He left his card, with a message that he would return later, and walked back the way he had come, wondering what his next step should be. A vision of Nessa's face last night, pinched and tired, rose before him. Miranda's doing. Well, he could make certain nothing of that sort happened again.

Most mornings, he knew, she could be found shopping on Bond Street, so he directed his steps there. He spotted her carriage almost at once, and headed toward it.

"Why, Jack, what a lovely surprise!" she exclaimed, emerging from a milliner's shop just as he reached her waiting carriage. Then she took a good look at his face. "Is something wrong?"

"You could say so. What possessed you to come to my home last night? I rather doubt my wife invited you."

Miranda tittered, though her expression held a hint of alarm. "I assumed it was a mere oversight. Certainly she welcomed me graciously enough."

"Nessa is always gracious." Jack bit out the words. "Your presence there upset her, however, and I'll not allow that to happen again."

Miranda seemed unmoved by his vehemence. Glancing languidly over his shoulder, she said only, "Let's not stand talking on the street in all of this wind, Jack. Come, we'll sit in my carriage to discuss it."

He glared at her, but she was already moving toward the vehicle, a few yards away. As he hadn't yet received any assurance from her that she would leave Nessa— and him—alone, he had perforce to follow. Careful to seat himself as far away as the confines of the carriage would allow, he faced her again.

"Do you understand me, Miranda? I'll not have you upsetting my wife. What once existed between us is in the past, and will remain there."

She pouted at him. "Then you no longer find me attractive, Jack?"

"Of course you're attractive, but I am no longer attracted to you. I love my wife." There. He'd actually said it aloud. Ironic that Miranda should be the first to hear it.

"Now isn't that sweet!" A sneer abruptly robbed her face of much of its prettiness. "I wonder, however, whether you'll ever get her to believe it? She knows all about us, you know."

"I told her before we married," he snapped. "Nothing

of substance has occurred since, despite whatever gossip her sister has heard."

Miranda now displayed genuine amusement. "Oh, her sister has heard quite an earful, I assure you, Jack. I made certain of that."

A sense of foreboding gripped him. "Do you mean to say you've spoken to Lady Creamcroft yourself? What lies have you told her?"

"Lies? Such an ugly word. Perhaps I might have exaggerated a bit—merely wishful thinking on my part, of course. But combined with the evidence of her own eyes, I likely created a powerful impression—one she no doubt felt compelled to share with her sister, your *beloved* Lady Foxhaven." Her words now dripped venom.

Jack realized he had underestimated the potential fury of a woman scorned. In the past, he'd generally managed to break things off cordially with one paramour before moving on to the next, with one or two notable exceptions. Of course he hadn't had a marriage at stake then.

Or love.

"Do not doubt for a moment that I'll see you ruined—or worse—if my wife suffers due to your machinations," he said icily. "Certain information dropped into certain ears and you could find yourself facing a charge of treason."

She blanched visibly, her eyes wide. "Jack, you wouldn't—that is, I'm sure you'll manage to patch it up. I—I leave for a house party in Surrey in two days' time, in any event." She managed a placating smile. "So there'll be no more machinations from me. I'm sure I've done enough."

Fearing he'd be tempted to do her an injury if he remained a moment longer, Jack slammed out of the carriage. Striding away, he glanced at his watch. Damn! He was due to speak on the Corn Bill under discussion in Parliament in less than an hour. He'd have to call on Lady Creamcroft this afternoon.

Nessa rang the bell of the Creamcroft Townhouse, then bit her lip while she waited for an answer. After what seemed like minutes but were probably only seconds, Clarendon opened the door.

"Pray tell Lady Creamcroft that her sister is here to see her." Nessa spoke more haughtily than she intended, so strictly was she schooling her voice to suppress all emotion.

"Lady Creamcroft has gone shopping," replied the butler just as stiffly, "but is expected back momentarily."

"I'll wait then, if I may." Returning to Foxhaven House would be to risk seeing Jack again—something she wished to avoid until she'd had a chance to talk with Prudence.

She was shown into the drawing room, where she took a seat, picking up a book that lay on a nearby table in an attempt to divert her thoughts. As it was a treatise on morality by Hannah More—one of her father's favorites—the attempt was not entirely successful. Fortunately, Prudence returned home before too many minutes had passed.

Setting aside the book with relief, Nessa rose to greet her. "Thank goodness you are back! I really must speak with you. I hope you don't mind my waiting for you here?"

"Not at all," replied Prudence, removing her bonnet and cloak. Once Clarendon had departed with the garments, she closed the door. Despite her assurance, Nessa thought her sister looked decidedly ill at ease.

As she was herself.

Still, she had to know what she was up against. "You said last night that Jack had been spending time—recently—with Mrs. Dempsey," Nessa said without further preamble. "How did you discover this?"

Prudence sat down opposite her and took Nessa's hands in hers. "Believe me, Nessa, I wish I had not said anything. Lord Foxhaven cares for you, I am certain of it. Perhaps—"

"How did you find out?" Nessa demanded, disengaging her hands.

Fluttering her own hands helplessly, Prudence sat back in her chair. "I saw them together myself once—no, twice. And Lady Mountheath made a point of telling me that they were seen at Bellamy's coffeehouse a few days since."

Nessa breathed a little easier. Three public meetings scarcely constituted a torrid affair.

Her relief must have shown on her face, for Prudence said, "I'm . . . afraid that is not all."

"What else?"

Now Prudence looked acutely uncomfortable,

actually fidgeting in her chair. She avoided Nessa's eye as she answered. "I . . . I actually spoke with Mrs. Dempsey myself—or rather, she spoke to me. She made it . . . quite clear that she and Lord Foxhaven were . . . involved."

"That trollop!" Nessa's anger, banked since leaving Jack at the breakfast table, suddenly flared to life. "She knew, of course, that if she told you I would come to hear of it. 'Twas no doubt her intent."

Clearly this had not occurred to Prudence. "Oh! But could any woman truly be so shameless . . . ? She seemed to let the information drop by chance, but I suppose . . . "

Nessa snorted in a most unladylike manner. "I'll wager she did. And knew precisely what she was doing. But," she added, "she could never have done so had Jack not given her the opportunity. Even if she exaggerated the matter, he is hardly blameless." A tiny voice reminded her of his explanation this morning, but she silenced it, in no mood for forgiveness.

"Nessa, what do you intend to do?" asked Prudence worriedly. "You knew of Lord Foxhaven's reputation before you married him."

"And you'd be perfectly justified in saying 'I told you so' at this juncture," Nessa admitted. "But that scarcely helps now. I have made my bed. Now I must determine in what position I intend to lie in it."

Prudence gave an odd little gasp, then covered her mouth. To Nessa's surprise, her sister appeared to be stifling laughter!

"I'm sorry, Nessa, truly I am," she sputtered in response to Nessa's thunderstruck expression. "But the most wicked idea has just occurred to me."

If anything, the thought of Prudence entertaining a wicked idea shocked Nessa even further. She felt her eyebrows arching ceilingward. "Indeed? Pray share it, if you can." Already, though, her sister's uncharacteristic mirth had infected her and she felt a vague lightening of her heart.

"If what you suggest is true, and Mrs. Dempsey is merely attempting to win Lord Foxhaven's affections—and he cares far more for you, I am certain of it—then perhaps you could—" She broke off, suddenly flushing scarlet. "That is to say," she continued, "as his wife, you have more opportunity than she to—"

"Seduce him?" Nessa finished, finally understanding what her sister was driving at.

Prudence turned an even brighter red and again covered her mouth at such plain speaking—but she nodded.

"Why Prudence, I am astonished!" But Nessa spoke playfully now, as she toyed with the possibility.

Recovering herself somewhat, Prudence leaned forward earnestly, though her color was still high. "I do hope you will try, Nessa. I was not going to mention this, but Amanda Leverton claims to have seen them together less than an hour ago, on Bond Street. She made a point of telling me that she saw him leaving her carriage."

Nessa's levity abruptly disappeared. "He joined her

in her carriage? This very morning?" He must have gone straight to her upon leaving the house. So much for his promises!

"Miss Leverton wished me to . . . congratulate you on taking her advice after all. It would appear she heard about your reception of Mrs. Dempsey last night."

"Her advice!" Nessa seethed. "That is the last thing I wish to follow. No, I believe I shall take yours, instead." She managed a shaky smile. "Truly, Prudence, I believe your suggestion has merit—shocked as I was to hear *you* of all people propose it! Dare I hope this means you have begun to find more of pleasure than duty in your own marriage bed?"

Her sister's complexion had nearly returned to its normal color, but at that it flamed again. "Really, Nessa! 'Tis not my marriage under discussion just now. It is perfectly satisfactory."

Despite her own troubles, Nessa could not suppress a grin at her sister's expression. It would seem she had hit the mark indeed! "I'm pleased to hear it. And I thank you for your advice. Scandalous or not, I believe it may be just the thing. After all, what choice do I have?"

What choice indeed? Short of abandoning her marriage vows entirely or living in celibacy—which would surely punish her more than it would Jack—what else could she do?

She stood in sudden decision. "You are the best of sisters, Prudence. Your idea may well be the saving of my marriage—and my sanity."

"Then I will have repaid my debt to you," Prudence

replied. Though her cheeks were still bright, she smiled as she met Nessa's eyes—a smile that admitted to the new pleasures she'd discovered in her husband's arms.

Glad that she'd been instrumental in improving her sister's marriage, Nessa gave her a fervent hug, then took her leave, ready to do battle on behalf of her own.

Two hours later, Jack was shown into the room his wife had so recently quitted.

"How pleasant to see you, Lord Foxhaven," Lady Creamcroft greeted him, looking up calmly from her needlework. "I'm sure if Nessa had known you planned to call here this afternoon, she would have waited."

Jack paused midway through his bow. "She was here? Today?" So much for his hopes of explaining Miranda's duplicity to Lady Creamcroft before she could pass along yet more damaging tales.

His hostess nodded. "She came seeking sisterly advice. I fear you have given her some cause for distress, my lord."

"I have," he admitted cautiously, taking a seat. "But not as much cause as you might think."

"Oh?" she asked mildly.

"I, er, learned today that you may have been told . . . things . . . which were not entirely true. I assure you, Lady Creamcroft, that I have not been unfaithful to Nessa, either in thought or deed." There. Now he'd counteracted whatever lies Miranda had told her.

But Lady Creamcroft appeared not at all surprised. "I'm pleased to hear it, of course, though I am not the one you need to tell. Your judgment seems questionable in this, as in other matters, my lord." At his frown, she continued. "Joining another woman in her private carriage is scarcely the sort of thing designed to alleviate a wife's suspicions."

Jack felt his eyes fairly start from his head. "Good God!" he exclaimed, then quickly added, "I beg your pardon, my lady. But I begin to believe a network of spies is at work to make my every move public in short order."

"Bond Street is scarcely a private venue, my lord, and gossip travels quickly in London, as you are no doubt aware."

"And now Nessa knows about that, as well," he said with a groan. "Pray believe me, Lady Creamcroft, it was not at all what it appeared. I will not be seeing Mrs. Dempsey, publicly or privately, in future. I have made certain of that."

She lifted her shoulders slightly. "Again, I am not the one who needs to hear this. I recommend you tell your wife."

Jack rose. "I'll do that—immediately. Thank you, my lady. I give you good day."

Ten minutes later he entered Foxhaven House, having spent the intervening walk rehearsing what he hoped was a suitably groveling speech. Soon this whole ugly misunderstanding would be behind them, and he and Nessa could resume where they had left off two days since.

"Daniels, is Lady Foxhaven at home?" he asked the

new butler as he relinquished his top hat and greatcoat. On being assured that she was, he headed up the stairs, only to be greeted by a vision as he turned at the first landing.

Nessa, dressed in a breathtakingly low-cut sapphire gown, was just descending from the second story. Her chestnut hair was piled high and studded with sparkling gems. A necklace of diamonds and sapphires, a Fox-haven heirloom, encircled her throat, its large central jewel suspended between her breasts, emphasizing her cleavage. Jack swallowed, his body responding instantly to the alluring picture she presented.

"Why Jack, are you not dressed yet?" she asked in apparent surprise while he groped for the opening words of his speech. "We are due at the Beckhavens' in an hour."

"We . . . we are?" With an effort, he wrenched his eyes away from her nearly-exposed bosom to focus upon her face. She wore an enigmatic half-smile.

"Yes, indeed. They have invited us to a dinner party preceding their musicale. From there, we are engaged to accompany Lord and Lady Norville to a reception at the Russian embassy. What a mercy we did not sched-ule our soirée for this evening!"

Jack blinked. Nessa was acting as though their con-versation that morning had never taken place. "I . . . Yes. I suppose it is. I'll, um, go up and change directly."

"I shall await you in the parlor. I've ordered the car-riage in forty-five minutes' time." With a stunning smile, she continued past him down the stairs, leaving a tantalizing whiff of exotic perfume in her wake.

He watched after her for a moment before dazedly proceeding upstairs to his bedchamber. Parker awaited him there, with his evening clothes already laid out.

"Will this be acceptable, my lord?" he asked, indicating the dark blue tailed coat, matching waistcoat, and buff breeches.

"Fine, Parker, fine," replied Jack absently. "Did you see Lady Foxhaven?" It wasn't normally the thing to discuss one's wife with one's valet, but just now he felt the need of a clearer head to supplement his own.

"Indeed, my lord. Most striking. I chose this coat to complement her gown. You'll be a perfect match."

Jack regarded his valet closely. "Do you think so?"

Parker gave one of his cryptic smiles. "A well-matched pair requires equal exertion from both. Practice and a willingness to accommodate will generally assure a smooth pace."

It was as enigmatic as any of his valet's speeches, but Jack knew better than to request an explanation.

After taking even more care than usual over Jack's cravat, his valet finally pronounced him fit to leave the room. Hurrying downstairs, Jack glanced at his pocket watch. He would have only a few minutes to speak with Nessa before the carriage arrived at the door. He'd best make those minutes count.

"My dear . . . " he began as he entered the parlor, but Nessa did not give him an opportunity to continue.

"Ah, there you are, Jack. Tell me, do you think I made

the right decision with these curtains? I'd thought the blue and cream would complement the rest of the room, but now I begin to believe the pattern is too busy."

He glanced impatiently at the curtains in question. "They look fine, Nessa. The whole house looks fine. You did a splendid job with it, as dozens of people informed you last night. What I'd hoped to talk about—"

"Why, thank you, Jack!" she cooed, smiling most bewitchingly as she came toward him. "I meant to tell you how much I appreciated your praise of me to our guests, but I . . . was a bit distracted and forgot to do so."

Was she trying to tell him all was forgiven? He scarcely dared to hope so. She seemed to be playing some role, the purpose of which he hadn't yet divined.

"I said nothing that wasn't true," he said, trying to imbue his words with additional meaning. "You have accomplished miracles in short order—on several fronts." Certainly, no other woman had ever managed to secure his love—or even his inward admission that such a thing existed.

For a moment, her glitteringly seductive façade seemed to slip, revealing the Nessa he knew. "Really, Jack?" Her eyes probed his, seeking . . .

"Milord, milady, the carriage," intoned Daniels from the open doorway.

At once, Nessa whirled away from him. "Precisely on time. We mustn't keep the horses standing. Let us go, my lord."

A footman appeared with their cloaks, and then accompanied them to the coach to open the door and lower the steps. Now he would have his chance to talk to her, Jack thought, joining Nessa within.

"Nessa, I wish to apologize," he said the moment the door closed behind him, before she could introduce any other extraneous topic. "I subjected you to gossip, however unintentionally, and to distress. I promise not to let it happen again."

She stared out of the carriage window for so long that he began to wonder if she had heard him. Finally she turned, but in the dimness he could not read her expression. "I appreciate your concern, Jack, but pray do not make promises you cannot keep."

"But I——"

She put up a hand to silence him. "I knew of your reputation when I married you, Jack. In fact, it was one of the things that attracted me in the first place, as I've said before. When you told me that all debauchery was behind you, my first reaction was one of disappointment rather than relief. So it was quite absurd of me to become angry upon hearing evidence to the contrary. In fact, I should have been delighted."

"Delighted?" Far from following her reasoning, Jack felt completely out of his depth.

She nodded. "My first marriage was deadly dull, not to mention terribly restricting. In agreeing to marry you, I consoled myself that an alliance with a rake—even a former rake—was bound to be more entertaining, allowing me the freedom to experience a side of life I had hitherto only dreamed of."

The vague uneasiness that had begun when Nessa

first greeted him upon the stairs earlier crystallized into foreboding.

"Imagine my dismay," she continued airily, "when I discovered you were serious about becoming thoroughly respectable—for your grandfather's sake—only days before our wedding. 'Twas nearly enough to make me cry off. But I'd become rather fond of you by then, so I chose to go through with it, contenting myself with our nightly : . . lessons."

"Contenting yourself?" he fairly exploded. "Don't try to tell me you haven't found our lovemaking as enjoyable as I have, for I'll not believe it." What on earth was he saying? He'd never had to defend himself in this manner to a woman before. Far from it!

She laid a gloved hand on his cheek. "Oh, you're *very* good in bed, Jack. Thoroughly skilled. I've enjoyed your instruction enormously."

"Honored to be of service, of course," he said icily, not at all mollified. What had gotten into her?

"Still, I'll admit that playing the proper little wife all the rest of the time has been wearying—just the sort of thing I'd longed to escape. And now, I shall do just that. Really, Jack, I should be thanking you rather than hearing your apologies."

His foreboding deepened to dread. "What do you mean?"

"Ah, here we are!" she exclaimed breezily, peering out of the window as the carriage pulled to a halt. She picked up her reticule. "Come, Jack, we have a full evening ahead of us."

❧ *18* ❧

"Hazel! You look lovely tonight," Nessa greeted Mrs. Beckhaven as she and Jack entered the moderately sized Townhouse. "I hope our last-moment acceptance of your invitation did not discommode you."

In fact, Nessa had initially declined this invitation, as they were already attending the embassy reception. Besides, the Beckhavens did not move in the best circles and therefore could not advance her goal of elevating the Foxhaven name. Now, however, her goal had changed.

"Not at all, not at all! I'm so pleased that you could come after all, Lady Foxhaven," replied her hostess, beaming all over her good-natured face.

"Please, call me Nessa. I'm certain we shall become great friends."

Hazel Beckhaven's eyes widened at this honor, sure to elevate her social standing. "That would be lovely . . . Nessa."

Jack bowed over her hand then, and they were ushered in for introductions to the rest of the company. It was a friendly, lively gathering, perfect for Nessa's purposes.

"Why, Sir Lawrence! I have not seen you for an age," she greeted one of her former admirers.

As handsome and eager as ever, the young gentleman stepped forward to kiss her hand. "You are more lovely than ever, my lady. I was never more devastated than when I learned that Lord Foxhaven had taken you from us. Now at least I may worship from afar."

"At least that," she said playfully, flirting her fan, before turning to greet another slight acquaintance. She carefully avoided looking in Jack's direction, for fear her resolve might waver. She was determined to enjoy herself this evening.

And every other evening to come.

While she planned to follow the spirit of Prudence's advice to win back her husband, she fully intended to have a lovely time doing it——and give him back a bit of his own medicine into the bargain. After all, she'd just begun to kick up her heels a bit when Jack had offered for her, so it stood to reason that he found that side of her——the scandalous side she'd always denied——attractive.

"Might I lead you in to dinner, my lady?" asked young Sir Lawrence at her elbow. Spotting Jack out of the corner of her eye conversing with Mr. Beckhaven and the Norvilles, Nessa consented.

Mrs. Beckhaven had dispersed her guests about the table so that no gentleman sat with his wife, encouraging a greater variety of conversation. Nessa found herself with Lord Norville on her left and Mr. Pottinger, another erstwhile admirer, on her right. Sir Lawrence was directly across from her, and Jack two places to his left. Quite satisfactory.

"I cannot tell you how delighted I am to see you in Town again, my lady," Mr. Pottinger said as the soup was served. "I quite feared Lord Foxhaven meant to keep you tucked away in the country, depriving us of your sparkling presence."

Nessa gave him what she hoped was a sparkling smile. "I should never have allowed that, I assure you, Mr. Pottinger. I'm far too fond of Town life."

He tilted his graying head in Jack's direction. "Ah, but men of your husband's—ahem—stamp are so well versed in the temptations London holds that they are inclined to overprotect their wives when they eventually marry—particularly when the wife is as lovely as yourself."

"You are too kind, sir," she murmured. "I know from experience, however, that upstanding gentlemen are also prone to immure their wives in the country, to keep them safe from the pleasures of London."

He responded with a loud, braying laugh, as though she had just imparted some clever witticism rather than the simple truth, and she abruptly remembered why she had not encouraged Mr. Pottinger last fall. Still she smiled, since Jack was watching them from just down the table.

When the fish was served, she turned her attention to Lord Norville. He was an intelligent man of about

Jack's age, and a welcome relief from Mr. Pottinger's vapid attempts at flirtation. She quietly asked him a few questions about the current issues concerning Parliament, receiving sensible answers that helped her to understand what Jack had been doing there of late.

She spent the meat course exchanging demurely flirtatious looks with Sir Lawrence across the table. That young man seemed in a fair way to becoming infatuated with her, which she might be able to use to her advantage.

With the fowl and sweetmeats she again had to listen politely to Mr. Pottinger's extravagant compliments, but she had the satisfaction of knowing that Jack was watching closely and doubtless trying to hear as much as possible.

They adjourned to the drawing room just as the other guests began to arrive for the musicale. Sir Lawrence made a beeline to Nessa's side, but Jack was quicker.

"I've a mind to sit with my wife during the performance, if you don't mind," he said, taking her arm. His voice was pleasant, but Nessa detected a steely glint in his eye.

Sir Lawrence, clearly flustered, took himself off. "Certainly, certainly. Don't hesitate to call upon me, my lady, should you need me at any time."

Nessa smiled after her young gallant, but Jack growled, "Don't encourage the lad. He'll develop a *grande passion* for you, and I'd be obliged to put a bullet through him at twelve paces."

"My lord!" exclaimed Nessa, both astonished and amused. "Surely you cannot consider poor Sir Lawrence any sort of threat?"

Jack merely snorted.

Her plan was proceeding quite nicely.

There was no further opportunity for private conversation until they were back in their carriage some two hours later, en route to the Russian embassy.

"It must be nearly midnight," complained Jack with a yawn, leaning back against the squabs. "Must we really put in an appearance at this thing?"

Nessa was feeling a bit tired herself, but immediately sat up straighter. "Why, is this the Jack Ashecroft I heard so much about? The man who diced and drank till dawn every night of the week? I hope married life has not taken all the fire out of you, my lord."

At that, Jack seized her arm and pulled her against him. "I'll show you fire, you little vixen!" He lowered his mouth to hers.

For a moment she yielded, the familiar heat flaming up within her at his touch. Then, recalling her plan, she pulled away. "Now, Jack, we don't want to appear at the reception disheveled. People might talk."

"I thought you didn't care about that anymore." When she didn't reply, he continued, more urgently. "Nessa, you must believe that Miranda Dempsey was nothing to me. She is leaving London anyway, and I'll not see her again, even in the most innocent way, when she returns. Pray cease whatever game you are playing at and let us return to the way we were before."

Nessa gave him a long look. "And there are no others waiting to take her place while she is gone?"

"None, I promise you." His earnestness almost made her yield—but then she thought of what she would miss if she did so.

"Good," she said. Turning to look out of the window, she considered her plans. Though she suspected now that Jack had not truly been unfaithful, she still wished to teach him a lesson—and to enjoy herself while doing so.

With no competitors to worry about, she could afford to play the untouchable coquette for a week or so, spurring his desire for her to a fever pitch. Then she could finally, deliciously, give in. It would be just the tonic their marriage needed.

Dared she hope it might even prompt a declaration of love?

Jack made an impatient movement. "So, may I direct the coachman to take us home?"

She turned to him in mock astonishment. "Of course not! We agreed to accompany the Norvilles, remember? That is their carriage just ahead of us. Besides, I wish to make the acquaintance of the Countess Lieven. I dare not risk offending one of the patronesses of Almack's by failing to honor an invitation I've already accepted."

Nessa had scandalized Simmons with her choice of gown tonight, one she had bought when her mourning first ended but which she had never had the courage to wear. Remembering what the countess had worn to the theater on a prior occasion, however, she doubted their hostess would be shocked. And certainly it had produced the desired effect in other quarters. She slanted a look at Jack through her eyelashes and smiled.

A few moments later they arrived at the reception and Nessa stepped once more into the role she had assumed for the evening. Once through the receiving line, she glanced about the room and spotted Mr. Galloway standing near a curtained archway. He looked up and saw her at the same moment, his eyes widening with undisguised admiration. He started forward, but then paused with a frown as Jack placed a hand on her arm.

"Shall I fetch you something to drink, my dear?" Clearly, he had not noticed the admiring gallant—yet.

She nodded. The moment Jack left her side, Mr. Galloway resumed his approach. "You have returned to grace London with your presence, my lady! Suddenly the dull month of February takes on a new glow."

Nessa could not take him seriously, of course, but his flattery was pleasant nonetheless. "You always know just what to say to a lady, Mr. Galloway. 'Tis pleasant to see you again, as well."

He moved closer, after a quick glance around. "Should you ever grow tired of domestic life, I'd be more than willing to show you some alternatives," he said suggestively. "In fact—" He broke off then, hastily stepping back.

Nessa was not surprised to hear Jack's voice at her elbow. "Give you good evening, Galloway. Your lemonade, my dear. I see you are renewing yet more old acquaintances."

Mr. Galloway must have heard the edge in Jack's voice, for he bowed most properly, murmured something incoherent about paying his respects, and decamped.

"Skittish thing, isn't he?" Jack commented. "If you're trying to make me jealous, my dear, you'll have to choose gallants with more backbone."

"He approached me, not I him," Nessa pointed out, refusing to let him nettle her. "Nor did I give him any particular encouragement." Not that it would have done much good. Still, it was yet one more incident to keep Jack on his toes.

Indeed, he remained close by her side for the remainder of the evening. They chatted with the Norvilles, who introduced them to various people they had not yet met—Jack because he had not mixed with the upper crust until recently, Nessa because she'd spent so little time in London.

As soon as they could do so without giving offense, Jack suggested they leave. This time, Nessa offered no resistance. Playing the sparkling, flirtatious woman of the world took more energy than she had expected. Tiring or no, however, it had been a most enjoyable evening—the most enjoyable part being Jack's response to her changed demeanor.

Now, however, would come the real test, she realized as they drove back to Foxhaven House. What excuse would she use to keep Jack from her bed? After chiding him earlier for being tired, she could hardly claim fatigue, and he must know her monthly courses were not due for some time yet. Besides, she had discovered she did not much care for sleeping alone.

Fortunately for her plan, though not for her peace of mind, Jack himself gave her the excuse she needed. "I've some correspondence to attend to in the library, if I can stay awake long enough," he informed her as they entered the house. "I'll join you upstairs shortly."

Suddenly wondering whether her plan was as clever as she'd thought, Nessa headed up to her bedchamber alone.

Jack poured himself a small measure of brandy and propped his feet up on the library desk. His correspondence was fictitious—or, at least, there was none he needed attend to tonight. What he needed to do was think, away from Nessa's intoxicating influence.

What was she up to? She hadn't actually accepted his apology, and clearly still intended to make him pay for the distress he'd caused her. Fair enough, he supposed. But he'd never been one to allow another to control his actions or emotions, and he wasn't about to start now—no matter what he felt for his wife.

Not that he'd admitted those feelings to her yet— nor would he, while she was playing at this game of hers. Certain words she'd said earlier rankled still. "Contented herself," indeed! And "rather fond of him." No, now was not the time to bare his heart to her. That would only give her more ammunition for whatever campaign she was launching to put him in his place.

In fact, he'd do best to keep his distance until he'd figured out her scheme. She had an uncanny ability to cloud his thoughts—particularly in bed. Nor did he believe she'd wish to go long without further "instruction," as she'd shown herself such an apt and eager pupil. He smiled into the crackling fire.

Yes, he'd wait until she asked him to her bed again. It wouldn't be long, he was certain.

At least, he hoped it would not.

Over the next few days, however, Jack found it more difficult than he'd anticipated to adhere to his resolve. Nessa persisted in dressing provocatively, though never quite crossing the line into vulgarity. She found some engagement or other for them to attend every single evening, whether it was a card party or simply accompanying others to the theater.

Those evenings were torture, for Nessa was always at her most bewitching—but directing her scintillating smiles and conversation more often toward others than to him. He'd reached the point where even an oblique invitation to join her in bed would have been accepted like a shot—but she continued to behave coyly toward him. More coyly than she appeared to behave toward others, in fact.

More than once he regretted his promise to make no attempts to control her behavior, now that it seemed in dire need of control. Still, he would not break that promise. In fact, it occurred to him that this whole campaign of hers might be an elaborate test of that very promise.

During the day, at least, he was able to find distraction in the House of Lords, where controversy surrounding the impending Corn Bill was mounting. One day when the weather was unexpectedly fine, however, he'd taken his horse instead of the carriage. Riding home by way of Hyde Park Corner, he saw a familiar profile in a high-perch phaeton entering the Park just ahead of him.

Without thinking, he spurred his mount forward. "I bid you good afternoon, my lady. I'd thought to suggest a drive myself when I reached home, but I see you are already engaged."

Nessa and Sir Lawrence, for it was he driving the phaeton, turned with varying degrees of surprise and alarm.

"Why hello, Jack," his wife greeted him with one of her bright smiles. "The sunshine was so lovely that I couldn't bear to refuse when Sir Lawrence invited me out. I'd no idea you'd quit your legislative duties so early."

"Obviously." Jack couldn't help glowering a bit, if only to enjoy the effect upon Sir Lawrence. To his surprise, however, the young man met his eye squarely, if nervously.

"It seemed most unfair for Lady Foxhaven to be trapped indoors on such a rare winter's afternoon," he declared, as though defying Jack to contradict him.

Nessa chimed in, "Yes, now that the redecorating is completed, I find time hangs rather heavily on my hands on those days when I have few callers."

"Indeed." Why, Jack wondered, did he seem unable

to utter more than a single word at a time? Neither his wife nor her young gallant showed signs of guilt, so he'd not give Nessa the satisfaction of displaying any jealousy, however sharply its tooth might bite him.

His taciturnity had an effect upon Sir Lawrence, however. "We were just driving into the Park, my lord," the stripling all but babbled. "I don't suppose you'd care to accompany us?"

"Thank you. I believe I would." Turning his horse, he kept pace alongside them. "I wish you'd informed me, my dear, that you've begun to find Town life boring," he said languidly. "There are several remedies I might suggest."

He was rewarded by a stare from Nessa and a glare from Sir Lawrence. The latter spoke first. "Lady Foxhaven don't need any more work piled upon her slender shoulders, my lord. Ain't she done enough already, redoing *your* house from cellar to attic?"

Jack raised his brows. "Have I overworked you, my lady? I must apologize, in that case."

"Of course not, my lord," she responded with a distinct twinkle in her eye, reminding him of the Nessa he knew. "I quite enjoyed the task."

"What else could she say?" muttered Sir Lawrence, almost but not quite under his breath.

Jack kept his eyes on Nessa's. "The truth, I hope. Always."

She colored slightly and glanced away. "Look! Is that an early crocus?" she asked brightly, pointing off to the side.

Obligingly riding over to investigate, Jack reported that it was. "It would appear that spring is nearly upon us—nearly, but not quite. The sun has gone in, and the breeze grows chill. I suggest we head for home."

The others agreed—Sir Lawrence reluctantly—and they turned onto the path leading back to the Park gates. Upon reaching Foxhaven House a few minutes later, Jack quickly dismounted, handing his horse over to the waiting groom.

"No need for you to climb down, Sir Lawrence. I can assist my wife to the ground."

Though he pouted a bit, the young gentleman remained where he was while Nessa exited the carriage into Jack's waiting arms. "I'll see you at the Duke of Clarence's ball tonight, will I not, my lady?" he inquired, looking after her more longingly than he had any right, in Jack's opinion.

"Of course," she responded lightly. "I'll—we'll be there. Thank you for the drive, Sir Lawrence."

With a tip of his hat and a final lowering glance at Lord Foxhaven, he shook the reins and departed.

Jack chuckled, forcing down his irritation. At Nessa's indignantly inquiring glance, he sobered a bit. "You're running a risk with that one, madam wife. He's in a fair way to becoming besotted enough to challenge me over some imagined slight. You don't want his blood on your head, I presume."

"You said that once before, and it's as absurd now as it was then. Sir Lawrence is merely a friend. Besides," she continued with a bewitching smile, "what makes you so certain you would best him in a duel? Perhaps he's a crack shot."

"Perhaps. Do you really wish to find out?"

She paled slightly at his seriousness. "No, of course not. 'Tis absurd, as I said. The matter will not arise."

"Good." The quick glance she shot him showed she recognized the parallel to an earlier conversation. Jack smiled to himself as she turned away to precede him into the house. He was in control again, which was where he preferred to be.

Half an hour into the royal duke's ball, however, he realized he had congratulated himself too soon. He'd had his first misgivings when Nessa had emerged from her chamber, clad in that scandalous gown of pale peach gossamer satin. When she moved, it gave a disturbing impression of near-nudity under the transparent gauze overdress. Judging by the way other men's eyes followed her, Jack was not the only one to notice.

In the carriage, he'd noticed she wore a new scent, subtle but intoxicating. She sat just close enough to tempt him without quite inviting his touch. Did she have any idea how maddening she was? He rather suspected she did.

"What an amazing assemblage," she commented now from his side. "And to think I was proud of the attendance at *our* little soirée."

Her eyes were wide, reminding him forcibly of the innocent Nessa he'd met last autumn. That memory, combined with her seductively sophisticated appearance now, produced in him an almost overwhelming surge of desire. Clinging to the remnants of his hard-won control, he nodded.

"It's to be expected when one of the royals throws a ball, it happens so seldom. In no way does it diminish your own triumph."

She smiled up at him, but something of his desire must have shown, for she quickly became coquettish again. "I trust I'll do you credit tonight, as well. Surely having my dance card already full can be construed as another sort of triumph?"

"I am astonished we were not trampled to death in the stampede when we arrived," he said dryly. "You did save me a waltz or two, did you not?"

"Three, in fact, to include the supper dance. You *are* my husband, after all." She dimpled up at him until he didn't know whether to shake her or kiss her breathless.

"I'd nearly forgotten," he teased, then decided abruptly that he'd gone far too long without certain husbandly rights. His resolve to stay out of her bed suddenly seemed absurd. She was his wife, damn it. Tonight would see the end of this silly estrangement, he was determined.

The dancing started then, opening with the traditional minuet and followed by a waltz. Nessa danced both with him, and her airy grace wrought his frustrated desire to a fever pitch before he was forced to relinquish her to another partner.

Watching her go down the room on the arm of Mr. Pottinger, he redoubled his resolve. Before he slept tonight, Nessa would be totally his again!

Nessa left Jack's arms reluctantly. This standoffish role was becoming more and more difficult, she thought as she allowed Mr. Pottinger to lead her into the country dance forming next. All she really wanted to do was go home with Jack and resume those "lessons," which had been in recess for far too long.

"You are beyond stunning tonight, my lady," declared Mr. Pottinger in his affected lisp as they took their places in the dance. "Every other woman here is cast completely in the shade." His gaze swept over her admiringly and she had to force herself not to flinch.

Again.

Not for the first time, she regretted her choice of attire. Somehow, this gown had not appeared nearly so scandalous when she'd had it fitted in the modiste's shop a few days ago. She'd had her first misgivings when her looking-glass confirmed Simmons' shocked exclamations, but had decided it was just the thing to break through this odd reserve Jack had erected against her of late.

What the deuce was wrong with the man? The more outrageously she flirted with him or tried to invoke his jealousy against others, the cooler and more controlled he seemed to grow. This gown had been a last-ditch effort to incite his desire—and it seemed to be working. Unfortunately, every other man present appeared similarly affected, a consequence she foolishly hadn't considered.

Mechanically, she went through the intricate figures of the dance, her mind still occupied with her husband. Her scheme to simultaneously punish him and enjoy herself had been less than successful. Oh, flirting and feeling desired by numerous men had its appeal, but as the novelty waned, the appeal grew less and less. Tonight, she had to fight the urge to hide herself from leering eyes. Perhaps, just perhaps, she had gone too far.

The sight of her sister's face as the dance concluded confirmed her fear.

"Nessa!" Prudence exclaimed in a strangled whisper the moment Mr. Pottinger took his leave of her. "What can you be thinking?"

Philip, Nessa noticed, was discreetly averting his eyes. She fought down a blush. "I'm merely taking your advice, Prudence."

Her sister flushed to the roots of her pale brown hair. "I meant for you to carry it out in *private*, Nessa! Not for all the world to witness! How——"

But then Sir Lawrence appeared to claim Nessa for the next dance, and Prudence had perforce to contain herself——though her shocked eyes still spoke volumes. Lifting her chin defiantly, Nessa accompanied Sir Lawrence to the floor. Even if Prudence were right——as a niggling voice told her she was——she would carry off this evening with aplomb.

Sir Lawrence appeared to be struck completely

speechless, which Nessa thought was just as well. She was sick of fulsome, lust-barbed compliments tonight. The hours she must still endure stretched endlessly ahead. Perhaps a fictitious headache . . .

"You look pale, my lady." Sir Lawrence finally found his voice. "Perhaps we should sit out this dance until you feel recovered."

The thought of escaping all of the eyes—both lecherous and condemning—appealed mightily. "Yes, let's," she said eagerly. "Somewhere . . . out of the way."

"I know just the spot." Taking her hand, he led her between the dancers to the opposite side of the enormous room, then through a curtained alcove. A dimly lit hallway opened onto at least a dozen rooms, most with doors ajar. The sounds of low conversation and laughter came from more than one of them.

He did not lead her into any of the rooms, however, but past them, through another archway and down a half-flight of stairs, then around a corner. When he finally stopped, they were in a sort of miniature conservatory filled with greenery and blooming hothouse flowers. The room would have been dazzlingly bright during the day, as half the ceiling and all of one wall were of glass. Now it was lit by at least a dozen hissing gas lamps.

Nessa looked about at the fairyland surroundings in surprise and more than a little misgiving. "Sir Lawrence, I don't believe—"

Before she could finish, however, he released her hand and clutched her to him, pressing his mouth against hers. For a moment she froze in complete shock, then began to struggle. He released her at once, and she backed away from him, drawing the back of her hand across her mouth. "Are you mad? What can you be thinking?"

She turned to go, but he blocked her way, going down upon one knee in the doorway. "My lady— Nessa—pray forgive me. I was overcome by your beauty, by your sparkling wit, by . . . everything about you."

Frowning, she stepped to the side, attempting to go around him. Yes, she had definitely been an idiot to wear this gown! "Very well," she said severely, "just never let it happen again. I'm going back to the ballroom now." Jack had been right, it seemed. "My husband—"

"Does not deserve you," interrupted Sir Lawrence, his handsome face eloquent with feeling. "'Tis a violation of all that is right that a woman like you should be bound to such a reprobate instead of worshipped as you deserve. As I will worship you."

Worse and worse! She *had* to escape before Jack came seeking her, or she really would have this foolish boy's blood on her head. "Sir Lawrence, I'm very flattered, of course, but—"

Again he interrupted her. She was beginning to find that irritating. "Come away with me, now, tonight! We can be in Dover by morning, in France tomorrow. Once in Paris, no one will find us. I'll shower you with—"

"No, you will not!" she interrupted him in turn. "Stop this at once. I am a married woman, and fully intend to remain so. If I have raised any expectations I am truly sorry, but I cannot go to Paris or anywhere else with you. Now let me go!"

"I recommend you do as the lady asks," drawled Jack's voice from the hallway. "Unless, of course, you'd care to answer to me?"

19

Enraged as he was on discovering his wife in a tryst with another man, Jack rather enjoyed the effect his words had on the pair before him. Nessa gasped, a hand flying to her throat and her eyes widening with horror. Sir Lawrence, still on his knees, nearly fell on his face as he attempted to turn and rise simultaneously.

"Jack!" Nessa squeaked. "How did you—?"

Sir Lawrence regained his balance and planted himself directly in front of her, facing him. "Ungallant of you to spy on your wife, my lord," he sputtered. "And it'll do you no good. I mean to take her—"

At that point, Jack's precarious hold on his temper snapped. Almost without his volition, his fist shot out to connect squarely with the young man's nose. Sir Lawrence fell heavily onto his posterior, his mouth open in amazement and pain. He groped for a handkerchief to staunch the blood suddenly spurting from his nose and struggled back to his feet.

"I think not," said Jack coldly before the other man could act or speak. "You're welcome to name your seconds, of course, but if I were you, I'd not want it generally known that I was knocked down in my pursuit of another man's wife. I suggest you occupy yourself elsewhere."

Sir Lawrence glowered for a moment, though the effect was rather spoiled by the bloody handkerchief he held to his face. As Jack held his eye with the steely glare that had intimidated bolder men than he, Sir Lawrence's defiance wavered, then crumbled. With one apologetic glance at Nessa, he fled the conservatory.

Jack now turned to his wife, who still stood in shock, both hands covering her mouth. "Let us hope I adequately discouraged him from calling me out. I trust your modesty will not be outraged if I fail to challenge him on your behalf?"

Wide-eyed, she shook her head. "Please . . . please do not." Her voice was barely above a whisper. "I never thought—that is, I had no idea—"

"What effect you have on men?" he asked, moving closer to her. "Oh, I think you had a very good idea, my dear. Why else would you have worn this dress, so obviously designed to elicit desire?"

The horror faded from her eyes and she regarded him candidly. "I only meant to elicit it in yourself, my lord, not in every man present. I seem to have achieved quite the opposite effect, however."

He took another step toward her, so that they were nearly touching. "Opposite? Hardly that." Her perfume surrounded him, intoxicating his senses. "In fact, I should say you have succeeded rather too well."

"I have?" she breathed, swaying toward him.

By way of answer, he gathered her into his arms and lowered his lips to hers. This time she did not resist, but responded with a fire rivaling his own. Her arms twined about his neck, pulling him closer until his body molded to hers, their tongues urgently stroking each other. Jack groaned, deep in his throat. His nether garments suddenly felt far too tight.

"Oh, Jack, I've wanted you so," she gasped. "Why did you not come?"

"You never asked," he murmured, tracing his lips along her jawline to the sensitive spot below her ear.

She shuddered slightly. "I'm asking now," she whispered, sliding one hand down to cup him through his breeches.

Now it was Jack's turn to shudder with longing, though her forwardness in such a setting amazed him. "Let us go home, then. I'm certain I'll not last out the evening after this sort of encouragement."

But Nessa pulled him in for another heated kiss. "I'm not certain I'll last till we get home," she sighed a moment later. "This is a lovely place, and I see a divan over there, by those ferns. Perhaps, if we lock the door . . . "

"Nessa!" Jack's laughter was tinged with urgent longing. "Pray do not tease me like this. I've half a mind to call your bluff."

"Who's bluffing?" she asked, slanting a seductive glance up at him through half-closed lashes. "Don't tell me that in all your colorful career you never did anything more scandalous?"

At the moment, Jack could barely recall anything he'd ever done with any other woman. His every sense, every nerve, was focused on Nessa. Her perfume, mingling with that of the flowers about them, her touch, her voice . . . "I've never been more tempted to, that's certain."

"Well, then?" She slid her hands up and down his back, then around to his thighs, urging him beyond rational thought.

"Very well, my naughty wife. Just a moment." He turned and closed the door, only to find no key to lock it from the inside. Still, what were the chances of anyone finding them here? He shoved the heavy iron doorstop in front of the door, so they'd at least have warning should it open, then turned back to Nessa.

"If you're not serious about this, now is the time to tell me."

By way of response, she grabbed his hand and pulled him toward the divan. Screened from the door by three small orange trees surrounded by exotic flowers, it nestled amid towering ferns near the far wall. Casting caution to the wind, Jack sat down and drew her against him.

"Perhaps we need a conservatory at Fox Manor," he murmured, attending to her throat again with his lips. "What say you, madam wife?"

"Hmmm . . . Let's see how this one works before we make any rash decisions." She loosened his cravat and ran her fingers through his hair, then began to unbutton his coat.

Snatching at the last vestiges of his control, Jack grasped her hands. "My darling, if you insist upon having me here and now, we'll have to forego disrobing entirely. We must be prepared to look innocent in short order, should any discover us here."

"I rely upon your expertise," she said with a smile that nearly sent him to the edge again. "Show me."

Fumbling somewhat in his haste and need, Jack began to undo the front fastening of his breeches. At once, Nessa reached to help him, clearly as eager as he. Lifting her skirts, he was pleased and relieved to discover she wore nothing beneath her garters and petticoats. Touching her, he found her wet and ready for him.

She had now freed him from the upper portion of his breeches, so he shifted until he lay on his back upon the divan, which was luckily long enough to support him. Before he could direct her, Nessa took the initiative, climbing astride him. She lowered herself upon him, engulfed him, and the world receded, narrowing to only the two of them.

Nessa had never been so aroused, not even in the earliest days of her marriage when sexual pleasure was new to her. Perhaps it was the risk of being caught, perhaps it was her brief estrangement from Jack, but she wanted him as never before. With an ecstatic gasp, she impaled herself upon him, driving him deeply into her until he filled her completely.

Jack reached up to fondle her breasts, already hard with desire, through the thin silk of her gown, propelling her to even greater desire. Slowly, then faster, she began to rock, riding him toward mutual release. Gripping him convulsively, she climaxed, a soaring sensation more intense than any before. At once, Jack tensed beneath her, driving upwards once, twice, then pulling her down upon him as he shuddered with his own release.

"Oh! Oh, Jack," she breathed, her heart still hammering as the urgency of passion slowly ebbed. "That was amazing. You are amazing."

He breathed a long sigh of satisfaction. "As are you, my love."

She swallowed. It was the first time he'd called her that since their marriage. Did it mean more now, or was it still simply a careless phrase to him?

As her heartbeat and breathing slowed, she became aware of other sounds—of something that sounded like distant cheering. Jack apparently heard it too, for he frowned questioningly at her, then moved to rise. She extricated herself from him and they separated far enough to sit up on the divan. The cheering seemed to be coming from behind the ferns, beyond the wall. Turning, horror slowly dawned. The wall of glass.

She turned to face Jack, her eyes wide, and at the same moment he began to curse, softly but fluently. Turning his back to the wall, he quickly refastened his breeches. Belatedly following his lead, Nessa pulled down her skirts and adjusted her disarranged bodice.

One breast had sprung free, and she hurriedly pulled the neckline of her gown back into place.

"You don't think . . . they're not actually watching *us*, are they?" she asked shakily. "The ferns——"

He glanced up at the blazing gas lights above them. "I'm not certain, but I doubt those ferns offer us much cover, given how bright it is in here and how dark outside. That must be the courtyard."

Panic began to grip her. "Then those are not merely passersby on the street, but other guests here tonight?"

He nodded ruefully. "I fear so. I should never have let you persuade me to this, my dear. I did know better, though the composition of the wall quite escaped me."

Nessa groaned. "I knew it was glass—or, at least, I noticed it before, but forgot. Still, Jack," she nestled against him, and the renewed cheers from outside confirmed her fears, "it was worth it, I think."

His look was quizzical. "Certainly I think so, but have you considered how we are to leave? We'll have to face at least some of them. Or shall we hold our heads high and pretend nothing is amiss?"

Nessa closed her eyes for a moment in mortification, but then began to laugh—though her laughter held an edge of hysteria. "What have we to lose?" she asked. "But first, let us move away from this enormous window!"

Ten minutes later, having passed each other's inspection (though Jack's cravat and Nessa's hair could not be what they were, without valet or abigail), the two of them reentered the ballroom. Ten seconds later, it was obvious their liaison was already general knowledge. Titters and curious stares followed them across the room.

Nessa knew her face was flaming, but she kept her chin high, though she did perhaps grip Jack's arm more tightly than usual. A glance showed her that his color had deepened as well, though he appeared on the verge of laughter. Quickly, Nessa averted her eyes for fear she might start giggling uncontrollably. People were staring enough as it was!

A dance had just ended and another was about to form, but though Nessa knew she was promised to someone for the next one, she was not particularly surprised when no one came forward to claim her. Gathering her courage, she looked about the room. One or two older gentlemen stared back boldly, but most seemed unwilling to meet her eye. Then she saw the Creamcrofts nearby, in conversation with another couple. How on earth could she ever face *them* again?

She was about to tell Jack that she'd changed her mind and would prefer to leave after all, when Prudence turned and saw her. Rather to Nessa's surprise, she murmured something to Philip, then came to greet her, eyes filled with concern.

"Nessa, my lord, surely——*surely*——the tale I've just been told cannot be true?" Prudence looked from Nessa to Jack and back, and must have had her answer from their conscious looks and heightened complexions. She opened her mouth, then closed it again, then drew Nessa aside with a stern glance at Jack.

"What exactly happened?" she whispered when they

had taken a few steps away. "I have no idea what to say to people!"

Though mortified as much for Prudence's sake as her own, Nessa was glad of the chance to get her confession over. "I took your advice rather too literally, I fear, Prudence. Finding myself alone with Jack in the conservatory, I, ah, took advantage of the situation . . . as did he."

Her sister blushed, but persisted. "'Twas shockingly bad judgment on both your parts—but how were you discovered? Surely you were not mad enough to leave the door open. Who walked in upon you? It seems everyone here is aware of it already!"

"Have you seen the conservatory, Prudence?" Her sister shook her head. "Well, it would seem that it has a, um, glass wall which is adjacent to the courtyard, screened only by some ferns. Somehow that escaped our notice until it was too late."

Prudence stared at her for a moment as her import sank in, then covered her mouth with a gloved hand. Her shoulders began to quiver, and for a moment Nessa thought her sister was on the verge of tears. But then a gasp escaped from behind the concealing hand and she realized her prim and proper sister was struggling with laughter!

For the second time in as many weeks, Nessa regarded Prudence with astonishment. Was this the prudish sister she'd known all her life?

"So your, ah, display was quite unintentional?" she gasped after a moment.

Nessa nodded, her own lips beginning to twitch.

"We must have put on quite a show, I fear."

For a moment the sisters clung to each other, struggling to subdue their mirth. Then, abruptly, Prudence sobered. "Oh, Nessa, 'twill be the talk of London by morning! Whatever are you going to do? Perhaps a discreet return to Kent . . . ?"

Nessa turned to see Jack a few paces away, regarding them with a curious frown. "Perhaps. I'll discuss it with Jack. Thank you, Prudence, for not abandoning me! I fear most will be less forgiving."

"We are sisters," said Prudence stoutly. "And besides, I have you to thank for . . . " She glanced over her shoulder at Philip and pinkened again. "For certain improvements in my own situation. Let me know if there is any way I can help."

Squeezing her hands, Nessa smiled. "You already have, Prudence. More than you know. Now go back to your husband, and I'll return to mine, to discuss how we are to weather this development."

Jack came forward the moment Prudence departed. "What was that about? Did I actually see Lady Creamcroft *laughing*?"

Nessa grinned. "Prudence has loosened up considerably in recent weeks, and seems the happier for it."

"So have you, my love." There was that word again, but Nessa tried not to set too much store by it. That they could be affectionate toward each other again was enough—for now.

"I suppose I have. However, I'm not sure Society as a whole will see it as an improvement." She lapsed into thought for a moment. "How does one get to the court-yard, my lord? I have a mind to see it."

He gave her a crooked smile. "Yes, I suppose we'd best discover just what we're up against, hadn't we? This way." He led her through a set of French doors at one end of the ballroom, both of them resolutely ignoring the laughter and whispering that marked their progress.

A marble terrace led down into a large garden area, still winter-bleak and only dimly lighted, primarily from the surrounding windows. Paved paths wove between intricately laid gardens which would doubtless be a blaze of color in a few months' time. Now, however, they were either clean raked or masses of low, leafless shrubs.

"There," said Jack, pointing.

Nessa looked. One floor above them was a wide expanse of glass, providing the bulk of the courtyard illumination. From here, the conservatory appeared nearly as fairylike as from within, a lush jungle of vegetation and flowers ablaze with light. And there, barely screened at all by the airy ferns, stood a backless divan— the very one the two of them had so recently . . . occupied.

"Oh, my," she breathed. "We might as well have been on stage!"

"I fear so," Jack agreed. Then, glancing about the nearly deserted courtyard, "Someone must have done quick work to assemble a crowd out here so quickly. I suppose such an inducement overcame the cold, how-ever, for many of the guests."

Nessa managed to pull her eyes away from the divan above. "I had hoped this would be an entertaining evening, but I little thought to provide the entertainment myself!" In spite of her renewed mortification, she could not suppress a rueful laugh.

"Nor I. But Nessa——" His voice suddenly became more serious. "I heard you earlier, saying you regretted being unable to accompany that young jackanapes to Paris. Why did you never tell me you wished to go after all?"

"I didn't . . . that is, Sir Lawrence was trying to convince me to run away with him, and I refused in no uncertain terms." She paused, looking up at him curiously. "Do you mean *you* would be willing to take me to Paris?" Sudden excitement flared within her.

"After this evening's events, it occurs to me that it might be to our benefit to discreetly remove ourselves from the London scene for awhile, until a new scandal arises to dim the memory of ours." He grinned down at her. "I'd thought of simply returning to Fox Manor, but a belated wedding trip to Paris would serve as well—— and might also serve another purpose."

Paris! She could finally see that fabled city of glitter, excitement, and sophistication. But——"What other purpose do you mean?"

His smile now was cryptic. "We shall see. I'll simply say that in Paris you may see enough of scandal to finally satisfy your curiosity——if this evening's exploits have not already done so."

She tilted her head saucily. "If they have, you can

hardly expect me to admit it, and thereby endanger my visit to Paris, my lord! When shall we leave?"

He shook his head, as though in disbelief. "You, madam, are incorrigible. Let me see . . . I have a few matters to attend to in Parliament yet. We can stop at Fox Manor on our way to Dover, so that I may take care of estate business there. I should say we might take ship within a fortnight or so."

"A fortnight!" In Paris, she could broaden her horizons far past what was possible in London, she was sure! What sights, what people, what experiences must await there—and in only two weeks' time!

"I'll be ready well within a fortnight, I promise you," she declared. "I can scarcely wait!"

As it happened, it was a fortnight to the day before they finally boarded the packet bound for Calais. Nessa had spent a busy, if rather lonely week, preparing Foxhaven House and its staff for their extended absence. Very few people had called, and those who did were not ones she felt disposed to receive. Most were scandalmongers, undoubtedly hoping to glean additional details to embellish their gossip. Pleading a lack of time—quite truthfully—she refused them all.

Only Prudence did she admit, and she did not stay long. But at least her motive was beyond question.

"Philip and I are expecting a child," she informed Nessa with obvious delight. "I'm not certain which of us is more thrilled. He feels the Season will be too much for me, under the circumstances, so we shall return to Herefordshire and likely remain for at least a year. You *will* come to visit me, will you not, Nessa?"

Nessa jumped up to hug her sister. "Oh, Prudence, what marvelous news! And of course I'll visit, as soon as we return from Paris." And she had perforce to explain her own plans.

Prudence expressed some concern, but was clearly too happy to dwell upon it. "I will trust you to do what is right," she concluded. "Certainly by now you have learned your lesson! I only hope Jack, er, Lord Fox-haven will make you as happy as Philip has made me."

She took her leave shortly thereafter, leaving Nessa to the remainder of her preparations. A day or two later, when Jack announced his current business in London complete, they loaded up the traveling coach and headed for Fox Manor, where they had agreed to spend a week.

Nessa found herself peering ahead as they neared the estate, eager to see it again. In fact, she realized, this was the closest to a feeling of homecoming she'd ever experienced. Returns to Cherry Oaks as a child had always been marred by fear of an almost inevitable scolding. As for Haughton Abbey, even when she'd grown comfortable there, she had never learned to love it. Fox Manor, however, felt like home.

Part of the charm, of course, consisted in the heal-ing of the rift between Jack and herself. They were now back to the easy camaraderie—and passionate nights—of the early days of their marriage. Sometimes Nessa even dared to hope that his feelings for her went deeper than a combination of lust and friendship, but she was careful not to press for any sort of declaration.

Still, if any place might elicit such a development, it would be Fox Manor, she thought. Almost, it was enough to make her suggest a longer stay here, putting off the excitement of Paris.

Almost.

As the day of their departure approached, Nessa's excitement mounted. Even more than London, Paris promised to show her a side of life she'd previously only imagined. And now, at last, they were on their way.

Forgotten was the chill drizzle that had pursued them from Fox Manor to Dover. Even the thin fog through which the packet made its way could not dampen her spirits.

"Thank you, Jack, for suggesting this," she said as they stood side by side at the rail.

He draped an arm over her shoulders, driving away the cold she'd scarcely noticed, and looked ahead as she did. "Wait to thank me after you've had a chance to absorb some impressions from what is reputed to be the wickedest city on earth," he said teasingly. "You may find Paris more than you've bargained for."

Nessa grinned into the mist. "I hope so!"

∾ 20 ∾

"Here we are," Jack announced, as the coach taking them the final stage of their journey reached the outskirts of Paris. "We should reach our hotel in ten minutes or so. Unless my message missent, a room will be ready for us. You'll wish to rest before launching yourself upon the city, I imagine."

Nessa pulled her face away from the window with obvious reluctance. "Oh, I am not at all tired, Jack! How could I possibly rest when all of Paris awaits?"

He chuckled, trying to ignore his misgivings. When he'd suggested Paris, he'd had more in mind than leaving London until the talk died down. He was counting on this most wicked city to finally cure Nessa of her craving for the seamier side of life—a side he knew far too well. He just hoped he wouldn't regret bringing Nessa here, to the site of so much he had put behind him.

His wife had amply proved she was no longer the prude he'd married. What if Paris, rather than giving her a disgust for debauchery, only increased her appetite?

Warily, he glanced back to her rapt face, avidly taking in the street scene.

"Here we are. The Hotel des Cinq Astres." The coach stopped even as he spoke.

"How lovely!" Nessa exclaimed, stepping out the moment the stairs were lowered—into ankle-deep sewage. "Oh, bother! I'd forgotten what you told me about the gutters. Now I shall have to change my shoes and stockings before we can explore."

She wrinkled her nose, but seemed otherwise undaunted by her first step into filth. Carefully avoiding the free-flowing sewage, Jack helped her onto the relatively cleaner walkway before the front door of the hotel.

Ushering Nessa inside, he approached the concierge at the broad marble desk. "Rooms for Lord and Lady Foxhaven and their servants," he said in flawless French and saw Nessa's eyes widen.

The concierge snapped to attention and began issuing instructions to various lackeys, and within a very few minutes they were shown into a luxurious suite on the third floor. A basket of fruit, wine, and mouthwatering French pastries awaited them there.

"How perfectly lovely!" said Nessa again. *"Merci, monsieur. C'est magnifique!"* Jack smiled. Her accent was quite passable. She must have learned the language under the tutelage of a true Frenchman.

Simmons and Parker began the unpacking at once, while Nessa sampled one of the pastries, exclaiming at its delicacy and flavor.

"You'll not wish to spoil your appetite, my love." Jack smiled indulgently. "Once we have dressed, I mean to take you to Rocher de Cancalle, where you may experience the finest cuisine to be found this side of heaven."

"Oh, I remember reading about it in one of the London papers," she said excitedly. "'Tis said to be worlds above anything in England. And we are to go there tonight? Shall we visit Tortoni's while we are here, for its famous ices? And the Louvre—perhaps tomorrow we may view the artworks there? Oh, and the Palais-Royal! 'Tis *the* place to see and be seen, is it not?"

Jack laughed at her childlike enthusiasm. He loved it when she forgot to play the sophisticate. "Yes, yes, my love, we shall go to all of those places, and more. But one step at a time. I will leave you to dress for dinner, while I do likewise. Come, Parker."

He retired with his valet into the adjoining chamber. Half an hour later, impeccably attired, he tapped on the bedchamber door and then entered. Nessa, resplendent in pale blue satin, stood up from the dressing table, where her maid had just put the finishing touches on her hair.

"Well?" she asked, twirling for his examination. "Shall I avoid disgracing England, do you think?"

He came forward to take both her hands in his. "Indeed, my dear, after one look at you, the French-women will abandon their flounces and outrageous bonnets to imitate your elegance. You are exquisite."

And she was. He was tempted to suggest having dinner sent up so that he could have her to himself, in fact. But no, he had promised her Paris. Helping her into her wrap, he led her downstairs, and out into the now-twilit streets.

"Stay close to me," he cautioned her. "Paris is not Mayfair, neither as well lit nor as safe, even in the better areas."

She drew nearer, her eyes wide as she took in the scene surrounding them—the thronged humanity of all social classes, the scrawlings upon the walls, proclaiming, "*Vive l'empereur!*" in defiance of Napoleon's defeat. Prostitutes lounged in doorways, street vendors hawked their wares in French and broken English.

Instinctively, Jack wanted to protect Nessa from the evils that he knew lurked around every corner and within every alleyway. He'd been mad to bring her here.

"This is wonderful! Amazing!" she breathed. "I've never seen anything like it. How exciting!"

He groaned inwardly, not only at her words, but at the memory of his own similar enthusiasm upon his last visit to Paris—and of the wild excesses it had led him to. Was he so certain that he could not be similarly tempted now? That Nessa would not? It would be best, he decided, if their visit here were kept short. Tomorrow he would make certain inquiries. . . .

They reached their destination none too soon for his taste. Jack's anxiety receded as he watched—and shared—Nessa's enjoyment of gustatory pleasures beyond her dreams. Whatever else he might say against Paris, the food here was the best on earth.

"Now I understand the wages true French chefs command in England," Nessa commented when she finally pushed back from the marble table after their prolonged and leisurely meal. "And I begin to believe those who claim to travel to Paris solely to dine here. That was magnificent."

"Now that you have experienced the best Paris has to offer," he teased, "we may as well return to England. Anything else we do here is bound to be anticlimactic."

"Oh, I think not," she replied, her eyes dancing. "The very atmosphere of this city inspires me to things most climactic, in fact."

Jack grinned, his body responding instantly to her innuendo. "Indeed? Then I suggest we return to our hotel without further ado."

Nessa stretched luxuriously upon awakening to her first full day in Paris. If last night had been any indication, she was going to thoroughly enjoy her stay here! A fabulous meal, followed by even more fabulous lovemaking with the man who had made this possible.

Turning to express her gratitude yet again, she discovered that Jack had already risen. He was on the far side of the enormous room, almost finished dressing. Before she could speak, a tap came at the door. Jack opened it to receive a tray of something that smelled positively heavenly. The moment the door closed again, she sat up.

"Mmm! Is that our breakfast?"

He turned with a grin that melted her insides to

water. "It is indeed, and an excellent one, I should think. One reason I chose this hotel was the reputation of its kitchens."

She bounded out of bed, only belatedly remembering to snatch up her silk wrapper when Jack's eyes brightened appreciatively. "After breakfast," she promised. "You wouldn't want me distracted by that mouthwatering aroma, would you?"

His blue eyes smoldered. "No, I'll want your undivided attention, as I plan to give you mine."

Sitting at the small table, Nessa saw only familiar foods: eggs, meats, pastries, coffee. But everything was hot—something rarely experienced in England—and the quality set it apart as well. The coffee was the best she'd ever tasted—full, rich, and strong.

"That was nearly as good as last night's dinner," she declared as she drank the last drop, to wash down her final bite of croissant. "If we spend many weeks in Paris, I fear I shall become as large as a cow!"

"Then I must make certain you take enough exercise to compensate." Jack tossed his napkin onto the table and rose. "I have a particular activity in mind right now."

Nessa came to him eagerly, and soon they were engaged in a most pleasurable exercise indeed. As so often happened after she was sated, however, she had to fight the urge to tell him she loved him. She had faced that truth some time ago, but after the incident with Miranda Dempsey, she felt reluctant to voice feelings that might not be reciprocated. When it was time, she would know.

Wouldn't she?

Today, however, she refused to dwell upon the matter. Paris awaited! "Where shall we go today?" she asked, almost before her breathing had slowed to normal. "One of the palaces?"

"I am wounded! Could I distract you no longer than that?" But he smiled indulgently. "The Louvre, I believe. Then perhaps the Tuileries?"

"Oh, yes! And then, tonight, the Palais-Royal? Please?" She'd read and heard numerous stories of its shops, cafés, and gaming establishments.

For a moment she thought a fleeting frown crossed Jack's brow, but the smile never wavered. "Of course. Up with you, then! We have a busy day ahead of us, it would seem."

Back in the streets of Paris, Nessa again felt assailed by the odors—mostly unpleasant—and the crowds. Why, all of Europe must be here! English gentlemen and officers in their blue or red coats, Frenchmen in their more sober black, ladies of all nationalities in every color of the rainbow, in everything from simple English styles to the more ornate French and German ones.

Just ahead, she saw an English officer exchanging angry words with what must be a French officer. The Frenchman then slapped the other resoundingly across the face, and the Englishman bowed. Turning aside, they continued their conversation at a less audible volume.

"Does . . . does that mean they are to duel?" she asked Jack, amazed at such a display.

He nodded. "Unless things have changed since I was here in August, dozens are fought every morning. The French are a hotheaded race, and with no war to occupy them now, our own idled officers are more than happy to oblige their thirst for violence."

She looked at him uncertainly. "Did *you* fight any duels when you were here last summer?"

Again he nodded, not quite meeting her eyes. "A few. I'd like to think I'm a wiser man now, though. For one thing, I've more to live for." He winked at her.

Nessa felt chilled and warmed all at once. The very idea of Jack putting himself in such danger, doubtless over such trivial things as the cut of a coat or a turn of the dice, made her almost ill. In vain she reminded herself that he'd undoubtedly faced greater danger in the army. Somehow the thought did not comfort her in the least.

"Jack! Jack Ashecroft! Is it really you?" A shrill, feminine voice broke into Nessa's disturbing thoughts. With a swirl of puce skirts and heavy perfume, a plump, pretty blonde blocked their way. Seizing Jack by both arms, she planted a resounding kiss square on his mouth.

He grabbed her bare shoulders and set her away from him, looking more startled than upset, Nessa thought. "Peggy! I had no idea you were still in Paris."

She appeared ready to launch herself at him again, when Jack continued hastily, "Pray, let me introduce you to my wife."

The woman's rouged cheeks turned even pinker, as

she noticed Nessa for the first time. "Your wife?" she cried, her blue eyes nearly starting from her head. "Say it's not true, Jack!"

Jack released her shoulders, now that the danger of another attack had passed. "I'd rather hoped for congratulations, not disbelief. Lady Foxhaven and I were wed before Christmas."

Peggy cocked her head pertly to one side. "Foxhaven? Weren't that your grandpa's name? So you're a markiss now, are you? Well, don't that beat all! Guess you had to wed so you could get yourself an heir, eh?" She nudged Nessa with her elbow, her eyes twinkling again.

Nessa managed a smile, both attracted and repelled by the woman's forthright, vulgar manner. "We're working on it," she said brightly.

Both Jack and Peggy stared at her for a moment, then the other woman let out a loud peal of laughter. "Looks like you found yourself a right 'un, Jack! Glad to see you ain't stuck with some starched up society type. Bring her 'round tonight and I'll introduce her to the other girls." With a saucy wink, she turned to sashay away from them down the street.

Glancing up at Jack, Nessa saw that his color had risen considerably. He cleared his throat a couple of times before meeting her eye.

"That was Peggy," he said unnecessarily.

"So I gathered." She couldn't helped being amused at his embarrassment, even if the encounter had been rather unsettling for her, as well. "A good friend of yours, I take it?"

"Just a . . . a casual acquaintance, really." He didn't quite meet her eye. "Manners are freer here, and even the English who spend enough time in Paris tend to adopt them."

"Ah," she said noncommittally. "Shall we continue on?"

He nodded and they resumed their walk, but this was not the last such encounter. They had nearly reached the Louvre when a disheveled young man accosted them.

"Jack Ashecroft, as I live and breathe! And who is this pretty lady? 'Tis one I've not seen in Paris before. Did you import her from England, perchance?"

"Hello, Teddy. Still getting drunk before noon, I see. This is my wife, Lady Foxhaven." Jack, Nessa noticed, was careful to interpose himself between her and this newcomer.

"So Uncle Luther stuck his spoon in the wall, did he? And you've become a sober married man. Guess there's no use in my suggesting a *ménage à trois* then, eh?" With an elaborate bow toward Nessa, he went off laughing.

Nessa looked curiously at Jack. "What did he mean?"

Again Jack began the throat-clearing that she now knew signified embarrassment. "Er, nothing. Teddy always was a nodcock. Wonder if his family even knows he's still alive?"

Though she suspected there was more to that comment than the literal meaning, "household of three," she allowed the subject to drop. "I had no idea I'd married such a very popular fellow." Nessa forced herself to speak lightly, though in truth she was rather unnerved by such flagrant evidence of his former lifestyle.

They entered the Louvre then, and Nessa forgot all other concerns in her awe at the artworks displayed there. They spent the next few hours lost in beauty and amazement, only recalled to reality by increasingly insistent hunger pangs.

Jack suggested Tortoni's for afternoon refreshment, and Nessa eagerly agreed. That celebrated establishment was crowded with people of all nationalities, but as Jack appeared to know several of those present, including the waiters, they were served in surprisingly short order. They had finished their meal and were just beginning the famed ices when shouting on the opposite side of the room rose above the general din.

A French officer and a man Nessa thought might be Prussian from his accent exchanged first words and then blows. A moment later, at least a dozen other patrons joined the fray. Chairs and tables were overturned, and a shot rang out.

"That is our exit cue, my dear," said Jack urgently. "This way." He ushered her outdoors, pushing his way through the crowd surging in the opposite direction to join or witness the melee. More shots sounded behind them, along with a piercing shriek.

"Goodness!" Nessa exclaimed shakily once they'd gone a safe distance down the street. "Does that sort of thing happen often in there?"

"There and most other places in this volatile city.

Are you all right?" Jack examined her face with a concern that warmed away her fear.

"Perfectly," she assured him. "I . . . had not realized Paris was such a dangerous place."

"Debauchery and danger often go hand in hand." He tucked her hand into the crook of his arm and turned toward the Tuileries. "When people lose respect for themselves and their own lives, 'tis but a short step to losing respect for others, and fiery young men must have an outlet for their passions."

Nessa swallowed. "And you were one of those?"

"I . . . suppose I was, though I pursued amusement more avidly than violence."

She wasn't sure whether that made her feel better or not.

During the remainder of the day and evening, Nessa began to realize that her girlish fantasies about wickedness had had little basis in reality. Here, the actuality was all about her, impossible to escape.

Prostitutes—they could be nothing else—boldly approached passersby in even the most genteel sections of the city. Gambling dens appeared to occupy almost every corner, and shots rang out frequently, either close at hand or in the distance. Wild laughter floated from doorways, and the moans of what must be sexual couplings from open windows above.

No longer did she envy the freedom of the women she saw everywhere displaying their legs and bosoms. Instead, she felt almost ashamed to share their gender. The Tuileries and its gardens, just beginning to hint at spring glory, were lovely, and the Palais-Royal amazing in its colorful variety, but by midway through the evening Nessa was both tired and oddly depressed.

Jack seemed to sense something of her mood. "Why don't we return to our hotel and have dinner sent up to our suite?" he suggested as they completed the circuit of shops and cafés. "I think we've both had enough of Paris for one day, don't you?"

Though she hated to admit it, Nessa had to agree. No doubt her enthusiasm for new experiences would revive after a good night's sleep, but for now she confessed herself sated by them.

The next morning, however, she awoke to a vague queasiness. "I fear all of this rich French cuisine has rather overset my digestion," she told Jack apologetically. "Can we perhaps ask that something simpler be sent up for today's breakfast?"

Immediately he was all concern. "Certainly, my dear! I'll send Parker down at once. Is there anything else you require?"

"Now, you needn't play the mother hen," she teased, though she could not help feeling touched. "I shall be fine, I am certain. Nor will you escape showing me more of Paris by exaggerating my little indisposition."

Indeed, after some tea and toast she felt much more the thing, and ready to see a few of the monuments which had been erected in Napoleon's honor. But though they took things easily that day, she found she could not summon up her former eagerness to see all that Paris had to offer. And there were still interruptions by some of Jack's former acquaintances, from noble to homeless.

It was all too easy, with the evidence before her, to imagine just the sort of life Jack must have led before she met him. Former officers referred to wartime exploits and the women who had followed them from camp to camp. Others made comments about the money they had lost to Jack or, less frequently, that he had lost to them.

And it seemed that every woman in Paris knew him far too well!

By the end of their fourth day in Paris, Nessa felt she'd seen enough of debauchery to last her a lifetime—though she could not yet bring herself to admit it to Jack.

For his part, Jack was finding Paris both tedious and unpleasant, with its constant reminders of a life he'd left behind—a life he discovered he did not miss in the least. Yes, there were occasional temptations to renew old friendships, but the drinking, dicing, and wenching no longer appealed.

Two months ago that knowledge would have disturbed him, but now he felt profound relief. Evidence that Paris' dubious charms were palling on Nessa brought him even greater relief. He began to realize that Nessa had a core of purity that even Paris could not touch, however she might try to hide it.

Still, he was worried about her. Her stomach had

been unsettled for the past three mornings, and though she always seemed to recover by early afternoon, he could not be entirely easy about her. No doubt the noxious atmosphere of Paris was taking its toll on her system, brought up as she had been to the clean air of the English countryside.

He'd meant to stay in Paris for a week at the least, but now he began casting about in earnest for alternatives. By the evening of their fourth day there, he had found one.

"What would you say," he asked her over dinner that night, "to spending the next two weeks in the French countryside rather than the city?"

Nessa set down her fork and looked curiously at him, both hopeful and wary, he thought. "The countryside? But how? Where?"

"I sent a message to an old friend who owes me a favor," he explained. "This afternoon I received his reply. He owns a charming little cottage less than twenty miles from Paris, on the outskirts of a particularly pretty village. I remembered visiting it last summer, which is why I inquired. He rarely stays there, and has agreed to let us make use of it for as long as we like."

Her eyes shone. "Oh, may we really?" But then she seemed to recall herself. "That is, I am enjoying Paris immensely, of course, but a change might be nice."

Valiantly, Jack kept his expression solemn. "Just what I'd thought, as well. We'll leave tomorrow, if you have no objection."

"No objection at all," she said with a smile, belatedly

adding, "Assuming, of course, that we may see the rest of Paris later on."

"Whenever you wish to do so," Jack agreed. He hoped, however, that she'd truly had her fill of Paris by now, as he rather suspected she had.

The next morning, the first of March, they left early, as Jack recalled that the roads they would traverse were not of the best. Though Nessa again woke to an upset stomach, she refused to delay on that account.

"I shall be fine within the hour," she promised. "I always seem to be."

By the time the carriage was loaded, her prophecy had been fulfilled. Two hours later, however, as they bumped along rutted, twisting lanes, she appeared to be in some distress again. Finally, she asked him to stop the coach so that she could step outside for a breath of air. A moment later, he was supporting her as she rid herself of her breakfast.

"I'm terribly sorry, Jack. Normally I'm not made at all ill by travel. Even that rough channel crossing we had did not upset me, if you'll recall."

"No need to apologize, my love." Tenderly, he brushed a few tendrils of hair away from her face. "These execrable roads would do up the strongest constitution."

She smiled up at him gratefully. "You are so good to me, Jack. Thank you for salvaging my pride—not only now, but also about Paris. I wanted to leave desperately, but was too proud to admit it. I'm not quite the woman of the world I'd like to believe, am I?"

Jack had to swallow the lump in his throat before replying. "You're the best woman in the world, Nessa. I honestly believe that." He bent to kiss her, but she held up a hand.

"Not until I've rinsed out my mouth, Jack! But I certainly can't doubt your sincerity now." She grinned weakly.

He chuckled and helped her back to the coach, where she took a sip of the wine they'd brought along. Truly a remarkable woman! Why on earth had he not yet told her he loved her?

That question occupied him for much of the remainder of the journey, as Nessa dozed with her head on his shoulder. He'd told Miranda Dempsey, of all people, but had not yet summoned the courage to tell Nessa herself. Why?

Fear, he finally admitted. Fear that she would laugh, or, worse, parrot the sentiment automatically—as he'd done to so many women—without meaning the words. He didn't think he'd be able to bear that, not from Nessa.

As twilight fell and they neared the end of their journey, he finally faced the unpleasant truth. Jack Ashecroft, celebrated hero of Salamanca, Vitoria, and Paris, was a coward.

∽ *21* ∽

Nessa awoke from her doze when the bumpy forward motion of the carriage suddenly ceased. "What has happened?" she asked drowsily. Were there highwaymen in France?

"Nothing, my dear. We have finally reached the cottage." Jack helped her to sit up just as the coachman opened the door. The fresh, cool air streamed in, reviving her at once.

She peered out and caught her breath at the scene before her. The little house nestled cozily in its garden. Rose vines on trellises, leaves just unfurling, covered its whitewashed walls. Diamond-paned windows twinkled, reflecting the setting sun in wondrous hues of crimson and violet, making it seem like something out of a fairy tale.

"Oh!" Nessa gasped. "Oh, how perfect! And we're really to stay here?"

Jack grinned at her response as he helped her from the coach. "We are indeed. I said it was charming, did I not? A bit rustic, of course, but we can obtain necessities from the village. No food of Paris quality, but this is still France, so you won't starve, I promise you."

He walked up the raked gravel path, took the key from his pocket, and opened the door. Pulling her wrap close against the evening chill, Nessa followed him into the cottage. Though not furnished with fashion in mind, everything within was comfortable and clean, save a thin patina of dust which showed it had not been inhabited for some time. She and Simmons at once set about remedying that small defect, however, and by the time the luggage was brought in and fires lit in the parlor, kitchen, and bedrooms, all was as neat and cozy as she could have wished.

"Now, my dear, that's quite enough of that," said Jack, coming back into the parlor as Nessa finished dusting the oaken mantelpiece. "You sit here by the fire and get warm and rested, while Parker and I go into the village to get dinner."

"Dozing all day in the coach was scarcely tiring," she pointed out. But even as she spoke, she realized that she still felt lethargic. She sank luxuriously into the deep armchair nearest the fire. "See if the bakery has any of those lovely croissants. Nothing in England compares to them."

Jack saluted her. "Your wish is my command, madam wife."

He and Parker left, while Simmons went into the bedroom to unpack the trunks. Nessa leaned back against the cushions and closed her eyes. Already she could feel the tight-wound frenzy of Paris seeping away, to be replaced by the serenity of the country. What an excellent idea of Jack's, to come here! It was just what she—what their marriage—needed.

She had hoped that the vaunted romance of Paris would infect their relationship, but romance was not what she'd found there. Debauchery, she now understood, was not romantic in the least. But without love, what separated her relationship with Jack from what the Parisian courtesans shared with the men there?

At first, the heady discovery that there was pleasure—great pleasure!—to be found in the marriage bed was enough for her. But more and more, of late, she was finding herself dissatisfied with mere physical pleasure, odd as that sounded. There was a part of her she had yet to surrender to Jack, and a part he had not surrendered of himself. Until their hearts were involved, until they could trust one another completely, their marriage could never be complete.

Nessa opened her eyes and looked around the cozy room with its chintz curtains, simple woodwork, and deep upholstery. Surely here, in the quiet of the country, with no distractions from Society or Jack's estate, they could finally find each other? She was determined to try.

She must have dozed, for the next thing she knew, Jack and Parker had come in through the kitchen and were making quite a racket as they put things away. Rising, she hurried in to see what they had obtained.

"There wasn't much selection, as two of the three shops in the village had closed already," Jack said in response to her query. "But we were able to buy bread, butter, eggs, and milk."

"That should be sufficient for tonight, I should think. Is that a root cellar?" she asked. "If there are potatoes or onions, they will round out the meal nicely."

There were both potatoes and onions, as well as a quantity of garlic in the small root cellar. Simmons made it quite clear that she considered kitchen duty far beneath her, but grudgingly agreed to help.

"If I can do it, certainly you can," Nessa pointed out to the affronted lady's maid.

"Hmph," was Simmons' only comment as she stoically cut up potatoes and put them into a pot to boil.

An hour later, the four of them sat down to their simple but hearty dinner at the large table in the kitchen. Simmons and Parker had both resisted this arrangement as beneath the dignity of their master and mistress, but were won over by Jack's argument that there really was no other suitable table in the house.

"Very well," Parker said, "but only this once. I cannot but think sharing your meals in this way must undermine the romantic atmosphere of this setting."

Nessa started and stared at the man, but he had turned his attention to his bread and potatoes. Jack merely chuckled and shook his head.

The moment the meal was over, Parker ushered Jack and Nessa into the parlor, then pressed the tight-lipped Simmons into service to help with the washing up.

"That was lovely," Nessa declared, sinking back into the comfortable armchair she'd occupied before.

"Lovely? My dear, you are absurdly easy to please, I must say."

Though she knew Jack was teasing, she answered him seriously. "I don't require fancy food and elegant surroundings to be happy. A peaceful setting, with you at my side, is enough."

He looked at her strangely, and she felt a twinge of panic. Had she said too much, revealed her feelings too clearly? Or was he merely unable to share her sentiment, and baffled by it? His next words reassured her somewhat.

"I can't promise your surroundings will always be peaceful, but I shall do my best to be a part of them. I had always believed that I would wither without excitement, myself." His voice deepened. "Now I come to realize that excitement takes many forms."

Even as she felt her body responding to the suggestiveness of his tone, Nessa couldn't help wondering whether he saw their lovemaking as simply an agreeable way to pass the time. Was he counting on her to keep him amused—excited—in this rustic exile?

Still . . . "It does indeed," she agreed. She would not let this odd obsession she'd developed to tap Jack's deepest emotions deprive her of the pleasure she found in his arms. "Will the fire in the bedroom have warmed it yet, do you think?"

He rose and took her hand. "Let's go find out."

Though tiny in comparison to their chambers in London, Fox Manor, or even the Paris hotel, the bedroom was as comfortable and cozy as the rest of the cottage. The bed dominated the room, piled high with feather mattresses and pillows under its colorful counterpane. One glance at it, and Nessa felt desire and sleep begin to wage a battle within her.

"As Parker and Simmons are otherwise occupied, I suppose we must make shift to undress each other," Jack said, closing the door behind them.

"I suppose so." Without further prompting, Nessa began loosening the intricate folds of his cravat.

Encircling her with his arms, he unfastened the row of tiny buttons down her back, one by one. Pausing occasionally for long, leisurely kisses, they worked their way downward until both were stripped to the skin.

"And now," said Jack huskily, sweeping her into his arms to carry her the two or three steps to the bed.

The mattress was even softer than it had looked. A moment later, both of them were nestled under the covers, their whole lengths pressed against each other. Nessa felt wonderfully comfortable, and even with Jack's lips upon hers, she felt a great lassitude sweeping over her.

"Mmmm," she murmured, as he trailed his lips down her throat to the hollow between her breasts. His hands massaged the back of her neck, her shoulders, loosening muscles she hadn't even realized were still knotted by the day's journey. Exquisitely relaxed, she burrowed deeper into the mattress, inhaling the masculine scent that was Jack, her own hands moving more and more slowly over his body.

Nessa blinked. Sunlight streamed through the chintz curtains, falling on her face, dazzling her.

"What . . . ?" In complete confusion, she struggled to sit up and look around at the cozy little bedroom, where just a moment ago, it seemed, she and Jack had been settling in for a night of lovemaking and sleep. The morning was well advanced, and Jack was nowhere to be seen.

"I fell asleep," she groaned aloud. Right in the midst of their lovemaking, she must have dropped off. She sat back against the pillows with a sigh. Poor Jack! He'd been so eager, and she'd . . . Goodness! What must he think of her? of himself? She hoped she hadn't insulted him beyond forgiveness.

A light tap sounded upon the door. "Come in," she called out, her spirits rising. She'd apologize at once, explain how tired she'd been—

Simmons walked into the room. "Will you be wanting to dress and have a bite to eat, my lady?"

"Oh. Certainly. Ah, where is Lord Foxhaven?"

"He and that Parker have gone into the village for more provisions. He'll be back within the hour, I should think."

Nessa thought for a moment. "Very well. I believe I'll wear my new rose morning gown—the one I bought in Paris." Jack had expressed admiration for the dress when she'd purchased it. Perhaps it would put him in a better frame of mind to hear her apology when he returned.

She smiled to herself. She intended to follow that

apology with more tangible restitution, if she could get him back into the bedroom. After nearly twelve hours of sleep, she felt beautifully rested and ready to advance her romantic plans.

Or almost. Upon standing, a twinge of the queasiness which had plagued her for the last week returned. Swallowing, she managed to fight it down, then turned to see Simmons watching her with a most knowing expression on her thin face.

"A bite of toast and a sip of tea will help you to feel more the thing, my lady."

Nessa frowned. "Yes, it usually does. But why? Do you know what is wrong with me, Simmons?"

To her surprise, her rigid abigail gave her an almost motherly smile. "I believe I can guess, my lady. If you'll forgive my asking, how long has it been since you last had your monthly courses?"

A sudden light broke upon Nessa. "Why—several weeks, now that I think on it. Oh, Simmons, do you truly think I may be with child?"

The abigail nodded, the crinkles at the corners of her eyes making her look more approachable—more human—than Nessa had ever seen her. "I do indeed, my lady. This morning queasiness is a classic symptom. Not to worry, however. It should pass in a few weeks."

"I'm glad to hear it." Despite the lingering upset, though, Nessa's heart was suddenly light as a feather. She carried Jack's child! She would be a mother! And Jack—

She turned abruptly back to Simmons. "Pray say

nothing to Lord Foxhaven—nor to his valet, either—for the present. I'd like to be absolutely certain before raising his hopes."

Actually, she felt quite certain Simmons' guess was correct. But if she told Jack now, might he not voice emotions he did not truly feel out of simple gratitude that she was providing him an heir? Contrary as it might be, she didn't want that. She wanted to know first that he loved her for herself, all other considerations aside. If he did.

"Certainly not, my lady." Simmons sounded faintly shocked. "'Twould not be my place to mention such a thing. Though . . . I rather think Parker may suspect already, even if His Lordship does not. You'll not be able to keep it a secret for long."

"No, of course not," Nessa agreed. But if all went well, she wouldn't have to.

Shifting the awkward parcels in his arms yet again, Jack decided he'd been foolish to leave the carriage behind. He'd hoped a walk to the village and back would help to clear his mind, but if anything he had more questions than when he'd left.

"Almost there, Parker," he called back encouragingly. His valet carried even more packages than he did, though he hadn't uttered a word of complaint about his master's questionable judgment.

Was Nessa seriously ill? Jack wondered. She'd never before fallen asleep right in the middle of his love-making—indeed, no woman ever had! If not, he feared it boded ill for their relationship—not to mention the blow to his pride. Of course, he'd far rather absorb such a blow than discover she had some life-threatening illness, he told himself quickly. What a self-centered cad he was!

Snorting in self-derision, he set down his parcels so that he could open the kitchen door. "Just leave everything on the table," he told Parker. "No doubt when Mme. Guignard gets here she'll organize everything her own way."

Belatedly realizing how absurd it was to expect a valet, a lady's maid or, worse, Nessa herself, to do the cooking and housekeeping, he'd arranged for a woman from the village to spend a few hours there each day for the duration of their stay.

"No doubt, my lord," agreed Parker. "You'll wish to check on Her Ladyship now, I presume."

Nessa rose as Jack entered the parlor and came forward to greet him, a vision in soft rose—a color he thought suited her particularly well. Her hair was simply but charmingly styled, caught back with a pink ribbon to cascade down her back. Best of all, she was smiling.

"Good morning!" she exclaimed. "For a little while longer, at least. I apologize for being such a slugabed."

He clasped the hands she held out to him. "Are you well, Nessa? I've been concerned about you." Just now, however, she looked the picture of blooming health, making his query seem rather foolish. Still, she seemed touched by it.

"Thank you, Jack." She met his eyes directly, and he

saw nothing but warmth there—and perhaps a hint of a question. "I'm perfectly fine, now that I've caught up on my sleep. My . . . timing last night was unforgivable, however."

He brushed that aside. "Think nothing of it," he said, just as though he hadn't spent most of the morning agonizing about it. "You were tired."

"I was," she conceded. "But now I am not, and should like the chance to make it up to you." There was no mistaking her words, or the seductive glance she slanted up at him.

Instantly he responded, both physically and emotionally—a powerful, almost frightening combination far beyond anything any other woman had ever produced in him. "I'd like that," he managed, huskily.

She squeezed his fingertips, then gently drew him in the direction of their bedroom. He followed most willingly. The moment the door was closed, she turned to face him again.

"The pleasure you bring me, Jack, is the greatest I've ever known. Never doubt that." She pulled him down for a kiss.

Jack obliged, but couldn't help wondering what it was she was trying to tell him. Was this a convoluted good-bye? Sudden fear shot through him, distracting him for a moment from his desire. Perhaps she really was desperately ill, and knew it! Perhaps—

He held her away from him, examining her face, trying to read her thoughts. "Nessa? Are you *certain* you are all right?"

To his amazement, she giggled. "I'll admit, my phrasing was rather melodramatic, but I simply wanted to convince you that my falling asleep so inconveniently last night was no reflection on you. I . . . wouldn't cause you pain for anything, Jack."

"Nor I, you," he declared, making it a vow. "Never again. I . . . " Yes, it was time. He owed her this much. "I love you, Nessa." He underscored the words with his eyes, putting every ounce of sincerity he possessed into his expression.

Her eyes widened. "Do you, Jack?" she breathed incredulously. "Do you truly? I'd hoped . . . sometimes imagined . . . Oh, Jack, I've loved you for months— since before we were wed. I—"

But he silenced her with another kiss, this one deeper, fuller, infused with more meaning than any they'd shared before. She fairly melted into him, her rapture, her *love*, clearly communicated. Jack thought for a moment that he might collapse with delight and relief, but instead he carried her to the bed, as he had last night.

This time she showed not the slightest inclination to sleep. As eager as he, she helped him to strip off her gown and his shirt and breeches, their efforts punctuated by frequent kisses. No words seemed necessary as they hurried to consummate their newly declared love.

As she had in the duke's conservatory, Nessa climbed astride him, fastening her mouth to his yet again as she eased herself onto his waiting shaft. No sooner had she begun to rock in that oldest rhythm, however, than Jack pulled her even closer, then rolled them both over so that he was now above her.

"Not so quickly, my love," he murmured into her ear. "I want to make this last."

Slowly, agonizingly, he took his time, kissing and fondling her, bringing her closer and closer to the brink, until finally neither of them could wait any longer. In a mutual explosion of passion—of love— they shattered in a climax beyond any they'd yet shared, holding nothing back from each other.

Gradually, the little bedroom came back into focus, obscuring the heavenly realm they'd visited. Jack smiled gently at the precious woman he held with his arms and his heart. "I never knew such happiness existed on earth," he whispered.

"Nor I. But Jack, I have something to tell you that may make you happier yet."

"Not possible," he stated, but the eager excitement in her eyes aroused his curiosity. "All right, tell me."

She hesitated for a moment, biting her lip, her eyes searching his face, suddenly serious. "I believe—in fact, I am all but certain—that I am with child. Our child."

"You . . . We . . . Nessa!" He pulled her close, to say with his kiss what he couldn't seem to manage in words.

The next two weeks were the most idyllic Nessa had ever known—even taking her almost daily queasiness into account. And Jack felt the same. At least, he told her so regularly. When the weather permitted, they wandered the surrounding countryside, exploring every little lane and byway. They exclaimed over each crocus or jonquil they found in bloom, watched clouds or birds in flight, delighting in the world around them and in each other.

Simmons, Parker, and even the capable Mme. Guignard left them completely alone, appearing only when their services were needed before fading discreetly into the background again. During their walks, or in front of the parlor fire on inclement days, Jack and Nessa talked, discovering more and more about each other—likes, dislikes, pasts, and future hopes. Now that all danger to Wellington was past, Jack told her the whole story of his meetings with Miranda Dempsey, to her great relief. He also confessed how their marriage had benefited him financially. As she had similarly benefited, Nessa could not hold it against him.

When they tired of talking, they walked or sat in companionable silence, or retired to the bedroom for yet another rapturous round of lovemaking.

Though Nessa knew this perfect, private time could not last forever, she sighed when the day came that Jack suggested they consider a return to England.

"I cannot neglect the estate forever," he pointed out, seeming as reluctant as she to end this special retreat from the world. "Too, I'll rest easier knowing that should you have any health problems, Mr. Mooring, our family physician at Foxhaven, is within easy reach."

Unable to argue against his touching concern, Nessa agreed. "But perhaps someday we can come back here," she suggested. "This house will always have a special place in my heart."

"And mine." Jack kissed her tenderly.

The next morning they headed back to Paris, where they intended to remain only one night before continuing on to the coast, and thence to England. It was now mid-March, and spring was beginning in earnest. But though the weather was milder, the roads were more rutted and muddy than before, making their journey even more tedious. Night had already fallen when they reached the outskirts of Paris.

"It seems . . . different," Nessa said, peering forward through the window of the coach. She wasn't sure at first, however, just what had changed—other than herself.

Jack was able to put his finger on it, however. "It does indeed. The crowds are still here, but their composition has changed. More of the common folk, fewer of the nobility, I'd hazard a guess."

"I wonder why?"

But Jack only shrugged.

As they neared the center of the city, Nessa's unease increased. The people outside seemed agitated, either very happy or fearful, she was not sure which. Glancing over at Jack, she saw that he was frowning as well.

"I haven't seen a single English officer," he commented at length. "I wonder . . . "

The coach halted. They had not reached their hotel, but were as close as the traffic in the streets would allow at present.

"Wait here a moment," Jack said. Before Nessa could respond, he opened the door and leapt down, melting almost instantly into the shifting throng on the walkway.

Nessa waited, her heart pounding in anticipation of she knew not what. As the minutes passed, she felt more and more certain that something was wrong, terribly wrong. But what?

After ten minutes of agonized waiting, Jack suddenly reappeared. Climbing into the coach, he secured the door behind him and turned to face her, his expression grim.

"Napoleon has escaped from Elba," he said flatly. "He is in France at this moment, marching toward Paris, and is expected within days. The royalist troops are deserting in droves, joining his forces."

Across from her, Simmons gasped, and Nessa felt the blood leave her own face. "The king?"

"Still here in Paris, it would seem, but whether the city will support him or Napoleon it is impossible to say. His troops in Grenoble and Lyons have already allied themselves with Bonaparte."

That explained the mixed emotions she had sensed from the streets, and also the absence of English officers. "What . . . what should we do?"

Jack took a deep breath. "As far as I've been able to determine, we may well be the only English left in Paris. We must follow the others and make our way to the coast as quickly and secretly as we can. Our freedom, perhaps our very lives, are at stake."

❧ 22 ❧

Though he spoke matter-of-factly, Jack was fighting to master an all-engulfing fear—not for his own safety, but for Nessa's. In her delicate condition, what would be the consequence of capture? He didn't dare think about it. He would simply make certain they were *not* captured. He must.

"Were you recognized?" Nessa asked.

He shook his head. "I don't think so, though I fear the fact that I'm English will have been obvious." He looked down at the blue superfine coat he wore. "I should never have gone out there dressed like this."

"You had no way of knowing beforehand," Nessa pointed out. "But what are we to do now?"

"First, we must find a less conspicuous place to make our plans." Jack opened the trapdoor on the roof of the coach to direct the coachman, only to find the man gone. "Damn. It seems our driver has heard the news as well. I hope he'll not feel it his patriotic duty to betray us."

"I'll drive, my lord," volunteered Parker.

Jack clapped him on the shoulder. "Good man! See if you can find a relatively unoccupied alley nearby."

The valet climbed atop the coach, and a moment later they were in motion again, though slowly. They turned, went more quickly for a minute or two, turned again, then stopped.

Parker opened the trap door. "Mayhap this will do, my lord."

Peering outside, Jack saw that they were in a narrow lane between tall buildings. It stank to high heaven, but appeared to be deserted. "Excellent, Parker! Now, unfasten that smaller trunk and I'll help you to bring it down."

A few minutes later, he had the trunk open and was rifling its contents. Ah! Here were just the things he wanted. "Nessa, you'll need to change into this." He held up one of her abigail's plainer gowns. "'Twill be a bit tight, I fear, but that can't be helped. Parker, I'll wear this black coat of yours—it's the Frenchiest thing in here, I believe."

He turned to examine the servants. "Mrs. Simmons, you'll do well enough, but I'd advise you, Parker, to divest yourself of the ruffles at your wrists and throat. You're rather too obviously a gentleman's gentleman as you are now." He and Parker then left the women in the carriage so that Simmons could help Nessa to change, and completed their own transformations outside in the alley.

"If anything goes wrong," he murmured to Parker as they adjusted their clothing, "get my wife to the coast and on a ship to England. Nothing else matters." Parker nodded silently.

A few muffled exclamations from within the coach attested to the difficulty of carrying out his instructions in such close quarters, but eventually the door opened. Nessa emerged, clad in the black stuff gown and a voluminous shawl.

"Some of the hooks in the back would not quite hook," she explained, "but the shawl should disguise the fact."

Jack nodded his approval. "It covers your hair as well. Excellent. Now to discover whether we can leave Paris as easily as we entered it."

This time Jack took the reins, while the others rode inside. With some difficulty, he managed to back the horses and carriage out of the alleyway. Turning them, he then headed northward, taking back streets wherever possible. Most of the activity seemed to be centered near the Tuileries and Palais-Royal, so that once they'd gone a mile or so, the traffic lessened considerably.

They were nearing the city wall, and he was beginning to breathe easier, when he saw the blockade. Though it did not look particularly official, a few burly Frenchmen had apparently taken it upon themselves to search each conveyance leaving the city. Cursing, Jack turned the coach again, to seek another route, only to find the next exit similarly blocked by zealots eager to earn their emperor's gratitude.

Halting yet again, he looked about for a likely alternative when the thing he had most dreaded occurred.

"Is this Jack Ashecroft I see?" exclaimed a female voice in French. "I should have known that if any Englishman had the fortitude to still be in Paris, it would be you."

"*Bonsoir*, Collette," he responded, realizing that attempting to ignore or evade her would likely do more harm than good. In fact, if she still held any tender feelings for him, she might be induced to help. "You are a sight for sore eyes." And indeed, his onetime paramour was as lovely as ever.

"Finding yourself in difficulties?" She sauntered close, looking up at him with a half-smile.

"Rather," he replied. "I returned to Paris only this evening, after visiting friends in the countryside, to discover this." He indicated the blockade a few hundred yards ahead. "Has the arrest of all English been ordered?"

She shook her head. "Not ordered, no, though the silly English behaved as if it had. And now that the emperor is expected momentarily, some of my countrymen seek to curry his favor by acting on their own."

"Can you help me, Collette? For old times' sake?" He smiled down at her, summoning all of his charm— for Nessa's sake.

She glanced at the coach. "Who do you have with you? English friends?"

"Just my servants," he said quickly. Too quickly, it seemed, for Collette now looked suspicious.

"Indeed?" Before he could prevent her, she opened the carriage door. Jack jumped off the box to stand beside her.

"My valet," he explained, pointing to Parker, "an under-housekeeper, and a maid." He indicated first Simmons, then Nessa. "The two women were employed at the house where I visited. They wished to return to England, so I hired them."

Collette's glance lingered on Nessa. "I can imagine what you hired this one to do!" She flashed a knowing glance at Jack. "And yet you wish me to help you?"

Jack glanced negligently at Nessa. "A pretty face, but nothing out of the ordinary," he said, wishing Nessa's French were not so good. "She can't hold a candle to you, of course, Collette!" He forced himself to keep his eyes on the Frenchwoman.

"That goes without saying," she agreed. "Very well, *mon Jacques*, for the sake of what was—and what may be again—I will assist you. Help me up, so that I may sit beside you."

Jack gestured for the others to reenter the coach, then boosted the woman onto the box before climbing up to take the reins again. To his surprise, she directed him back toward the first barricade he had seen.

"Raoul there, on the right, is my cousin," she told him as they approached. Then, more loudly, "Raoul! Are you minded to fill your pockets tonight?"

The burly man scowled up at her. "Helping English to escape, Collette?"

"Only peasants, servants left behind to make their

own way by their curst, cowardly masters—but with the money to pay passage."

"How much money?" Raoul's eyes gleamed in the dim torchlight.

Recognizing his cue, Jack reached into his pocket and pulled out a gold sovereign. The man snatched it from him, then carried it closer to the light, to examine it suspiciously. He then returned to open the carriage door.

"Not that I don't trust you, Collette." He stared at the three inside for a moment, then grunted and closed the door. "Very well, then. Odds are they'll never make the coast anyway, before our emperor conquers the English for good." With an uproarious laugh, he waved them past the barricade.

"Thank you, Collette," said Jack, when they had gone half a mile down the road. "Now, if you can give me directions to the most likely route to the coast, I'll be forever grateful. You'll want to return to Paris, will you not?" He slowed the coach.

But she shook her head. "I live in this direction, and you'll be needing a place to spend the night safely. Continue as you're going—it's only a few miles away."

Collette had been pure Parisian, as Jack recalled. No doubt it was her parents who lived up ahead. At any rate, she was right. They'd need to stop soon for the night, for the sake of the horses as well as themselves. It was more than an hour later that Collette directed him down a long track off to the right, which eventually led to a sturdy farmhouse.

"Wait here," she told him, then clambered down and hurried into the house—to apprise her parents of company, he presumed. A moment later a tall man slammed the door open and strode to the carriage. While Jack was still preparing his speech, the man reached up and pulled him roughly to the ground.

"So, Jacques Ashecroft! I have longed for an excuse to do this," he roared in French. Before Jack could regain his balance, the man planted him a stunning blow to the face.

Falling to his knees, Jack looked up confusedly. He could feel the blood running freely from his nose. A muffled scream came from inside the carriage, but he resolutely ignored it, silently willing Nessa to remain where she was.

"Have I offended in some way, monsieur?" he asked, in what should pass for native French.

The man's chuckle held a vicious edge. "Offended? Offended? Why should your seduction of my wife offend me? Only the thought of the emperor's reward keeps me from killing you here and now. I confess I once doubted her story of how you forced her, but Collette has now proved her faithfulness by bringing you here." He glanced back to where she stood in the open doorway of the house, her arms folded across her chest.

"There are three more in the coach," she told him. At Jack's incredulous stare, she merely shrugged.

"They are but servants," said Jack. "You will gain nothing by holding them here."

Collette stepped forward. "Two are servants. The third? I think not." She pulled open the carriage door and gestured, with the pistol he only now noticed she held, for the occupants to get out.

Jack's mouth went dry. *Hell hath no fury like a woman scorned.* He was seeing the proof of it yet again. Somehow he had to convince them to let Nessa go. She stood there bravely, glaring at her captors.

"You're right," he said abruptly. "She's not a servant. She's a whore I picked up in Paris, who promised me her favors for free in return for passage to England. As I seem unlikely to collect now, you may do what you wish with her." He struggled to stand, but the hulking Frenchman immediately grabbed him by the collar.

At that moment Parker's foot shot out, kicking the pistol from Collette's hand. Grabbing Nessa with one hand and Simmons with the other, he bolted for some nearby trees. With a strangled oath, Collette scrambled for the pistol.

"Stop," her husband barked. "Let them go. We can't guard so many anyway, nor do I wish to feed them. I have the only prize I need in one of Wellington's most valuable officers."

Jack offered up a fervent prayer of thanks for Nessa's escape, just before a savage blow to the back of his head made everything go black.

For a minute or two, sheer panic kept Nessa's legs moving. She scarcely noticed the undergrowth snagging her skirts or the branches stinging her face. But as reason overcame fear, she slowed, pulling against Parker's iron grip on her wrist.

"Wait! Wait," she panted. "We can't leave Jack. They'll kill him!" Remembering his last words, she almost felt he deserved it—but no. Surely he'd said that only to save her. Still, right now she rather wished she didn't know any French at all.

Parker pulled her forward again. "They won't kill him. They want a live prize to give the Corsican when he arrives. He should be safe enough for now."

Nessa stopped resisting and trotted by his side. "For now? But what if he fights? Tries to escape, come after us? Mightn't they kill him then?"

"His lordship won't come after us," Parker assured her. "His first concern will be your safety. I'm to get you to the coast at all costs. Those were his orders."

"Do you mean he *expected* this to happen?"

"Of course not. But he's a man who likes to be prepared for every—"

Just then Simmons, who'd been panting more and more loudly, stumbled over a root and nearly fell. Parker released Nessa's wrist to support her.

"There, now, mum, we can walk for a bit," he said kindly. "I hear no sounds of pursuit, so we should be safe for the present."

Nessa considered taking the opportunity to bolt back to Jack, but realized that would likely only endanger him more. In fact, without her along, he would never have been in this predicament at all. Remembering how he'd disappeared into the crowd in the Paris streets, she was certain he could have escaped the country easily, had he not had her safety to consider.

They walked now, conserving their energy, Parker murmuring encouragements to the flagging Simmons. Nessa followed along, deep in thought. She'd brought Jack little but trouble from the moment he'd met her, she realized. Far from giving him the respectability he'd sought, she'd embroiled herself—and him—in one scandal after another, each worse than the last. 'Twas her fault they'd had to leave England, and now it would be her fault if Jack were imprisoned or killed by Napoleon's forces.

Jack's last words came back to haunt her again. Perhaps he really *did* think of her as little more than a whore! And he'd told Collette earlier that Nessa couldn't hold a candle to her . . . But no. Jack had told her he loved her, and she would not, could not believe he hadn't meant it. Not after the last two weeks they'd spent together, sharing their hearts. She owed him her faith, and her loyalty.

"—extremely well, ma'am. You're a very brave woman, Mrs. Simmons," Parker was saying softly.

"It's . . . it's miss," replied Simmons, almost shyly.

But Nessa scarcely noticed this oddity. "Parker," she said suddenly, "you were with Jack in the wars, were you not?"

He nodded.

"Then no doubt you and he faced dangers at least this great. What would Jack do now, were he in our place?"

Parker slowed, considering. "There *was* a time, on

the Peninsula, when half a dozen or so of his soldiers were captured."

"Yes?" prompted Nessa eagerly. "And what did he do?" She realized now that though Jack had told her much of his childhood, his hopes, his dreams, he'd told her almost nothing of his years in the army.

"He waited until all but the sentry were asleep, then created a diversion."

"A diversion?"

Parker nodded again. "Some pigs, as I recall. The French forces had occupied a farmhouse and its buildings. His Lordship contrived to release a herd of pigs, and in the resultant confusion he was able to get his men out."

Nessa had to stifle a giggle, and saw that Simmons' lips were uncharacteristically twitching as well. "Pigs! Oh, my. But"—she thought hard for a moment— "mightn't we do something similar now, tonight? Wait a few hours, till everyone is likely to be asleep, then get Jack out? If anyone is about, we could create a diversion, just as he did on that occasion."

But Parker shook his head. "His Lordship would never forgive me if I put you in such danger, my lady. Once I have you safely to the coast and bound for England, I shall return and endeavor to rescue him myself." Simmons nodded vigorously in agreement.

"But that may be too late!" Nessa exclaimed. "It would be days—perhaps more than a week—before you could return. Napoleon is due in Paris at any moment, and once they turn Jack over to his forces, you'll never get him out. He might even be"—she swallowed—"executed."

Parker made no reply and Nessa could see, by the dim moonlight that filtered through the now-sparse trees, that the man was torn between concern for his master and obedience to his orders. She pressed her point.

"If he dies, what good is my safety? I'd sooner die myself than live without him, I assure you." Abruptly, she stopped and sat down on a large stone. "In fact, I'm not going a step further. I rather doubt you can carry me all the way to the coast. I'll escape you at some point, and go back for Jack. I'm certain I'd have a much better chance of freeing him with your help, but if I must, I shall attempt it alone."

Simmons began to sputter something about unseemliness, but Parker sighed. "Very well, my lady, you win." Nessa thought he looked almost relieved. "If we plan carefully and are exceedingly cautious, we may have a reasonable chance of success. 'Tis certain they'll not expect us to return, especially not tonight."

He turned to Simmons. "We passed an abandoned shelter of sorts a short way back. Do you wait there for us, and get some sleep if you can. It would be as well if at least one of us is well rested. If we fail to return, you must make your way north as best you can. Do you see that star?" He pointed and waited until Simmons nodded. "That is due north. Between that, and recalling that the moon rises in the east, like the sun, you should be able to manage."

Simmons looked more than a little frightened, but raised her chin bravely. "I trust you *will* return, and with His Lordship—but I'll be quite all right. Pray do not worry about me."

Nessa regarded her abigail with new respect. Just now, however, she had other things to think about. "Here's that shed now," she commented. "Ah, good—there is dry straw and bracken inside. This heavy cloak will only hinder me, so I'll leave it here for you to lie on, Simmons. Try to sleep, and we will be back before you know it." She fervently hoped her words would prove true.

Jack awoke to darkness. The first thing he noticed was a pounding headache. The next was that his hands and feet were bound by thick rope, and that he was lying on something prickly and smelly—dirty straw was his guess. Straining his eyes in the blackness, he saw a few chinks of dim light, outlining just enough of his enclosure to reveal it as a stall in a barn. Listening intently, he heard the shufflings and snortings of nearby animals, but no obviously human sounds.

Struggling into a half-sitting position against the rough boards of the wall, he wondered how long he'd been unconscious. Not terribly long, perhaps, as it was still obviously night. Would Nessa and Parker have made it to relative safety by now? He devoutly hoped so.

He'd been mad to entrust Nessa's safety to someone like Collette, he realized now. The woman had been more bitter than most when he'd broken off their brief relationship upon discovering she was married. He should have known she'd jump at the chance to revenge herself upon him. Had his experience and knowledge of women deserted him, or had it always been but a figment of his imagination? He rather suspected it had.

Which meant he might not understand Nessa as well as he believed, either. Certainly, he'd done little to make her life better. First he'd denied her the very thing she wanted: the freedom to live her life her own way. Wasn't that the same thing he'd always demanded for himself? Why shouldn't she have the same chance? And now he'd put her in terrible, perhaps deadly, danger.

A cold finger of horror touched him. Not only was Nessa in danger, but their unborn child as well. Her desperate flight to the coast, now without his protection, might well cause her to miscarry—in which case he would never forgive himself. For a moment he struggled uselessly against his bonds, out of sheer frustration, then lay back, exhausted. No, he must conserve his strength against the chance of escape. In the morning someone would come to feed him, surely. Then, perhaps, he could contrive—

A soft rustling, resolving into distinctly human footsteps interrupted his thoughts. The steps were light. Collette? Might he still have a chance of persuading her to free him? He lay perfectly still and waited.

"Jack?" came a soft whisper. *No! It couldn't be!* Then, distinctly in English, "Jack, are you in here?" It was Nessa.

Hope and terror simultaneously reared up within

him. How could she risk herself like this? How could Parker allow it? He'd explicitly told the man—

"Jack?" came Nessa's voice again, closer this time.

"Here," he called softly. "Nessa, I'm in here."

She gave a gasp that sounded suspiciously like a sob, and hurried toward the sound of his voice. He heard her fumbling with the door of the stall, then opening it, only to trip over his outstretched legs and fall right on top of him with a soft "oomph."

She felt wonderful.

"Oh, Jack! I was afraid I'd never find you!" She gave him a quick hug, then scrambled off of him. "I've been—but there's no time for that now. I must get you untied, then let Parker know, so he can—"

"Parker?" Jack whispered sharply. "He actually brought you back here? He's dismissed." Nessa laid her fingers across his lips. Even amid the danger and his fury at Parker, he had to fight the temptation to kiss them.

"I gave him no choice," she said. "But no more talk now, please! If all goes well, we'll have plenty of time later. Goodness, but these knots are tight!" She'd been tugging at the rope about his wrists as she spoke. "There, I think I . . . yes! It's undone. Can you manage the one at your ankles? We haven't much time."

His hands now free, he clasped her quickly to him for a brief, hard kiss. "You'll both have a lot of explaining to do, my dear. But yes, I'll untie the rest. Be careful!"

Returning his kiss just as fiercely, she left as quietly

as she'd come. Jack made quick work of the double knot securing his ankles, then staggered to his feet, stamping to get the blood flowing again and biting his lip against the pins and needles. After a minute or two, he could walk normally. He left the stall, then paused. The big barn door was to the left, but he was certain Nessa had gone to the right. Which way was he to go? Suddenly pandemonium broke loose outside the barn door—wild squeals, and shouting. Pigs! Parker had released the pigs! Chuckling, Jack headed in the opposite direction and found a small opening at the back of the barn. Parker and Nessa reached it just as he did.

"That should keep them busy for a few minutes, my lord, and with luck we'll be long gone before they think to check on the prisoner. Can you walk?"

"I can run, if need be. Let's go!" He grabbed Nessa by the hand and they raced through the yard behind the barn, trusting to the commotion on the other side to drown their footsteps. Reaching the fence at the edge of the yard, Jack easily lifted Nessa over it, before vaulting it himself.

A moment later, they were safe under the cover of the trees. "Do you need to rest before we go on?" he asked Nessa then.

"Not yet, though I'm not sure I can run much further. Once we return to where we left Simmons, we can all rest for a bit."

They continued on at a brisk walk, Jack supporting Nessa over the rougher patches of ground. As they went, she and Parker explained what they'd done.

"Her Ladyship thought to release the pigs, my lord, after I told her the story of the time you used that ruse."

"And you mustn't be angry at Parker," Nessa chimed in. "I flatly refused to go on without you, so short of knocking me on the head and carrying me over his shoulder or leaving me behind, he had no choice. I can be most stubborn."

Jack gave her a squeeze. "Don't I know it! I suppose it was unfair to expect Parker to have more success in changing your mind than I ever have. And I must say I'm most grateful to you both! But it'll be a challenge still to get to the coast on foot. It must be all of a hundred miles."

He noticed then that Nessa was leading him off to the left. "These will help then, I imagine." There, tied to trees, were four saddled horses. "Parker and I agreed that it doesn't count as theft, as we did leave them the carriage and four in exchange."

"Whatever ill-advised risks you've taken, this has been a most efficient rescue," Jack exclaimed with a laugh. "Now we can put some distance behind us before we find a place to hole up for the day."

Leading the horses, they soon reached the abandoned barn where Simmons waited. She'd clearly not slept, but seemed quite eager to continue the journey nonetheless—though she exclaimed at the impropriety of having to ride astride.

"Oh, buck up, Simmons," said Nessa cheerfully. "No one will ever know. Think of it as a chance to do something wild and adventurous."

"I've had enough of adventure for one lifetime," she muttered, but allowed Parker to lift her onto the smaller mare.

Now they were able to make better time, especially as the trees thinned. Soon they reached a narrow road leading roughly northwest. Spurring the horses to greater speed, they cantered under the light of the setting moon and had put more than fifteen additional miles behind them before dawn.

As the sun crept above the horizon, they dismounted and tied the horses in a small copse about half a mile from a tiny village. They must have food if they were to continue, so Jack decided to risk a brief foray. To his relief, news of Napoleon's march appeared not to have reached this out-of-the-way place yet, and he was able to buy ample provisions to keep them going for the next day or two, as well as a few blankets.

After a frugal breakfast, they all settled down to sleep in the copse, exhausted after more than twenty-four hours of wakefulness, exertion, and danger. Nessa snuggled against Jack, laid her head on his shoulder, and was asleep in moments. He stayed awake for a few more minutes, smiling down at his wife's sweetly slumbering face. Despite the miles and dangers they still faced, Jack felt sure that he must be the luckiest man alive.

Nessa watched the French coast recede with profound thankfulness. The past week had been the most harrowing she'd ever experienced, with several near misses and severe frights along their journey. Upon reaching the coast, they'd had to wait two more agonizing days before they could bribe their way onto a packet bound for England. The weather was still uncertain, but the real danger was behind them now.

Jack came up to stand beside her, draping an arm over her shoulders just as he had on their voyage from England a mere month ago. It seemed more like years to her, so much had happened.

"Have you, like Simmons, had enough adventure to last you a lifetime?" he asked her.

She chuckled, for Simmons had repeated that phrase so often that it had become a joke between them. "Enough to last me a year or two, at any rate, I believe. I find the wilder side of life is not so appealing as I once thought it would be, somehow."

"And I'm finding all the excitement I need in my wife." He squeezed her shoulders. "When that year or two is up, promise to discuss it with me before you go seeking any more adventures."

Nessa tilted her head up for his kiss, enjoying the fine salt spray that blew over them both. "I promise."

❧ *Epilogue* ❧

EARLY MARCH, 1816

Jack stood in the doorway of the nursery at Fox Manor, enjoying the scene before him for a few moments before announcing his presence. Nessa and Prudence both sat on the floor, while their sons clambered over them. Though little Robert was a month older than his cousin, young Geoffrey was the bolder one, crawling away from his mother to investigate the crackling of the fire a few yards away.

Nessa scooped him up with a laugh. "Oh, no you don't, you little rascal! You'll find out soon enough that lovely yellow thing burns, but I'd as soon it wasn't today."

Prudence shook her head. "You're going to have your hands full with that one, Nessa. And I thought my Robert was becoming more than I can keep up with! When we return home, I've finally promised to give more of his care over to his nurse."

"But you'll stay yet awhile, will you not, Prudence? We so enjoy having you all here, and see how good

Geoffrey and Robert are together. I'd love to see them raised almost as brothers."

"We are in no hurry," Prudence assured her, smiling. "In fact, Philip is out today looking at a property here in Kent, with an eye to purchasing it. If all goes as we hope, we may relocate here permanently."

Nessa hugged her sister in delight, and Jack waited until her raptures had subsided before clearing his throat. At once she whirled to greet him with a sunny smile that belied the gray day outside.

"Jack! How long have you been standing there? Did you hear what Prudence just said?"

"I did indeed," he said, coming forward. "And I am as delighted as you are. If the property Creamcroft is inspecting today will not do, I will endeavor to help him find another." He leaned down to kiss first Nessa, then his wriggling son, keeping one hand behind his back.

Nessa noticed at once. "What are you hiding there? Another toy for Geoffrey? He must have more than any infant alive already."

"No, my dear, this toy is for you." He extended the rolled up parchment and she took it, clearly puzzled.

Unrolling it, she read its contents through before looking up at him incredulously. "You've bought it? Our little French cottage? Oh, Jack!"

"Consider it an anniversary gift. It was one year ago today that—"

Handing their son to Prudence for a moment, she stood and put her hands into his. "I remember," she said softly. "I, too, will ever consider that day the anniversary of our true marriage. The day we dropped all pretense and pride, and admitted our love."

He bent to kiss her, not caring that Prudence and both babies were watching. A long while later he lifted his head. "That was the day my real life began," he said, "my scandalous, virtuous love."